SHADOW 81

SHADOW 81

LUCIEN NAHUM

A DRUM BOOK
1986

To Vita, whose gentle, affectionate prodding convinced me.
I'm glad I listened for a change.

PART ONE

CHAPTER 1

Grant eased himself into the cockpit and was almost immediately overcome with nausea. He cursed as he strapped himself into the seat of the TX-75E fighter-bomber.

He never could get used to the constant stench of excrement that floated around Da Nang Air Base. He should have joined the Navy, he thought. On a carrier you could breathe a little fresh air once in a while. You knew that, after having dropped your bombs, you'd be coming back to an air-conditioned ship, instead of this hellhole.

A cloud of red dust, kicked up by a jeep patrolling the perimeter beyond the fence surrounding the sprawling military complex, drifted into the open cockpit. Particles of it stuck to the back of his throat, making him gag as he taxied into takeoff position together with the three other airplanes assigned to the flight. He coughed and felt the vomit rising as he tried to spit out the grit that had invaded his mouth and nostrils.

That was another thing, this clinging red dust around the area. As far as he was concerned, if the North Vietnamese wanted it, they could have it.

It wasn't yet 1000 hours and Da Nang was steaming. The shimmer of the boiling damp air rising from the ground created a mirage that almost hid the end of the runway from sight. Grant's sharp eyes strained to make out the scorched hills in the distance beyond the jungle foliage.

He could hardly distinguish the outline of the infamous Monkey Mountain. More planes and helicopters had cracked up in freak accidents on that piece of rock than had been shot down by the Viet Cong. The chopper pilots loathed the job of ferrying men and supplies to the observation post on the top of that mountain. Helicopters, however, were the only means of reaching this stronghold. Airplanes had a different problem. Monkey Mountain, which looked like a sore thumb jutting into the sky, was practically in line with Da Nang's two parallel north-south runways. During the monsoon season, sheets of rain obscured the peak, which became a deathtrap for landing aircraft.

Grant was melting. The sweat dripped from under his helmet into his eyebrows and flowed down to his eyes, causing alternate stinging and burning sensations as he tried to read his checklist.

This cockpit was made for a dwarf, he thought as he wriggled in his seat trying to find a comfortable position for his six-foot-two-inch frame. He reached to the instrument panel to set his directional gyro to the magnetic course of the runway.

Screw the pilot. The space is needed for missile guidance systems.

The four airplanes stopped briefly in front of a row of hangars to give way to an ambulance transport on its way to Saigon. Grant noticed a group of men busily unloading a large crate from a C-130 "Hercules" cargo plane. On its side was a message stenciled in six-inch letters. "The San Diego Chapter of the Daughters of the American Revolution is proud to offer this piano to our fighting men in Vietnam."

"A fucking piano," Grant fumed. "Maybe we can serenade the VC out of the jungle."

Grant was Number Four man on this mission, making him wing man for Number Three taxiing ahead of him. The plane he was following stopped short while attempting to avoid a piece of debris on the ground. Grant clenched his teeth, instinctively pulled back on the power and slammed on the brakes just before he rammed him. The oleo strut of the nose gear sank almost all the way down, causing the fighter-bomber to dip sharply forward, accentuating Grant's nausea.

"Stupid bastard!" he yelled over the deafening whine of the turbines, shaking his fist in frustration. He suddenly loosened his straps, leaned over the side, and threw up, spewing his breakfast along the fuselage.

"Great way to start the day," he muttered angrily as he fastened up once more. "What is a nice, blond, thirty-year-old boy like Grant Fielding, from Stamford, Connecticut, doing in a dump like this, in Charlie country filled with amateurish morons? He should be dodging the draft at Harvard or Yale, studying sociology." He closed the canopy.

"Right! Sociology to help the poor, emerging, underdeveloped nations who will one day surely grab us pampered suckers by the balls."

Major William Harrison, the flight leader, called on the radio.

"Vampire flight—check in."

"Vampire Two," replied the pilot in second position, confirming he was ready to go.

"Vampire Three," said the man ahead of Grant.

"Vampire Four," Grant acknowledged, as he adjusted his oxygen mask.

Major Harrison called the tower.

"Vampire flight is ready."

"Cleared for takeoff, Vampire. Temperature is 98 degrees—wind is from 210 degrees—6 knots," the tower answered laconically.

"Roger, here we go," Harrison said as he added power while the Number Two man nuzzled in behind his right wing, following his every move.

After an incredibly short run of less than two hundred feet, the two birds of prey broke ground together and started to climb almost vertically above the runway.

The Number Three man and Grant, like members of a precision ballet team, lifted off a few seconds later. They rapidly rose virtually straight up with very little forward motion and rejoined them in formation flight.

The four fighter-bombers banked steeply to the left, making a graceful 180-degree turn, heading north over the sea. They quickly came up over the sparkling white sand of China Beach, next to Da Nang Harbor, congested, as usual, with countless freighters waiting their turn to unload their military supplies.

About eight minutes after leaving Da Nang they leveled off at twenty-five thousand feet, picked up a northwesterly course, and followed the coast a few miles out over the sea.

At this altitude Vietnam didn't seem so bad. The succession of immaculate beaches along the rugged shoreline and the magnificent nuanced blue shadings of the sea looked like a four-color spread in a travel brochure.

The temperature in the cockpit was now set at 73 degrees, and Grant really had little to do for the moment except follow the aircraft ahead. For a second, he let his mind wander. Just like a Hollywood version of the tropical paradises of the South Seas. Wait till Hilton gets into this place after the war, he thought. He conjured a picture of himself stepping out of the hotel and running toward the water holding hands with an appetizing, suntanned blonde in a microbikini.

"Vampire flight, switch to channel two," the flight leader ordered.

Grant left his imaginary girl on the beach, sighed, and turned the knobs on his UHF radio to the prearranged frequency of 223.1. In a cool, professional tone, he checked in as Vampire Four after acknowledgment by Two and Three. "What the hell am I doing playing vampire games with a bunch of grown men instead of getting laid on one of those beaches? It's insane!"

Now that he was in the air, the butterflies in his stomach vanished. He experienced a strange sense of relaxation. Vomiting had helped. He felt absolutely fatalistic. What was it the Arabs said? "*Maktoob*"—it is written. Loosely translated, Grant remembered, it meant that a man's destiny is programmed in the great ledger of heaven before he's even born. He accepted that philosophy.

To Grant, a product of the Air Force Academy, it had been a pretty antiseptic push-button war. Vietnam was just a piece of real estate to be bombed and strafed because, as they claimed in Washington, "the vital interests of the United States were at stake in Southeast Asia." This was a conflict strictly for professionals, at least so far as the Air Force was concerned. Grant had never really felt personally involved. To become a career man, a carbon copy of the pock-marked Harrison, he just had to obey orders—like Calley at My Lai—log flight time, and accumulate seniority. If he kept his nose clean, he would eventually be promoted from captain to major—maybe general someday.

The victims on the ground meant nothing to him. They were perfectly anonymous—casualties of a surgical operation. He felt no sense of guilt. He had never seen the results of his work at close range. Newspaper pictures of children burned by napalm, of dismembered corpses piled up in smoldering hamlets, and of hordes of refugees fleeing in terror were about the extent of his knowledge. He occasionally saw these things in the Bangkok papers or in the New York *Times* brought in by a new arrival. *Stars and Stripes* was what he read the rest of the time and, for obvious reasons, the paper of the Armed Forces did not delve deeply into horror stories.

Grant felt very detached from it all. He had never mingled with the locals, whom he regarded with contempt. He hardly ever set foot in downtown Da Nang or Saigon. Smelly streets, beggars, bars, and whores did not interest him, to say nothing of the risk of getting the clap. He had preferred to cast himself in the role of a vulture operating at high altitude, oblivious to what was taking place on the ground.

Harrison, the flight leader, thought Grant was the personification of the eager, up-and-coming officer. Yet Harrison was unaware that something had recently happened to make Grant change his mind.

In perfect close formation, the four airplanes proceeded along the coast. Pretty soon they spotted Hue, the ancient imperial capital, scene of bloody massacres during the 1968 North Vietnamese Tet holiday offensive, then Quang Tri. Harrison broke the silence as they were coming up abeam the demilitarized zone at the seventeenth parallel, still over the sea.

"Vampire flight, switch over to channel three. Proceed as per briefing."

Together, the fighters entered a slight left turn, then rolled out after having established a heading of 320 degrees to follow the narrow gullet separating the wider parts of North and South Vietnam. Maintaining twenty-five thousand feet, they cruised, as planned, at 0.75 Mach, or roughly 385 knots.

The briefing had been pretty standard. It stressed the need to look out for reported new surface-to-air missile sites. It meant keeping your eyes open for an occasional token MIG, although they seldom really bothered you. To Grant, it boiled down to risking your ass to bomb a worn-out railroad track, a depot, or a couple of dikes to cause the flooding of a few rice paddies. This was called "hitting them where it hurts—in the breadbasket—" under the illusory belief that the weedy North Vietnamese could be starved out. Last but not least, in case you were hit there was the procedure for destroying the plane in the air as you ejected, even if it meant you blew up with it.

This aircraft was not to fall into enemy hands at any cost. The

Russians and the Chinese were both itching to get one in relatively good condition to find out what made it tick.

It was the latest version of the TX-75E, one of the most sophisticated weapons in the arsenal of the United States: the most versatile and efficient multirole vertical takeoff and landing fighter-bomber ever conceived. At economy cruise speed, it had a "top secret" endurance of almost ten hours as opposed to less than five for the next best operational fighter-bomber in the world. Stingy on fuel consumption, it only burned two hundred gallons per engine per hour on long-range ferry flights. Its top speed and maximum ceiling remained classified, but they couldn't even be approached by any other airplane. The aircraft could do everything. This twin jet marvel performed at subsonic and supersonic speeds. It could also carry and deliver six thousand pounds of bombs plus four thousand pounds of air-to-air and air-to-ground missiles, miscellaneous rockets and shells for its 30-mm cannons. It was an acrobatic battleship of the skies with highly destructive firepower while being practically invulnerable to enemy defenses.

The aircraft was of the "swing-wing" type, allowing it to extend or retract the airfoil for any type of speed configuration. When at rest, the drooping wings could be folded neatly along the fuselage for easy and compact storage. It weighed a little over fifty thousand pounds when fully loaded, and when empty it could be shipped anywhere without difficulty to any theater of operation or combat zone. For transportation, it could be stowed in a container about the size of a large furniture van. The aircraft could hover, take off, or land in anyone's back yard—just like a helicopter. No runway was needed. For security reasons, however, it operated out of regular air bases, guarded around the clock. Crews of mechanics and electronic experts constantly lavished their expert attention on this unparalleled product of American technology and know-how.

Grant often wondered why they even needed a pilot on this fully automated monster, which looked like a bat on the ground but metamorphosed into a beautiful sleek hawk in the sky. Everything was computerized. Inertial guidance systems for pinpoint navigation, radar scopes with a 400-mile sweep, microwave equipment for poor visibility landings, vertical scale instruments, and a maze of multicolored buttons, switches, and levers. The airplane, which seemed to have a mind of its own, reduced the role of the man at the controls to that of a baby-sitter.

But each of these babies was worth twenty-two million dollars, not counting the cost of the ordnance, which, of course, was expendable.

Grant had been quite flattered to be selected for training on what was considered to be the apple of the Pentagon's eye. It had been a tremendous ego trip to be the envy of the rest of the guys still relegated either to antiques of F4 Phantom vintage, or to clonkers with fancy names, such as "Skyraider," "Vigilante," "Intruder," and, best of all, "Crusader." That last one really tickled him. Some crusade!

"Vampire flight, switch over to channel four. The weather looks OK. Primary target still on," Harrison said.

Grant changed to 222.4, checked in, and mentally reviewed the technical details of the raid.

It was to be an all-out attack on Hoa Binh, about 60 miles southwest of Hanoi. This mission was only a diversion in a series of massive air raids scheduled for that day all over Vietnam, with the accent on B-52s pounding Hanoi. The giant bombers would also concentrate on giving nearby Haiphong Harbor a good pasting.

According to Intelligence, Hoa Binh seemed to have developed into an important regional routing center for men and supplies and was to be wiped out. There was no point, however, in risking B-52s over this objective—for the moment at least—or until such time as things really got out of hand. Recently, SAMS had been swatting the heretofore immune B-52s like flies and several mobile batteries had been reported in the area. Four nimble fighter-bombers, with heavy firepower, operating with great flexibility at low level, would be sure to inflict, at lesser cost, damage comparable to that of the B-52s.

The strategists had determined that a succession of saturation bombings at this time would bring Hanoi "to its knees, begging for mercy." The official communiqués euphemistically spoke of "protective reaction strikes" in retaliation for unwarranted attacks against "unarmed" American planes conducting "routine reconnaissance" operations over North Vietnam. These terror raids were supposed to "paralyze the enemy." The well-intentioned goal, as advertised by the State Department, was to reduce "infiltrations"

15

into the South. This, the Pentagon insisted, was the principal danger to American lives.

Personally, Grant preferred the Ho Chi Minh Trail jobs. You bombed the jungle in Laos or Cambodia, hit a truck or a bicycle once in a while if you were lucky, and then went home for dinner.

This was the fifth time in two months that Grant was assigned to Hoa Binh. The fighter-bombers had always escaped unscathed. It had almost become a milk run, and he was now familiar with every wrinkle in the mountainous terrain. The main thing to remember was to stay close to the man ahead of you so as not to get hit by the blast from his bombs. You also had to pull up fast after dropping your own bombs before you hit any number of dead ends formed by the sinuous topography. A couple of evasive maneuvers as you gained altitude and, according to the briefing experts, there was nothing the guys on the ground could do to you.

Part of Grant's job as Number Four man was to protect Number Three's wing. Once over the target, the flight leader and Number Two would take care of a sector. With Number Three, Grant would tackle railroad cars and a truck depot located between two mountains a couple of miles farther to the west. Two or three passes should do it. After the attack, the four airplanes were to rendezvous at twenty-five thousand feet over Cho Bo, about 5 miles south of Hoa Binh. The return flight southward would be conducted over the interior of North Vietnam via Phong Nha instead of coming back over the sea. From that point, the four airplanes would proceed to the demilitarized zone and continue to Da Nang by way of Quang Tri.

Deep into enemy territory now, still over the sea, the four fighter-bombers flew abeam Dong Hoi and Ha Tinh. The weather was clear and, in the distance, to the west and south, along the border of Laos and South Vietnam, Grant could make out enormous black patches in the jungle, the work of napalm and defoliation. The chemicals used for defoliation, "to flush out Charlie," were just as lethal to the vegetation as were the fires caused by napalm, though they left traces of a different color. They were huge, sad-looking, reddish-brown scars, reminiscent of the shade of dying autumn leaves in New England. B-52s also left a distinctive trademark—monstrous moon-like craters dug out by carpets of bombs. The gigantic bowl-shaped cavities were themselves peppered with enormous potholes—open sores in the soil caused by lesser explosions. Grant thought it would probably take a lifetime, if not more, for the jungle to become green and intact once again.

The sight of all this waste and destruction was pretty depressing when seen from a lonely cockpit at twenty-five thousand feet. The Vietnamese were going to be saved from communism at all costs, even if it meant that the whole country would be destroyed. Democracy was going to be rammed up their asses whether they wanted it or not—even if they all had to die for it.

What bothered Grant most was that so many pilots like himself, constituents of a very elite group, had "bought the farm"— been killed—while trying to rid the jungle of a few leaves.

Two years of Vietnam had disillusioned Grant. None of his immediate superiors suspected it, but he had lost interest. One thing was sure: he had absolutely no intention of buying any farms in this dump. If he was going to risk his behind, it would be for something worthwhile—himself. Blowing up a bunch of VCs was no real way to make a living when all the smart asses were calling him a murderer back home. What the hell was the President doing in Peking toasting the Premier with Mao Tai and signing communiqués about technological assistance, satellite stations, and cultural exchanges? Why the hell did he have to go to Moscow to kiss the ass of the Secretary General of the Communist Party? There was his picture, right there in *Stars and Stripes*, drinking vodka and trying to peddle a few boatloads of wheat. What kind of crap was that when the Russians were supplying the North Vietnamese with the very missiles that could destroy his airplane? What was the point of killing, or getting killed, when there were "diplomats" in Paris negotiating every conceivable sellout at the very moment that he was preparing to bomb Hoa Binh?

Grant had put his life on the line a sufficient number of times to justify early retirement and full exploitation of the system for his own ends. He was going to be rewarded for his efforts and begin to enjoy the benefits of the free society. Free enterprise, so be it!

The four-man flight was approaching Vinh, flying almost due north now. Sam Son, on the coast, was the next checkpoint. When it came into sight, the fighter-bombers banked to the left and, for a short while, headed squarely west, over rice paddies, toward Bai Thuong. Once again, they turned to the right and proceeded on a northwesterly course. In the heartland of North Vietnam, over Vu Ban, about 40 miles south of their objective, they prepared to attack Hoa Binh.

CHAPTER 2

"Jimmy" Fong was not an inquisitive man by nature, especially if his clients paid cash in U.S. dollars.

He was a rotund, congenial, impeccably dressed little man of about fifty, with an eternal smile on his wrinkled face. Early in his career, he had learned that it was mandatory for a Chinese operating a business in Hong Kong to call himself "Jimmy" or "Charlie." It made things much easier for the foreigners who couldn't pronounce or remember Chinese names.

From the moment he noticed the tall Occidental walking around the shipyard with one of his foremen, Jimmy sensed a big deal in the offing. As he watched from his office window, the man stopped frequently in front of ships of the same approximate tonnage and asked many questions. He seemed to be an American. Jimmy Fong's guesses were usually correct. He worked for Peking, who used his business as a front. In fact, Jimmy's shipyard was a clearinghouse for a multitude of currencies sorely needed for foreign trade by the People's Republic of China. Yet Jimmy's professional competence and integrity were of the highest caliber. His personal honesty was beyond question. He always delivered.

Fong was compulsively neat. His ultramodern teakwood-paneled office was spotless and smelled slightly of furniture polish. He was very proud of his huge glistening mahogany desk. One of his men was assigned to polish it thoroughly for hours every night. Except for a telephone, a blank sheet of paper, and a fountain pen, the top of the desk was bare. Fong detested clutter and became very upset if anything was out of place. He had a fetish about being well organized. He knew where everything was in his shipyard, and nothing made him happier than to be able to find things in the dark. For instance, he could remember that he had exactly forty-two paper clips carefully laid out in little rows in his otherwise empty right-hand drawer. In Jimmy Fong's business every nut and bolt, every tool, and every man was accounted for.

His desk, flanked by two magnificently carved armchairs, was squarely planted in front of a large window through which he glanced occasionally at swarms of workers scurrying all over vessels of every size and description. This was a major three-shift, twenty-four-hour operation, servicing ships from all over the world. At night, Fong could survey the scene with the aid of swiveling spotlights anchored to the exterior wall. He did not have to step outside to aim the lights; he manipulated them with knobs next to the air conditioner beside the window.

Fong spoke excellent English, having studied naval architecture in Scotland. He had also spent two years of apprenticeship at the "Can Do" Brooklyn Navy Yard during World War II. He had gained enormous respect for American efficiency and, for some reason, the expression "let's get on the ball" had stuck in his mind. It conveyed a sense of urgency which suited his temperament and he had tried to find an equivalent figure of speech in Chinese. He had given up, however, when one of his foremen had respectfully asked for clarification as he couldn't see the connection between a ball and a cranky bilge pump in need of quick repairs.

He rose as the American was ushered into his inner sanctum and walked toward him, delicately toying with the visitor's calling card as he held it by the edge between his right thumb and index finger. "Mr. . . . Dentner . . . Mr. . . . Harold . . . Dentner . . ." Fong said, enunciating each syllable as he read the card, which bore no address or telephone number.

The visitor waited for the door to close behind him, then stood still, holding his ground, looking at the shipyard owner.

Fong examined Dentner. He was six foot one or two and trim. He wore dark slacks, black loafers, a blue shirt open at the neck, and a lightweight sport jacket, all in excellent taste. A beret was perched on the side of his head. The hair beneath was most unkempt. Fong couldn't see his visitor's eyes, as they were hidden behind large, dark prescription glasses. He was mostly struck by the thick beard and mustache. They could pass as genuine to a less observant eye, though he was quite sure it was a proficient make-up job. The streaks of white and gray looked too neat, too symmetrical. The same applied to the hair, but he couldn't be absolutely certain because of the beret. He could not be much more than thirty, although he was trying hard to look fifty or more.

Dentner remained perfectly still and silent by the door. Fong made the first move.

"I'm Jimmy Fong. Welcome to my shipyard, Mr. . . ." he squinted again at the card even though he remembered the name perfectly well, ". . . Mr. Dentner. What can I do for you?" he said smiling, extending his hand.

"I'm in the market for a ship," Dentner replied pleasantly enough. He shook Fong's hand but still stood firmly by the door, not moving a muscle.

Fong noted that the man's speech was delivered with a pronounced Southern drawl.

"I'm at your service, Mr. Dentner. Please have a seat," Fong said, motioning to one of the armchairs as he went back to his desk. "Who recommended you to us, sir?"

Dentner walked deliberately to the armchair on the right of the desk, caressed the shiny top of the back rest lightly with the tip of his index finger, but did not sit down. He looked at Fong. "This is the most beautiful desk I've ever seen. These armchairs are works of art, Mr. Fong."

"You flatter me, Mr. Dentner. I am really quite fond of this furniture. A man needs pleasant surroundings when he is working. But, please, do make yourself comfortable or I will be embarrassed."

Dentner selected the armchair to the left of Fong and sat down gingerly, seemingly hesitant to make himself at home in such intimidating surroundings.

"I appreciate a man of good taste," Fong beamed. Then he repeated his question, "How did you find us, Mr. Dentner?"

"I looked you up in the classified directory, then called the tourist bureau to check up. They said they weren't allowed to vouch for anyone in particular but added that your reputation was exceptionally good."

"Ah yes! They're very nice at the tourist bureau," Fong said, not believing a word of it. "Many GIs from Vietnam come here on R and R. But perhaps you are not familiar with this abbreviation for rest and recuperation. Some of them want to purchase

Chinese junks or sailing ships to take back to the States after their tour of duty. By your accent, they probably thought you were a soldier visiting Hong Kong when you called, Mr. Dentner."

"That's possible. But, as you can see, at my age, my fighting days are over, Mr. Fong. Now, I am yearning for solitude. Is it all right to smoke?"

"Of course," Fong reassured Dentner. Without looking, he reached into the second drawer from the top, on the right of the desk, and produced a jade ashtray. He rose and deposited it on a small shiny round table next to his visitor's armchair, making it rather obvious he didn't want any ashes on his desk.

"You are an interesting man, Mr. Dentner," Fong said as he returned to his leather swivel chair. "I think we will get on very well, even if we do not do business. Please call me Jimmy. What is your field of endeavor, that it requires solitude, if I may ask?"

Dentner lit a cigarette and carefully deposited his match into the ashtray. "I'm a writer, Jimmy. I would also be happy if you just called me Harold."

"An author, how fascinating! I'm an avid reader, Harold. What kind of writing do you do?"

"Mysteries." Dentner flicked an ash and cleared his throat.

"I love Agatha Christie, also Spillane, Chandler, and Fleming. But . . . I don't think I've read any Dentner novels."

"I use pseudonyms," Dentner replied dryly.

Fong got the message. He changed the subject. "What kind of vessel did you have in mind?"

"I need a rather unique form of transportation, Jimmy. This ship must be of very shallow draft and, at the same time, it must be able to cross the Atlantic, the Pacific, or the Indian Ocean without refueling en route."

Visions of smuggling flashed through Fong's fertile mind. His face, however, did not reflect surprise at this strange request. He just nodded, removed the cap of his fountain pen, and began making notes in Chinese on the solitary sheet of paper on his desk. "How many men will you have for a crew?" he asked.

"I'll be alone. The ship must be rigged for a one-man operation," Dentner replied evenly as he put out his cigarette.

Fong stopped writing and lifted his eyes from his sheet of paper. In all his years in the shipping business, this was the first time he had been genuinely startled. He looked questioningly at

Dentner, who gave him a broad smile, the first since he had entered the room. Fong was disturbed because he couldn't read the man's eyes behind the dark glasses.

"Relax, Jimmy," Dentner chuckled good-naturedly. "I know you think I'm probably nuts. The fact is I'm just a little eccentric."

Fong answered with a sickly grin and nodded.

"You see," Dentner went on, "I like to be alone. I work better that way. I want to be able to steer this ship right onto a deserted beach and ram the bow into the sand." He slammed his right fist into his open left palm, making a loud smacking noise that jarred Fong's nerves. "I want to park it there for a while. I can live on the ship and take walks along the beach if I feel like it. When it's time to leave, I wait for high tide, back up, and go."

Fong's eyes grew wider and wider. He looked sheepishly at Dentner. "Would you, perhaps, like some tea?"

"No thanks, no tea."

"Something else, then. Scotch, gin, bourbon . . ."

"Scotch will be fine."

Fong pressed a button on the phone and a man appeared at the door. "Scotch," he ordered, pointing to Dentner. "On the rocks?" Dentner nodded. "On the rocks," Fong confirmed, "and tea for me." The man left. "Go on, Harold," he said.

"What I have in mind is something like a whaler or, maybe, a small coastal freighter or even, perhaps, a miniature tanker. It would have to be modified for my purpose, of course."

Fong opened the middle drawer of his desk, reached inside without looking, and produced some loose sheets of graph paper, together with a black felt-tipped pen. "We have such types of vessels on our docks. Perhaps even a large junk could be adapted to your needs."

Dentner made a face and Fong realized a junk was not the answer. He quickly added, "Just a suggestion, of course. We can take a look later to see if there is something more suitable. What are your specifications?"

"I'll need a large rectangular area of relatively flat deck space. It must be at least sixty-five feet long and no less than twenty-five feet wide. I wish to live aboard when I am anchored. You will, therefore, have to build a large cabin. I like high ceilings, so the perpendicular measurement is to be sixteen feet."

Fong blinked.

"You need a sixteen-foot ceiling?"

"Yes. I eventually intend to transform this into a duplex. When I'm ready, my wife and children will join me. I will then subdivide into separate quarters."

"A duplex. I see. Would you like us to stack two separate sections, each eight feet high, one on top of the other?"

"No. For the moment all I want is a big rectangular crate, sixty-five feet by twenty-five feet by sixteen feet, with a top that can be removed easily. Provisions must be made for a railing along the perimeter of the roof, as I will use it as a sun deck."

Fong raised an eyebrow. "A large hatch or maybe a container of sorts."

"Precisely."

"A container," Fong repeated, "about the size and shape of a railroad boxcar. The removable top would also serve as a sun deck."

"That's it," Dentner nodded as he lit another cigarette.

There was a knock at the door. A man carrying a brass tray delivered the scotch and the tea.

Dentner, much more relaxed now that he was getting through to Fong, raised his glass in a friendly gesture, took a sip, and waited until the man was gone. He carefully set his wet glass on a coaster which had been placed next to the jade ashtray. "There is more, Jimmy."

Fong looked into his cup of steaming tea but did not put it to his lips. "Please continue."

"The floor of the cabin must be able to take a load of sixty thousand pounds." The American noticed the incredulous look on Fong's face. "I know it's unusual but I intend to build a home on a remote island. I'll have to bring my own supply of bricks and cement and I don't want to make too many trips."

Even if he was lying, the man obviously knew what he wanted and had come prepared. Fong wrote down the weight on the sketch of the ship he had begun to draw on his graph paper.

"I'll also need a sixty-by-twenty-foot platform capable of sustaining thirty tons, and it's to fit without difficulty into the container-cabin. Naturally, I'll require an adequately powerful crane to lift this kind of load. It must be either telescopic or in easy-to-assemble sections and capable of extending about twenty to twenty-five feet over the side. It is to be located in the bow, as far forward as possible, taking the center of gravity of the ship into consideration. This will give me enough room to load and unload my supplies through the removable top of the container."

"Anything else?" Fong asked, not knowing quite what to say. Dentner replied with rapid-fire instructions.

"Twin diesel engines. The ship must be able to cruise at about 17 to 18 knots. Inboard fuel tanks all around the hold. I don't really care where you put them as long as you give me a range of eight thousand nautical miles. You can place them all around the container, if you wish. I'll also want a separate tank for fifteen hundred gallons of kerosene which I will use for lighting and heating, etc., on my island. You are to supply the kerosene. Fully automatic pilot enabling the ship to proceed when I'm asleep. Put a bunk and a cooking stove in the wheelhouse for me. Radar scanner coupled to an audible collision warning buzzer in case I'm not on the bridge. Long-range radio navigation equipment and all the necessary receivers for plotting fixes, shortwave, etc. The hull should be painted black. I'll furnish you with the list for food, canned goods, and beverages when the time comes."

Fong had kept pace with the swift dictation. He put down his felt-tipped pen. "What will the ship's registry be?"

"Panamanian, of course," Dentner said.

"Naturally," Fong smiled, "and the name?"

"*Solitude.*"

"I will need identity pictures for the registry," said Fong.

"You will have them on the day of delivery," the American replied.

Dentner took a sip of scotch. Fong had forgotten all about his tea, which was tepid by now. He looked at his notes.

"What you're really asking for is a World War II Landing Ship Tank like the LSTs used by the Marines during the assault on the beaches of Iwo Jima. It must also be a deep sea trawler, an ocean-going tug, a coastal freighter, a pocket oil tanker, a yacht, and the *Queen Elizabeth* all combined. I'm surprised you don't also want it to be an amphibious submarine."

"You've summed it up perfectly," Dentner said.

Fong was in deep thought. "It could be done . . ." he mused, drawing a few lines on his sketch. "In fact, I believe I have a ship that could be modified . . ."

Dentner showed the first sign of excitement. He rose, took a gulp from his drink, and, glass in hand, went behind the desk to look over Fong's shoulder.

"I think I have the answer," Fong continued, obviously very satisfied with his great competence in his field. "We will have to install a heavy retractable keel, weighing about thirty or forty tons, I would say, to prevent capsizing in heavy seas when crossing the ocean. Since we will have a crane capable of lifting such a load, we could also use it to lower or pull up the keel when required. This way, the ship can be beached when the additional keel is in the up position. The bow will have to be strengthened, of course, to prevent damage when you drive it into the sand."

Dentner was visibly thrilled. He absent-mindedly set his wet glass on Fong's desk and slapped him on the back to express his contentment.

Fong was horrified. A wet spot on his mahogany desk. The ultimate sacrilege!

Dentner immediately realized the extent of his *faux pas* and apologized profusely. He promptly removed the glass and put it back on the coaster by the armchair. Fong had jumped out of his seat and was busily rubbing the spot with a white silk handkerchief.

"Once again, I'm sorry. Please believe me," Dentner said.

Fong was slowly regaining his composure. The damage was imperceptible now, but he knew it was still there. He would have it erased that night. "Let us go outside, I want to show you something," he said.

Dentner followed him to the docks, where the noise of chipping hammers and the flashes and hissing of welding machines contrasted vividly with the serenity of the air-conditioned office.

Fong led him to a dock where a tiny tanker stood covered with rust. This obsolete derelict was the cause of his troubles with Peking at the moment. It was the first time he had been criticized for making a bad deal. He had allowed ten thousand U.S. dollars for it, as trade-in value, on a small freighter he had sold to a Portuguese operator in Macao. In the course of an audit, Peking had assessed the worth of this "garbage" at two thousand dollars if it would ever fetch that much from a scrap metal merchant. Fong had been very insulted. His judgment had been questioned upon being told that the treasury of the People's Republic of China could ill afford such folly. He had been given one year to get rid of the tanker. It had now been sitting in his shipyard for eight months and was giving him nightmares.

There had been talk of transferring him to other duties in Peking. Fong dreaded the idea of being recalled to China. He loved his homeland dearly, but cultural revolutions upset his sense of order.

Dentner banged on the decaying hull a couple of times. It made a drumlike sound.

"This ship is one hundred and ninety-two feet six inches long, with a twenty-eight-foot beam," Fong said cheerfully. "It displaces nine hundred tons and has no engines at the moment, so I can put in the diesels you want."

They climbed onto the deck. Fong made a rectangular gesture with his hand and indicated his men could cut out a section sixty-five feet by twenty-five feet and lower the container-cabin into the hold. He estimated the sides of the giant crate would protrude about six or seven feet above the spot on which they were standing. This would not interfere with the visibility from the wheelhouse, which was situated in the stern, eleven feet above the deck. There would be plenty of clearance, he assured Dentner.

"Sounds OK," the tall American said. "You can make the container out of wood. It doesn't have to be expensive stuff. In fact, the cheaper, the better. I'll want portholes with printed curtains all around the area protruding above the deck. Cut them out at a point about halfway between the deck and the railing you'll install around the removable ceiling."

Fong nodded. "No problem. How many portholes do you want?"

"Spacing them about fifteen feet apart—ten altogether. Three on each of the sixty-five-foot sides and just two on each of the twenty-five-foot sides."

Fong made a note. "That's easy," he said as he started to climb down to the dock.

"Just a minute," Dentner called, stopping Fong in his tracks. "I'll need a second boat."

Fong came closer.

"A sort of large runabout," the American continued. "A forty-footer or something like that. It, too, must be capable of operating on the high seas and have a range of about a thousand nautical miles. I also want it to fit into the container-cabin of the larger ship."

That was a new one on Fong. A ship within a ship. Definitely a smuggling operation of some kind, he thought. But what? He was intrigued but tried not to show it. Heroin? . . . Cocaine? . . . Opium? . . . No, Dentner wouldn't need that much space. Hashish? . . . Could be, that was bulky enough. Marijuana from the Mexican coast to California sounded logical. That's where the second boat would probably come in. Yet Dentner didn't seem to be the drug-peddling type, but it could be huge amounts of pills, barbiturates, who could tell? Cigarettes? . . . liquor? . . . No, too small time. Maybe a super secret CIA operation, since the man was disguised. He thought he had it! arms for Palestinian terrorists or anti-Portuguese guerrillas in Mozambique. That was obviously the answer.

The two men went on another tour of the shipyard and found a dilapidated fishing vessel, slimy, clumsy, ugly-looking, and smelly —but unquestionably sturdy.

"Thirty-six feet long, diesel engines, twenty tons, three-foot draft, practically unsinkable," Fong claimed. "It is slow, however, I must tell you. About ten knots at best. Too small for a profitable fishing operation nowadays but, as a runabout, it will do. It can go about five hundred nautical miles but I can fit extra tanks or give you drums of fuel that would be securely lashed on the deck. I can give you a good price on it," Fong declared as they walked back to his office.

Back in his armchair, the American said the fishing vessel would be acceptable with fuel drums on the deck. "How much for that one?" he asked.

"Fifteen thousand U.S. dollars, plus the cost of refurbishing," Fong said.

"No refurbishing will be necessary. I'll take it as is, provided it is seaworthy and mechanically sound."

"We will test it, Harold, and I guarantee satisfaction."

"Good," said Dentner, lighting a cigarette and taking a deep drag.

"What do we christen it?" Fong inquired, on the lookout for ashes that might float down on his precious desk.

"*Privacy*."

"Panamanian also?"

"Yes," Dentner said simply, then asked how long the modifications would take to be completed on the larger vessel.

"It will be a minitanker when it is finished," Fong said. "It will take . . . oh . . . I would say . . . about seven or eight months to do the job," he added. He vibrated at the thought Dentner was seriously considering the purchase of this eyesore, thus getting Peking off his back.

"Too long. I want both ships in two weeks. Three weeks, at the very most."

"It is out of the question. I have a full schedule. My men are already working around the clock."

"Put them on overtime, hire some more help. For what they earn here, they'll be delighted to work a few extra hours."

Fong resented the implication that he was paying coolie wages. "That will be very expensive," he hedged.

"How much?"

"I really don't know," Fong said. "I have to make many calculations. I will call you tomorrow at your hotel."

Dentner decided to drop all pretense.

"Fong, I don't want you to know where I'm staying. But you've already gathered that, I'm sure. Since we're on the subject, I know you're curious to find out why I need two ships in that kind of setup. I would suggest you do not attempt to pry into my affairs or to have me followed. Let's keep this strictly a businesslike relationship, we'll both be better off. You sell ships. I'm buying! How much?"

It was a difficult moment for Fong. He couldn't take a chance on overpricing the larger ship and yet he couldn't give it away. The eye of Peking, he felt, was on him at that very moment. "I have to think . . . to talk to my foreman . . . I need a little time . . ."

"You know damn well what the approximate cost is going to be for this piece of junk, otherwise you wouldn't be in the position you're in today," Dentner interrupted. "Give me a ball-park figure for delivery in three weeks."

The prospect of getting rid of the rusty tanker, of not losing face with Peking, brought a glimmer to Fong's eye.

"I cannot say for sure. This is not a commitment, you understand. I would estimate roughly 210,000 U.S. dollars for the larger ship . . . plus $15,000 for the little one . . . makes about $225,000."

"You're full of shit, Fong, and you know it," Dentner cut him short, his voice a trifle higher. "You know you can't unload that heap of crap. But it suits my purpose—at the right price. Now you want to take years to deliver, plus screwing me on the money. I don't want any more of this fucking around," he said with great irritation. "Are you capable of fast delivery and at the right price? Yes or no?"

Fong's feelings were hurt. Not only was Peking doubting his business acumen, but this American dog was now adding further insult to injury with his insolence.

"Two hundred thousand is the best I can do for the converted tanker, with all the extra equipment you want, plus $15,000 for the little vessel. I can have the big ship ready for actual sea trials, including beaching it, in exactly twenty-one days," he stated, staring at a calendar he had pulled out from his left-hand drawer.

"I can give you $180,000—package deal—both ships. Save on paint. I don't care what they look like. I want them to work—that's all."

Fong looked for a long moment at the man's dark glasses, studied the beard and the mustache again, and simply replied, "I will prepare the contracts."

"No papers. No traces," Dentner said, stopping him as Fong reached into his desk.

"As you wish. I will need a deposit."

Dentner rose and dominated Fong's sitting figure. He fished into his pocket and brought out a roll of one-thousand-dollar bills. He flattened the wad on the desk, quickly counted out ninety, and returned the rest to his pocket.

"Here you are, Fong. Half down, the other half upon completion of the shakedown cruises for both ships. OK?"

Fong smiled.

"We will get on the ball—right away," he said energetically as he put the money in his middle drawer.

Fong was delighted. After almost thirty years, he had finally found someone who could understand his favorite American expression.

CHAPTER 3

Dentner walked from Fong's shipyard to the ferry terminal. He made the crossing three times from Kowloon, through the busy harbor, to Hong Kong, carefully watching the passengers as they got on and off to make sure he wasn't being followed. Leaving the ferry in Hong Kong, he took a taxi for the short ride to the Mandarin Hotel.

He paid the fare while en route to his destination and got out before the cab had come to a full stop in front of the main entrance. He walked rapidly through the crowded lobby and exited via a side door. He waited a few minutes, saw nothing suspicious, then hailed another taxi.

Continuing this circuitous route, Dentner proceeded to the nearby Hilton. This time, he went in the back entrance. He waited for a moment before deciding to go up to his room, where he was registered under the name of Chadwick Sloane.

He made sure he was alone in the elevator, then pressed the buttons marked 4, 6, and 8. He stepped out on the sixth floor, looked up and down the corridor, crossed quickly to the fire exit, ran up one flight of stairs and let himself into Room 712.

For the next three weeks, Dentner hardly left his room, where most of his meals were brought up. He rented cars on two occasions, from Avis and Dragon Hire. He drove around the island a total of seven times, each trip lasting six to eight hours. He stopped frequently to satisfy himself no one was behind him but, especially, to observe the activity on the beaches. From a vantage point on Victoria Peak, he watched, through binoculars, the traffic of sampans and ships in the harbor.

Dentner made five quick shopping trips.

The first was to a mannequin factory which excelled in the production of realistic store-front dummies of every imaginable ethnic background. Dentner put in an order for an Oriental girl with small breasts, a black woman with an Afro hairdo, and a young, healthy-looking, suntanned California surfer type. He also made arrangements for the delivery of three white men. One of them was to be young and tall with long hair, the other two middle-aged, with beer bellies, bald and crew-cut respectively—the rich, semi-retired American tourist type. The manager looked surprised when Dentner specified that all the mannequins should have pubic hair that matched the hair on their heads.

The manager was convinced he was dealing with a closet sex maniac who didn't dare give way to his fantasies by ordering in the States. Dentner was paying cash, in advance—2,200 U.S. dollars. Since the manager did not object to a little fun himself, he had kept a straight face. He was just puzzled by the man's haste. Dentner wanted his mannequins within ten days. The Fong shipyard, in Kowloon, had seemed a peculiar address for the delivery of the dummies.

The second purchase was made in an elegant boutique where Dentner selected half a dozen sexy bikinis, low-cut beach dresses, a variety of men's Bermuda shorts and terry-cloth outfits.

At his third stop, a surplus dealer, the bearded American acquired six air mattresses, scuba diving equipment, two inflatable dinghies with paddles, two small outboard motors, four heavy-duty axes, and several camouflage nets.

On his fourth errand, this time to a drugstore, Dentner bought considerable quantities of vitamins, Alka-Seltzer, pain killers, motion sickness, wake-up and pep pills.

Finally, he went to a camera store where he bargained for a Polaroid, an automatic self-timer to trigger the shutter, and a few rolls of black and white film. In his hotel room, he positioned the camera on a dresser, sat on a chair a few feet away and, after a few tries, managed to take four passable pictures which he would later remit to Fong for the registry of the ships.

Except for a few calls made from public telephones to find out how Fong was coming along, Dentner kept very much to himself. He pored over charts of the Pacific. He studied the paths of regular shipping lanes and the patrol patterns of U.S. warships of the Seventh Fleet operating in the Gulf of Tonkin and the South China Sea. He scrutinized the characteristics of currents, prevailing winds, weather trends, and lists of radio navigation frequencies.

Fong had organized a special team of twenty-four men, working three eight-hour shifts, seven days a week. Time was too short to draw up blueprints for his foremen. Therefore, he decided to supervise the modifications personally. He carried the plans in his head and was often on the deck of the *Solitude* to instruct the workers as to how he wanted things done. To Fong, it had become a point of honor to convince Peking that no one ever put anything over on him when it came to buying or selling ships. Furthermore, he felt compelled to prove to Dentner that nothing was impossible once he set his mind to it.

A telescopic crane was salvaged from a dredging barge ready for scrapping and installed on the bow of Dentner's ship. Two diesel engines and their propellers were cannibalized from a small Norwegian tramp freighter, which had run aground on a reef with considerable resulting damage to the port side. Fong had inherited this useless vessel for the small cost of the tow, figuring he could always use it for parts.

The large cabin presented no particular problems. It was constructed of six separate panels of inexpensive wood. The sections were lowered into the large rectangular hatch, which had been cut into the deck and assembled below. The roof, which could be lifted and lowered by the crane, was in fact a lid for what the workers had nicknamed "the big box." Holes were drilled around the perimeter of the lid for the installation of a railing, and things began to take shape.

A retractable keel weighing thirty tons was fitted into a snug, leakproof, V-shaped section cut out of the bottom of the hull. Cables connected to both ends of the upper part of the extra keel were run to the deck, fore and aft. They emerged at the bow, in front of the crane, and at the stern, just ahead of the wheelhouse. By an intricate arrangement of pulleys, of Fong's design, the crane, once hooked up to the cables, could easily raise or lower the extra keel, which would be let down in heavy seas and pulled up when the ship was to be landed on the beach. Fong's estimations had been very precise. When raised, the top of the keel reached a point about an inch below the floor of the large cabin on the inside of the hold. On the outside, its bottom was flush with the regular hull.

Supplementary fuel tanks were welded into every nook and cranny with connections to the main pumps. Fong calculated the ship would have a range of 8,200 nautical miles at about 17 knots. A radar scanner was installed on the stubby mast of the *Solitude*. An automatic pilot and all the radio equipment listed by the American customer were put into the wheelhouse together with an electric cooking range and a cot. The man on the bridge would have everything at his fingertips.

There were no complications as far as the fishing vessel was concerned. All it required were engine tune-ups and the installation of extra fuel drums on the deck.

Fong sat in his office and did some figuring. Counting the basic price of $10,000 for the larger ship, indispensable new parts, electronic equipment and manpower, the net cost of refitting the *Solitude* would amount to roughly $122,000. To that, he added $6,000 which represented his actual cost for the fishing vessel, including tune-up and extra fuel drums. He smiled, remembering that he had tried to squeeze $15,000 out of Dentner, although he would gladly have let the ship go at half the price. The total outlay came to $128,000, so the shipyard would make a quick profit of approximately $52,000. He decided to throw in a nice paint job —black—on both vessels, just to show Dentner that he could do it and that neatness counted at Fong Enterprises.

A startled worker came up to Fong one morning to report that several crates, some of which looked like coffins, had arrived for Dentner's ship. Fong wondered if he should take a peek. After much hesitation, he ordered one of the "coffins" to be pried open gently. He saw the body of a black girl through the crack. Fong's eyes widened. He had the cover removed. He poked through the straw packing, took a closer look, and became hysterical with laughter. So Dentner had a weakness for pretty girls—custom made —like everything else he wanted. Fong had the box closed and told his men not to say a word about its contents.

Dentner arrived at the shipyard at 8:00 A.M., carrying two suitcases, exactly three weeks after having purchased the *Solitude* and the *Privacy*.

"She is all fueled up and ready to go," Fong said with enthusiasm as he led him to the dock. "My best man took her out of the harbor three times. I went with him on one of the trials and am satisfied she is seaworthy."

Dentner walked up and down the dock, along the length of the hull, and looked the *Solitude* over. It was unrecognizable. Fong had transformed it into a playboy's den of iniquity and the glossy black paint made it seem brand new. From the outside, no one could suspect that the big cabin, which protruded about seven feet above the deck, was, in reality, nothing but an empty hatch. There were gaily printed chintz curtains on the portholes to prevent indiscreet eyes from looking inside. Fong had also thoughtfully placed two beach umbrellas, a table, and seven aluminum reclining chairs on the sun deck. Dentner guessed that Fong had seen the mannequins.

Fong showed Dentner the rest of the ship with particular emphasis on the engine room, which needed very little attention, and the wheelhouse, from where everything could be controlled. A separate tank in the bow contained the fifteen hundred gallons of kerosene Dentner had ordered.

Dentner was noncommittal. "How about the keel and the platform?" he asked.

"I will show you personally," Fong said.

The telescopic crane was bolted to the bow in front of the cabin. Fong started the powerful winch motor. He fastened the hook to cables connected to the keel and pulled a lever. Dentner heard a rumbling noise coming from below the deck.

"This attachment lifts and lowers the extra keel," Fong instructed Dentner. "No need to tell you that this operation should only be conducted when the ship is lying dead in the water. The forces of the rushing water on the keel would be too great and could certainly snap the cables if you tried to lift it while the vessel is in motion. The reverse procedure should be followed when you desire to leave the beach and lower the extra keel. If the weather is good and the seas calm, I would suggest you sail with the keel retracted. The lessened drag will add to your speed."

Dentner nodded, then operated the keel mechanism a few times. He listened intently to the sounds emanating from the hold and, by the fourth try, could gauge by a telltale thud when the retracted keel was flush with the bottom of the hull. He also made note of the number of coils around the winches when the keel was up or down. This would give him a reliable check on the exact position of the keel in case he would be too busy to go below to open a trap door for a visual inspection.

"Now the platform," Fong said as the keel was lowered for the last time and the cables went slack. He disconnected the keel attachments and hooked up the crane to four other cables. Each was bolted to a corner of the railing on the cabin roof, from which the umbrellas, the table, and chairs had been removed and stored below by workers. The roof was promptly hoisted and deposited on the dock. Fong then swung the crane toward a platform loaded with sandbags. Workmen quickly hooked up the crane to a heavy steel ring resting on top of the sandbags. As the hook of the crane began to tug at the ring, a series of vertical and horizontal cables became taut and the platform assumed the look of a giant bird cage. "Thirty tons," said Fong, pointing at the sandbags with obvious satisfaction. He manipulated the control levers and the crane lifted the platform from the dock without visible strain. The ship did not sway.

"This is the way you must do it," Fong explained as the platform dangled over the side. "Bring it in slowly, then, very gently, you position it like this, right above the cabin. You now let it down slowly, without jerking it, so as not to impose undue strain on the cables."

Dentner tried it. He had a little difficulty at first. The platform banged slightly against the sides of the cabin as he lowered it, but caused no damage. After a few tries, he got the hang of it. The platform was returned to the dock, where workmen began to remove the sandbags.

"So far, so good," Dentner grunted. "What's next?"

"My man will take you out and show you how to beach it," Fong said.

"No, not yet, Jimmy. Let's take the little one first while they unload the sandbags. It'll save time. I want you to come with me for the trials. I must be absolutely sure everything is perfect."

Fong hesitated for a moment, but decided to go along. "I will still need my man. He knows both ships inside out and is a better sailor than I. You can leave your suitcases here, since we will be coming back soon."

"OK, bring your man, but my suitcases stay with me. I don't want them out of my sight."

Fong called one of his workmen and told him to follow them to the fishing vessel with the suitcases and, after that, to inform the chief supervisor that they were ready to leave for the sea trials.

The *Privacy* looked presentable enough with a new coat of black paint, but it still stank. Fong apologized and said there was little he could do about the smell of fish, which would take years to fade away. Dentner's suitcases were deposited in the cockpit. A quick inspection confirmed the boat had no leaks and all the extra fuel barrels were on deck. Everything seemed to be in order.

Fong's man arrived. He was a jolly-looking young brute, about five feet seven, who introduced himself as "Sammy." With Dentner and Fong standing beside him, he started the engines. Dentner looked at his watch. It was close to ten. He told Sammy to show him the way out of the harbor eastbound, adding that they would go westbound on the mother ship tryout.

By noon the three men had returned, satisfied that things were in order. Dentner was now familiar with the relatively simple operation of the fishing vessel, which he docked next to the *Solitude*.

As he left the boat, Dentner requested that the tanks be topped off to replace the two hours of fuel which had been consumed during the test. He also asked that his suitcases be transferred to the wheelhouse of the *Solitude*. Fong was curious to know what other exotic sex apparatus Dentner had stashed in his luggage, yet he realized he would never know.

The sandbags had been removed from the platform, which had then been lowered into the cabin.

The *Privacy* was refueled, then hoisted from the water by workmen and placed into a cradle which had been sitting on the dock next to the *Solitude*.

Fong had lunch brought up to the wheelhouse while he, Dentner, and Sammy waited for the hull of the *Privacy* to dry. Workmen hastened the process with large sponges. Fong noticed that the bearded American still kept his beret on the side of his head, even while eating.

At about 1:00 P.M., Dentner said he wanted to place the fishing vessel into the hold of the *Solitude* by himself so as to get the feel of the crane. He hooked it up to the cradle supporting the *Privacy* and, except for a little wind which complicated things slightly, had no serious trouble picking it up from the dock and lowering it into the cabin. Next came the roof, which he replaced in its original position with no difficulty.

"Let's go," Dentner said.

Sammy brought the engines to life and let them idle. He then descended from the wheelhouse to the deck to haul in the bow and the stern lines, thereby confirming to Dentner that one man could handle the whole operation of getting under way. Dentner observed him attentively. He also noticed that the engines made a beautiful purring sound and hardly transmitted any vibrations to the ship. Sammy returned to the wheelhouse and, under his expert guidance, with Fong looking on, the *Solitude* sailed majestically out of the shipyard, into the harbor, heading west.

Once out of the harbor and on the open sea, Dentner told Sammy to proceed south and to sail as close as possible to the necklace of small islands and reefs surrounding Hong Kong. The American insisted on doing everything himself—with Sammy at his elbow.

The ship proved to be extremely stable with a full load of fuel. Dentner wanted to know how she would behave as fuel was consumed and she became lighter. Fong assured him that she would remain steady even when riding high in the water. He added that, if he had any doubts, he could always pump sea water into the empty fuel tanks as ballast.

They conducted speed trials around Aberdeen Island. As Fong had promised, the *Solitude* could cruise comfortably at between 17 and 18 knots. The fuel pumps could be fed directly from any of the regular tanks as well as from every one of the extra tanks installed by Fong. A fuel tank selector had been placed to the right of the wheel so Dentner could read the gauges at a glance to see which tank was being emptied and exactly how much fuel remained on board as the trip progressed.

Although crude, the automatic pilot was reliable. The ship would hold course well enough to permit Dentner to sleep for short periods. Fong warned him, however, that the autopilot would need supervision and that it would be advisable to reset it every three to four hours.

The radar scanner was tested for ranges up to 20 nautical miles. Dentner stretched out on the cot and closed his eyes as he would be doing when sailing alone. Sammy switched on the audible warning system. A piercing whistle, capable of waking the dead, brought Dentner to his feet. He looked at the scope. It informed him that the *Solitude* was on a collision course with an unidentified vessel 8 nautical miles dead ahead and coming up fast. Dentner smiled and asked Sammy to turn off the damn thing.

Harold Dentner sat down at a small metal desk surrounded by radio equipment. He tuned in several low frequency and LORAN (long-range navigation) stations and plotted bearings on a chart provided by Fong. Looking out of the wheelhouse, he saw they were presently due north of Aberdeen Island. He went back to the chart. It checked out. He tried the same thing with the ADF (Automatic Direction Finder). There was a small difference of less than a degree between the two plotted pencil marks on the chart. That was close enough. Finally, he selected a few frequencies on the two VHF receivers. Ship-to-ship and ship-to-shore communications came in loud and clear.

They left the vicinity of Aberdeen Island and moved on to Round Island, Beaufort Island, and Sam Kong Island, sailing around Hong Kong in an easterly direction. They then proceeded to Wanglan Island, a few miles east of Sam Kong, with Dentner at the wheel putting the ship through its paces.

The American stopped the ship dead in the water and tried the retractable keel. It still worked perfectly, just as it had when tied to the dock.

The ship was beached four times. Fong closed his eyes and swallowed hard on the first two tries as Dentner, under Sammy's direction, sadistically rammed the *Solitude* into the sand of a tiny deserted isle about 12 miles from the harbor. After a while, Fong stopped wondering whether he was ever going to get back in one piece, and actually began to enjoy the experience. He was surprised to discover that he liked the crunchy sound and feeling of the bow scraping the bottom as it neared the shore. The shipyard owner became even happier every time the engines were put into reverse and the ship pulled itself out without difficulty. Everything checked out beautifully. Fong was proud of his work.

Dentner wanted to verify a few things on the return trip. While Sammy steered the ship, he and Fong went below to see if there were any leaks as a result of the rough handling on the beach. The ship was dry. They checked the fuel tanks for cracks—particularly the forward reservoirs, which contained the fifteen hundred gallons of kerosene ordered by Dentner. No damage.

Some of the food supplies were stowed in a metal cupboard in the wheelhouse, and the rest were in a container in the hold behind the big cabin. There was also a small refrigerator for beverages and perishable items. Dentner figured he had enough food to keep him going for at least a month. Next to the food, he found the six boxes containing the dummies and three crates filled with items he had purchased from the surplus dealer in Hong Kong.

They also inspected the *Privacy*, which was sitting in its cradle in the hold. She was sound despite the successive assaults on the beach.

It was close to 6:00 P.M. when the *Solitude* returned to Kowloon.

Dentner gave Sammy a hundred-dollar bill as a token of his appreciation and asked him to see to it that the fuel used during the test be replaced at once. Sammy flashed a big, toothless smile and wished him good luck on his voyage.

Fong remained alone with Dentner in the wheelhouse. He shook his head disapprovingly. "That was a very generous tip; I'm afraid you're going to spoil my best man."

"Don't be cheap, Jimmy. He earned it," Dentner said as he opened one of his suitcases.

Fong looked over Dentner's shoulder but all he could see was a pair of pants and some sport shirts. Dentner reached into a corner and pulled out four Polaroid identity pictures and a roll of thousand-dollar bills.

"Let's go into my office," Fong said.

"No. We'll take care of everything right here. I'm leaving as soon as she's topped off."

"You mean you are going to go without resting?"

"As I said, I'm leaving now."

"As you wish, Harold," Fong replied as he opened an envelope containing the ship's papers.

Dentner gave him two pictures, opened his suitcase again, and took out a roll of double-faced Scotch Tape, a small jar of rubber cement, and a stapler. "As you can see, I'm a well-organized guy too. No need to go back to your office. You can stick the pictures on the papers right here. Name your weapon—Scotch Tape, rubber cement, or stapler?"

Fong glared at Dentner, took the rubber cement, and neatly pasted the pictures to the documents. With his index finger, he carefully rubbed off the excess adhesive that had squirted from the edges.

Dentner examined the papers, which listed Panama City as his legal address. They were in order.

"I'll need the other two pictures for the records in my office," Fong said.

Dentner remained silent for a moment, as if in deep thought. "I'm pretty sure you can live without them." He grinned, tearing up the pictures and putting the pieces in his pocket. "Just say someone mislaid them if anyone should ever ask you."

Fong shrugged his shoulders. There was nothing he could do.

Sammy shouted from the dock that the refueling was completed.

"OK," Dentner yelled back as he stepped out of the wheelhouse. "Stand by. I'll be casting off in a couple of minutes."

He re-entered the wheelhouse and went to the small desk. Fong was sitting on the cot. Dentner counted out ninety thousand dollars and handed them over to the shipyard owner.

"The ship's logs are in the bottom drawer of the desk on the right," Fong said quietly.

Dentner nodded, started the engines, and let them idle.

"We will need to type a ship's manifest and get customs to inspect the vessel before you sail. We will also have to obtain a clearance from them stating your destination. I will make the necessary arrangements immediately, and be right back," Fong told the American.

"Forget it," Dentner said. "If the authorities ask questions, you can tell them some American nut wanted to test this ship at night and he never came back. Look sad. Say you're worried the vessel sank and that your poor client probably drowned—without paying. That'll sound sincere. So long now."

Fong looked like a broken man. Couldn't this big bully do anything in a legitimate fashion? Didn't he have any consideration for his paper work? His neat files? His permanent records? Fong realized there was no point in discussing the matter further and contented himself with giving Dentner a dirty look. He became exasperated when Dentner flashed back a triumphant grin. Fong left the wheelhouse dejectedly and went down the ladder to watch the departure from the dock.

It was getting dark. Dentner went to the bow and hauled in the line. He nonchalantly walked to the stern and cleared the second line. The ship started to drift away from the dock very slowly.

Before climbing back to the wheelhouse, Dentner stopped amidships and leaned toward the spot where Fong was standing. He motioned him to come a little closer.

"Fong, the tests were okay. But if anything conks out on this trip, I'll be back to haunt you. You know what I'll do," he spat out, "I'll scratch your fucking mahogany desk."

Fong's complexion turned slightly bilious.

"You won't have any trouble, Mr. Dentner," he said with great deference. "The Fong shipyard guarantees its work."

Dentner went into the wheelhouse and waved a cheerful good-by as the ship pulled away from the dock.

CHAPTER 4

Picking his way carefully through a maze of sampans and ships at anchor, the captain of the *Solitude* left Hong Kong Harbor from the west side a little after 9:00 P.M. Once out on the open sea, he established a southwesterly heading of 220 degrees after having taken magnetic variation, current, and wind drift into consideration.

He adjusted the tachometers to 130 RPM—a setting that would correspond to a cruising speed of just under 15 knots. There was a long way to go and no sense in pushing the engines to their limit. They would be running at full throttle in due course.

As the lights of Hong Kong began to fade in the distance, the sea became choppy. He opened a suitcase and took out some Dramamine. He couldn't afford to get seasick. It would throw off his schedule.

On the desk, he placed binoculars, charts, and a large diary with twenty-four lines per page—one for every hour of the day.

He drew an X across a page marked Saturday and on the 2100-hour line wrote: "DEPARTURE OK." On the Sunday page, he struck a diagonal from top to bottom without comment. One entry was made for Monday: "ETA—0600."

Whenever he spotted the lights of ships, he altered course temporarily to keep his distance.

At midnight, he washed down two pep pills with a can of orange juice. There would be no sleep on this trip.

He removed a gun from the second valise, put it in his pocket, and checked the remaining contents—another gun, dynamite, detonators, caps, and fuses.

After setting the autopilot and audible radar warning system, he busied himself with charts and radios through the night. The anticollision whistle was not triggered.

At daybreak, on Sunday, breakfast consisted of coffee, two more pep pills, and half a pack of cigarettes.

The ship was steady. There was no visible traffic in the area. Only a jetliner, probably bound for Hong Kong, broke the monotony.

An afternoon meteorological broadcast announced that a warm front accompanied by heavy rains and severe thunderstorms, presently over Malaysia, was slowly progressing toward the *Solitude*. Quick calculations confirmed he would beat the weather system and reach his destination well before things got rough.

The second night of the journey went smoothly. Now more familiar with the ship, he could take occasional leisurely strolls about the deck.

On Monday, 0545, he scanned the horizon through binoculars and spotted his destination.

"Right on the button."

A few hundred yards from the crescent-shaped beach, he stopped the ship, activated the crane and hauled in the retractable keel. Resuming normal speed, he cruised along the shore for an hour, looking for submerged hazards and a sheltered landing spot.

He selected a spit of sand within the curved hooklike edge of the western tip of the island which afforded the best measure of protection against the elements.

At 0715, under cloudy skies and light rain, he put on full power and rammed the beach.

He affectionately patted the ship's wheel and stopped the engines.

"It was a hard bang, baby, but we made it."

Less than thirty-six hours after leaving Hong Kong, the *Solitude* was beached on one of the most isolated spots of the uninhabited Paracel archipelago in the South China Sea. It was an islet, about six miles south of Bombay Reef, at the eastern extremity of the island chain.

Scattered between the sixteenth and eighteenth parallels—running more than 700 miles north to south—the string of some sixty atolls, lagoons, cays, coral reefs, and shoals was claimed by several countries.

There were simmering disputes at the United Nations about these shredded remnants of volcanic activity situated approximately 250 miles south of the Chinese mainland, 300 miles off the coast of North Vietnam, 200 miles east of South Vietnam, 600 miles west of the Philippines, and 700 miles southwest of Taiwan.

Japan had utilized some of these forlorn islands as military outposts during World War II but had renounced its claims in 1951. Since then, Peking, Taiwan, Hanoi, Saigon, and Manila had all asserted sovereignty. They adamantly demanded recognition of their "historic" rights to these remote specks of land.

Somber warnings of "appropriate actions" and other verbal saber rattling had become commonplace but were not taken seriously. Some of the countries in litigation solemnly declared they were ready to go to war if the question of the Paracels was not settled promptly in their favor. For reasons of "national pride," they pompously insisted, the fate of these islands presented a threat to the security of the area and even to world peace.

When questioned about reports of possible offshore deposits in the region, all these nations loudly and piously denied that oil had anything to do with it.

For the moment, however, the numerous claimants cautiously steered clear of the area, fearing the Vietnam conflict might be escalated to the Paracels. It was a possibility everyone shied away from—particularly the United States—by now unwilling to complicate any further its involvement in the Southeast Asian quagmire.

This was the ideal place to be alone and unobserved.

Immediately after hitting the beach, the captain of the *Solitude* lowered two anchors from the bow and flung an ax onto the shore.

He climbed down a rope ladder and began chopping into the rocks and coral. Each anchor was laboriously dragged a short distance over the sand, placed at right angles to the bow, and firmly imbedded into the crevices.

43

The ship could now be left unattended.

After inspecting his gun, a quick thirty-minute exploration of his domain confirmed the tiny island was deserted.

He let go two more anchors over the *Solitude*'s stern and donned his scuba gear. Slipping into the water, he swam to the bottom to make sure they had dug into the coral. He checked the tautness of the chains by using them for chin-ups and nodded with approval.

At 9:00 A.M., the crane lifted the cabin roof and deposited it on the beach. The *Privacy* was then extracted from the hold, lowered into the water, and tied to the port side of the mother ship.

The front forecast earlier was now passing through, bringing torrential rains and high winds.

Hurriedly, he began hacking at the *Privacy*'s wooden carrying cradle and carefully gathered every sliver into a neat pile on the deck. Now underwater, he kept chopping until the former fishing vessel was freed of its shackles. Each bobbing remnant of timber was methodically retrieved from the churning waters.

It was 9:45 A.M.; the storm was interfering with his plans. He waited it out in the wheelhouse, where he peeled off his diving suit.

Thirty precious minutes passed before the gale-force winds abated and the skies began to lose their ominous darkness.

The crane's next job was to pick up the platform inside the hold and lower it onto the beach. The hook then went into the container-cabin, lifted a large crate, and swung it over the side to the deck of the *Privacy*. Two more crates were deposited next to the wheelhouse of the mother ship. He pried them open, pulled out several camouflage nets, and threw two of them on the beach.

Hooking the corners of the webs to the anchors, he spread them over the chains and the platform as he worked his way back to the *Solitude*. He weighted down the nets with large rocks and chunks of coral until he was certain not even a typhoon could budge them.

The crane rumbled into action to lower the two crates from the deck of the *Solitude* back into the hold. It then hoisted the roof from the beach and replaced it atop the cabin.

He now meticulously camouflaged the entire surface of the *Solitude*, from the mast and the wheelhouse right down to the water. The webbing was secured with wire at strategic locations so it would stay in place even in high winds. Additional nets were spread over the *Privacy*, covering it from stem to stern.

Ashore once again to inspect his work, the skipper smiled with satisfaction; the camouflage blended perfectly with the surroundings. From the air, and even as close as two hundred yards out at sea, it would be virtually impossible to discern the presence of the two ships.

By noontime he was finished with his preparations. Close to exhaustion, he set an alarm clock, turned on the fan in the wheelhouse, fell onto the cot and sank into a deep sleep.

Jolted by the piercing insistence of a buzzer, he felt in the darkness for the alarm. The lights in the wheelhouse were never turned on in the unlikely event the glimmer might be spotted by passing ships or low-flying aircraft. He was still groggy, having completely lost track of time.

He groped for a flashlight, shaded with a red dimmer, to check his calendar-watch and diary. It was 11:00 P.M.—still Monday. He had been on the island for sixteen hours and had slept for more than ten.

Aiming his flashlight at the diary, he tore off the Saturday-through-Wednesday pages, stuffed them into his pocket and replaced the diary in a drawer of the desk. He turned on the stove and put up a large kettle of water.

He went on deck for a breath of fresh air. The front had passed, leaving clear skies and a bright moon.

The *Privacy* had to be readied for departure. He removed its camouflage nets and stored them on the *Solitude.*

By the time he was finished, the water was boiling. He made a huge amount of instant coffee which was poured into thermoses and transferred to the *Privacy.*

A final look around the *Solitude* confirmed all switches were off and the vessel was secured.

As he abandoned the mother ship to board his new command, he felt that he was re-enacting a Humphrey Bogart scene from *Key Largo.* He tossed the classic parting remark over his shoulder: "So long, sweetheart, it's been swell."

Now at the helm of the *Privacy,* he started the engines, untied the lines to the *Solitude,* and weighed anchor.

Before getting under way, he trained the flashlight on his diary pages: on the Tuesday, 0100 line, he jotted: "DEPARTURE OK." On the Wednesday page he noted: "ETA—2100."

Maneuvering at minimum speed to avoid the danger of running aground, the *Privacy* sailed away from the island.

Once out to sea, he applied full power. The engines were humming. He didn't care how much they'd be abused running wide open. There would be no further use for them once this trip was over.

He estimated his speed at just under 10 knots. The voyage of approximately 420 nautical miles would last forty-three to forty-five hours.

This time, rest was out of the question. There was no autopilot on the former fishing vessel and the radio was scratchy. Except for the compass and a sextant, the boat's few rudimentary instruments were generally unreliable.

At 0400, he had a cup of coffee, then lashed the wheel to maintain a northwesterly heading of 345 degrees.

He unfastened an oil drum, rolled it toward the stern, and poured its contents into the tanks. The overpowering diesel fumes, combined with the stench of fish which still permeated the vessel, made him dizzy.

The captain gouged deep holes in the drum, which was tossed overboard. It sank immediately, leaving no trace.

This procedure was repeated every two hours with the remaining fuel drums. He fought his nausea each time.

The remnants of the wooden cradle which had supported the *Privacy* were systematically chopped into unrecognizable pieces and flung over the side at hourly intervals.

He leaned over the stern and, with the ax, scraped off the words "PRIVACY—PANAMA CITY."

As the day progressed, the skies grew cloudy but the sea remained calm. He sighted a few ships but made no effort to evade them. Were he accosted, he could claim to be an eccentric recluse on a solitary trip around the world.

At lunchtime, rummaging through a cupboard, he glanced with distaste at the array of canned tuna, Spam, biscuits, and soft drinks. He decided he wasn't hungry after all. For the past three days, he had subsisted entirely on this most unappetizing menu.

In the evening, dead reckoning navigation confirmed that he was no more than 10 to 15 miles off course. He lashed the wheel and allowed himself a few half-hour cat naps, being sure to set the alarm. It was a rough night.

By Wednesday morning, the skipper had disposed of all the bits and pieces that had once been the *Privacy's* cradle, as well as the twenty-four fuel drums. The ship was now running on its own reserves with seven hours to destination.

He inspected the contents of the crate transferred from the *Solitude*—an inflatable dinghy, into which he loaded paddles, a small outboard motor, a waterproof knapsack, a life preserver, and a swim suit. The box was reduced to splinters and thrown away.

Just before sunset, he went below to deface the serial numbers on the engines. He combed the ship, systematically destroying any remaining evidence that could possibly link him to the *Privacy*.

At 1900 hours, he spotted lights in the distance. The navigation charts and diary pages could now be burned and their ashes scattered. The sextant was dropped overboard.

He flung his clothing to the winds, climbed into the swim suit, and slipped a knife under the waistband.

The lights dancing on the shore were getting brighter.

Just before 8:00 P.M., about 2 miles from his goal, he stopped the engines and went below with his ax.

Almost fainting from the lingering, repugnant stink of rotting fish, he crawled into the vessel's tunnel-like hold. He hacked into the hull, from stem to stern, until the water shot through like geysers. Completely drenched, he scampered to the deck.

The *Privacy* was going under rapidly.

He threw the ax and his gun over the side, donned the life preserver, lowered the dinghy, slid aboard and briskly paddled away from the wash of the sinking ship.

He clamped the outboard motor to the stern bracket and pulled the starter cord. It caught on the third try.

About two hundred yards from his destination, he cut the motor, strapped on the knapsack, and slashed the rubber boat, sending it to the bottom.

At 9:00 P.M., Wednesday, he swam into Stanley Bay.

He was back in Hong Kong—exactly four days after leaving Fong's shipyard.

The beach was deserted.

He pulled a suit, shirt, tie, underwear, shoes, and money from his knapsack. His swim suit and life preserver were stuffed in their place.

Once dressed, he began the long 12-mile hike to the ferry.

Before discarding his knife, he ripped the knapsack and its contents to shreds, strewing the tatters along the way.

At 2:00 A.M., Thursday, he walked into an all-night restaurant located near the terminal. He politely declined all suggestions of fish dishes, ordered a sumptuous hot meal, and savored every morsel.

It was daybreak when he crossed to Kowloon and took a taxi to Kai Tak International Airport.

In the baggage storage room, he exchanged a claim check for a suitcase containing his passport and a plane ticket.

Customs was no problem. Mr. Harold Dentner's week-ender held nothing but the usual, personal travel paraphernalia.

At 9:00 A.M., the Air France Boeing 707 was climbing on course to Bangkok.

He ordered a double gin and tonic, downed it in one gulp, and fell asleep.

He needed it!

CHAPTER 5

"This is Vampire One. Let's go," Major Harrison's voice came over the radio 10 miles south of Hoa Binh.

In quick succession, Numbers Two, Three, and Four acknowledged the flight leader's order to strike. They made last-minute verifications of all flight and weapons systems.

Grant felt an uncomfortable tightening in his stomach. He bit into the right corner of his lower lip as he scanned the instrument panel. No warning lights. Everything was go. He glanced at the clock. It was just past 1100 hours. There was a thin cloud cover about ten thousand feet over the target area.

"One," Harrison said, "we're on our own now. Let's keep in touch."

This was the cue for the pilots to switch over to the prearranged frequency of 226.1. Radio silence, which had been maintained since the departure from Da Nang to prevent the enemy from tracking their progress, was no longer necessary. They could now talk freely to keep themselves abreast of any unforeseen danger or targets not covered in the briefing. No names would be mentioned—only their respective position numbers.

Eavesdropping was unlikely, since the radio settings were known only to the pilots. Even if the enemy dialed every possible combination of frequencies, the Americans would probably be long gone before they tuned in on the right channel. In any event, the jargon of the pilots was practically incomprehensible to the uninitiated American, let alone to a South or North Vietnamese. Although the mission might seem an eternity to the hunters and their victims, it should last no longer than about fifteen minutes. By 1120 hours, the attackers should be on their way home.

Still in tight formation, the sun at their back, the four fighter-bombers suddenly screamed down at an acute angle from twenty-five thousand feet toward their objective. Hoa Binh came into view as they broke through the clouds; big white flashes streaking at them from the mountainous terrain signaled the unleashing of unguided rockets.

The ground gunners were at a disadvantage. They were looking into the sun. Their rockets were way off. The 23-mm and 57-mm antiaircraft batteries were brought into action. The flak was thick but stayed wide of the mark.

"So long, see you guys later," Harrison said through clenched teeth, as they reached the southern edge of town.

The flight leader and the Number Two man peeled off to the right, then swooped down upon their target—an ammunition dump. They scored on their first pass, pulled up sharply, and disappeared into the clouds. Pandemonium broke loose over Hoa Binh.

In the confusion, the Number Three man and Grant continued straight over the town, almost at treetop level, before banking steeply to the left. Houses were in the gunners' line of fire and provided some small measure of protection for the two aircraft. They headed toward their first objective—a railroad depot—which they attacked with cannons.

"Nice work, Three," Grant said as the two planes pulled up, wing in wing, their noses pointing straight up at the sky.

Grant glanced at the ground. He saw that they had demolished three or four boxcars. They were lying across the tracks, now ablaze with fireworks shooting in every direction. Terrified civilians were running for cover.

"Hey, Three, seems like ammunition too," Grant commented as he felt his pressure suit automatically tightening around his thighs and stomach to keep the blood from rushing out of his head under the 4G force of the pull up.

The North Vietnamese defenders recovered quickly from the initial surprise of the attack. Heavier cannons—85-mm and 100-mm—were rolled out of caves. By now, the antiaircraft rockets were getting closer to the fighter-bombers.

A light wind from the south was blowing heavy black smoke from Harrison's ammunition dump toward the town. It interfered with the visibility. It was Number Three and Grant—Number Four—who were now at a disadvantage. Dodging rockets and flak, through the sooty pall hanging over the hills and mountains, was becoming an extremely difficult task. It was like asking a skier to attempt a championship slalom during a raging blizzard with just his instinct to guide him. Still on the outskirts of town, about 6 or 7 miles east of Number Three and Grant, the flight leader and his wing man were better off. Antiaircraft fire was less dense in their sector. The smoke was blowing away, enabling them to pick their targets more carefully.

As Number Three and Grant entered their dive for their second pass, they heard Harrison calling his wing man.

"OK, Two. I'll take those trucks. You get that building on the left."

"Roger. Did you see that cross painted on the roof? . . . Seems to be a hospital."

"Yeah, I saw it . . . fuck 'em . . . don't let them con you . . . they've got no business storing ammunition next to what's supposed to be a hospital . . . blow it up . . . how're you doing out there, Three?"

"Uh . . . We're coming up on the railroad yard . . . second pass . . . I'll get the tracks . . . Four . . . you hit the boxcars . . . still some left near the station . . ."

"OK."

"One. Expedite. We're getting pretty heavy rocket fire now . . . how 'bout you?"

"Three here. It's bad . . . but we're keeping low . . . using the buildings on the west side as shields . . . but they're shooting rockets at us from the north now . . . houses in the way, though . . ."

"OK. We don't have too much protection on this side . . . in and out of the open right now . . ."

"Holy shit . . . Hey. Did you see those beds flying all over the place? . . . seems it was a hospital after all . . ."

"Tough . . . but you can't trust 'em . . . pull up . . . let's get back into those clouds . . ."

The North Vietnamese defenders were readying radar-guided and heat-seeking, high altitude, surface-to-air missiles. They were ineffective for the moment, however, with the fighter-bombers so close to the ground. Both sides knew there was no point in wasting them. As usual, the SAMs would be fired as soon as the raiders began climbing to make their escape.

Harrison and Number Two had completed their third pass and were circling for the fourth and last. They would then turn south and climb to the rendezvous point to rejoin the other two airplanes.

It was now just past 1115 hours and the lightning attack would soon be over.

"Hey, Three," Grant broke in, "that briefing was full of shit . . . as usual . . . look at that crap."

"Where?"

"Over there . . . on the left side of the mountain dead ahead . . . nobody ever said anything about heavy tanks . . . at nine o'clock . . . about a dozen of 'em on the flatbeds . . ."

"I got 'em."

"Want to take care of that, Three? . . . I'll hit the fuel tanks up the valley . . ."

"OK."

Number Two called. His voice betrayed a note of excitement.

"Two here . . . just spotted a couple of MIGs . . ."

"Where?"

"Just south of us . . . six o'clock . . . looks like they're at about twenty thousand . . ."

"I got 'em . . . Three and Four, you got contact?"

"Three. No contact this side . . . too busy . . . too much smoke . . . be pulling up in a second . . . they looking for trouble?"

"Don't think so . . . they know better . . . seem to be steering

51

clear . . . of the two of us, anyway . . . maybe decoys . . . you finish up . . . we'll go get 'em . . . keep 'em off your back . . ."

"OK. We'll be through in a couple of minutes . . . you get on their tail . . . we'll be right up . . . any SAMs up your way?"

"One. No. Too early yet . . . the cocksuckers will probably wait till we go after the MIGs . . . they're just bait . . . they want to get us up there for a clean shot . . . you guys watch your asses . . ."

Number Three interrupted.

"Hey, Four, you there?"

"Right behind you."

"Did you see that bull's-eye on the tanks? . . . Must've knocked off half of 'em."

"Nice job, Three . . . I'm going after the rest."

A rocket fired from Grant's left wing made a blazing trail. Its guidance system directed it straight to the center of the gasoline complex. A towering mushroom of billowing smoke, sparks, and flames shot up three or four thousand feet. It spread out, settling gradually over the valley, obscuring the ridges.

"Hey, One? You still around? . . . Four just got a farm of fuel tanks . . . must've had ammunition or explosives around there too. Man . . . what a blast . . ."

"We're just completing last pass . . . going after those MIGs . . . how long you guys going to be?"

"Still plenty of stuff in the valley west of you . . . just saw some heavy artillery not too far from where I am . . . going to take a look . . . stand by . . ."

"Hurry it up and let's get out of here . . ." Harrison said.

Grant called.

"There's a whole depot of oil drums in that valley . . . Three, how about you hitting the heavy guns . . . I'll take a last shot at those drums . . . Man, there must be thousands of 'em . . . you see 'em, Three?"

"I got 'em . . . you go ahead . . . I'll get the guns and the trucks to the left of the oil drums . . ."

"Roger."

Harrison called. His tone was pressing.

"We're through here . . . going after those MIGs . . . they're about five miles from where you are . . . make it snappy . . .

they're getting close to us with rockets and flak . . . can't stay here much longer . . ."

"Three. OK. Be right back . . . you go to rendezvous . . . this is our last pass . . . you ready, Four?"

"I'm with you. You just keep going . . ."

The two airplanes entered the cloud of smoke, wing in wing, Number Three concentrating on the trucks and guns while Grant prepared to drop bombs on the fuel drums. The smoke was getting thicker. Number Three could no longer see the reassuring wing of Grant's plane behind him.

Number Three unloaded his remaining rockets, missiles, shells, and bombs on his two targets and pulled up fast, heading for the cloud cover. Grant dropped his bombs on the fuel drums. The tremendous force of the explosion and the resulting shock waves made the airplane yaw violently, forcing him to devote all his attention to his instruments to keep things under control. The smoke had cut visibility down to zero. The flak was intense. Anti-aircraft rockets were still bursting all around.

Harrison called.

"Where the hell are you two guys?"

"Climbing . . . passing through eighteen thousand . . ."

Someone cried out, "I've been hit."

Harrison reacted instantly. "Who's hit?"

Three came right back. "Where are you, Four . . . quick, where are you?"

"Don't know for sure . . . the smoke's too thick . . . I think I got a fucking firecracker up my ass . . . lost pressure on one engine . . . maybe it's a dud . . . didn't explode yet . . ."

"Vampire lead . . . Number Three . . . I've lost visual contact with Number Four . . . He's . . ."

Harrison cut him short.

"I heard. No contact here . . . chasing those MIGs . . . where is he? . . . Hey, Four . . . any chance of you making it up here? . . ."

"Don't think so . . . losing pressure on the second engine, too . . . got smoke in the cockpit . . . must be one of those goddamn heat-seekers . . . damaged both exhausts . . . trying to climb . . . just trying to get over that mountain . . ."

"If you can't make it, eject and destruct . . . hear me? . . .

53

eject and destruct . . . bail out, Four . . . we'll come take a look soon as we can . . ."

"Trying to climb . . . stand by . . ."

Number Three was circling over the cloud cover at twenty thousand feet, looking down at the spot where he'd last seen Grant before the fuel drum explosion. Harrison and Number Two, about 10 miles away, gave up trying to bag the MIGs. The Russian-built fighters had eluded them and were heading for the sanctuary of the Chinese border.

Radar-guided SAMs were now coming at the fighter-bombers through the clouds. They looked like harmless, orange balls of fire as they kept climbing. At preselected altitudes, they would suddenly explode with stupendous force, setting the sky ablaze and radiating shock waves that could be felt for miles.

Number Three kept circling, wondering whether he should go down to look for Grant or climb to rejoin Harrison and Number Two. He called the flight leader.

"Number One, I can't see him through this smoke . . ."

"Hang in there . . . we'll be right with you . . ."

An unexpected movement down below caught Number Three's eye just as he was about to give up. It was Grant's airplane shooting almost vertically through the cloud cover. Three yelled.

"Hey, Four, I've got you in sight, you OK?"

"Negative. Just zooming now . . . Can't keep the nose up . . . Both engines gone . . . Goddammit! There goes the stick shaker . . . Gotta dive her right now . . . ejection mechanism malfunction . . . can't bail out . . ."

Harrison called.

"Where is he, Three?"

"Right below me . . . Jesus . . . he's in a dive now . . . going right into those mountains . . . you see him, One?"

Harrison and Number Two arrived on the scene and joined Number Three as they helplessly watched Grant go into a nose dive. Harrison called.

"One and Two here with Three. Got you in sight . . . SAMs all over the place. Can you set her down? Pick a soft spot . . . a rice paddy or something . . ."

"Unable rice paddy . . . don't think I can glide it that far . . . Little control over the airplane . . . doing the best I can . . ."

"OK then . . . put her down anywhere . . . destruct as you

clear. . . Repeat destruct. . . Four? . . . Four? . . . One to Four, do you read? . . ."

There was no further response.

About twenty seconds after the last call, Harrison, Numbers Two and Three saw a big red flash through the cloud cover, above a peak bordering the valley.

It was just past 1120.

"There's nothing more we can do," Harrison said. "Those SAMs are getting too close. Let's get the fuck out of here."

The three fighter-bombers climbed to twenty-five thousand feet. As scheduled, they came up on Cho Bo at 1125. They were now about 5 miles south of Hoa Binh; out of immediate range of the SAMs. The frequency was changed to 220.9 in case the enemy had tuned in the previous channel. The pressure was off. The pilots began to relax.

"Vampire lead—Two. Think he had a chance?"

"Didn't look good," Harrison replied. "Seems he bought that farm on the mountain . . . Who the hell knows? . . . Maybe he was lucky . . . the ejection system might've worked before he hit."

"Shit, man, I thought we had it made," Number Three cut in. "He was right behind me when he hit those drums . . . we were supposed to play chess this afternoon . . . you know that sonofabitch plans fifteen moves ahead?"

"OK, let's get back to work," Harrison said, ending the eulogy.

They arrived over their home base at 1230. Because of heavy traffic, they were cleared by Da Nang tower to dispense with the runways and to hover down directly next to their hangar.

The maintenance chief ran up to Harrison's airplane. "Where's Grant?" he inquired, dreading the answer.

"Lost him," Harrison said. "They got him at Hoa Binh."

The sweat was running down the wrinkles of the pudgy maintenance chief's face. There was nothing more to be said. He turned to the crew standing by the hangar doors and shouted, "OK, let's put 'em in the barn. Get moving!"

General "Zach" R. Enko had just returned from lunch, munching on a cigar as he walked up the three steps to his office next to the briefing room. He saw Colonel Bernie McSnair standing in front of his door, nervously cracking his knuckles.

"I'm afraid I've got bad news," McSnair said, trying to avoid the General's piercing black eyes.

"What is it now?" Enko growled.

"Harrison's back from Hoa Binh. I think we may have lost an airplane there."

"What do you mean you 'think.' Why must you always be so noncommittal? Who the hell was it?"

"Seems it was Grant Fielding, sir. He was Number Four man."

"I've already told you, McSnair, stop this 'seems' shit. What happened to him?"

"Don't have all the details yet, sir. Captain William Keegan is conducting the debriefing."

"I guess I'd better go in and get it firsthand instead of listening to a lot of double talk later. You come with me."

Lieutenant "Chuck" Dow was sitting at the desk barring the entrance to General Enko's office. He had overheard "Zach the Terrible" chewing out McSnair but had pretended to be busy shuffling files. Zachary R. Enko would be in a vile mood for days. The TX-75E was his pet and he'd have a fit if they even got scratched by enemy fire. It would be best to keep away from him until he cooled off.

Enko and McSnair marched into the debriefing room. Harrison, the other two pilots, and Captain Keegan rose and stood stiffly at attention.

Enko didn't waste any time on greetings.

"Let's have it," he barked.

Captain Keegan, a thin, rosy-cheeked incompetent, cleared his throat in an effort to show he was not intimidated.

"Based on preliminary appraisal by the rest of the members of the flight, General, it appears that Captain Fielding was incapacitated by a heat-seeking missile . . ."

"Cut out the bullshit and shut up," Enko snapped. "Harrison, I want to hear it from you. Did you see what happened?"

"Only the last few moments, sir," Harrison replied. "Number Two and I were chasing a couple of MIGs when he got hit. Number Three had just lost him. By the time we got back, we all saw him go into a nose dive west of the target area. There was the flash of an explosion through thin cloud cover when he stopped acknowledging our calls. I told him to destruct, General," Harrison added prudently.

"Well, did he?"

"Hard to say, sir. Doesn't seem to me he could have had the time to clear out and activate the self-destruct system. The explosion was probably caused by the airplane impacting with full force. If he still had any bombs aboard, they might have blown up along with his remaining rockets and destroyed the airplane."

"Huh," Enko grunted. "You think he might have gotten out in time?"

"To be truthful, sir, I doubt it. From the way he spoke, his canopy seemed to be jammed. Whether the malfunction was caused by enemy fire or by a mechanical defect couldn't be determined. Knowing Grant, I'm sure he would have tried to destroy the airplane, even if it meant he'd go with it."

"There should be more like him," Enko remarked soberly. "He was a good officer. He had a sense of responsibility. Do you have anything to add to Major Harrison's comments?"

The other pilots shook their heads.

"That's about it, sir," Number Three said.

"I can't think of anything else, sir," Number Two replied.

"OK, Harrison," Enko went on. "Tell me, what did we get in return for Fielding and twenty-two million dollars' worth of airplane?"

"We destroyed two ammunition dumps, a fuel farm, a stockpile of oil drums, railroad tracks, boxcars, tanks, heavy artillery, and a couple of SAM sites."

"Was it worth it?"

"I think so, sir," Harrison answered, trying to keep his temper under the General's probing.

"What about you two?" Enko insisted.

"We did a lot of damage, sir," Number Two stated.

"I concur," said Number Three.

"Don't you kid yourselves," Enko snarled. "We lost one of our best men and those goddamned bastards will be back in business tomorrow. You weren't supposed to take any risks with that airplane. Harrison, I want a complete report explaining why you permitted an aircraft like this to be lost in exchange for a few cans of gasoline. You'd better make it good."

Enko turned to McSnair and Keegan. "I want to know what happened to that TX-75E. All I can tell you is that there'll be hell to pay if those Gooks got hold of it. It's too bad about Fielding. But right now, our main concern is the fate of the aircraft. I want all airplanes operating in the vicinity of Hoa Binh to take a good look at the spot where Fielding disappeared. Harrison, you brief the crews accordingly. Next, send a couple of F4s to take a look around and monitor the emergency frequency. They should be able to pick up his distress beeper on two forty-three point zero. If he's still alive, that is."

Captain Keegan was dutifully noting the General's instructions with Colonel McSnair looking over his shoulder and nodding.

"I want Skyraiders and Jolly Greens to take a look around also as soon as practicable. They're slow enough to do a good spotting job at low altitude. The helicopters are to get close enough to take detailed pictures of the wreckage—if they find it. We've got to know exactly what happened to that plane. We must find out if the flash that Harrison and the others saw was the self-destruct mechanism activated by Fielding or if the airplane blew up. Last, let's try to find Fielding. He's the only one that can really tell us what happened. I don't want to lose any more airplanes, is that clear?"

"Yes, sir," Colonel McSnair said. "I'll get on it immediately."

General Enko tried to puff on his cigar, but it was extinct. He threw it on the wooden floor and stormed out of the briefing room, went into his office, and slammed the door behind him.

That same night, in the United States, the seven-o'clock news on ABC, CBS, and NBC TV opened with the usual report on the Vietnam situation.

Grim-faced anchor men described the vicissitudes of American troops in Southeast Asia. They referred to various statements emanating from U.S. Headquarters in Saigon, stressing the vital importance of each hamlet that had been under attack that day.

ABC had a front-line report from one of their correspondents. He was in army fatigues, with a five-o'clock shadow, playing to the hilt the part of the intrepid reporter doing live stuff in the thick of battle. He held his foam-rubber-covered mike close to his mouth and panted that he was under heavy fire from the Viet Cong at a Marine outpost "somewhere in South Vietnam." In case the viewers were not convinced of his temerity, he held the mike at arm's length for a moment and told them to listen for enemy gunfire. Under the eye of the camera he then threw himself into a ditch. Still out of breath, he signed off, telling his audience he would be back with more reports of the day-to-day activities of the fighting men defending freedom in the jungle. One thing he didn't mention—he was hoping for a raise.

On CBS, the anchor man announced that heavy raids had been conducted that day over North Vietnam, inflicting crippling damage to Hanoi, Haiphong, and Hoa Binh. He said reports from the U.S. Command in Saigon conceded that one B-52 bomber and four other aircraft were missing in action. Hanoi, he added, claimed eight U.S. airplanes had been downed.

Grant Fielding had become just another statistic.

CHAPTER 6

Colonel Bernie McSnair got on the telephone and called Nakhon Phanom Air Base in Thailand.

Also known as "Naked Fanny," Nakhon Phanom was an "ultra-hush" facility with an eight-thousand-foot runway located on the border between Thailand and Laos, about 250 miles northwest of Da Nang. Neither of these countries was supposed to be directly involved in the Vietnamese conflict. Washington, however, was pouring enough money into the government coffers of Bangkok and Vientiane to keep corrupt officials looking the other way.

A1H "Skyraiders"—single-engine prop planes with tandem seats, nicknamed "Sandys"—were based here. The pilot occupied the front seat and, when required, a combination navigator-observer sat in the back. Although unsuited for modern air combat, these planes were ideal for reconnaissance operations. One of their assignments was the patrolling of "McNamara's Fence," named after the latest brain storm of the onetime Secretary of Defense. This electronic barrier, strung along the demilitarized zone between North and South Vietnam, had made computer and microwave equipment manufacturers delirious with joy. And needless to say, very wealthy. This was the Pentagon's ultimate answer to North Vietnamese infiltrations into the South via the DMZ or the Ho Chi Minh Trail, which snaked through Laos and Cambodia.

Sensors could give the precise co-ordinates, speed, and direction of a supply truck operating in the vicinity of the demarcation lines. "Sniffers," the electronic equivalent of bloodhounds, were supposed to distinguish by the exhaust fumes whether the trucks were French, Russian, or Chinese. Remotely controlled "miracle" gadgets could theoretically detect so much as a suspicious footstep about to cross the border. Maniacal enthusiasts of the System envisioned the day when the Sniffers would be able to discern, from the smell of their breath, whether the infiltrators were North Vietnamese, Cambodian, or Laotian.

Pentagon officials had become hysterical when cynical reporters, taken on a grand tour of McNamara's Fence, had not been overly impressed. Some of their articles had suggested that empty beer cans strung on a clothesline across the border might be cheaper and more effective.

Crammed with "black boxes," the Sandys would travel up and down the Fence. Specialists on the ground would activate the electronic equipment aboard the planes. The "black boxes" would instantaneously relay the queries and interrogate the sensitive equipment planted along the border. The computers occasionally went haywire, triggering false alarms. Headquarters would then needlessly send out swarms of jet fighters or bombers.

Even if nothing was accomplished, it was considered to be good training for everyone concerned, thereby justifying the millions of dollars spent on this inane project.

The Sandys were also used extensively for search and rescue missions. Their slow cruising speed of about 120 knots and excellent maneuverability permitted them to take a long, close look at the ground and to play bird dog for HC-53s—multipurpose jumbo helicopters nicknamed, "Jolly Green Giants." The Sandys usually preceded the Jolly Greens, pinpointed the rescue area, awaited their arrival, and stood by to suppress ground fire as they picked up survivors.

With Captain Keegan standing respectfully at his elbow, Colonel McSnair, somewhat agitated and fumbling for his glasses, relayed General Enko's orders for an immediate search and rescue operation in the Hoa Binh sector.

The Colonel then told Keegan to advise the U.S. Command in Saigon. Headquarters would order bulletins to be posted in every briefing room, at every base and on every aircraft carrier. Until further notice, the crews on all types of aircraft operating in the vicinity of Hoa Binh would remain on lookout for the missing pilot and/or plane wreckage.

At 1400—two hours and forty minutes after Grant Fielding's disappearance—three Sandys, tuned to the emergency frequency of 243.0, were on their way. They were soon followed by two Jolly Greens, which would take about two hours to cover the 240-mile distance separating Nakhon Phanom from Hoa Binh via a 100-mile stretch over Laotian territory.

The Sandys were greeted by heavy enemy flak, which erupted the instant they came into view of Hoa Binh.

It was just past 1600 and the cloud cover had thickened over the area. The ceiling had dropped to less than six thousand feet, forcing the Skyraiders to operate at lower altitude, where they were more vulnerable.

The gunners on the ground wondered why there was such intense activity by the U.S. Air Force in their sector that day. As far as they knew, no more men and supplies than usual were transiting the town. There seemed little justification for the Americans to risk successive waves of fighter-bombers and reconnaissance aircraft on such run-of-the-mill objectives.

The three airplanes concentrated their search on the southwest edge of town, not bothering to return enemy fire. Most of the heavy smoke resulting from the attack of the Vampire flight had cleared. Individual blazes smoldered here and there. One could possibly be the debris of Grant's airplane.

The Sandys stubbornly combed the area hoping they could spot the remnants of a wing, fuselage, or tail section. They found nothing. There was complete silence on the emergency frequency Grant would be using if he were still alive and not captured by the North Vietnamese.

The rescue team tried to raise Grant on the voice channel of the emergency transmitter. All calls of "Beeper, Beeper, come up voice" from the Skyraiders to the ground remained unanswered.

By this time, the Jolly Greens were approaching the search zone.

The helicopter flight leader called his counterpart in charge of the Skyraiders.

"Jolly One to Sandy One. We're about ten miles out. Do you want us to get any closer?"

"No. Got nothing for you yet . . . we're looking . . . better stay put . . . too much action for you guys right now . . . you OK where you are?"

"Roger," Jolly One replied. "No problem for the moment . . . keep in touch."

"OK."

The ground fire was becoming intense. One of the Skyraiders was hit in the tail. The pilot called to say no one was hurt and that he would try limping home.

The Skyraider leader, in charge of the entire operation, assigned one of the helicopters to follow him.

With the second helicopter standing by, the two remaining Sandys continued their search for a while longer.

The weather was getting nasty and the flak heavier. MIGs had certainly been alerted by now and would soon be on their way to attack the Sandys, who were no match for them.

The Skyraider leader decided it was time to go. He told the remaining Jolly Green to make a 180-degree turn back to base, then ordered the other Sandy to climb through the cloud cover and head for Nakhon Phanom.

It was almost 1630. The search and rescue mission had lasted thirty minutes, producing no tangible result except for a crippled Sandy, which, hopefully, would make it back home.

Captain Keegan got the bad news from Nakhon Phanom at about 1900 hours. The first S and R operation had been unsuccessful, but the Sandys would try again the next day.

Keegan found Colonel McSnair at the Officers' Club and relayed the information.

McSnair lambasted Keegan, who was rewarded with a little speech stressing how dumb he was and not fit even to be a messenger boy. Keegan was getting it from all sides. This was definitely not his day.

Hoping for a negative reply, McSnair checked with Lieutenant Dow to find out if General Enko was in. The General's right-hand man told him to report at once.

A few minutes later, McSnair knocked timidly on Enko's door.

"Well, McSnair, what have you got for me?" He did not invite the fidgety Colonel to sit down.

"Nothing much, sir. The first search was unproductive. The Sandys got a good look for about thirty minutes, though. No trace of the airplane. No beeper. No voice. The area was heavily defended. One of the Sandys was hit. No casualties."

"How many aircraft participated in the search?"

"Three Skyraiders and two HC-53s, sir."

Enko stared at McSnair, deliberately making him uncomfortable. He rose, lit a cigar, and walked over to a map hanging on a wall to the right of his desk.

"That's too bad," Enko finally said, looking attentively at the map with his back to McSnair. "Fielding should now officially be listed as missing in action," he continued. "Better advise his next of kin."

"Will do, sir."

McSnair stopped cringing. Enko seemed to be taking things a little more calmly now. He was sparing his sarcasm—a good sign. The Colonel noticed that, as usual, and despite the oppressive heat, the General's uniform was impeccably pressed. He was fifty-three, but looked ten years younger. His jet black hair was gray at the temples and blended perfectly with the hard-chiseled face. He was a trim six-footer, weighing about 180 pounds with an unusually broad chest on which rows of campaign ribbons were proudly displayed. He radiated authority. Only a fool would not be intimidated by this man. McSnair was at a disadvantage. Only five foot eight, at thirty-nine, he was paunchy and losing his hair.

Enko motioned the Colonel to come closer. He traced a broad circle with the wet tip of his cigar around Hoa Binh.

"Extend the search to a 50-mile radius of the target area. He may have succeeded in gaining some ground, even with reduced power."

"Yes, sir."

To McSnair's surprise, General Enko adopted a paternal tone and asked him to sit down.

"As you know, Colonel, I'm due in Washington in nineteen days for a staff conference. Although you might sometimes think me harsh with you, I've decided to leave you in charge while I'm gone."

McSnair felt a lump in his throat and made an unsuccessful

effort to smile to show his appreciation. He pulled out a handkerchief and mopped his balding pate.

"I'll be away about two weeks. You think you can handle it?"

"Oh yes, sir."

"You're aware, I'm sure, of the responsibility I'm entrusting to you. I hope I won't be disappointed."

McSnair nodded respectfully.

"You won't be, sir. I'll do my best."

"I know you will, McSnair." Enko sounded almost kind. "Now back to our present business. We've had our growing pains with TX-75E."

"Haven't we, though, sir," the Colonel hastened to agree.

"The press back home goes into an uproar every time one of them is lost. It's become a political thing. The enemies of the Pentagon claim it's a defective toy that cracks up by itself without the help of enemy gunfire. Some dodoes in Congress want to cut out appropriations for further development of the airplane from next year's budget. I'll probably be called in to testify about the airworthiness of the aircraft."

"I don't envy you, sir," McSnair said solicitously. "Those senators just don't understand our problems. All they think about is money."

"They represent the taxpayers. There's nothing much you can do about that. True, the airplane still has a few bugs, and it doesn't always perform to specs. But I don't buy the theory about that weakness in the wing structure which is supposed to cause the crack-ups. We need time to perfect it and that means money. This is a first-generation model. It will serve as the basis for streamlining the Air Force."

"If only these politicians could see the light," McSnair agreed.

"They don't want to see any lights. They want to cut costs." Enko spoke with contempt. "Do you know some want to ground the airplane? Others have suggested we dump them on the Australians for whatever we can get. They want to give away twenty-two-million-dollar planes just because they don't have the guts to stick it out. Jesus, that burns my ass."

"I know, sir. You've nursed those airplanes ever since they were on the drawing board."

"You're damn right. I conducted the initial flight tests. It's a

64

good airplane. I put my life into it. I'm not going to let them scrap it. I'll bring this project to completion if it kills me."

Enko's eyes were flashing. For a fleeting moment McSnair thought he detected a hint of lunacy in them. The Colonel decided it best to humor him.

"I'm sure you'll convince the right people to keep the project alive, sir."

Enko wasn't listening.

"If these idiots in Congress and the newspapers only knew how badly the Russians and the Chinese want to get hold of this airplane, they'd change their minds fast. But we can't publicize this. It's supposed to be a secret weapon. But it won't be for long, with all those goddamned leaks in Washington."

"Why do politicians always have to learn the hard way?" McSnair laid it on with the tingling feeling he was becoming the General's confidant.

"Because they wouldn't be doing what they're doing for a living if they had any brains," Enko snarled. "Anyway, McSnair, let's get back to the subject. If the airplane isn't found by the time I leave, I want you to continue the search. I sincerely hope Fielding managed to bail out and activate the self-destruct mechanism. But if he didn't I hope to God the airplane blew up when it crashed. I want to be reassured as soon as possible by having that wreckage spotted—preferably in tiny bits and pieces. Then, at least, we'd know the enemy couldn't reassemble the airplane. Remember, McSnair, this is my baby."

"You can count on me, General," McSnair said solemnly. "I will leave no stone unturned. I promise you that."

General Enko stood up. In an unprecedented emotional gesture of friendliness he accompanied McSnair to the door, put one arm around his shoulder, and shook his hand.

"Thanks, Colonel," he said. "You're a good man."

CHAPTER 7

The circumstances of Grant's disappearance over Hoa Binh as witnessed and reported by Major Harrison had become fact.

What actually took place during the rapid and confusing sequence of events which had occurred in the heat of battle was a different matter.

For Grant, things began to happen very quickly after his distress call.

He distinctly heard Harrison's pressing order to "eject and destruct" at the very moment he plunged into the overcast and the rest of the formation lost visual contact with him.

Grant was completely familiar with the terrain from previous missions.

Just as he broke through the cloud cover, he saw the ground coming up fast.

He took deliberate aim, fired a missile at a heavy gun emplacement on the flank of a mountain directly below, and banked steeply to avoid the blast.

The resulting explosion of the antiaircraft ammunition illuminated the sky, infusing a pinkish glow to the base of the clouds. This, he knew, would be remembered by his three teammates watching over him.

If everything went according to plan, this would be a masterpiece of premeditated misdirection.

Still under the clouds, extremely tense at the prospect of being seen by either Harrison or one of his escorts, Grant abruptly descended to treetop height and added power. He then flew straight and level on a westerly course for two minutes—away from the town and the other three pilots.

Once out of immediate range of the flak, he turned to the right and hedgehopped as he described a wide circle that took him around the northern outskirts of Hoa Binh.

The antiaircraft gunners did not expect another fighter-bomber

66

to return. In the few seconds they took to react, Grant was due east of the town and fast getting out of reach.

As he hugged the ground to remain invisible to radar, Grant switched his radio dials. He selected the prearranged frequency scheduled to be used after rendezvous.

He listened intently to the chatter of the pilots and did not begin to relax until he heard Harrison saying he thought Number Four was a goner.

Grant, nevertheless, kept monitoring the channel.

He stopped sweating after Harrison told Numbers Two and Three to call it quits for the day and return to Da Nang.

Grant removed his oxygen mask and took a deep breath.

A broad smile lit his face now that he was certain no one was coming back to look for him.

He made sure his transmitter was off and let out an ear-shattering yell.

Grant's relief was only momentary. The most critical and hazardous phase of the trip was just beginning. Until out of enemy territory, he would have to stay dangerously close to the ground to avoid radar detection. He must remain alert, not just for natural obstacles protruding from the rough terrain, but for antiaircraft shells and rockets as well. Peasants were another potential danger, since they would certainly try to take potshots at him.

While dodging enemy fire Grant would have to search the sky constantly for fear of being noticed by MIGs or, even worse, as far as he was concerned, American airplanes operating in the area.

He had two good reasons to feel jumpy about U.S. planes. Since he was flying alone, he could be mistaken for an enemy aircraft by some pilot with an itchy trigger finger and get shot down by his own side. On the other hand, if he were recognized as a friendly plane lost or in trouble, some well-intentioned American airman might try to be of assistance. This would complicate matters, since Grant had absolutely no intention of ever going back to Da Nang.

Only a few feet above the ground, in hot, muggy, overcast weather, Grant had to pay close attention to his navigation. His perspective was very limited, and his radios useless for homing at such low altitude. Everything was a blur, the features of the land hard to distinguish.

Raids were in progress over Hanoi and Haiphong, about 50 miles north of his immediate whereabouts. Grant steered clear by threading his way around the towns of Phu Ly and Nam Dinh—both well to the south of the combat area.

No matter what happened, he mustn't go too far south and get close to the demilitarized zone. He couldn't take the chance of being detected by the electronic gadgets along McNamara's Fence and have all hell break loose.

When Grant spotted Phat Diem coming up on the horizon, about twenty minutes after leaving Hoa Binh, he knew the North Vietnamese coast was next.

It was only after he crossed the shoreline and let down to thirty feet over the South China Sea that he began to breathe normally.

He established a southeasterly heading which would take him over the Gulf of Tonkin, far below the Communist Chinese island of Hainan.

Grant pushed the throttles forward and set his cruising speed at just under 700 miles per hour. He could have gone supersonic, but he did not want to attract attention by triggering any booms.

Flying this low and zigzagging over the swell, he ran the risk of spray hitting the aircraft with fatal consequences. Going any higher would mean taking the chance of being detected and tracked by U.S. warships patrolling the area.

At his present altitude the only snag was that his own radar was as ineffective as those that might be looking for him. He could not spot the ships electronically and had to rely strictly on eye contact to give them the slip.

Grant saw the contrails of Navy fighters crossing his path at about thirty thousand feet. This gave him a jolt. They were in and out of clouds, on their way to North Vietnam, coming from the southeast. He changed course to evade their carrier.

At 1230 on that fateful day, or just about the same time Harrison and the other members of the Vampire flight were landing in Da Nang, Grant came up on Bombay Reef at the southeastern tip of the Paracel archipelago. He had covered the 600-mile distance from Hoa Binh in just under one hour.

He climbed to 250 feet and slowed down to 140 miles per hour.

Grant turned squarely south, looking for a landmark. He found it quickly and brought the airplane to a standstill in the air.

He made the fighter-bomber hover over the tiny island while he looked around, making sure it was deserted and that no one had followed him. Gradually, he brought the aircraft down on a wooden platform hidden by a camouflage net. He cut the engines, opened the canopy, and let himself down to stretch his legs.

He walked around the airplane, inspected it for damage, and found none. He checked the nose wheel and the main landing gear. They were firmly planted on the platform.

Grant went aboard the camouflaged *Solitude*, took off his helmet, removed his flight suit, and deposited them in the wheelhouse. He opened a can of orange soda. It was warm but he drank it with relish. Clad only in a pair of tennis shorts, he picked up a gun in the wheelhouse and put it in his hip pocket.

From one of the two large crates in the hold he took out a camouflage net, a small aluminum ladder, cables, a can of gray paint, a brush, and a sharp knife, which he lowered onto the beach.

Climbing on the ladder, he quickly spread the netting over the airplane.

In a very happy mood now, whistling while he worked under the netting, Grant anchored the airplane's landing gear to the platform.

He opened his can of paint and blocked out all identification markings on the wings, fuselage, and tail. He replaced the lid on the can and took it, together with the brush, back aboard the *Solitude*.

Next, Grant ran a hose from the bow of the ship to the airplane and pumped out all the fuel remaining in the wings. It went into forward tanks of the vessel. Drained of twenty-four thousand pounds of fuel and minus its full six-thousand-pound load of bombs dropped over Hoa Binh, the aircraft and its remaining armaments of missiles, rockets, and 30-mm cannon shells now weighed just under twenty-one thousand pounds. Grant propped the ladder against the fuselage and climbed into the cockpit. Using internal battery power, he activated the retraction mechanism which neatly folded the empty wings along the fuselage. He made sure all switches were off, stepped back on the ladder, and closed the canopy.

Back on the beach, he used his knife to cut out the netting around the platform. A long rectangular section still remained pinned under the wheels of the landing gear. Alternately tugging at the mesh and making incisions, he struggled to pull the rest of the net loose from beneath the wheels. The platform was now free of all entanglements and completely exposed.

Grant looked at the time. It was close to 1600 hours; he was getting hungry. He ate a can of corned beef and drank another can of soda while reviewing the next few chores to be accomplished.

He removed the camouflage nets which covered the ship, grappling with them for a good hour. They were stored inside the crates in the hold.

With the crane at the bow of the *Solitude*, he picked up the roof of the cabin and deposited it on the beach.

He went ashore and once again climbed on the ladder to remove the net which had served to hide the airplane.

Grant began to hurry now that the ship and the plane were no longer camouflaged.

He hooked up the crane to the platform and gently hoisted the airplane, which was gently lowered into the cabin.

Swinging the crane over the beach, he picked up the roof and replaced it over the hold.

He quickly gathered up and stored the last of the remaining nets still on the beach. The anchors wedged into the rocks and the chains linking them to the ship were now exposed.

Grant donned scuba gear. He swam to the submerged stern anchors and pried them loose.

Back on the shore, he loosened the other two anchors on the beach, dragged them to the bow, and hoisted them aboard with the crane.

Grant was sweating profusely, but there was one last thing to do.

He picked up a broom in the wheelhouse, went ashore, and began to sweep away all the traces of his presence from the sand.

Walking backwards toward the *Solitude*, he smoothed out the imprints of the chains and erased the marks of his footsteps as he went along.

Grant's heart skipped a beat just as he was about to climb back aboard the ship for the last time. The ladder was still lying in the sand next to where the platform had rested. He cursed himself for almost having forgotten this last detail, and heaved it onto the deck.

Grant swept away the traces of the ladder, threw the broom aboard, and took a final look at the beach.

No one would ever know he had been there.

He went aboard the *Solitude* and started the engines.

It was almost 1930 hours.

Just as Grant Fielding was being officially listed as "missing in action" in Da Nang, the *Solitude*, her engines in reverse, was slowly pulling away from the beach.

CHAPTER 8

When dawn broke, Grant found himself under cloudy skies 200 miles due east of the Paracels. With the aid of the autopilot and collision warning system, he had managed to sleep about four hours.

He unfurled a Panamanian flag and flew it from the stern.

The weather forecast predicted possible rain and rough seas for the next twenty-four hours. He lowered the extra keel. This would steady the ship but reduce his cruising speed from an average of 17 to 15 knots.

From a drawer of the small desk in the wheelhouse, Grant produced a large diary and several charts which he spread out to plot his course along the great circle route. This would be the shortest distance between his present position and destination. He would have to make detours, however, weaving in and out of heavily traveled shipping lanes to avoid being sighted—especially by warships of the U.S. Seventh Fleet.

Grant calculated that, even at 15 knots, he would cover a minimum of 360 nautical miles per day. The trip would take no more than three weeks. But if he could retract the keel for part of the way, and take advantage of the easterly flow of the Japan Current, he might complete his 7,200-mile voyage in 18 to 19 days.

He set the autopilot on a heading which would take him past the northeastern extremity of the Philippines, between the islands of Bataan and Taiwan. The weather was breezy with the sun occasionally peeking through the clouds. Grant filled his lungs with fresh air, relaxed, and began to enjoy the journey. He made numerous trips from the hold to the sun roof to bring up the six boxes containing the mannequins, air mattresses, two beach umbrellas, a folding table, and seven aluminum chairs. Since the mannequins were to be his companions on this trip, he decided to name them according to the phonetic alphabet. "Alfa" seemed to fit the bald, semiretired appliance-salesman type. The muscular, long-haired beachcomber became Bravo. The middle-aged, beer-bellied, crew-cut tourist was dubbed Charlie. The Oriental girl was named Delta. The black beauty with the Afro, Echo. And the sun-ripened, appetizing California kitten, Foxtrot. The hair on the mannequins had become flat and tangled during their cramped stay in the dampness of the hold. Grant went to the wheelhouse for a comb and brush.

For an hour he became a high-fashion stylist; fluffing up the hair, applying make-up to the girls, and dressing his "passengers." Foxtrot was last to be groomed. When he was finished, he patted her on the derrière to express his satisfaction with her appearance. "Not bad for a first try," he said aloud.

Delta was gorgeous in her microscopic swim suit. Echo looked much better topless, so he removed her bra. As for Foxtrot, he decided to leave her bottomless.

Charlie was given a pair of tight-fitting trunks and propped against the railing, leaning forward, as if looking out to sea. Delta was placed on his left, her right arm around his waist. The breeze ruffled her long hair, blowing it across her face into Charlie's, making them appear like lovers engaged in tender conversation.

The pudgy and balding Alfa was issued a pair of ridiculous, baggy Bermuda shorts that hung way below his knees, and a sun visor that partially covered his face. Grant fastened him to the railing on the starboard side. Bending his right arm over his head, he placed a yellow handkerchief in his hand. Alfa looked as if he were waving at passing ships.

The table was set with a large red plastic cooler surrounded by cans of beer. The reclining chairs were scattered about the sun roof under the beach umbrellas.

Grant inflated all six mattresses and taped them to the deck. He put one along the railing on the port side. Foxtrot was placed face-down on this mattress, her head between her arms, her little round bottom sticking up. The long-haired Bravo was placed beside her. Bravo's head was made to rest on Foxtrot's back, the face to one side, the arms around her waist.

"This is charming," Grant said, "but something's still missing." Breaking into laughter, he ran to the wheelhouse and returned with a purple felt-tipped pen. With painstaking care, he traced a large heart on the upper part of Bravo's left arm and carefully inscribed "MOTHER" inside the tattoo.

Grant sprawled the topless Echo in a lazy position on a reclining chair. He put a can of beer in her left hand, perched a white floppy hat atop her Afro, and tilted it over her eyes.

He went to the bow to contemplate his window dressing from a distance. This really looks convincing, he thought, I could swear these dummies are real people. Grant had successfully accomplished his aim.

It was past 0900. Grant reset the autopilot, tuned in rock music from Manila, and made some coffee. Donning a striped swim suit, beach hat, and sunglasses, he went on deck and stretched out in a chair beside Echo. "Here's to you, baby," he said, raising his coffee mug.

He set the alarm on his calendar wrist watch and made himself comfortable as he listened to the music.

"Keep a sharp lookout, Alfa. You too, Charlie. Bravo, my boy, don't overexert yourself with that chick. As for me, boys and girls, it's time for a little siesta."

Grant allowed his thoughts to drift. By now, his parents should have been advised that their only child was missing in action and presumed dead. That bothered him, but there was nothing he could do about it. His father must have taken the news stoically. Grant was certain that, as usual, he had caught the 7:42 A.M. from Stamford to New York and put up a dignified front for the benefit of his colleagues at Central Architecture and Engineering, Inc. Grant had a soft spot for his old man. He had never made the big time as an architect and, at fifty-six, had resigned himself to his fate. Well, that was the price you paid if you lacked the guts to aim high. Who knows, he might have been another Frank Lloyd Wright.

Nonetheless, Grant Fielding, Sr., had been a good provider. The family owned two cars, a thirty-foot cabin cruiser, and the house was paid off. He voted Republican, never cheated on his income tax returns, and was for "peace with honor" in Vietnam. A mem-

73

ber in good standing of the "silent majority," he would become angry whenever his son called it the "silent mediocrity."

Grant's thoughts focused on his mother. She had probably fallen apart and blamed her son's death on her husband—a typical reaction whenever things went wrong. Elvira Fielding had never understood her son's early fascination with airplanes and had attempted, without success, to talk him out of taking lessons in those "dangerous contraptions." True to form, his father had preferred to ignore the situation, thereby giving Grant his tacit approval by default. It was only after Grant became a "legitimate" pilot in the Air Force that his mother finally gave up.

The alarm woke Grant at noon. He went to the wheelhouse and switched from Manila to the Hong Kong news broadcast: The Vietnam peace talks were still progressing in Paris and, barring any unforeseen complications, hostilities would soon be over.

Grant didn't believe a word of it. From the preparations he had witnessed in Da Nang, the United States had no intention of tiptoeing out right now. True, the elections at home were soon due, and the President was posing as a man of peace. Yet, he still advocated negotiations from a position of strength. In plain English, that meant continued bombing of North Vietnam until Hanoi made major concessions.

The announcer went on to say that the monsoon season was hampering American raids. Many operations scheduled over North Vietnam were now suspended because of heavy rains.

Good, Grant thought. This would also prevent the search and rescue teams from looking for the "remains of his aircraft" now in the hold of the *Solitude*.

By 1400, the weather had improved. He pulled up the retractable keel and began to make better speed. Then he went below to check the engines. Everything was in order.

Back in the wheelhouse, he adjusted the autopilot and switched over to the aft fuel reserves. He would now have to change tanks every few hours to trim the ship.

Grant took some bearings. The *Solitude* was exactly halfway between Manila and Hong Kong and making good time. He estimated she would be abeam Laoag, at the northern end of the

Philippines, by nightfall and reach the vicinity of Bataan by daybreak.

Getting bored, he pulled out a magnetic chess set and a book recounting famous matches. Opening a can of beer, he set up the chessmen and replayed an epic battle between Bobby Fischer of the United States and Russia's Boris Spassky.

At 1800, just as Grant Fielding was rounding Laoag, Colonel Bernie McSnair reported to General Enko in Da Nang.

"Two attempts were made to locate Captain Fielding, today, sir."

Enko looked up from behind his desk. "Well?"

"Heavy rain cut the visibility to almost nothing around Hoa Binh. The search and rescue teams had to turn back."

"How about the B-52s? They bombed Hanoi through the cloud cover. Did they pick up any beepers?"

"No, sir. All the reports are in. No beepers. But even if he did turn on the emergency locator, the batteries would be getting low by now. He's been missing for over thirty hours."

"What's the weather outlook?"

"Pretty bad for the next four or five days, sir. It's the rainy season, all right."

"We've got all the luck, don't we? At least there's one thing going for us. If the airplane did crack up on a mountain, it's just as difficult for the enemy to get to it as it is for us. One more thing. If our guys do find that plane and it's not completely demolished, let them shoot some rockets at it. I want it pulverized."

"Will do, sir."

"OK, McSnair. I know you're doing your best. Keep me advised."

Grant crossed the 120th meridian east of Greenwich and set his watch one hour ahead.

By 2300, he was fast asleep, his alarm set for 0300.

He awoke feeling fit and vigorous—treating himself to tea instead of his usual coffee. He opened his diary, logged a few notes, and took cross bearings. Grant estimated he'd pass between Bataan and Taiwan at about 0900.

The *Solitude* was getting lighter as she consumed fuel. Grant determined the amount of diesel oil burned during the first thirty-six hours of the trip. The engines were performing smoothly as per specs. The fuel flow was normal.

At 0730, the weather turned warm and hazy. Grant went up to the sun deck. He sat on a mattress next to Alfa, who was still waving his yellow handkerchief at nonexistent passing ships.

Grant drank some tea as the ship rocked gently on course. He felt like a millionaire on a private yacht living the carefree life. A numbing feeling of peace permeated every muscle of his body. The throbbing of the engines made him feel wonderfully drowsy as he stretched out luxuriously. He didn't try to fight the slumber induced by the hot sun and the wind's gentle caress.

A piercing whistle shattered the air. Grant jumped to his feet and looked at his watch. It was almost noon. He had slept four hours. He ran to the wheelhouse and switched off the warning system.

There were two large blips on the radar—the first at one o'clock, 18 miles distant and closing in—the other at eleven o'clock, 20 miles away, following the first blip. He felt a knot in his stomach.

Grant nervously lit a cigarette, letting it dangle from his lips, as he took cross bearings. The *Solitude* was 30 nautical miles northeast of Bataan on a heading of 070 degrees.

The two targets could mean big trouble if they were U.S. warships proceeding from Japan to the Subic Bay Navy Base in the Philippines on their way to Vietnam.

Grant turned on his VHFs and rapidly dialed through a multitude of standard civilian and military frequencies hoping to intercept exchanges between the two vessels. A jumble of words poured through the static. He turned up the volume and adjusted the squelch. The nuclear carrier U.S.S. *Enterprise* was calling the battleship *New Jersey*, recently taken out of mothballs and put back on active duty.

From the drift of the staccato dialogue, Grant learned that the ship closer to him was the *New Jersey*, now only 15 miles away and converging. The *Enterprise* was asking the *New Jersey* to perform a visual check and identify a small vessel, behaving erratically and possibly in difficulty, presently on radar on a course of 070 degrees. The carrier added that it preferred to remain clear of all ships for the moment.

Grant checked his charts. He had either forgotten to reset the autopilot or it had momentarily disengaged while he had been asleep, letting the ship zigzag all over the ocean. No wonder the *Enterprise* thought something was amiss and that he could be in distress. He pushed the throttles full forward and turned away to the left on a heading of 050 degrees, trying to put as much distance as possible between the *Solitude* and the *New Jersey*.

The *Solitude* was on the high seas, in international waters, and the *New Jersey* had no right to intercept a civilian vessel flying the Panamanian flag. But it was not uncommon in these troubled waters for ships to be boarded for inspection, even if apologies had to be expressed later. Remember the *Pueblo*, he said to himself, recalling the incident of the American spy ship captured by the North Koreans. The boarding of the *Solitude* was out of the question with that TX-75E sitting in the hold.

The *New Jersey* was now 12 miles away. The *Solitude* could not outrun it. The *Enterprise* continued on course, widening the distance between her and the *New Jersey*.

Grant had no choice but to implement his contingency plan.

His face contorted with rage and apprehension as he quickly planted dynamite charges in the bow, the stern, and under the aircraft in the hold.

He returned to the deck carrying a rubber dinghy, which he inflated with a CO_2 cartridge, a small outboard motor, a telescopic mast, a sail, paddles, and cans of food. Then he ran to the wheelhouse and prepared his scuba equipment.

Should the *New Jersey* attempt to intercept him, Grant would have to blow up the *Solitude*. But he would escape by donning his scuba gear, lowering the dinghy from the blind side of the *New Jersey*, and then igniting the fuses. As the *Solitude* went down, he'd remain submerged, clinging to one of the dinghy's ropes, hoping the battleship would think the rubber craft was simply part of the debris. After the *New Jersey* left, he would climb into the little boat and make for Bataan.

Grant's plan had always ruled out rescue. It meant trial for high treason, and execution, if any piece of the aircraft were to be found. Even if the ship sank without a trace, the best he could hope for would be a court-martial for desertion.

His decision was irrevocable. There would be no survivors on the *Solitude*.

He remained glued to the radar screen. The battleship was gaining steadily. Although the *Solitude* was operating at maximum speed of 18 knots, the *New Jersey*, at over 30 knots, was closing in fast.

It was 1215. The battleship had picked up 3 miles in the last eleven minutes and was now only 9 miles away. The *Enterprise* remained at the edge of the screen, about 20 miles distant.

On the theory the lookouts were communicating by walkie-talkie with the bridge of the *New Jersey*, Grant tried to intercept the exchanges on FM, VHF, and UHF, but to no avail. He concluded that the battleship probably was using an intercom system. Grant and the *Enterprise* were unable to listen in.

Clad in his scuba gear, dripping with perspiration, Grant cursed venomously in frustration as the *Solitude* pitched and rolled in the moderate swell. He lit another cigarette which he would use to ignite the fuses if the battleship got any closer than 2 miles. He watched intently as the radar blip grew nearer.

At 1240, the *New Jersey* was 4 miles away, still coming at him. It turned slightly toward the starboard side of the *Solitude*, readying to cut across her bow.

Two more miles—blip . . . blip . . . blip . . . blip . . .

The rhythmic pulse on the radar screen began to reverberate in his brain . . . his temples were pounding . . . his heartbeat quickened . . .

Blip . . . blip . . . blip . . . 1245 . . . blip . . . blip . . .

If he had to make the move, now was the time. "Goddammit," he cried out, "all this fucking work for nothing!"

For no apparent reason, the blip became stationary—the *New Jersey* was reducing speed. Why?

Grant was jolted by a blast over the VHF. He instinctively turned toward the radio, as he realized that the battleship's intercom had been patched into the open frequency with the *Enterprise*. The carrier and Grant could now listen to the conversation between the *New Jersey*'s bridge and the lookouts.

Ensign Bud Baker, efficient and ferret-faced, called one of the spotters.

"This is Mr. Baker, on the bridge. The Captain says we're close enough now. We can't make out much down here. What about you?"

Boatswain's Mate Third Class Irwin Rosenthal, a jolly, blubbery butterball armed with binoculars, replied.

"It's pretty hazy, sir . . . It's a small ship . . . about seven hundred to a thousand tons, I would say. Looks like a coastal freighter converted into a private yacht, or something like that, Mr. Baker."

"Can you make out anything else, Rosenthal?"

"Hard to focus, sir . . . Wait a second . . . There seems to be someone on the starboard side . . . It looks like some fat slob in Bermuda shorts waving at us, sir . . ."

"Never mind your personal opinions, Rosenthal," Baker remonstrated. "Just tell us what you see."

Grant froze. Alfa and his yellow handkerchief had been spotted. He couldn't just let him stand there with his arm over his head. It would soon be obvious that this man wasn't moving. He grabbed a can of beer, ran out to the sun deck, and stood to the right of the mannequin, waving his beer at the *New Jersey*.

"Sir," Rosenthal said, as Grant heard him clearly over the radio blasting from the wheelhouse, "there's another guy standing next to him now. He came out of the bridge . . . He's waving too . . . He's holding something in his hand . . . It's a can of soda or something."

"What flag is she flying? What's her name?"

"Can't see too clearly, sir. Let me clean these lenses . . . Be right with you . . ."

Grant put his left arm around Alfa's waist, then grabbed the mannequin's right arm, wrapping it around his own shoulders, as he continued waving the beer can.

"Mr. Baker, sir? . . . I think she's Panamanian, as far as I can make out . . . Yes . . . She's definitely Panamanian."

"Oh, one of those. What's she called?"

"Poor angle of vision . . . Wait . . . She just turned slightly into the swell . . . I can make out an S as the first letter . . . Then an O . . . Shit, she just moved the other way . . . Uh, beg your pardon, sir . . . I lost the rest when she rolled, Mr. Baker."

"OK, OK. What else do you see, Rosenthal? On the deck, I mean?"

"There's a table, chairs, a cooler, beer . . . Hold it . . . There's a girl on one of the chairs."

"Well, what about her?"

79

"She doesn't have any bra on, sir . . . She's sleeping . . . Topless . . ."

"Yes . . . Continue . . ." Baker swallowed, noticeably interested.

"I can see a little better now, sir . . . The man who came out of the wheelhouse is helping the fat guy toward the girl's chair . . . The fat guy seems to be bombed out of his mind . . . His friend is helping him to lay on top of the girl, sir . . . Christ . . . A jelly-belly like that . . . He must be loaded with dough . . . Some guys have all the luck."

"Get on with it, Rosenthal," Baker said, trying to remain serious in spite of the grimacing expression of the Captain and the other officers, all fighting to keep a straight face, as they listened in with him on the bridge.

"Well, Mr. Baker, do you want me to tell you everything I see? . . . I mean . . . Can I speak frankly, sir? . . ."

"Of course, Rosenthal. Now hurry it up. We don't have all day."

Grant went into an exuberant jig on the deck, waving beer cans in both hands.

"It's a party, sir . . . Some sort of a wild orgy . . . Must be a bunch of dee-generate pre-verts on that ship, sir . . . Wait . . . I can make out the name now . . . it's called the *Solitude*." Rosenthal let out a belly laugh.

"*Solitude*," he repeated. "They gotta be kidding . . . It's a floating cathouse, sir . . ."

"OK, Rosenthal. What else?"

"There's a couple up forward, sir . . . They've got their backs to us . . . Good-looking pair from behind though, if you ask me . . ."

"All right, Rosenthal, that's enough. Anything about the ship look suspicious?"

Rosenthal was no longer listening.

"Man, would I love to be on that ship . . . There's this other chick . . . Can't see her face . . . She's bare-assed, sir . . . She's getting . . . She's getting . . ."

"She's getting what?" Baker asked impatiently.

"She's getting . . . If you'll pardon the expression . . . Uh . . . Can we get any closer, sir?"

"Relax, Rosenthal," Baker said, clearing his throat. "I think the Captain's satisfied. Come back down."

Baker called the *Enterprise*. He was informed the comments had been heard, and he need not elaborate. The *New Jersey* was asked to rejoin the carrier.

Grant went back to the wheelhouse and, through binoculars, saw the *New Jersey* turning away. His eyes widened and he broke into uproarious laughter as a mad scramble burst loose on the top deck of the battleship. Scores of sailors, alerted by Boatswain's Mate Third Class Irwin Rosenthal, raced to the railing and fought for binoculars to catch a glimpse of the dreamboat *Solitude*.

It was now 1300. Grant's ordeal had lasted almost one hour.

He went to the sun deck, grabbed a can of beer from the cooler, opened it, and took a long swig. "I think I deserve an Academy Award for this performance," he said aloud, as he watched the stern of the *New Jersey* disappear into the distance.

CHAPTER 9

Five days after leaving the Paracels—three days after his memorable encounter with the *New Jersey*—Grant was 600 miles south of Yokohama. He was on the open North Pacific, enjoying full freedom of the high seas, still proceeding eastward.

He had already covered 1,800 miles. His great circle route had taken him well north of Guam, keeping him at a respectable distance from Okinawa and Iwo Jima, where further brushes with the U.S. Navy would have presented a threat. With the help of the Japan Current, the ship was now averaging better than 20 knots.

Grant had become so accustomed to the *Solitude* that he anticipated her every shudder and could tell in his sleep if she strayed off course.

He had settled into a routine of four hours on and four hours off, which allowed him to systematically reset the autopilot and switch fuel tanks. Inspection of the engines, minor maintenance, housekeeping, and navigation kept him busy, but he no longer had to ration his time with an eyedropper.

Grant set the clock ahead as he crossed time zones. Every completed page of the diary was burned and the ashes thrown to the wind as he progressed uneventfully on international waters. So far, he was a little ahead of schedule.

In Da Nang, Colonel Bernie McSnair was still looking for Grant's airplane and reporting daily to General "Zach" R. Enko. Thus far, only three missions had been launched to find the missing TX-75E. McSnair pleaded that the monsoon was responsible for this meager total. Enko told him he was getting tired of excuses.

As a matter of routine, the International Red Cross was notified that Grant Fielding was missing in action and presumed captured. Since Hanoi consistently refused to release POW lists, there was little hope of this organization discovering if Grant were alive or dead. The Pentagon still believed it was worth a try—even if the North Vietnamese persisted in ignoring the Geneva Convention.

General Enko was due to leave for Washington in a few days to attend the strategy conference to which he had been summoned. He was getting impatient.

The Secretary of Defense had written Enko personally, directing him to bring along a "full and detailed" report on the missing airplane; a complete rundown on the performance of the other TX-75Es, and pilot evaluation summaries regarding the aircraft's reliability. The Secretary insisted on accurate figures as to the number of sorties conducted during the last six months, an itemization of the type, and extent of damage sustained in action and statistics on maintenance problems.

This was a bad omen for the future prospects of the airplane. The General concluded that pressure was being exerted on the Secretary from congressional quarters. Still, he felt under attack for his role in the development of the aircraft and took it as a personal affront.

The letter had arrived at a most inopportune time. Enko was much too occupied with preparations for the conference. He delegated the responsibility for the investigation to McSnair, impressing upon the Colonel that he was now acting under direct orders from the Secretary of Defense.

Knowing what the airplane meant to the General, McSnair would find a way to make it look good in the report. Furthermore, he would intensify the search for Fielding's aircraft during every break in the weather. This was his chance to get into Enko's good graces. He wasn't going to blow it.

Colonel Bernie McSnair felt his time had come: He was now the General's right-hand man—a direct pipeline to the Pentagon.

On the afternoon of the twelfth day of his voyage, about 1,000 miles southeast of Amchitka, in the Aleutians, Grant crossed the International Date Line. The moment he passed through the imaginary boundary became the corresponding instant of the preceding day. It was a Monday, and Grant found himself reliving Sunday. He had traveled 4,400 miles, steering well north of Wake Island and Midway. One week to go before he reached his destination.

Grant disposed of several items at daily intervals: The two huge crates in the hold and the six boxes which had contained the mannequins were chopped to pieces and cast away. He kept only one large camouflage net, throwing the rest over the side together with the can of gray paint and brush which had served to block out the airplane's identification markings. The charts for the completed legs of the journey were burned and dispersed with empty cans and other garbage.

He experienced one restless night during the trip. He had tossed, turned, and dreamed, reliving a scene that had really happened.

In his dream, Jennifer, his girl friend, had come to see his parents, although they disapproved of her. As usual, the meeting had been cold. Her eyes were red and swollen, making her appear older than her twenty-four years. She knew that Grant never really loved her, nor had he encouraged her to love him. But her tears upset him. He saw himself in the dream telling her what he had said to her in reality: he didn't want a brood of brats with runny noses, or a lawn to mow, or household chores to attend. He refused to start at the bottom of the ladder flying for some airline while she taught the sixth grade. He wanted freedom of action, although he knew that she clung to the illusion that he might change his mind. All at once, she stooped to make an appeal to his parents. She had come to tell them that she didn't believe their son was dead, and she would wait for him. His parents had just sat there, motionless—like his mannequins on the sun deck.

Grant woke up with a start, tired, drenched with perspiration, and feeling guilty.

Colonel McSnair had begun to take himself seriously. Cloaked in the dignity of the trust General Enko had placed in him, he assumed little airs of importance. He was giving everyone a hard time, particularly Captain William Keegan, whom he had appropriated as his "special—and permanent—assistant." McSnair bullied Keegan, called him names, often referred to him as "the baby-faced moron," and made his life generally miserable. He was getting even for the days Enko had persecuted him.

Keegan feverishly worked around the clock to compile statistics for the Pentagon report McSnair was supposedly preparing for Enko. He spent the better part of his days interviewing TX-75E pilots in the debriefing room. At night, he sifted through accident reports and maintenance logs.

McSnair had decided to go on a diet and to do a little exercise. He wanted to look athletic—just like the General. In the afternoon, while his "slave" Keegan pored over weather maps and search and rescue accounts, he played handball in the hope of tightening some of that excess blubber around his jowls and stomach. His uniform was now beautifully pressed at all times and he stuck out his chest.

The Colonel was acutely aware that he would be in charge, albeit for only two weeks after Enko's departure for Washington, and he didn't let anyone forget it. At the Officers' Club, he often dropped subtle hints as to his newly found status and influence. When speaking of the General, he'd casually refer to him as "Zach." After a few drinks, he'd inevitably bring the conversation around to "Zach told me this, or Zach believes that . . ." McSnair was oblivious to the snickers of his fellow officers.

But McSnair still cringed in Enko's presence. He never dared address him as anything but "General" or "Sir."

Seventeen days after his disappearance over Hoa Binh, Grant was 1,200 miles northeast of Honolulu. His trip log showed he had covered 6,300 miles and had another 1,100 miles—or three days—to go before he reached his destination.

Grant tuned in to news broadcasts on shortwave regularly. Negotiations between the United States and North Vietnam had progressed considerably in Paris during the last two weeks. Paradoxically, the bombings had resumed as soon as the weather had lifted. Hanoi was being reduced to rubble.

Events were moving faster than Grant had anticipated and he feared they might upset his timetable. He yearned for someone to throw a monkey wrench into the works which would delay the signing of a peace treaty until he finished what he had set out to do.

Something else was irking him—that nightmare about his parents and girl friend. In the dream, Jennifer had worn a POW bracelet. He had broken out in a cold sweat when he had seen his name vividly engraved on it—a most repulsive gesture as far as he was concerned. It bothered him to think that either Jennifer or his parents believed he was in some horrible compound in North Vietnam. He didn't want them to join organizations, sign petitions, or tearfully relate their plight on some local TV newscast.

Grant knew he'd horrify quite a number of people who would call him cynical, but he felt very little sympathy for the POW cause. He was fed up with the propaganda regarding the POWs, who had become just another tool used by the Administration to play on the heartstrings of uninformed voters.

Sure, he felt sorry for some poor draftee infantryman who got captured in the jungle and sent up North. But the great majority of POWs were pilots—career officers who knew the risks they were taking and accepted them. They had it good in peacetime, pushing airplanes around the sky on maneuvers or airlifts. That was a cushy deal—a glorified cabdriver. You saw the world, with or without your family, courtesy of the Pentagon, as you moved from base to base. Germany, Spain, Japan—not a bad life while waiting for a pension.

But, when the chips were down, you were expected to make up for the good times by putting your life on the line. That was the deal in exchange for the job security offered by the Armed Forces.

So, a few guys got captured. So what? They were alive, weren't they? Naturally, they'd get worked over a little by the peasants they'd been bombing. Who could really blame the Vietnamese for seeking revenge after their villages had been devastated and their families wiped out by fragmentation bombs.

Grant's ideas on the matter were absolute: If you weren't prepared to put up and shut up, you had no business getting into military life.

His thoughts drifted back to the briefings in Da Nang—the possibility of getting captured.

According to the Military Code of Conduct, you were supposed to comport yourself in a professional manner from the moment you fell into enemy hands until such time as you were released. Simply put, you were to keep your mouth shut no matter what pressures, mental or physical, were exerted upon you—just like a "soldier" working for the Cosa Nostra.

Squealing, no matter how insignificant the information, in return for favors of any kind, even urgently needed medical attention, would not be tolerated. Fraternizing with do-gooders from the States, such as pseudo-pacifists, or movie stars who were allowed to come to Hanoi, was a no-no. If you stepped out of line and sent messages via visiting American hippies or on Hanoi radio, your file wouldn't look too pretty when you came out.

You were also subtly reminded that a few crew-cut, patriotic, gung-ho types would be in prison with you. They'd be sure to keep an eye on things and make their reports upon termination of hostilities. In other words, you were warned to watch out for "stoolies" from your own side.

Finally, if you remained loyal and silent, you'd be given a hero's welcome, back pay, a bonus for time spent in captivity, and, very probably, a well-deserved promotion. If you weakened, you'd become a pariah.

What really galled Grant was the sickening spectacle of those apple-pie-eating wives waiting faithfully by the fireside. He felt sorry for their children, certainly. But the wives, those paragons of virtue—what a farce! Some of those broads were collecting full pay and never wanted their husbands to come back. Jesus!—what a great act they were putting on while two-timing those poor bastards. There were going to be a few unanticipated babies and a good number of divorces when they returned after five or six years of captivity. There would be lots of tears and a few nervous breakdowns at the time of reunion. Grant was certain of that. Many of the men would have fits of jealousy. They'd ask numerous questions and feel betrayed and disgraced regardless of the answers.

The POWs would get over it eventually. Some would receive over a hundred thousand dollars in back pay and bonuses. That would sweeten the pill and help them with a fresh start—advancement up the military ladder or good jobs in civilian life. All things considered, a good many guys would be prepared to sacrifice a few years of freedom for that kind of money.

Grant no longer wanted any part of the military life. He was convinced his participation within it had been hypocritical. He was tired of being used and manipulated. He'd had enough of war, of listening to lies, of killing people.

That airplane in the hold was his ticket to freedom. He would use it for a good cause—himself!

Two days before reaching his destination, Grant heard some good news on the radio—at least as far as he was concerned.

There was a snag in Paris. Hanoi had cried foul. It was loudly protesting against the renewed bombings and claiming the Americans were acting in bad faith. Washington was clamoring for the North Vietnamese to respect the Geneva Convention and release the names of the POWs. Legal experts were saying that, since the U.S. had never formally declared war on North Vietnam, the conflict was not subject to the Convention rules. The whole bargaining process had become a mess.

The U.S. and North Vietnamese representatives were no longer talking to each other and had returned to their respective capitals for "consultations."

Grant celebrated the event by toasting his mannequins with a beer while dancing a jig on the sun deck. Anyone observing the scene would think he had gone berserk.

Colonel McSnair remitted a voluminous file to Enko on the eve of the General's departure for Washington. McSnair waited for a moment, expecting some sort of recognition for a job well done.

Enko stuffed the papers into his top desk drawer, told McSnair he'd look at the report during the night and let him know if it was satisfactory in the morning. He pointedly added he would make the necessary corrections aboard his flight to the States. Struggling to hide his disappointment, McSnair went to the Officers' Club for a drink to bolster his sagging morale and to remind a few adversaries that, in less than twenty-four hours, he'd be in charge. Captain Keegan was seated at the bar, exhausted from the sleepless nights spent preparing the report for McSnair. His chin was resting on his hand as he talked to a lieutenant. Keegan was quite drunk.

"Give a little prick a big job and you know what? . . . he becomes a big prick!" Keegan slurred. He grinned sheepishly at the Lieutenant. "I read that in a book somewhere . . ." Keegan sighed.

"How true . . ." the glassy-eyed Lieutenant hiccuped.

McSnair pricked up his ears.

"Those poor bastards," Keegan went on, unaware of McSnair's presence, "they're being sent on wild-goose chases . . . risking their asses to come back empty-handed . . . what a miserable job . . . all this for some general's toy . . . and some ass-kissing colonel . . ."

"Captain!" McSnair bellowed.

Keegan opened one eye, turned lazily, and looked up. The Colonel was bristling.

"I would suggest you get a little rest, Keegan. We've got a busy day tomorrow."

The Lieutenant saluted and left on tiptoe. Keegan assumed the air of a whipped dog.

"Sir, I was just having a little friendly . . ."

"We do not discuss our business with underlings," McSnair hissed. "It's bad for morale. For now, I'll overlook what I've heard regarding your views on anatomy."

"Yes, sir."

"And, for your further information, Captain Keegan, I want more sweeps. We'll continue the search. I want to find out what happened to that airplane before the General returns. The rest of the day-to-day operations are also going to run like clockwork. Is that clear?"

"Yes, sir. Good night, sir."

McSnair ordered a double.

General Enko looked preoccupied as Colonel McSnair and Captain Keegan escorted him to the C5A. The giant jet transport was about to leave for the States with a cargo of GIs killed in action and wrapped in "body bags."

McSnair had insisted on carrying Enko's briefcase bulging with files. Keegan shuffled behind toting the General's valise.

"The report's OK," Enko said. "I'll edit a few minor changes on the way. Contact me in Washington if there's anything new."

About 700 miles, or two days from his point of arrival, Grant began a little housekeeping. All items now listed as unnecessary went over the side at regular intervals: table, seven reclining chairs, six air mattresses, two beach umbrellas, cooler, beer, soft drinks, and superfluous cans of food. He burned the registry papers, ship's logs, manuals, diary, and all marine charts except for one covering the last leg of his journey.

Twenty days after leaving the Paracels, at about 1300, Grant spotted a chain of mountains in the distance.

He traveled up and down the coast for an hour, surveying the shoreline through binoculars, then proceeded with "burials at sea."

"So long, Alfa," Grant said sadly as he decapitated the mannequin with one swift stroke of his ax before removing his Bermuda shorts and the yellow handkerchief still fluttering in his hand. "It was nice having you aboard, you dirty old man, but all good things must come to an end and we must now commit your body to the deep," Grant sighed as he hacked Alfa into unrecognizable pieces which he threw overboard.

"And to you, Foxtrot . . . my thanks . . . and sorry," he said as he chopped up the bottomless suntanned kitten.

Grant had similar kind words for the four other mannequins as their remains and their beachwear were flung into the ocean.

In a final gesture of farewell to the drifting remnants of his former "passengers," Grant waved Alfa's yellow handkerchief before dropping it into the swell where it floated like a shroud.

Grant pulled up the keel and headed due east toward a small cove sheltered by a semicircular wall of towering cliffs at the foot of the forbidding chain of mountains. The place was inaccessible except by sea.

At 1430, the *Solitude* rammed the beach.

Grant had much to do before sundown.

The crane picked up the cabin roof and set it on the sand. It then slowly lifted the platform out of the hold and gingerly lowered the airplane onto the beach.

Grant went ashore, attached the hook of the crane to the nose strut, unfastened the cables which had secured the landing gear to the platform, and returned aboard the ship.

Very gently, he began to swing the crane back and forth, imparting a smooth forward rocking motion to the airplane as the hook tugged at the strut. The fighter-bomber gradually rolled off the platform and came to rest on the hard sand and coral.

He replaced the platform in the hold and hoisted the roof back atop the empty cabin.

The remaining camouflage net was dropped next to the airplane together with the aluminum ladder, which was propped up against the fuselage. Pushing the canopy open, he climbed into the cockpit.

On internal battery power, Grant activated the extension mechanism, which spread the wings of the TX-75E. He then rapidly stretched the camouflage net over the airplane to hide it from view.

With a long hose running from the bow of the *Solitude* to the wings, Grant pumped back the fuel he had drained in the Paracels.

He checked the cockpit gauges. They indicated approximately 2,750 gallons. A total of 4,000 was needed to top off the tanks.

Grant now connected the hose to the supply of 1,500 gallons of kerosene stored aboard the *Solitude*.

The airplane's manual specified that, although not recommended for normal operation, kerosene could be used in an emergency. It was compatible and blended readily with the regular propellant if mixed within the proportion of not more than one to three.

Grant kept pumping until the tanks overflowed.

Now with a full load of twenty-four thousand pounds of fuel and at the proper maximum endurance throttle settings, the aircraft could remain in the air for almost ten hours.

He looked at the time. It was just past 3:45 P.M., leaving him less than three hours before dark to complete his preparations.

He went into the hold and returned with a pup tent, which he pitched under the camouflage net by the nose wheel of the airplane.

Back in the wheelhouse, Grant put up a large kettle of water as he transferred the contents of one of the suitcases under the cot into a waterproof knapsack: clothing, shoes, gun, knife, ax, flashlight, passport, money, aerial charts, and a little black box.

About the size of a small transistor radio, the box was fitted with input and output jacks. It was also equipped with tone and modulation control knobs as well as a patchcord with microphone plugs at both ends.

With the boiling water, Grant made the equivalent of twenty cups of instant coffee which he poured into four thermoses. They went into the knapsack, together with an assortment of cans of food and drink.

Grant deposited the heavy knapsack under the tent, then brought ashore a sleeping bag, his flight suit, boots, helmet, and a ten-foot rope.

He climbed into the cockpit, tied one end of the rope to the tubular frame of the seat, then slid down to test its strength. It was sturdy. Now able to dispense with the ladder, he took it back to the ship.

At 6:15 P.M. the *Solitude* slowly backed away from the beach.

About three miles from shore, the crane lifted the sun deck, swung it over the side, and dropped it into the ocean. The platform went next.

Grant now fastened the hook to the wall of the hold on the port side, tugged until it was wrenched free and heaved it overboard. The other three walls, then the floor, were yanked, splintered, and wrecked in similar fashion. He sent them floating south with the current, away from the cove. The *Solitude* now looked like a derelict ore carrier whose hatch was indecently exposed.

As the ship progressed in a wide circle, Grant emptied the dynamite from the second suitcase onto the desk top in the wheelhouse.

He now tore, cut, chopped, and cast away the remaining items on his list: Panamanian flag, two valises, aluminum ladder, scuba gear, mattress, pillow, sheets, blankets, books, chess set, playing cards, cooking utensils, and all leftover food supplies. The last marine chart was burned, together with whatever papers were still in the desk drawers.

With his ax, Grant scraped off the words "SOLITUDE—

PANAMA CITY" painted across the stern, rendering the ship anonymous.

He went below and defaced the serial numbers on the engines in the improbable event they might reveal a clue as to the identity of the vessel's owner.

The fuel gauges indicated the ship still carried enough reserves for two days. Grant opened up all the valves to empty the tanks. While the diesel oil spilled into the ocean, he prepared four charges of dynamite with very long fuses. He taped them to the retractable keel, the wall of an empty fuel tank in the bow, a bulkhead in the engine room, and under the crane.

Grant inflated a rubber dinghy into which he loaded a small outboard motor and paddles. He then set the radarscope in the wheelhouse for its maximum range of 20 miles. The scanner showed no shipping within that radius.

He pushed the throttles full forward and looked at his cove through binoculars hanging from his neck. The camouflaged airplane was about 2 miles southeast of his present position. It was getting dark.

Surveying the coastline and the mountains to the north and south of his beach, he saw no lights, no signs of life.

Starved for fuel, the engines began to cough and sputter. They died at 7:35 P.M. The ship began to drift southward with the current.

Grant went below and lit a cigarette to ignite the fuses. First the one in the bow, next the engine room, then the keel, and, finally, the crane. He now had five minutes to steer clear of the explosion.

He threw his ax overboard, donned a life preserver, and lowered the dinghy from the stern. He slid aboard, clamped on the outboard motor, pulled the starter cord, and sped away from the scuttled vessel.

Grant was half a mile from the *Solitude* when he heard the four dull thuds followed by small flashes of light. There was no fire since no fuel or wood had been left on board.

With large, gaping holes in her bottom, the *Solitude* sank almost instantly in over three hundred feet of water.

"Good-by, sweetheart," Grant said with genuine regret. "You were a real lady to the very end. May you rest in peace."

He headed for the beach.

The stars were beginning to glitter when Grant neared the cove, just before 8:00 P.M.

He cut the outboard motor about two hundred yards from the beach, paddled in the rest of the way, and dragged the dinghy under the camouflage net.

Grant waded back into the water, knee deep, away from the cliffs for an unobstructed view, and looked out to sea through his binoculars.

The *Solitude* had sunk unobserved. No ship would come to its rescue.

He scanned up and down the coast, then examined the sides and the tops of the mountains in his field of vision. Still no lights. Not a soul around.

Grant was worn out and hungry. He ate some ham with melba toast and drank a can of ginger ale.

Fearing the glow might be noticed if he smoked on the beach, he went under the tent and lit a cigarette. He looked at the time. It was almost 9:00 P.M.

Grant unrolled his sleeping bag, dropped his ashes into the empty can of soda, stretched out luxuriously, and listened for sounds as he dozed off.

Nothing suspicious. Just the roar of the surf crashing on the cliffs protecting the cove.

PART TWO

CHAPTER 10

The fourteen high-ranking officers were already seated around the long oval table when General Lawrence F. Harmon entered the austere wood-paneled room at the Pentagon.

The startling news he was about to break would certainly cause controversy, and Harmon had come prepared to keep the squabbling among the brass to a minimum. He sat at the head of the table.

"Gentlemen, you've all been asked to attend this conference because this is the final big push. I know you have drawn up the requested plans for the orderly withdrawal of forces under your command. Those were the instructions given to you a month ago. But, since then, the situation has changed."

Harmon paused and took a sip of water from a glass set before him, allowing his listeners time to absorb the impact of his announcement.

"As you know, there's been a breakdown in the Paris negotiations, which are now at a standstill. We must impress upon the enemy that we mean business and will not back down."

Some of the participants began to fidget uncomfortably.

"The Joint Chiefs of Staff have decided to go all-out in an effort to 'stabilize' the situation in Vietnam before talks are resumed. Needless to remind you that public pressure for rapid termination of hostilities is mounting and time is running short."

General Harmon rose and turned to a large map.

"Full details on the rundown I'm about to give you are contained in the documents placed before you. I would prefer you wait until after the briefing before perusing them. At that time, you may also ask questions or state your viewpoints." He looked at his watch. "It's now ten-thirty and this preliminary meeting must be concluded by eleven forty-five, as I will be required elsewhere. So, we'll have to be brief."

The fourteen men silently nodded their understanding. Several of them turned in their swivel chairs to get a better look at General Harmon and the map.

"Effective immediately," he said, pointing at several targets, "the bombings on North Vietnam will resume full scale."

A few of the generals and admirals shot surprised glances at each other. Some cleared their throats.

Harmon, a man of sparkling intelligence and, at forty-six, one of the Pentagon's rising stars, remained impassive. He was a master at manipulating audiences and did not continue until all eyes were glued upon him once again.

"Naturally, air strikes, helicopter gunship action, and coastal naval bombardments will continue in South Vietnam during this time. Large-scale mopping-up operations will proceed with the object of inflicting as many casualties and as much damage as possible before the talks are resumed. We need leverage in Paris. We're depending upon you, gentlemen, to show Hanoi, Moscow, and Peking that we're reasonable people—willing to bargain—but that we have absolutely no intention of being run out of South Vietnam. That's the big picture for the moment."

Harmon returned to his seat. "Any questions?"

Admiral Alexander T. Marr raised his hand.

"Yes?"

"General Harmon, are the withdrawals to proceed during this new escalation?"

"We have to show our good faith," Harmon said, smiling. "Ground troops will continue to return home or will be redeployed in the Asian sector as per schedule. We will respect the withdrawal timetable of roughly fifty thousand men per month from South Vietnam as secretly agreed to in Paris."

Harmon leaned back in his chair and studied the expressions of his listeners for a brief moment.

"This is why we'll have to depend more than ever on the Navy and the Air Force for continuous pounding of the enemy during the 'lull' in negotiations . . . Yes, General Preener?"

"Could we have some idea when the talks are to resume, also when the peace accords are to be signed?"

"Based on information presently at my disposal from the White House and the State Department, the whole question hinges on a matter of appropriate timing. The North Vietnamese are trading on the lack of unity shown by Congress and on the antiwar demonstrations so widely publicized by our own media. They feel that if they can just hold out a bit longer, they'll win the war of nerves. They're especially gambling on our upcoming presidential elections. They hope to obtain major concessions from the incumbent by forcing him to make the 'popular decision' of ending the war at any cost to stay in office. His opponent has publicly hinted he's willing to 'crawl to Hanoi on his knees' to obtain the safe return of our POWs and put an end to the conflict. We have to convince them they're making a big mistake."

General Enko raised his hand.

"My old friend 'Zach the Terrible' has a question," General Harmon said with a twinkle of friendship for his old acquaintance.

"You still haven't answered General Preener's point. What kind of 'appropriate timing' are we talking about?"

Harmon wet his lips, visibly hesitating before he phrased his reply.

"It's hard to say, Zach. My guess is it'll be at least another five to six weeks. As soon as the polls consistently confirm that the President will be re-elected—no matter what he does in Vietnam —Hanoi will come around to his way of thinking. They don't want to be bombed 'back to the Stone Age,' to quote one of our now retired colleagues," he chuckled. "I would imagine the accords should be well on the way to being signed by Christmas."

Enko stood, staring coldly at General Harmon.

"Am I to understand that, while they're playing cat and mouse in Paris, we're to go on sacrificing good men and valuable equipment, just for show?—when we know in advance that, no matter what happens, it'll all be over by Christmas and we'll be leaving Vietnam come hell or high water?"

A few rumbles of dissent came from the rest of the participants: "Now just a minute, General Enko . . ."

"This is not the proper time to bring this up . . ."

"We're here to discuss military strategy, not politics . . ."

"Let's stop wasting time . . ."

General Harmon raised his hands.

"Hold it, gentlemen, please!" He was a little pale and his eyebrows were knitted into a frown, although he retained his perfect composure. "I said we'd have a discussion at the end of the briefing, not an argument. Now permit me to answer the General."

Harmon decided to meet Enko head-on.

"You're quite right, Zach, and you've put it very succinctly. This is a rear-guard action and, unfortunately, we'll have to make a few sacrifices."

Enko remained standing. His mouth was hard. He spoke bitterly.

"The first duty of an officer is to spare as many of his men as possible although he does expect a certain percentage of casualties. My record proves that I've achieved tangible results with minimum losses. But this is ridiculous! We're being asked to risk superbly trained men and multimillion-dollar equipment with no intention of even trying for a victory."

"General Enko," Harmon said stiffly, "I'm only transmitting political decisions made at the highest level. I repeat, 'the highest level.' I have no say in the matter. It's out of my hands."

"Well, it's not out of mine," Enko snapped back. "They're passing the buck. My pilots are highly intelligent people. They're flying the most sophisticated aircraft ever assembled. They're asking a lot of questions and they're right. Do you think I can brush them off by telling them what you're telling me?—that they have to put on a side show?—that they're going to get shot down by Russian SAMs, maybe become POWs, just to buy time for a few more days of haggling in Paris?"

"General Enko, we have no choice. Those are the orders," Harmon replied calmly.

The other participants had prudently decided that the best course of action was to stay out of the discussion.

"About three weeks ago, under similar orders, I lost one of my best men and a twenty-two-million-dollar airplane shooting up a few barrels of gasoline—'just to keep the enemy busy.' This is no way to run a war. Why don't we just go in there and get it over with?"

"We do exactly what we're told. We're carrying out and implementing political strategy. You, of all people, should be aware of that," Harmon said kindly, to show he appreciated Enko's frustration.

"Then give us some worthwhile targets if we're going to do it —not Mickey Mouse missions. It's a matter of morale if nothing else. It's hard to tell the men to risk their lives on insignificant punitive expeditions when the news media all over the world are breathing down their necks and calling them assassins."

"You're putting up a good fight, Zach, as always," Harmon said softly. "But those are the orders."

Enko sat down, seemingly subdued, but only briefly. He looked around the table and found he had no support. He tried one last time.

"Indiscriminate bombing will get us nowhere," he said quietly. "Couldn't we at least be permitted to select legitimate targets and eliminate unproductive suicidal missions? Could we give the 'negotiators' an opportunity to come to terms while giving our own boys a fighting chance?"

"You've got a valid point, Zach. I'll have to admit that. I'll take it up with the proper people."

Harmon stood up, looking at his watch.

"It's only 11:30. We're ahead of schedule. Good, that'll give us a chance to get some coffee. We'll all be back here in seventy-two hours—that's Thursday at 11:30. Bring tentative plans based on your availability of men and equipment while the withdrawal is proceeding. There'll be one more meeting on Friday, after which you're to return immediately to your respective commands. Thank you."

Enko was attempting to close his overstuffed briefcase when Harmon tapped him on the shoulder.

"Got a minute, Zach?"

"Sure, Larry."

"Wait till they're gone."

"OK."

Enko pretended to struggle with his papers until the door was closed and they were alone.

"Zach," Harmon said with great affection, "I can't forget you were my boss in Korea and that it's thanks to you I'm alive today. I also know you had a lot to do with my being where I am now."

"So?" Enko replied sourly.

"Please don't push me in front of the others. I'm not taking orders from you any more. It's the other way around," Harmon said gently, with considerable respect.

"I don't care about that. You know it, Larry. I didn't send you flying to your death in Korea when everybody got hysterical, and I was only a colonel then. Now I'm a general and you're asking me to be a butcher. I don't give a damn what happens to the North Vietnamese. I'm concerned about my men. I don't want to waste them, just as I refused to waste you. It's about time someone told you guys you're full of crap."

"Times have changed, Zach," Harmon said somewhat stiffly. "We're not fighting a war any more. We're now playing diplomatic games and you've got to learn the new rules. I know what you're going through and I understand, believe me. You're of the old school and you see your men as more than just digits on a computer. Now, if you want to be reassigned rather than handle what's required of you, that can be arranged."

Enko's eyes flashed with anger.

"Larry, or should I say 'General Harmon,'" he replied caustically, "I'm a professional and I don't have to prove a goddamned thing to you or anyone else in the Pentagon. You're pushing a pencil now. I'm working in the field. The day I can't cut it, I'll know enough to quit. No one has to give me any 'subtle' hints . . . If you'll excuse me, I now have to go fight with the Secretary of Defense about something else."

He picked up his briefcase and stalked out of the room.

Enko had lunch alone while scanning the Washington *Post*. As usual, the news was depressing. Not one good thing was happening around the world, especially in Washington, where every story concerned one scandal or another.

At 1300, he was shown into the office of the Secretary of Defense.

"Welcome home, General Enko, even if it's for such a short time. Please sit down," the Secretary said affably. "How did it go this morning?"

"Not too well, as far as I'm concerned, sir."

"Well . . . I haven't had a chance to get briefed by General Harmon, but I'm sure everything can be worked out. We'll know more in a couple of days . . . well . . . I've read your report."

"Yes," Enko said in a neutral tone.

"It's good . . . it's very good . . . but . . ."

"But what, sir?"

"I'm afraid we'll have to temporarily suspend production on the TX-75E. You can make do with other aircraft until we have completed a thorough re-evaluation of the program."

"In other words, you're killing it," Enko said quietly.

"No, no. Nothing like that. I know how much effort you've

put into it. But it's just that every one of the 158 delivered over the last three years has had a problem of some sort. Obviously, there's something wrong somewhere. We've lost fifty-two planes right here at home during training alone, of which seventeen disappeared over mountains or over the ocean without leaving a trace. Only one pilot survived to tell us that the right wing had fallen off as he changed the airfoil configuration for supersonic flight. In Vietnam, fourteen men managed to engage the self-destruct apparatus after being hit. We still don't know what happened to the last plane lost three weeks ago."

"We haven't located that one as yet," Enko said. "But I'm inclined to think the enemy didn't get hold of it either. As mentioned in the report, there's a 99.9-per-cent probability it destructed or blew up when it hit the side of a mountain."

"Ah . . . yes . . ." the Secretary agreed momentarily. "But there still remains that 0.1-per-cent possibility, farfetched, of course, that it might have fallen into the wrong hands. I must tell you the President is very concerned about it."

"What's the next step, Mr. Secretary?"

"We'll have to ground them, General. As I said, this is only a priority determination and not a terminal objective. When you're back here permanently from Vietnam, you'll be part of the task force assigned to reassess imputs to evaluate the feasibility of keeping the project alive as an ongoing challenge."

Enko realized the Secretary had lapsed into Pentagonese jargon to evade the issue and put his airplane on the shelf. There would be no point in pressing him right now.

"I understand, Mr. Secretary. But I'd still like you to know it's a hard airplane to hit. Why don't we mention all the Phantoms that have been shot down?"

"We're not discussing the Phantom, General. Right now we're concerned with the statistics of the fighter-bombers under your command."

"I'm sorry to insist, sir, but I maintain that careful analysis of the facts and figures will bear out my contention. The statistics on the over-all performance of the TX-75E are just as good, if not better, than the initial data on other aircraft which also had early growing pains but have since become reliable work horses."

"That may be so, but now is not the time to experiment. The budget won't allow it."

"One last thing, sir, and this is documented. I have repeatedly stated that the airplane was not ready for combat. We put it through its paces in Vietnam much too soon. In the long run, this aircraft will prove to be the best we've ever had. All it needs is a chance to show what it can really do."

Obviously bored, the Secretary was no longer listening.

"Er . . . well . . . yes, General. We'll take your recommendations under consideration. After all, you were the main force behind the project," he said pointedly. "I assure you that what you have to say will weigh heavily. In the meantime, do the best you can with what you've got."

He rose and shook Enko's hand.

"Good-by, General."

Enko took a cab to his home in Fairfax, an unpretentious five-room house he had purchased while still a colonel on temporary assignment to the Pentagon.

He walked straight to the bar, poured himself a double vodka on the rocks, and lit a cigar.

"Is that you, Zach?" Susan Enko called from the upstairs bedroom.

Enko gulped his drink. "Hmmm," he grunted.

Susan appeared in a terry-cloth bathrobe, her pink flesh glowing after a warm shower. She was drying her long dark hair with a towel. At forty-two, she was still a strikingly handsome woman. No one believed she was the mother of a twenty-one-year-old lieutenant stationed in Germany and a daughter of twenty-two in medical school at NYU.

"You're early," she said cheerfully as she came down the stairs. "It's not even three o'clock. How did things go with Harmon and the Secretary?"

"Lousy. It just wasn't my day," Enko grumbled, pouring himself another double.

"Don't let them bother you, Zach. What do they know? . . ." she said, kissing him on the cheek. "What you need is a little change of pace. I know what! Why don't we go to some fancy place for dinner."

"We'll see," Enko said, taking a big swallow before sitting on the sofa.

"Would you like me to call the Stinsons?—maybe they could join us. We haven't seen them in ages."

"No. I don't feel like being nice to anyone today."

He looked at Susan. The loose knot on her bathrobe had slipped, opening the garment and exposing her right leg as she stood next to him. He put his hand out and delicately caressed her thigh, gradually creeping upward. She remained quite still. He stared at her.

"Enough conversation," he ordered gently. "Take this thing off."

Susan awoke about an hour later. He had made furious love to her and she had dozed off in his arms on the sofa. He was in deep thought, taking sips of his vodka and stroking her hair.

"That was good," Susan smiled. "You'll have to rape me again sometime, General."

"For an old bag who's pushing fifty, you're not so bad yourself," Enko chuckled.

"Oh, the nerve! I'm not pushing fifty, you rat," she said playfully. "I'm barely over forty."

"Forty, fifty, sixty—what's the difference as long as the merchandise is of lasting quality?" Enko teased her further.

"General, you're a crude old bastard. But I'll forgive you because you're still a great screw." Susan cuddled up to him, draping her leg over his. "I love you, Zach," she murmured tenderly.

"OK, Susan . . . what's it going to cost me?" he smiled.

"Would you like another drink, Zachie?"

"Don't Zachie me, Susan," he laughed good-naturedly. "How much?"

"You have no feelings . . . but, since you bring it up . . ."

"Aha, I knew it . . ."

"Oh, Zach . . . I'm not happy living here. This place has turned into a military compound. All I ever see are Army wives who bore me to tears talking about their operations and nervous breakdowns. I'm ready for one myself. I want to move."

"We can't move now," Enko said very seriously.

"But Zach, I've been house-hunting for weeks and I found this lovely place in Silver Spring . . ."

"I'm not interested."

"It belongs to a NASA engineer who's being transferred to Houston. We can get it for a song . . ."

"The matter is closed."

"But Zach . . ."

"I like it fine right here."

"But you don't live here," she snapped, untwining her body and wresting free of his embrace. "You're away ninety per cent of the time, and I don't even have the kids for company any more. Besides, what difference does it make to you where we live?"

Enko remained stretched out on the sofa. He calmly lit a cigar. "Don't pressure me, Susan. You know better. I can't cater to your whims right now."

"They only want sixty thousand dollars and it's worth at least eighty thousand. By the way, I wanted to give them a deposit so they'd hold it until you could see it. But I found only three thousand dollars in our savings account. Where's the rest of our money?"

"I put it in a blind trust."

"Why on earth did you do that? Why didn't you tell me?"

"You're beginning to sound like a nag, Susan. But, if you must know, sooner or later I'm going to have big trouble because of my involvement with that airplane. Remember those aero-space stocks I bought? I don't want anyone to even hint at a possible conflict of interest. That's why I put everything into the trust."

"Well, that's your problem. I want you to get some money for the down payment," she shouted. "I don't care how you do it. I want to move."

An angry scowl came over Enko's face.

"Susan . . . don't force me to put you in your place. Just get off my back," he said, smacking her bare behind.

Susan slapped her husband hard across the mouth as she stood naked over him.

"Who the hell do you think you're talking to, you nasty sonofabitch? . . . One of your ass-kissing captains? I'm your goddamn wife. Don't you dare bully me."

Enko glowered at her as he remained very still on the sofa.

"You're becoming vulgar, Susan."

"Look who's talking about vulgarity? . . . Putting on airs with me! . . . Don't you realize I'm not afraid of you? . . . And let me tell you something else . . . that stupid airplane of yours will ruin you. I hear what's going on . . . you fool . . . I may be the only friend you have left. And that's only because I'm stuck with you. Maybe you won't even find ME here someday."

Without a word Enko stood and began dressing.

"Well . . . what do you have to say now, Mister Big Shot?"

"Susan, I never thought I'd see the day when you'd be as low as the rest of them."

"The rest of them? . . . Who are the rest of them? . . . Answer me . . . your Vietnamese tramps? . . . Answer me!" she screamed, incensed.

Enko put on his cap, picked up the bottle of vodka, and put it in his still-unpacked suitcase lying on the floor.

"Where are you going?"

"I'll let you cool off. I've got a lot of work to do for the Pentagon and I need a little peace and quiet. But first, I'm going on a binge. I'll sleep it off at some hotel. Don't try to get in touch with me. You'd only make us both look foolish. I'll come to say good-by before I leave for Da Nang."

Susan had put on her robe. She was crying silently on the sofa.

Enko picked up his luggage and left the house.

He hailed a taxi and told the driver to take him to the Sheraton.

CHAPTER 11

The $100-a-plate fund-raising dinner at the Century Plaza Hotel in Los Angeles looked like it would be a huge success. Local party chairman Vito Di Stefano was pleased.

All 2,500 invitations had been sold and, as he hopped from table to table, shaking hands with movie celebrities and old political cronies, Di Stefano was doing some quick figuring. After deducting the cost of the affair—about fifty thousand dollars including the liquor he had insisted should flow freely—there would remain approximately two hundred thousand dollars for the campaign chest.

Di Stefano, in a tuxedo, was not exactly the epitome of elegance. Chubby and balding, he was just under five foot six and his elevator shoes fooled no one. His little black mustache—which he dyed regularly—served only to accentuate his clumsy attempt to look suave and refined.

He had started his career as an obscure official in Local 231 of the Sanitation Workers' Union and stepped on countless people to get to his present position. The personification of the wheeler-dealer, he could strong-arm an impressive number of public figures into contributing generously to the election coffers. Some of the party big wigs found him offensive but could hardly ignore the fact that his efforts regularly produced close to two million dollars a year. They tolerated him as a necessary evil who still reeked of garbage.

At fifty-two, Di Stefano strived to project an image of paternal and effusive kindness. He had not been directly involved in labor rackets for the past twenty years and hoped this occasion would be the launching platform for his next step up the ladder—Congressman, perhaps even Senator from California. Second-rate actors had made it to the top, stepping right out of "B" pictures to Capitol Hill, ambassadorships, or governorships—why not an ex-sanitation worker? The federal government, in his opinion, was ready to be "sanitized." Di Stefano chuckled inwardly at his dubious, private little joke.

The master of ceremonies announced that baked Alaska would be served for dessert and that Mike Camew, the hottest comedian and impressionist on the West Coast, would entertain during coffee.

As loud applause and flickering lights greeted the performer's entrance on stage, Di Stefano quietly left the huge ballroom and went up to Suite 806. He adjusted his bow tie, patted his mustache, and rubbed his diamond pinkie ring before knocking timidly on the door.

"Come in, it's open."

Senator C. Felton Wadsworth was standing with his back to the door, in front of the full-length mirror in the living room, rehearsing his speech. He saw Di Stefano's reflection peeking in.

"We're alone, Vito. Come in and shut the door."

Di Stefano approached Wadsworth with abject deference.

"Senator, the comic's warming up the audience—he'll be through with his act in about twenty minutes."

"I'd better get dressed, then," Wadsworth said, dropping the typewritten speech he had been holding in his left hand on a dresser.

Di Stefano smiled. The Senator was in his shorts, an unbuttoned tuxedo shirt, and black socks. He put on his pants.

"Senator, I want to tell you we're really delighted to have you as our guest of honor. We need that shot in the arm. I've got the TV boys, the radio, the press . . . some of these fellows owe me a few favors. They'll make you look good. I guarantee it."

"I always look good," Wadsworth said, smiling condescendingly. "But we both know that no matter what I say, our presidential candidate just isn't going to make it. I'll go through the motions, though."

"You're right, as usual, Senator," Vito agreed unctuously. "The presidential race is a foregone conclusion. But I'm no longer concerned with this election. I'm looking ahead—to four years from now. It's too bad you didn't run for the White House this time. I think you'd have been a shoo-in. They were ready to draft you at the convention and, yet, you let us get stuck with Clinton."

"It's just as well. The Vietnam thing is dying out. Nobody really cares any more. Clinton better stop harping on it. We have no real issues. You tell me how we can force out an incumbent who's riding higher than any President before him. It's impossible."

"He's in solid—that's for sure."

"The next election will be another matter, Vito. Maybe, then, you'll even be able to make Senator on my coattails," Wadsworth said, grinning patronizingly.

"Don't talk down to me, Wadsworth," Di Stefano said in a harsh, insolent tone no longer in keeping with his customary servility. "You'll need fund raisers like me—no matter how wealthy you are—don't you forget it."

The Senator hardly expected Di Stefano's abrupt about-face. He stopped in the process of inserting a cuff link and gave the local party chairman a cold look. Vito stared back, just like a street fighter ready to settle things right there and then. Wadsworth contented himself with making a mental note of the incident. He changed the subject.

"What about my reservation to Honolulu?"

Once again, Vito reverted to the role of humble chief "advance" man.

"The four-o'clock United flight you wanted was booked solid.

It's the height of the season. But we found you a first-class seat on Pacific Global leaving at 1:00 P.M."

"Looks like I'm not going to get much sleep, then."

"I'm afraid not."

"Can I skip that party after the speech?"

"Out of the question, Senator. The big spenders have been waiting for this for weeks. They want to be seen with you, shake your hand, take pictures. We've got to give 'em their money's worth."

"And we can't let the fans down, can we?" Wadsworth sighed. "What about that farewell brunch tomorrow—can you cancel it?"

"You must be joking, Senator. Do you know who's coming to that brunch?—Clinton!"

"Oh no!" Wadsworth groaned. "He's supposed to be campaigning in Seattle."

"That's where he is right now. But I called his press man and told him it wouldn't be a bad idea if Clinton made a brief stop here on his way to Omaha. I've already got the Los Angeles *Times* photographers lined up. It'll look great, Senator. You and Clinton together . . . smiling . . . patching things up before you go stomping for him in Hawaii. I'll have the pictures wirephotoed to Honolulu immediately. They'll be in the papers before you arrive."

"I'm not thrilled with that idea at all. Why didn't you ask me first, dammit? It'll look phony as hell."

"It ain't gonna look phony one bit. You take Vito Di Stefano's word for it. We've got to close ranks and now's the time to do it. I'll also fix it so you get the biggest welcome in Honolulu you've ever had anyplace—even better than in your own home state."

"Leave it to you, hey, Vito?"

"That's right. I've never given our candidates a bum steer yet. You'll be met by Kirada. He'll have you covered with leis . . . hula girls dancing you all the way into the VIP lounge at the terminal . . . the whole bit. You just leave it to Vito. They'll think you're the nominee."

"That's all very nice, but when am I going to get some sleep?"

"You can get some shut-eye on the plane, Senator. I'll call a few connections and get you two seats way up front where no one will bother you. They'll remove the armrests so you can stretch out and arrive in Honolulu fresh as a daisy."

"OK, Vito. You win. Now, if you'll excuse me . . . I'll be down in ten minutes."

"Sure, Senator, sure. I'll be waiting for you at the side door."

Wadsworth went into the bedroom. He heard the door close and cursed softly as he put on his shoes. Why the hell had Vito saddled him with Clinton at that brunch? That *rapprochement* nonsense wouldn't fool anyone. If anything, it would embarrass him and the candidate.

He put on his jacket, looked at himself in the bedroom mirror, and flashed his legendary boyish smile.

At forty-eight, the lean, six-foot, virile-looking Senator was one of America's foremost television personalities. There was nothing noteworthy about his achievements in Congress to date and no introduction of bills of momentous import, but, nonetheless, everything he did received intensive coverage. If he watched his step and didn't get stabbed by Clinton until the election was over, he would certainly be next in line to carry the party banner.

On a personal basis, Wadsworth didn't particularly care for Governor Sherman S. Clinton. They really had nothing in common. Clinton was a bulldozer with a one-track mind and simplistic solutions. Vietnam?—PEACE NOW. The economy?—GIVE-AWAY PROGRAMS. Student unrest?—FREE TUITION. Unemployment?—GOVERNMENT JOBS. Minority rights?—RE-EVALUATION OF THE WELFARE SYSTEM. Drug addiction?—UNDERSTANDING, COMPASSION, AND METHADONE. Foreign policy?—SEMI-ISOLATIONISM (until he made up his mind).

The candidate's long-winded, self-righteous, repetitive pronouncements and platitudes had begun to bore to tears even the most loyal party followers. Clinton was a difficult product to sell the voters.

Wadsworth didn't need Gallup or Harris polls to tell him that Clinton would lose—and lose badly. His mission was to put up a front for the candidate. He would attempt to deliver his own state on election day, getting as much exposure as possible for himself in the process, while playing the role of the loyal party regular anxious to mend fences. He needed at least four more years to make his own bid for the presidency, and Clinton was unwittingly supplying him with weapons for the next election.

"And now my friends . . ." Vito Di Stefano shouted into the mike while waving his hands to restrain the applause, ". . . it is my pleasure to present the man we've all been waiting for . . . a man who has given unstintingly of himself for our party's cause and the cause of justice . . . our guest of honor . . . a great American who has the respect of Congress and the people . . . my friend and your friend . . . the workingman's friend . . . our beloved . . . Senator C. Felton Wadsworth . . ."

The standing ovation lasted a good two minutes. Smiling, the Senator waited for the cheering and applause to die down.

Wadsworth had a deep and resonant voice. He was eloquent, poised, and convincing, with undeniable charisma. The one-hour speech, confined to generalities and rhetorical questions, was interrupted nine times by thunderous applause.

In the last part of the address, Wadsworth went to bat for Clinton. He couldn't have done more if he had been his twin brother.

The audience loved every second of it and almost went into a frenzy when he concluded by raising his right hand while holding his pinkie down with his thumb in a gesture somewhat reminiscent of a Boy Scout salute. He spread out his three middle fingers, positioned his hand above his head in the glare of the spotlights, and said: "You see these three fingers? They form the letter 'W.' I want you to think 'W'—'W'—'W'—" he shouted, thrusting his hand rhythmically toward his listeners with each exclamation. "You know what that means?" he sang out. "It means: 'WE WILL WIN!' Now you remember that: 'WE WILL WIN! —WE WILL WIN!' Sherman Clinton will be our next President and I will be there to serve him."

The crowd went wild as it picked up the chant "WE WILL WIN— WE WILL WIN." Hysterical women in evening gowns ran up to the stage to kiss the Senator, to touch him, or feel a part of his clothing. Portly men rushed behind them for a chance to shake his hand.

Di Stefano quickly ushered Wadsworth into a dressing room where they would wait for the tumult to subside.

"I've got to hand it to you, Senator—you were magnificent."

"Thank you, Vito. I get thrilled myself when the crowd responds. When do I have to be at the party?"

Di Stefano looked at his watch. "It's ten o'clock. They'll start coming in about ten-thirty. Could you make it by eleven?"

"I'll be there, but I won't stay long. First, I want to go to my room and change my shirt. I got drenched under those spotlights."

The party lasted until three in the morning. There was a lot of drinking. Wadsworth had a few but watched his consumption carefully. He exchanged pleasantries with the local party wheels and danced with their wives, always maintaining the proper distance. He finally got to his suite and jumped into the shower.

As he stepped out of the bathroom, drying himself with a towel, Wadsworth heard a gentle knock on the door.

Not Vito again, he thought. Didn't he understand he had to get some sleep? "Who is it?" he asked gruffly.

"It's me," answered a delicate feminine voice.

A puzzled expression came over Wadsworth's face. Wrapping the towel around his waist, he opened the door.

The girl in the low-cut pink evening dress held a bottle of champagne under her left arm.

"I think you have the wrong room," Wadsworth said politely as he began to close the door.

"No, I don't," the tall brunette giggled, sticking the bottle through the opening.

"Who are you?"

"I'm Leila. Please let me in," she said, pushing the bottle a little farther.

He involuntarily stepped back. The girl entered, quickly closing the door behind her.

The Senator was still dripping. His hair was tangled, partly covering his eyes and face.

"Why, you just came out of the shower. You must be squeaky clean, all over, Senator," she cooed.

"Er . . . yes. What can I do for you, Miss . . . ?"

"Leila," she smiled. A long stockinged leg provocatively peeked through a slit in her gown. "Leila . . . my name is Leila . . ." she whispered, undulating slightly and running a tapered fingernail up and down Wadsworth's arm. "I want to be sure you're nice and comfy."

"Who sent you here?" he growled.

Leila's face fell. She attempted a weak smile. "Why, Senator, I'm one of your fans."

"I want to know who sent you here. You'd better answer me or I'll have you arrested."

Leila was unprepared for the Senator's reaction and frightened by the hard look in his eyes.

"The management of the hotel sent me," she blurted. "They wanted to know if you . . . needed anything . . ."

"You're lying. I'll ask you just once more. Who sent you?"

She began to tremble and tried to run for the door, but Wadsworth beat her to it. His towel fell to the floor, leaving him stark naked. He felt ridiculous.

"Please let me go, Senator," she begged. "I swear it was the front desk . . . I got a call telling me to come up here and to bring a bottle . . . that's all I know . . . please believe me . . . if I'd known it was going to be like this, I never would have come . . ."

Wadsworth relented. He picked up the towel and, once again, draped it around his waist.

"Tell your friends that Senator Wadsworth doesn't need any call girls or I'll see to it that your 'political groupie' career is finished. Now take your bottle and get the hell out of here."

He locked the door, got into bed, and turned off the light. It was past four-thirty and he was still wide awake.

I wouldn't put it past that sonofabitch Vito, he muttered to himself. Pictures of me in bed with a tramp—that's all I need—this time I'd be ruined for good!

The haunting mountain-climbing episode flashed through his mind once again, making his flesh crawl.

Mercifully, the public's memory had, as usual, been short. Nonetheless, two years after the incident, Wadsworth still felt vulnerable. He knew that, for a long time to come, he would be an easy target for ruthless political enemies who would relish resuscitating the skeleton in his closet if he became too ambitious too soon.

He fell into an uneasy sleep.

An inner clock awoke Wadsworth at nine-thirty, before the phone rang or the alarm sounded. He took a shower and called for his luggage to be taken to the lobby.

An hour later, he made his appearance at the brunch. Vito was there, nattily attired, greeting some two hundred guests. The drinking was already well under way. Clinton had not yet arrived.

Wadsworth smiled as he distractedly answered a few "hellos," put his hand on Vito's elbow, and led him to a quiet corner.

"I had a visitor in my room last night."

Di Stefano stood on tiptoes and raised his head as he waved at a new arrival. "Yes? Who was it?"

"You know damn well who it was, Vito. Don't you ever pull another stunt like that on me again."

Vito put his arm around the Senator's waist and gently prodded him to turn so that they both faced the wall. "I don't know what you're talking about," he protested in bewilderment.

"If you don't, which would surprise me, then you'd better find out who sent that woman to my suite. She said she got a call from some man at the desk who'd been instructed to provide me with 'entertainment.' "

Vito looked genuinely aghast.

"There are limits to being crooked, Vito. That was a cheap shot."

Di Stefano pulled out a handkerchief and mopped his brow. He swallowed hard and closed his eyes in an obvious attempt to control his anger.

"You've just accused me of trying to set you up, Wadsworth. You'll have to make that up to me someday. Look . . . I'm on your side—remember?" Di Stefano rasped.

The Senator was stunned.

"I need you . . . and you need me, Wadsworth. If it'll make you happy, I'll find out who did it. That's no problem. Now, if you want to call it quits between us, that's OK with me too. You're not the only politician around, you know . . . I've gotta go now— have to welcome some friends."

Wadsworth was crestfallen. He stopped Vito as he turned to leave.

"Just a moment . . . please. I'm sorry, Vito . . . I was too hasty . . . I don't know what's come over me. I'm having problems with my wife again and I've been under great pressure lately . . . it's a grueling schedule. I guess I must be tired."

Di Stefano grinned victoriously.

"That's better, Senator. Forget the whole thing. No hard feelings."

Wadsworth took a deep breath, relieved the argument had gone no further.

But it was Vito's turn to show his displeasure.

"Since we're being frank, I'd like to tell you one more thing, Senator. I didn't want to upset you after your speech last night, but the big contributors in this state feel you're not aggressive enough."

"I'm not sure I understand," Wadsworth said, shaken once again.

"A lot of people think you're pussyfooting. Instead of just paying lip service to Clinton, you should openly challenge the powers that be and, by that, they mean the incumbent."

Wadsworth was stung by the criticism. "What do they expect me to do?"

"They want you to lead the congressional assault on the White House."

"I can't do that just now and you know it, Vito."

"Oh . . . the accident? . . . So, you were witness to an unavoidable tragedy. So what? It could happen to anyone. What have they got on you?—NOTHING. You have your rights, Senator—same as any other citizen. If the judge decided on a closed hearing, that's fine. No one will ever hold that against you. Let them try to make something of it. We'll stonewall it, that's all . . . Here's Clinton now . . . I'd better go take care of him. We'll talk about this later . . ."

The presidential candidate went directly to the lectern.

Wadsworth ordered a drink, listened politely to Clinton's ten-minute pep talk, and led the applause at its conclusion. He dutifully shook the Governor's hand and grinned with him as the photographers clicked away. Di Stefano got into the act, standing between them, beaming with joy.

Clinton left immediately for Omaha. Wadsworth remained a little longer to take pictures with the guests. He had a few more drinks and forgot the time.

At 11:45 A.M., someone mentioned that the Senator was going to miss his plane. Vito appeared miraculously from nowhere and told Wadsworth his bags were already in a chauffeur-driven limousine waiting at the main entrance.

It was a mad dash to LA International.

CHAPTER 12

Captain Burton Hadley was in luck. He easily found a spot for his Porsche in the cut-rate, long-term parking lot at LA International. He saw no reason to pay the exorbitant prices exacted closer to the terminal.

Unbuckling his seat belt, he reached for his uniform jacket on a coat hanger in the rear, put it on, and ran his fingers through his graying temples before donning his cap.

Carrying his three-suiter and heavy black flight case, he walked to the shuttle bus, mindful of keeping his lean, six-foot-three frame erect.

Barely forty-seven, Burton Hadley was one of the youngest senior captains with Pacific Global Airways. He had earned the respect of flight crews and ground personnel alike and was well on his way to becoming a check pilot.

Hadley had joined the company at twenty-seven, with a degree in economics, and after four years in the Air Force, including a tour of active duty in Korea.

He never assumed the prima donna airs affected by less experienced pilots. He didn't have to. Hadley was a total, no-nonsense professional and it showed.

At 11:30 A.M., the Captain strode into the operations office. Chief Dispatcher Louis Derosch spotted him at the counter, among a dozen or so other pilots.

Derosch knew Hadley's penchant for promptness and immediately went to brief him personally.

"Good morning, Captain."

"How are you, Derosch. What have you got for me?" Hadley responded warmly.

"You're going in the right direction . . . great weather all the way to Hawaii . . . would you believe it's already snowing back East?"

"No kidding. What kind of a load do we have?"

"You're light, Captain. Just about two hundred passengers. Don't have the final figures yet—they're still checking in. Not too much freight on this one either. You're fat on fuel. Should make excellent time."

"That's good. But why so few passengers? I thought we'd be full."

"From what I hear, we were supposed to pick up a connecting charter group from London, but their flight's been delayed twenty-four hours with an engine change."

"Well, we can't win 'em all, Louis. I hate to sound like a company man, but it really bothers me to see so many empty seats. What flight level did you select?"

Derosch opened a file. "We've got you at thirty-one or thirty-five with a choice of three routings. The computer says there's no more than a couple minutes' difference. Take your pick."

Hadley quickly scanned the flight plans.

"I think I'll take Number Three at thirty-five thousand feet. The higher, the better. We'll save fuel at that altitude—make the stockholders happy." Hadley smiled. "OK with you?"

"Anything you say, Captain. You're doing the flying. I'll get your clearance."

"Thanks, Derosch. Who's my co-pilot?"

"Hal Bessoe."

"Good man. And the flight engineer?"

"Herb Faust."

"Fine. We've got ourselves a good crew," Hadley said as he signed the routine departure documents. "Where's the airplane?"

"It's positioned at Gate Twelve. They're fueling up right now."

"Well, I guess I'll get out of your way. Please tell Bessoe and Faust that I'm on board. Have a good day, Derosch. See you soon."

"You too. Have a good flight, Captain."

At 1215, co-pilot Bessoe reported to the cockpit and went through the pre-takeoff check list with Hadley. Faust took up his station at the engineer's panel directly behind Bessoe and started logging the readings on the multitude of gauges before him.

The passengers began boarding the Boeing 747 at 1230. With cheerful greetings and warm smiles, the stewardesses directed them to their seats. Soft Hawaiian music wafted through the cabin, setting the leisurely mood of the flight.

Exactly on schedule—at 1300, the engines whined to life.

The warning light on the instrument panel indicated the main door was not locked. Captain Hadley picked up the intercom mike.

A stewardess answered immediately, reporting that a last-minute passenger was rushing down the ramp.

"Hurry it up. Let's get off the ground."

"He's here now, Captain."

Senator Wadsworth had just made the flight. The Captain's warning light went off.

Hadley called the tower: "Los Angeles ground, PGA 81 ready to taxi from Gate Twelve. We've got departure information 'ECHO.' "

"Pacific 81, you're cleared to Runway 25 left. Observe standard taxiing routes."

CHAPTER 13

Grant awakened as dawn was breaking over the Pacific.

He crawled out of his pup tent, stretched, and yawned as he ran his fingers over the stubble on his face. Shaving became the first order of the day.

Grant had been on the cove for a little over thirty-six hours. He had spent the whole of the previous day relaxing in the sun, swimming, studying aerial maps, and catching up on his sleep.

At 7:45 A.M., he looked through his knapsack then climbed into the cockpit with the little black box and microphone patchcord.

With double-faced tape, he firmly secured the tiny electronic apparatus under the instrument panel. He plugged the airplane's mike into the input jack of the black box then, with the patchcord, connected its output jack to the radio transmitters.

Grant flicked on the battery power switches. Snatches of rhythmic, Latin-sounding music came over the loudspeaker as he tuned one of the low-frequency receivers. He went back to the last powerful, static-free, station he had picked up and waited for the time signal.

A fast-talking, exuberant disc jockey announced:

"*Son las ocho de la mañana aquí—en la hermosa Ensenada—Baja California!*"

Tuned to this station, the needle of the Automatic Direction Finder confirmed the aircraft was located along the Mexican coastline—exactly 42 miles south of Ensenada.

Grant set the clock to 0800 and selected the forty-meter "ham" radio band on another receiver. He heard several brief exchanges in Spanish and English between amateur radio operators as he fine-tuned to 7286 kilohertz.

At precisely 0803, a call came in loud and clear:

"Bravo One—this is Bravo Two."

For the first time in twenty-two days, since his disappearance over Hoa Binh, Grant's voice was heard:

"Bravo One here. Ready for rendezvous. Any changes?"

"Negative. No modifications. Proceed per schedule. Bravo Two ready and standing by—out."

"Roger. Bravo One—out."

Grant turned all the switches off, stood up in the cockpit, and, stretching as far as he could, began slicing through the airplane's camouflage net. When he could lean no further, he slid down the rope to the beach and continued tugging and cutting.

Soon, the web was reduced to four long rectangular pieces which he folded, weighted with rocks, and rolled into neat cylindrical bundles.

Grant ripped up the pup tent and sleeping bag. He loaded them aboard the inflatable boat, together with the bundles, empty thermoses and food cans, tin-foil wrappers, cigarette butts, and a small jerry can of gasoline.

Half a mile from shore, Grant dumped his cargo, scattering the last vestiges of his presence. He topped off the little outboard motor and threw the jerry can overboard. He was back on the beach at 0915.

While the boat dried in the sun, he collected all remaining odds and ends—binoculars, knife, can opener, and a full thermos of coffee. He put them in the knapsack and hauled it into the cockpit.

Grant brushed the sand off the boat, which he deflated and placed into its canvas bag together with a CO_2 cartridge. He loaded it into the airplane, along with two snap-on paddles, and the small outboard motor.

At 1140, he went on a walk-around inspection of the ominous-looking drooped-winged aircraft. He checked the landing gear and the air intakes, then made sure the three missiles and four small rockets protruding beneath the wings were ready to be activated. The fighter-bomber was airworthy. He patted the fuselage in a satisfied gesture.

A sudden change overcame Grant as he put on his flight suit, life preserver, and helmet. His eyes narrowed. His lips tightened.

A final glance around the cove reassured him that no trace of his visit remained.

He smoothed over a few footprints with the soles of his boots as he walked backward toward the airplane, although he was certain that whatever tracks remained would be blasted away on takeoff.

At 1210, Grant climbed into the airplane and pulled up the rope.

The extra paraphernalia in the cockpit left him little room to move freely. He found the best arrangement was to place the boat on the seat and use it as a cushion. He put the knapsack and the tiny outboard motor on the floor between his legs.

Grant unfolded an aerial map and drew a line from the cove, northwest to a point over the ocean. It was situated exactly 100 miles west of Ensenada and 100 miles southwest of San Diego. From that spot, he drew another line due north. At the point where it intersected the U.S. mainland, Grant drew a circle—over Los Angeles.

The two lines totaled 265 miles. His plan called for the trip to last no longer than thirty minutes at various speed settings for an average of 550 MPH.

At 1225, Grant closed the canopy, switched on internal power, and, eyes glued to the instrument panel, fired up the engines.

The needles on the gauges jumped. All systems were functioning.

Grant gently "walked" the throttles to full power.

Like a lunar module blasting off from the surface of the moon, the aircraft slowly rose vertically in a blinding white cloud of sand and fragmented coral.

Grant felt the three small, reassuring thumps indicating the landing gear had retracted and locked. The triangular display of red lights on the panel confirmed the wheels were up and that the TX-75E was in streamlined flight configuration.

As if catapulted, the aircraft suddenly shot over the ocean, then stopped abruptly. It hovered for a moment at the edge of the beach.

From an altitude of thirty feet, Grant took a last look at the deserted cove. It was as wild and untouched as the day nature had created it.

Grant established a northwesterly heading and pushed the throttles forward.

Ten minutes after takeoff, skimming over the waves to avoid radar detection, he was 100 miles off the coast of Baja California and 180 miles south of Los Angeles. He turned north and reduced speed.

At 1250, a check on the ADF and the two VHF omnidirectional range receivers pinpointed his position. He was 10 miles west of San Clemente Island.

He continued on the same course and, four minutes later, was 15 miles west of Santa Catalina Island.

Approximately 30 miles southwest of Long Beach, Grant tuned in to the departure frequency of the control tower at LA International and listened intently.

Traffic was at its peak, generating incessant chatter between controllers and airplanes on the ground and in the air.

Grant strained to pick up what he was waiting to hear. He caught nothing. Thinking he might be too early, he checked his clock. It was exactly 1301.

He reduced speed to under 100 MPH and descended further, to just twenty feet above the water, on a direct course to the airport.

1302—still nothing.

Ten miles west of LA International, Grant decided he could proceed no further. It was now 1305. He began to circle slowly off the coast. He was already committed and had no choice but to hold.

Grant heard that only one runway—25 left—was in use at the moment. A controller advised that heavy earth-moving equipment was being hauled across Runway 25 right, which would be reactivated shortly.

He cursed upon learning that bulldozers were the cause of the temporary congestion in the normal flow of traffic. That was one foul-up he had not anticipated.

The tower cleared an American Airlines flight for takeoff direct to New York, then a Mexican jet to Puerto Vallarta. Still nothing of interest to Grant.

He looked at the clock. It was 1307. He began to sweat. Every minute lost was precious fuel consumed.

A controller told a TWA flight to Chicago and a Pan Am 707 on its way to South America that traffic was backed up. They would be Numbers Four and Five respectively for departure.

Then he heard it.

A cold shiver shot up his spine.

Pacific Global Airways Flight 81 announced it was ready for takeoff in sequence.

The tower answered that 25 right was now in use for departures only. PGA 81 was instructed to switch from 25 left to 25 right and to hold short of the runway threshold. It would be Number Three in sequence behind an Eastern Tristar and a National DC-10.

The 747 lumbered heavily down the taxiway and docilely lined up behind the two other jets like an elephant following the leader in a circus parade.

At 1314, the tower called:

"PGA 81—taxi into position and hold."

"Roger. Position and hold," PGA 81 acknowledged as it turned and lined up on the runway while extending its flaps.

Grant stopped circling, increased his speed, and headed for a point 5 miles south of the end of Runway 25 right. He arrived just as the National DC-10 became airborne.

The controller called the 747.

"PGA 81, you're cleared for immediate takeoff. Have a good one now."

"We're rolling—PGA 81—Aloha."

The jumbo jet accelerated slowly, gradually picking up speed down the twelve-thousand-foot runway. Soon the nose wheel left the ground, then the undercarriage. The airliner entered a steep climb as the landing gear and flaps began to retract.

Grant waited for the huge aircraft to pass over him.

He spotted it at 1318, at about five thousand feet, climbing fast on a southwesterly heading.

Grant added power as he made a left climbing turn, intercepting the path of the 747. He zoomed to altitude and caught up with the jumbo jet as it was passing through ten thousand feet.

He positioned the fighter-bomber half a mile behind the tail of the airliner.

At 1322, as the mainland was rapidly fading at the back of the two planes, Grant pressed his mike button:

"PGA 81—you are being hijacked."

CHAPTER 14

Captain Burton Hadley frowned. He shot a puzzled look at his co-pilot. Hal Bessoe was shaking his head in disbelief.

Glancing over his shoulder, Hadley motioned to the flight engineer to plug in his head set. Herb Faust seemed surprised at the request but immediately reached for his earphones.

Hadley pressed his mike button.

"Who was that calling PGA 81?" he asked calmly.

"Just keep climbing and hold your present heading," answered the disembodied voice.

Hadley was genuinely startled. This was a new one on him. No scribbled note demanding a ransom. No frantic stewardess on the intercom or knocking on the cockpit door saying a man was pointing a gun at her head. Nothing about going to Havana, Algiers, or some Middle Eastern sheikdom.

The possibility that it could be a prankster on the ground crossed Hadley's mind. The same thoughts were reflected on Bessoe's face. Lips pursed, eyes wide open, and eyebrows raised in surprise, the co-pilot's expression was comical. Shrugging his shoulders, he looked at Hadley and Faust. He threw his hands up in the air in a bewildered and questioning gesture.

Hadley spoke into his mike.

"Los Angeles Tower—PGA 81."

"Pacific Global 81—go ahead."

"Did you read that message a moment ago?"

"Affirmative," replied a controller's voice with the faintest trace of tension.

"What's the story?" Hadley asked.

"Stand by Pacific 81. We're checking it out. Trying to get a bearing on the location of the transmitting equipment."

"OK," Hadley acknowledged with poise. "Better expedite. We're passing through twenty-one thousand and still climbing."

"Roger, Pacific 81. First guess here is that it might be one of your passengers with a portable VHF or a walkie-talkie tuned to this frequency. Could someone in the crew check in the cabin and see if . . ."

Grant broke in on the exchange.

"LA Tower, this IS a hijack. Prepare to copy instructions. Captain PGA 81, listen in. Keep climbing to thirty-six thousand feet and hold your course—two one zero degrees."

Tom Bragan, the chief supervisor, was already alerted. As he hurried from his office toward the controller working PGA 81, his assistant confirmed all the tower's tape recorders were on and thrust a pad and pencil in his hand. Bragan put them on a console next to one of the mikes.

"Ready to copy," Bragan said, making an effort to sound matter-of-fact.

This was it. Grant spoke very deliberately so that every word would sink in.

"As you can see on your radar screens, I am about one hundred feet above and half a mile behind PGA 81. This is a jet fighter—fully armed. The 747 is a sitting duck. I can shoot it down instantly. Do you read?"

"LA Tower—we read," Bragan said evenly.

"What about you—Captain PGA 81?" Grant asked impatiently.

"We read—PGA 81." A note of uneasiness had crept into Hadley's voice.

Grant's heart was pumping wildly. His hands were moist.

"I want the entire area within a four-hundred-mile radius of Los Angeles Tower IMMEDIATELY AND COMPLETELY cleared of all aircraft and ships. I am equipped with long-range radar. If I see the slightest movement in my direction from anywhere within this boundary, either military or civilian, I won't ask any questions.

I'll just blast that 747 out of the sky. LA Tower—understood?"

"We understand," Bragan replied.

"I'll give you exactly ten minutes to notify all concerned to alter course or stay on the ground. Make everybody scatter. This includes the Air Force, the Navy, commercial and private planes as well as merchant vessels and pleasure craft. You've got thirty minutes to clear the area. In the meantime, monitor this frequency and tell everyone else to get off this channel. Prepare to mark the time. It is now . . . thirteen . . . twenty . . . four local. Mark."

"Mark—LA Tower," Bragan acknowledged. While the anonymous hijacker was talking, he felt a slight tap on his shoulder. Michael Ayno, his assistant, was standing behind him, surrounded by a small group of controllers.

The chief supervisor had been jotting down notes during the exchanges. He tore off the top sheet from his pad, switched off his mike, and stood up, his six-foot-four frame towering over the other men.

Bragan started rattling off rapid-fire directives, glancing occasionally at the piece of paper in his left hand and designating with his right index finger those he appointed to specific tasks.

"Bring in all airplanes on final or ready for final approach for the next eight minutes only. Tell the rest to get the hell out of here. Cancel all takeoffs. Instruct all departing aircraft to return to their terminals. Inform all inbound flights there's an emergency in progress."

"What do we do with the planes presently over the Pacific?" Ayno asked.

"All aircraft over the ocean within fuel range of Hawaii should return to Honolulu. Those approaching the mainland are to proceed at once to San Francisco. Give them PGA 81's position, relative bearing to their flight path and distance—but tell them to keep away from that guy and to make the necessary detours."

Ayno was making notes. "What about incoming flights over the mainland?"

"They should land immediately at the nearest airport or else make 180 degree turns and divert to San Francisco, Reno, Phoenix, or any point four hundred miles beyond Los Angeles—as long as they can make it within the next twenty-five minutes. Advise every airport within the specified boundary to ground all aircraft. They should activate all runways to rapidly process all incoming traffic. Call Honolulu and tell them to hold all eastbound departures."

"Do you want us to advise Canada and Mexico at this time?"

"Yes . . . of course—warn them," Bragan said. "Also tell our other control centers from coast to coast about the expected changes in traffic patterns until the situation is clarified. Confirm everything by teletype."

Ayno nodded. "I'll take care of the emergency procedures check list. I'll co-ordinate with PGA regional operations, get in touch with the FAA, call the Navy in San Diego and the Coast Guard."

"Right," Bragan approved. "Tell the Coast Guard to pass the word immediately to ships at sea to clear the area."

"OK. We'll get on it," Ayno said.

"Notify the others on the check list—the Pentagon, Vandenberg Air Force Base, Strategic Air Command, NORAD in Colorado Springs, and all other government agencies that might be of assistance. Also contact the nearest hospital—we may need ambulances."

"Will do."

"And don't forget the FBI and the police," Bragan added. "We're certainly going to call on them for help at some point."

"OK." Ayno pointed at one of the remaining controllers, thereby indicating that this last assignment would be his. The man nodded.

"There's one important thing, Ayno," Bragan said. "Tell the military authorities to sound the alarm and to stand by but, above all, insist that they stay put for the moment. Be sure to stress that we can't take any chances. Have them keep their airplanes on the ground. We don't want some trigger-happy idiot getting any bright ideas."

"They probably won't like our telling them what to do," Ayno interjected. "They may have their own ideas on how to handle the situation."

"I know, but it's a civilian aircraft that's being threatened. Right now, it's our responsibility, not theirs. Call the Secretary of Defense if necessary. Tell him we suggest that everyone do exactly as the hijacker says, for the moment, and until we know exactly what's going on. We'll take care of the liaison work right here."

Ayno turned to one of the controllers. "See if you can get the Secretary of Defense," he said. "I'll be at my phone in a minute."

Bragan put his arm around Ayno's shoulders and led him aside. "Keep the news media out of this as long as you can. We don't need any panic. I'll stay on the mike with PGA 81 and the hijacker for now. You watch over the rest. Keep me informed verbally when there's a break in the conversation—otherwise by short written notes."

Most of the controllers were on phones or on mikes executing Bragan's directives. One waved at Ayno:

"The Pentagon's on the line."

"Go ahead," Bragan said to Ayno. "Tell the Secretary I'll try to talk to him as soon as . . ."

The chief controller was interrupted by Grant calling the 747. The hubbub in the tower muted instantly.

"PGA 81. What's the Captain's name, also the co-pilot?"

Hadley looked at Bessoe and noticed his jaw muscles were tight. He cleared his throat before speaking.

"Captain Burton Hadley is flying PGA 81. Hal Bessoe is the co-pilot," he answered in a flat tone.

"Roger. Sorry it had to be you, Captain Hadley." Grant sounded almost apologetic. "From now on both you and the tower will refer to me as 'Shadow 81.' This will be my call sign. Acknowledge."

"Shadow 81—Roger," Hadley said.

"We copy—Shadow 81," Bragan replied from the ground.

Grant checked his instruments. They were about fifty miles out over the ocean and, of course, by now invisible to binoculars on the mainland. The weather was still perfect. No clouds but for a thin layer of stratus at approximately five thousand feet, roughly 20 miles to the south. A few cumulo-nimbus, announcing possible thunderstorm activity, were building up a few miles west of the stratus layer. He must avoid that area, he decided. Grant glanced quickly in every direction as he followed the jumbo jet. No airplanes or ships in sight. He suddenly noticed that the compass heading had changed slightly. The 747 was drifting imperceptibly to the left.

"Captain Hadley," Grant snapped, "please hold your course. I said two one zero. You're eight degrees off on a heading of two zero two. Don't try any evasive maneuvers. I can see those clouds just as well as you can. I will not keep repeating instructions."

"Unintentional," Hadley answered through his teeth, realizing

128

that the hijacker had immediately caught his feeble attempt to turn back toward the mainland. "Roger. Correcting to two one zero."

"That's better, Captain Hadley," Grant said soothingly. "I think we're going to get along just fine."

Grant looked at his altimeter. They had already reached thirty-four thousand feet and were still climbing.

"Hadley—Shadow 81."

"PGA 81—go ahead," Hadley sighed.

"Level off when we reach thirty-six thousand."

"OK—PGA 81."

Ayno approached Bragan in the tower.

"Why don't we ask this guy what he wants?"

"Not now. Give things a chance to settle down. Have you notified the proper authorities?"

"They've all been alerted. They're discussing the situation at the Pentagon and will get back to us as soon as they've decided what to do."

"We've done all we can then—for the moment. Now we'll just have to wait 'til he makes his next move."

"Hadley," Grant called as the two planes reached the altitude he had assigned, "fly straight and level. No turns unless I say so. Reduce speed very gradually—repeat—very gradually from your present 410 knots to 250 knots indicated, holding your course. No sudden maneuvers. I'm right behind you. If you pull back your power too fast I'm liable to run up your tail."

"Roger—PGA 81." Hadley nodded agreement to his co-pilot and pointed at Faust to handle the throttles. The flight engineer proceeded to change settings.

"OK," Grant said with a hint of satisfaction in his voice. He synchronized his own settings with those of the airliner as they both slowed down.

"Captain Hadley," Grant's tone was respectful, "how many passengers do you have on board?"

"Stand by," answered the Captain as Faust handed him a clipboard. He thumbed through the flight's documents.

"Shadow 81," Hadley called, trying to sound calm and detached, "we have 187 passengers . . ." he paused, "including three babies." He anticipated the next question. "Fourteen crew members—that's counting two extra stewardesses deadheading to Honolulu and myself. Total—201 people aboard."

"How many hours of fuel are you carrying?" Grant asked.

"Stand by one—checking."

Captain Hadley thought quickly as his eyes swept the gauges. Shadow 81 certainly seemed to know his business. No doubt he was aware that, on a flight from Los Angeles to Honolulu, the 747 would require at least six hours of fuel, plus about two more hours for possible weather diversion to an alternate airport and routine holding delays. There was really little point in lying.

Hadley turned to Bessoe and Faust. They were both quite pale; then he realized he probably didn't look too composed himself. He motioned to Bessoe to switch off the mikes.

"What do I tell this guy?"

"I don't think you can kid him too much," Bessoe said resignedly.

Faust had left his station and was now standing between the two pilots. He nodded in agreement.

"We left with ten hours," Bessoe continued. "We've used about thirty minutes' worth taxiing and climbing. He knows we can outlast him—but not exactly by how much. Maybe we can con him out of an hour or so. That would be close enough to the truth and we'd have something left in reserve."

"I don't think he'll buy that," Faust said glumly. "Better tell him what's what."

"I tend to concur with Bessoe," Hadley said, overruling Faust. He switched the mikes back on.

"Shadow 81—Hadley. We have about eight hours' range—give or take fifteen minutes."

"Should be about right, Captain," Grant said with a hint of irony in his voice, as if he had read Faust's mind. "But I'll allow a couple of extra hours anyway," he added derisively, "just in case you were thinking of doing a little cheating."

Faust looked at Hadley and Bessoe, shaking his head from side to side. His long, gaunt face reflected a perverse satisfaction at having judged their shadow correctly.

"I assure you I have no intention of misleading you," Hadley said, sounding a bit put out.

"Good. Let's keep it that way. We'll all be better off. I've got another question, Hadley. This time I want a quick answer with no hesitation. What's your minimum slow flight speed for maximum endurance?"

"With our load and at this altitude, I don't believe we can go much below two three zero knots," Hadley came right back. "It gets pretty shaky then . . . starts shuddering . . . almost stalling speed."

"Is that really the best you can do, Captain?"

"Are you going to question my word about everything?" Hadley asked with obvious irritation.

"I'm afraid so," Grant said cuttingly. "You've already tried to deceive me twice in the last twelve minutes. I wouldn't try it a third time, Captain."

Hadley stood firm. "I repeat. I cannot go below two three zero knots if I am to maintain proper control of this aircraft."

"That will have to do, then," Grant conceded. "For the moment, anyway. We'll take another look later as you burn fuel and get lighter. You'll probably manage to go slower. Right now reduce power and maintain two three zero knots—thirty-six thousand feet—same heading."

"Roger—PGA 81." Hadley, a disciplined pilot conditioned to verbal shorthand by over twenty-five years of flying, caught himself acknowledging these weird instructions as a routine matter.

"Hadley," Grant said, "I would suggest you tell your flight engineer to watch his power settings. I want maximum endurance at the slowest cruising speed. Better save all the fuel you can. You'll need it."

"We'll give you maximum endurance—PGA 81."

"Hadley—Shadow 81."

"Shadow 81—go ahead."

"We'll be 160 miles out of Los Angeles any minute now. When I give you the signal, start circling to the left. We'll hold there for a while."

"OK—PGA 81."

"Just keep making 360s—same speed and altitude. Your fix will be the following co-ordinates: 32 north latitude, 120 west longitude at the intersection of these lines of position: 200 degree radial—Los Angeles VOR and 240 degree radial—San Diego VOR. Your pattern is not to exceed a radius of 10 miles from that point. This means, Hadley, that you should get no closer than 140 miles to any spot on the mainland at any time. Check that figure constantly with your distance-measuring equipment tuned to Los Angeles. Do you read?"

"We read—PGA 81."

"Good. Stand by. Begin circling . . . now," Grant ordered.

"Roger. Circling—PGA 81," Hadley said as he entered a gentle left turn.

Grant looked at his clock.

"LA Tower—Shadow 81."

"Shadow 81—go ahead," Bragan answered.

"We're coming up on 1340 hours. How're you doing on clearing the area?"

Bragan looked up at Ayno and at the other controllers. They replied silently by raising their thumbs.

"Your instructions have been relayed to all concerned," Bragan confirmed. "You didn't give us much time but they're all scattering. It may take a little while longer to get them completely out of your radar scope but they're on their way."

"Tell them to hurry it up."

"I'm afraid we may not be able to abide in all cases by the 400-mile figure you specified because of fuel or weather problems encountered by some airplanes already en route," Bragan said. "Most aircraft have been told to divert to San Francisco, which is not quite 400 miles, Reno, or Phoenix. Is that OK?"

"Apparently, I didn't get through to you. San Francisco won't do. Tell them to go to Vancouver or anywhere they like. I said 400 miles and they'd better be off my screen by 1354. You work it out. Is that clear?"

Bragan cursed under his breath in frustration before pressing his mike button.

"It's clear. Doing our best, Shadow 81. We'll keep you advised."

"You do that. Who's the controller in charge?"

"Bragan. Tom Bragan. I'm the chief controller on the mike right now."

"Glad to meet you, Bragan," Grant said as if he were shaking hands. "You sound like you're on the ball."

"Thanks," Bragan said dryly.

"Bragan," Grant continued, ignoring the sarcasm in the chief controller's tone, "I'd appreciate your staying on the mike. Save us all the trouble of breaking in somebody new."

"Roger—will do. Bragan."

"Take it easy, Bragan. You're doing fine. Just don't try to pull any fast ones like Hadley did a while ago and everything will be OK. Now, next step: All airplanes inbound for the mainland or still in my immediate vicinity should drop at once to five thousand feet or below. As you've heard, we're circling at thirty-six thousand. I don't want anyone above us, especially unfriendly military guys with the sun at their backs. That, Bragan, would make me very, very nervous. I'm sure you understand what I mean. So, how about relaying that?"

"Roger—five thousand or below," Bragan acknowledged while signaling Ayno to comply.

"Stand by for further instructions," Grant said.

About twenty minutes had elapsed since he had intercepted PGA 81, and he now had to make some calculations before proceeding to the next stage.

Grant studied his instrument panel and wrote down a few numbers in a notebook resting on his lap.

From the left breast pocket of his flight suit, he took out his manually operated dead reckoning aerial navigation computer.

In the groove between the four-inch-diameter metallic discs of the circular slide rule, he inserted the long, flat, ten-inch sliding rectangular grid used for determining drift correction. In the center of the grid, which protruded about three inches on either side of the compass rose face of the computer, he plotted his speed and headings with pencil marks.

Rotating the compass rose to the proper bearings, he quickly solved the basic vector problems of wind drift and head wind component.

He flipped the computer over to the circular slide rule side and used the rotating logarithmic scales for time-speed-distance and fuel consumption assessments.

At his actual cruising speed of 230 knots, Grant could remain in the air about eight more hours. So far, everything was right on the button.

Grant could have relied on the sophisticated electronic instruments in the fighter-bomber's panel to have instantly arrived at the same conclusions. He preferred, however, to make doubly sure using the old-fashioned method. If he first determined his figures by hand with the navigation computer—still the pilot's best friend

—he would be ready to cope should anything go wrong with his electronic equipment.

He needed about an hour in reserve to make his escape. That left him seven hours net. Another quick check around the cockpit to make sure that all systems were functioning normally and he'd be ready to resume contact with LA Tower.

Grant had kept a careful eye on PGA 81's tail. The giant 747 was circling obediently.

CHAPTER 15

Senator Wadsworth looked forward to this trip. As an Army captain during World War II, he had spent five months in Honolulu, a place of fond memories, and had since returned many times as a campaigner.

He ran his fingers through his hair as he leaned over in his seat, attempting to catch the eye of a stewardess. Thick curls at the back of his neck reminded him that he had to get a haircut as soon as he arrived at the hotel. Long hair was in right now, but no need to overdo it.

The cavernous first-class section of the 747 was virtually unoccupied except for a quartet of middle-aged, closely cropped executive types. They had appropriated the back row next to the partition separating first and economy class and were exchanging remarks in hushed tones. One of them, the youngest-looking, plunged into his briefcase before the airplane had taken off. He came up with a batch of typewritten sheets, with which he was obviously trying to prove a point.

Probably a flunky, Wadsworth thought. He recognized the servile look. He couldn't stand this breed of eager-beaver rah, rah, rah, company men. As voters, he had discovered, these supposed upper-echelon decision makers rarely succeeded in making up their minds about major issues.

What did he care anyway? he asked himself. All he wanted right now was a drink and a little peace and quiet. The speech he would make that evening in Honolulu was memorized. Except for the injection of local color, on which he would be briefed later, it was standard material. The address would be tailored to the audience. He would tell them what they wanted to hear—the same empty words.

He knew he'd be a big hit, as usual. For the moment he needed that drink and a few hours' sleep.

"Miss?" Wadsworth said suavely, flashing his best smile.

Chief stewardess Laura Hines, who was returning from the economy-class section, smiled back.

"Yes, Senator, what can I do for you?"

"I'd like the newspapers, please. I don't think I'll have any lunch later. I'm going to catch a nap. But how about a double scotch on the rocks—Johnnie Walker—Black Label—if you have it."

Laura had seen Wadsworth on television. Although accustomed to meeting celebrities in the course of her work, she was, nevertheless, instantly conquered by the rich depth of his melodious voice. His charming grin reminded her of a naughty boy asking for something he really knew he wasn't supposed to get.

"We have everything on PGA, Senator," she laughed. "You've picked the right airline."

She leaned toward him so as not to be overheard by the four men behind and took a mock conspiratorial air.

"I'm sure you know we're forbidden to serve drinks until we reach cruising altitude," she whispered, her lips almost brushing his ear. "But, for you, Senator, I'll make an exception. Don't you go telling anybody now," she said, winking.

"You can count on me," he chuckled.

Laura disappeared into the galley, and quickly returned with a cup on a tray. She also brought the Los Angeles *Times*, the *Wall Street Journal*, and the New York *Times*.

"Your tea, Senator," she said aloud for the benefit of the passengers in the rear.

Wadsworth looked up. "My . . ."

He saw Laura's eyes twinkling mischievously.

"My tea . . . of course. You're adorable. What's your name?"

"Laura Hines."

"Lovely name."

"Thank you, Senator. Just press the button if you need anything else."

Wadsworth lit a cigarette and glanced through the L.A. *Times* to see what coverage he had received on his speech.

As Vito had predicted, his picture was on the front page. The three-column headline and the subheadlines read:

CORNY BUT CATCHY
SENATOR WADSWORTH COINS NEW THREE "W" CAMPAIGN SLOGAN
"WE WILL WIN"
Vows support for Clinton despite party split

Wadsworth smiled and read the article as he sipped his scotch. He pressed the button for Laura.

"I'd like some more tea," he said, handing back the cup.

He certainly can put it away fast, Laura thought. She took the cup and went back into the galley.

But Wadsworth never got his second drink.

As she picked up some ice cubes, Laura suddenly realized the plane was slowing down and entering a left turn.

She called the cockpit to find out if anything was wrong. The other stewardesses and some of the more seasoned passengers would be sure to notice the aircraft was behaving erratically and they would soon be asking questions.

"Tell them we're rerouting because of weather—nothing serious —and that an announcement will follow shortly . . . Laura," Captain Hadley added, "come up to the cockpit as soon as you're through."

Although she thought Hadley sounded tense, which was most unusual, Laura reacted immediately. Her reassuring voice came over the cabin loudspeakers.

"Ladies and gentlemen, this is chief stewardess Laura Hines. Your pilot, Captain Burton Hadley, wishes to inform you that he has just been instructed to reduce speed and to alter course due to unexpected weather conditions. There is no cause for alarm and he will give you further details in a moment. Refreshments and lunch will be served in a few minutes, so please remain seated and enjoy your trip. You may smoke but please keep your seat belts fastened until we reach our final cruising altitude. Thank you."

Hadley heard Laura's explanations and was impressed with her poise. He had flown with this girl on a number of occasions. Not only was she cool and efficient, he thought, she was also a damn good-looking blonde.

Senator Wadsworth was scanning the New York *Times*, when he sensed an abnormal engine power reduction. Then he heard Laura's announcement.

His intuition told him something was wrong. He could recognize a phony speech when he heard one. Out of the corner of his eye, he noticed that Laura, instead of bringing him his drink, was rapidly climbing up the spiral staircase leading to the first-class lounge and cockpit.

In a flash, Wadsworth unfastened his seat belt and began to follow her, but then stopped dead in his tracks. The four men were staring at him. They looked worried.

Realizing that he should act casually, the Senator smiled, pretended to yawn deeply, and stretched his arms. He gave them a friendly wave and walked nonchalantly toward the staircase saying he was going to take a nap in the lounge. That seemed to reassure them.

By the time Wadsworth got upstairs, Laura was gone. He tried to open the cockpit door but found it locked.

"Captain, what is it?"

Hadley took his eyes off the horizon and saw that Laura was standing behind him. He put his index finger to his lips and motioned to Bessoe to make sure the mikes were off.

"We've got problems, Laura," Hadley said. "We're being hijacked by a jet fighter sitting on our tail. I don't have a clue who this guy is or what he wants, except he's told us to circle right here for the moment."

The smile which had illuminated Laura's delicate features faded gradually as Hadley briefed her.

"What do you want me to do, Captain?"

"Nothing much you can do—yet. Better tell the girls about this and instruct them to supply the passengers with anything they want to drink—compliments of PGA. Give them the liquor individually. Don't roll out the serving carts. We may have to make sudden maneuvers and we don't want anyone to get hurt. Stick to the weather delay story for now. Come back here as often as you can and I'll keep you advised. I'll let the passengers know what's really going on as soon as our friend lets us in on his intentions."

Laura swallowed hard, nodded her understanding, and started back for the cabin.

Wadsworth startled her when she found him standing behind the cockpit door. She quickly tried to close it, but the Senator had wedged his foot into the opening. His grin had disappeared.

"I want to see the Captain," he said grimly, in a tone usually reserved for the underlings in his Washington office.

"I'm sorry, Senator," Laura objected with a strained smile as she tugged at the handle with both hands to prevent him from entering. "No one is allowed in the cockpit, you know that."

"I couldn't care less about your regulations. I know something's going on and I want to find out what it is. Now please step aside, like a good girl."

With that, the Senator pushed past her. He was standing next to Hadley by the time she grabbed his sleeve in a fruitless effort to lead him back to the lounge.

"Captain, I'm Senator Felton Wadsworth. What's happening?"

Hadley was busy scanning his instrument panel when the unfamiliar voice broke his concentration. He glared over his shoulder at the tall intruder and saw that Laura, looking helpless, was behind the Senator.

The Captain was furious.

"I don't care who you are. This is none of your business," he shouted. "You'll be advised like the others when I'm good and ready. Now get the hell out of here and go back to the cabin where you belong," he commanded.

"Captain," Laura interjected, "I tried to stop . . ."

"Get him out of here. Now!" Hadley interrupted.

Wadsworth flushed. He wasn't accustomed to being treated in this manner. He was on the verge of losing his temper when he noticed the co-pilot was rising out of his seat with a menacing look. Wadsworth instantly reverted to diplomacy.

"Gentlemen," he said softly, pretending not to notice Laura still tugging at him, "I thought I could be of some help. You have a lot of worried passengers down there. Perhaps I could calm them. I've been through a few sticky situations and I'm certain I can cope with this one if you tell me what it is."

"There's nothing you can do," Hadley cut him short.

"You fellows look pretty busy up here," Wadsworth continued, undeterred. "Most of the people in the airplane will recognize me. My presence could be reassuring in that crowded economy-class section, don't you think, Captain?"

Wadsworth's little speech, delivered with all the sincerity he could muster on such short notice, made the expected impact.

"You may be right at that, Senator," Hadley conceded grudgingly. "Let go of him, Laura. Better go and take care of the passengers, honey."

Laura felt relieved. At least Hadley was no longer mad at her.

This time, she looked through the peephole in the door before she opened it. There was no one in the lounge.

"We've got some nut in a jet fighter tailing us and threatening to blow up our plane."

The Senator's face fell.

Hadley quickly filled him in on the details.

"I see," Wadsworth said gravely. "Sorry if I upset you, Captain. May I remain here for the moment and listen in?"

"You might as well stay, since you're here now. But please don't say anything unless I signal you the mikes are off."

"Of course, Captain, of course."

Grant's voice broke in.

"I'm going to be talking to LA Tower now. You listen in, Hadley. But first, let's clarify a few matters in case you or your crew get any bright ideas. You can't make a run for it. I can fly circles around your Boeing—so forget it. Don't try to duck into any clouds in case the weather changes. My weapons have infra-red seekers for terminal homing. Even if I should lose you—which is unlikely, since, pardon the language, I'm right on your ass—I can fire everything I've got in your general direction. Something is bound to hit you. One more thing. Don't give me any bull about sudden mechanical failures. As long as I'm in the air, you fly. Do we understand each other?"

Hadley's voice quivered slightly.

"I understand—PGA 81."

"Fine. Settle down, Hadley. You too Bessoe. Relax. This is going to be a long ride. Might as well enjoy it. LA Tower—Bragan —did you copy?"

"We copy—LA Tower."

"Shadow 81—PGA 81. One question."

"What is it, Hadley?"

"Can I tell my passengers about this? They're naturally wondering what's happening. Also, can we give them something to eat?"

"If the tower abides by my instructions, I don't see why not. I'm a civilized guy, Hadley. But maybe you'd better check with LA first. It's OK with me if it's OK with them. Did you read, LA?"

"Roger—stand by," Bragan acknowledged. "We've summoned PGA's Regional Operations Manager and the FAA to decide on the best course of action regarding the passengers. Can you hold that off for a few minutes, PGA 81?"

"We'll stall the food for a while—Hadley."

"In the meantime, Bragan," Grant cut in, "let's get down to business. I have a little shopping list for you. Are you ready?"

"Ready—Bragan," the chief controller replied in a neutral tone. Only those in his immediate vicinity realized he was getting edgy.

"I want twenty million dollars in gold—repeat—twenty million dollars in gold—to be brought immediately to Los Angeles International Airport. Ten million must be in five-kilogram ingots—that's one thousand bars. The other ten million in one-kilogram ingots—that's five thousand bars. It's all to be delivered by 1700 hours local time at the latest. It is now 1346 local."

In the 747 cockpit, the four men stared incredulously at each other, stunned by the enormity of the demand.

"Twenty million, in gold?" Bragan gasped. "Where do you expect us to find it on such short notice?"

"That's your problem," Grant rasped. "Why don't you try Fort Knox? They should have it, unless the country's gone broke. By the way, you can tell the boys back there I'm giving them a break. I'm not even figuring this at the present official rate, but at the free market quotation. I'm giving a discount of almost seventy dollars or sixty-six per cent per ounce."

Bragan was at a loss for words.

"Stand by," he said, and turned for advice to his assistant.

Ayno was standing at his elbow with PGA's Regional Manager, the head of the FAA in Los Angeles, and the local FBI chief. He consulted with them briefly and returned to his mike.

"Shadow 81—Bragan."

"Go ahead, Bragan."

"I've just checked around. I'm pretty sure we can raise this amount in cash locally and . . ."

"No cash," Grant cut him short. "Repeat, no cash. That's final."

"Even if we get the gold in Fort Knox, how do we bring it from Kentucky to LA and meet your deadline? That's over eighteen hundred miles," Bragan argued.

"Now come on, Bragan, don't play games with me. You're not stupid. You know damn well the Air Force has supersonic fighters. There's a whole slew of them around Godman Air Force Base, right at Fort Knox. If not, some can be sent at once to Godman or to Standiford Airport at Louisville, which is only about thirty miles north of Fort Knox."

"I'm not sure I understand."

"Here's your answer, Bragan. According to my calculations, you'll need ten planes to split the load of twenty-two thousand pounds of gold. They can stow it in the bomb racks. These planes fly close to Mach 2. They can cover the distance in about ninety minutes and make it easily by 1700. It'll be good training for them to see how fast they can scramble when the chips are down. Do you get the picture now?"

"Roger. I'll have to contact the Air Force."

"That's right, Bragan. Tell them I want the supersonics to approach directly from the east. They are to slow down to two hundred knots and fly no higher than two thousand feet above ground level when they report over San Bernardino. Remember, Bragan, only ten planes. Get moving."

"I'll do the best I can," Bragan said. Then, as an afterthought, "How do you intend to pick up this stuff?"

"That's my business," Grant replied icily. "I'll let you know when the time comes."

"I'll get back to you as soon as possible."

"You'd better hurry. You don't have much time. It is now 1354 local and I'm glad to see all blips have disappeared from my screen. Begin countdown for the gold delivery. It is now . . . T minus three hours and five minutes and counting."

"Roger—understood—T minus three hours and five minutes and counting—LA Tower."

CHAPTER 16

Barney Alcott was sitting at his desk in the pressroom of LA International Airport reading *Time* magazine. The telex behind him was silent. He had nothing to report and no one had anything to say to him.

The only event of the day would be the arrival of a minor Japanese trade delegation on a Pan Am flight due in at 2:00 P.M. He could hardly bear the excitement.

Not quite sixty-five and resigned to the reality of forced retirement in four months, he was a frustrated man. The Los Angeles *Times* had eased him out of his job as chief of the city desk five years before. As a consolation prize, they had given him the title of "Aviation Editor," and put the old fire horse out to pasture at the airport where he covered arrivals or departures of VIPs and other assorted nonsense.

The city desk had been handed over to one of his former reporters, Terry Fransdale, a man in his thirties whom he disliked intensely. Terry was a graduate of the U.S.C. School of Journalism and Barney distrusted him. A newspaperman, in Barney's opinion, was born and not made by any school. Barney admitted bias in this respect. He had served his apprenticeship as a copy boy for the San Francisco *Chronicle*. His main responsibility at the time had been to run errands for editors and reporters too lazy to walk down one flight of stairs and across the street to buy sandwiches and coffee. But, by keeping alert, he had picked up a lot of pointers around the various desks. One of the first things he had learned was that any reporter worth his salt always sweated over a story which appeared, to the reader, to have been written effortlessly.

Long ago, an older reporter in a moment of drunken depression had said, "Every story is a difficult childbirth—a cesarean operation." The phrase had stuck in his mind.

Thirty years later, when Barney became chief city editor for the

L.A. *Times*, he still froze for a second every time he inserted a blank sheet of paper into his typewriter.

Barney knew he was no Pulitzer Prize winner, but this stuff at the airport was for morons. To sweeten the pill, the *Times* management had told him he could free-lance for anyone who cared to use his services. They had thereby confirmed that the importance of his stories was minimal—fillers to plug the holes in the back pages.

Now they had given him the *coup de grâce*. He had just been assigned a twenty-two-year-old beginner to gradually take over his functions. To add insult to injury, Harvey Dubbs was a graduate of a school of journalism.

Barney had tried to be friendly by offering to introduce Dubbs to his contacts at the airport, but the cocky young reporter had curtly replied that he would make his own friends.

The old man thought he would have a stroke but had eventually calmed down. He would show this pip-squeak that his experience would prevail if and when a story broke.

Barney looked at the time. It was getting close to 2:00 P.M. He tuned the pressroom's VHF set to the tower frequency. He'd get ready to meet his Japanese delegation after he'd heard the controllers giving the Pan Am flight clearance to land.

He picked up something about a gold shipment and looked at the VHF dial to see if the needle was on the right spot. It was.

What the heck were they talking about? He recognized Bragan's voice. That was unusual! Bragan rarely handled the mike these days, except for practice. Barney's instinct told him something was up.

Where the hell was that Dubbs kid? He would have sent him to the tower to find out what was going on. The arrogant little bastard was always late.

He picked up the phone and dialed the tower.

The helpless jumbo jet and its shadow, circling at thirty-six thousand feet, were now silent, waiting to hear from Bragan.

The chief controller remained seated at his console for a minute, rubbing his eyes, forehead, and the back of his neck in an effort to relax. Finally, he stood up and motioned one of the controllers to sit by the mike.

"Stand by. Call me if they say anything."

143

As he started for his office, Bragan caught simultaneous exchanges on a number of different frequencies between airliners and the controllers.

Unaware of the situation, some of the captains were trying to give the tower an argument about being diverted. A few were demanding explanations.

For the first time, Bragan showed his temper. He stopped in front of an unmanned console, rapidly flicked a succession of selector switches on the control panel to the "ON" position, and picked up a mike.

"All aircraft on these frequencies stop transmitting at once," he ordered in a tone which left no doubt as to who was in charge. "This is the chief controller. You are to do exactly as you're told without further protest. For your information, a 747 in your area and operating on a different channel is being followed by an unidentified fighter plane threatening to shoot it down. Comply at once with our instructions unless you want to endanger that airliner and also run the risk of getting that fighter on your own tails. No need to acknowledge this message. Just get on the ground, wherever you're told to land. If you're not in the air, taxi back in sequence to your departure point as soon as possible."

Bragan looked out of the tower's glass walls.

All airliners which had been lining up on the taxiways or standing by at runway thresholds were slowly turning around and starting back toward their terminals.

Bragan made his way to his glass-enclosed office in the center of the room followed by Ayno, PGA's Regional Operations Manager, the FAA director, and the local FBI chief. He sat at his desk and lit a cigarette.

"Ayno, better see to it that announcements are made and repeated in all terminals as well as on every aircraft on the ramp. Departing passengers and those already aboard airplanes must be notified that there is no sense in stampeding the counters of other airlines. They have to be told not to attempt to transfer to other carriers, as all flights have been canceled. Ask the police to erect barricades at all airport entry points. They must turn back every car bringing in passengers. They're not going anywhere."

"OK. I'll take care of that right away. I've spoken to the Pentagon. They'll give us full co-operation. The Air Force is on alert,

144

but no fighters will take off without your approval. The Secretary of Defense wants to talk to you. I'll get him on the line."

"Good, I'll tell him about the ten supersonics. Also, track down the Secretary of the Treasury. Speak to him about the gold at Fort Knox. He's the only one that can give the proper authorization. Stress that we don't have a second to lose."

The scene in the crowded cabin of an American Airlines trijet DC-10 preparing to leave for Phoenix was typical of what was going on aboard every airliner on the ground at LA International and elsewhere within 400 miles.

Passengers were fidgeting in their seats, wondering what was taking so long to get airborne and asking the cabin attendants all sorts of questions they couldn't answer. The announcement from the cockpit stating that the aircraft was returning to the departure gate provoked outbursts of loud protestations.

Most of the passengers started to fumble for their tickets with the intention of having them endorsed to another airline. They stopped fussing when the pilot told them that this was not the only cancellation, departures having been suspended for all companies until further notice.

Mike Ayno entered Bragan's office and pointed at the telephone.

"Barney Alcott's on the line, Tom."

"Oh no! Stall him. Tell him I'm tied up."

"He was listening on the VHF. He seems to know what's going on."

"I'd better talk to him, then." Bragan picked up the phone. "Hi, Barney."

"I know you're very busy, Tom, but I thought it would be best to handle this thing the right way rather than go off half cocked."

"Barney, I'd appreciate it if the word didn't get around just now. Can you hold it for a while?"

"I'm afraid not. Anyone with a VHF can listen in. I heard it and a thousand other guys can also hear it. What I'm trying to say is that we should approach the problem in a professional manner."

"I just don't want the press all over the airport. First thing you know, it'll be on the radio. That's as good as telling the hijacker what we're thinking and doing because he'll be listening too."

"It's inevitable, Tom. This is America, with the fastest news media in the world. You're not going to hide anything for too long. And you don't want some amateur reporter jumping to conclusions and overdramatizing this thing. It'll do more harm than good."

"Barney, we've known each other a long time. I've always cooperated with you on emergencies and other hijackings. Please hold off for a while. Give us a chance to get organized. We'll get back to you."

"Tom, I've always given the straight facts and made you guys look good too. But this is a FIRST and I want to be in on it. You might as well face it. The news will get out anyway. If it's not me, it'll be someone else."

"What do you suggest?"

"I'll make you a deal, Tom."

"Go ahead."

"You tell me what's going on and I'll tell my paper and the news wires. This way it'll be the official version. No speculation. I won't mention names for the moment. I'll quote you as an authoritative source."

"What about your colleagues who'll start bugging us?"

"Very simple, Tom. You just have someone tell them that the tower is too busy to talk and refer them to me. I'll be your unofficial spokesman, if you like. This way, all you have to do is talk to one person—me. I'll be your press office and public relations combined. Believe me, Tom, it'll save a lot of time and aggravation for everyone concerned."

"I don't know, Barney."

"Everything I report will be factual. I guarantee it. You tell Ayno to keep me informed and I'll centralize and relay. I'll be the press pool. Otherwise, Tom, I'll be on my own and so will you."

Bragan looked at Ayno. From the drift of the conversation, he had understood what Barney wanted. He nodded at the chief controller.

"OK, Barney. We'll keep Ayno's line open for you. But, please, play it down for the moment."

"I'll do the best I can. But keep in mind that once I put it on the wire it goes through many editors before it's announced or printed. I'll tell them to be very careful. Thanks, Tom."

146

"So long, Barney."

Ayno perched on the corner of the desk and offered a cigarette. Bragan took one.

"I think you did well," Ayno said, giving Bragan a light. "Barney's an old pro. At least we know who we're dealing with."

"He didn't give us much choice."

A controller knocked on the glass door.

"A captain from United who landed just after the emergency wants to talk to you."

"Tell him I don't have time to listen to any complaints."

"He says it's urgent."

Bragan exhaled a cloud of smoke, crushed his cigarette, and picked up the phone.

"Who? . . . Say again your name, please. . . ." He reached for a note pad. "Where was that? . . . You're sure? . . . Where can we reach you? . . . OK, I've got it down. Please keep it quiet for the moment. Thank you, Captain. You've been a big help."

Bragan's mood had changed slightly for the better.

"That captain saw the fighter as it was climbing behind PGA 81. All identification markings on the airplane have been erased. He's sure, however, that it's a TX-75E fighter-bomber. He says he's a colonel in the reserve and has seen them at close range at Edwards Air Force Base."

"That's a lead, anyway."

"Mike, call the Pentagon. They should be able to trace which TX-75E is missing from its base and determine the identity of the pilot who stole it."

Terry Fransdale made a face when the switchboard operator told him Barney Alcott was on the line.

The pace was frantic in the newsroom of the L.A. *Times*. His city desk had other things to worry about besides the announcement of insignificant arrivals by the old has-been.

"Tell him to dictate his stuff to one of the girls or to put it on the telex. I don't want to talk to him."

"He said that would probably be your attitude but that you'd be sorry if you didn't listen to what he had to report," the switchboard operator insisted. "He's on 6712."

"OK, OK." Fransdale pushed the flickering extension button. "Yes, Barney. . . . So it's another hijacking. There's a dozen every day. So what? You mean to tell me you're disturbing me for that crap. That's no longer news. It can wait. Put it on the teletype . . ."

"Terry," Barney shouted, "you don't seem to grasp the situation. Stop being paranoid. I'll give you one last chance, otherwise I'll feed the story to the wire services first. Now do you want to listen or don't you?"

From the tone of Barney's ultimatum, Fransdale realized that this was not a run-of-the-mill situation.

"OK, go ahead. . . . I see," Fransdale exclaimed nervously. "Why didn't you say so in the first place?" He took notes feverishly. "Go on. . . . I've got that. . . . Go on. . . . OK, that's enough for now. Call me back. . . . Where's Dubbs? . . . Late again, huh? . . . You tell him I'll take care of him later. Remember, Barney, we get first crack at whatever you've got. Then you can call the wire services. I'll be waiting to hear from you."

Fransdale screamed for a copy boy. Several scrambled to his desk.

"One of you run to the composing room and tell them to hold the late final. I have a last-minute bulletin. I'm typing it now. There should be a by-line: By Barney Alcott, Aviation Editor."

Harvey Dubbs walked nonchalantly into the pressroom wearing his usual insolent look.

"Hiya, Alcott, old boy. Did the Japanese guys get in all right?"

"Don't you ever call me old boy," Barney roared. "Get your ass to that telex and type what I'm going to dictate to you. Shmuck!"

At Naval Headquarters in San Diego, the communications complex was swamped with radio messages. All surface ships were being advised to steer clear of the area specified by the hijacker. Some of the units were beginning to acknowledge receipt of the instructions and to confirm immediate compliance.

The Coast Guard nerve center at Long Beach was also the hub of intense activity. All merchant vessels and pleasure craft were being told to remain in port or, if at sea, to stay outside the boundaries indicated by the fighter pilot. All marinas from Seattle to Baja California were being contacted and instructed to let no boats leave their moorings until further notice.

All private airports within 400 miles of LA International were being contacted by the FAA. The message was to ground all general aviation traffic, including executive aircraft, air taxis, and private planes.

At Skylark Airport, on Lake Elsinore, 70 miles southeast of Los Angeles, a group of fifteen suited-up skydivers were stopped just as they were about to climb aboard five single-engine Cessnas for a collective jump. They were told all flying activities were canceled for the day on orders from the military authorities. No reasons or explanations were offered. It was a big disappointment for the discomfited free-fall enthusiasts, especially with such perfect weather. Howls of protest erupted against the Armed Forces and the establishment, who thought they could push everybody around.

At the Pentagon, General Raymond Prominowe, of Military Intelligence, was put in charge of the investigation.

A handsome, quiet, and unemotional man in his fifties, Prominowe was delegated the task of co-ordinating all activities relating to the hijacking and to the safe return of the PGA 747.

He had received orders from the Joint Chiefs of Staff telling him to work closely with Tom Bragan at LA Tower but to interfere as little as possible with his actions. It was, after all, a civilian airliner and the military should remain inconspicuous for the time being.

Prominowe summed his right-hand man, Captain Fred Scarlata, a deceptively innocent-looking computer whiz-kid. He arrived within seconds.

"Scarlata, I just received a call informing me that a hijacker is at the controls of a TX-75E. Tell your boys to run this type aircraft through the computers for every U.S. airbase in the world—Germany, Korea, Japan, Vietnam, Guam, and, here at home."

"No problem, sir."

"But that's not all, Scarlata. Just in case it's not a TX-75E, I want you to give me figures on every type of fighter of every nationality no matter how old or new—surplus stuff, that sort of thing—there must be a missing fighter someplace."

"That'll take some time, sir, but I'll do the best I can."

"One more thing, Scarlata. Call LA Tower. Get a copy of the

taped conversation of the fighter pilot, the airliner, and the ground. See if we can learn his identity through voice prints."

"I'll be back as soon as I can, General."

In a network TV studio newsroom in Los Angeles, Josh Prentice, the newscaster, was idly reading the insipid copy unraveling on the teleprinters.

It was a little past 2:00 P.M. and he had plenty of time to get ready for his three-minute roundup spot at 2:55 P.M. during the half-time break of a football game aired live from the East Coast.

"Gorgeous Josh," as the camera crew dubbed him, noticed one of the news wire machines had stopped. Bells started clanging.

He took a closer look at the printer. Words began to appear at high speed.

BULLETIN

HIJACKING—LOS ANGELES

A PACIFIC GLOBAL AIRWAYS JUMBO JET WAS HIJACKED AT ABOUT ONE THIRTY PM (PST) TODAY. IT HAD JUST TAKEN OFF FROM LOS ANGELES INTERNATIONAL AIRPORT FOR HONOLULU (HAWAII).

(MORE)

URGENT

HIJACKING—FIRST LEAD—BY BARNEY ALCOTT—LOS ANGELES

THE HIJACKER IS AT THE CONTROLS OF AN ARMED JET FIGHTER. HE IS TAILING PGA FLIGHT 81, A BOEING 747, CARRYING 187 PASSENGERS AND 14 CREW MEMBERS. HE HAS THREATENED TO SHOOT DOWN THE AIRLINER UNLESS HE IS PAID TWENTY (REPEAT TWENTY) MILLION DOLLARS RANSOM IN GOLD WITHIN THE NEXT THREE HOURS.

(MORE)

Prentice ripped off the copy from the teleprinter, buzzed his producer for permission to interrupt the football game, then raced to his prop desk before the TV cameras.

"Set up," he shouted, interrupting the cameramen's coffee break. "I have a bulletin. Prepare the title slide."

"Gorgeous Josh" took a few seconds to adjust his tie. He then looked lovingly at his image in a mirror which he quickly took out from the desk drawer. He slicked down his eyebrows, patted his hair, polished four front teeth with his index finger, and flashed his famous smile. Only then did he give the OK to his floor manager.

Prentice focused on a studio monitor.

The football game was interrupted. A bulletin slide appeared on the screen.

The newscaster's face filled the monitor. He was now wearing an appropriately somber expression.

"We interrupt our regularly scheduled program to bring you the following bulletin. An unprecedented hijacking is now taking place . . ."

In a downtown Los Angeles bar, a redneck type, drinking beer, became enraged. "They have a helluva nerve blacking out the football game for this bullshit. I've got a big bet on that game."

He kept on ranting and raving.

"They can afford to go on vacations to Hawaii?—Screw them. Who cares, anyway? Besides, I can't stand that goddamn announcer."

No one in the bar listened to him. So this time, his barrage was directed to the TV set itself.

"Put the game back on, you stupid bastards, you!"

CHAPTER 17

The PGA ticket counter at LA International was mobbed by relatives and friends of the passengers on Flight 81. They had heard the news on their car radios as they were returning home, and had immediately doubled back to the airport. All were clamoring to be told what was going on.

Harried airline employees were on telephones, begging family members and acquaintances not to come to the airport. They kept repeating there was nothing they could possibly do to help and that their presence would only add to the confusion.

TV crews had arrived and were setting up their cameras and sound equipment to shoot the scene. They were soon joined by newsmen from several radio stations carrying tape recorders, and newspaper reporters.

The cameras began to roll. Correspondents darted to stick their mikes into the faces of relatives of the passengers for human interest comments:

"What thoughts are running through your mind right now, knowing your daughter is on board, with your baby grandson, at the mercy of a killer—completely helpless?" asked a TV reporter, making sure he was facing the camera with a look of proper concern.

"What do you want me to tell you, you jerk—that I'm happy about it?" screamed a semihysterical man in his fifties. "Of all the inconsiderate, imbecilic . . ."

Another relative, a small man in a seersucker suit and a straw hat, pushed his way up to the mike and butted in.

"All I can tell you bad news buzzards is that the government better do something about this. They can't let these people get shot down in cold blood. We demand to be protected. Why don't you announce that, you creep?"

Everyone began to gather around the reporter with menacing looks. Fearing he was about to be lynched, he beat a hasty retreat.

A monster traffic jam was building up in front of the terminal. Worried parents, wives, and children simply abandoned their cars in the middle of the road to run to the ticket counter.

Exasperated cops were blowing whistles and excitedly gesturing at drivers to keep moving, but to no avail. Tow trucks were summoned.

At Vandenberg Air Force Base, 135 miles northwest of Los Angeles International, twelve jet fighter pilots, wearing helmets and oxygen masks, were sitting in their planes, at the edge of the active runway, ready to take off.

General Paul Fregouze, a nervous man whose glasses perpetually seemed about to fall off his nose, was pacing up and down in the tower. He stopped once in a while, pushed his glasses back into place with the middle finger of his right hand, and looked out at the fighters lined up in position.

A thin, gray-complexioned individual close to retirement, the General had received a disturbing phone call from the Pentagon. To his dismay, he was now in charge of co-ordinating all West Coast military activities in connection with the thwarting of the hijacking.

Since Vandenberg was also a satellite launching station, tracking from outer space of the 747 and the fighter following it had also been requested. A telescope platform for astronomical observations was presently orbiting over the area approximately every ninety minutes. High-resolution pictures were to be taken.

This was a situation Fregouze had never had to face before and it made him more agitated than usual. Satellites couldn't work at close tolerances when it came to zeroing in on such small targets as two airplanes following each other. They should have known better at the Pentagon.

The satellite would now have to be rotated as well as tilted to point at the ocean. Fregouze could only hope the remote control signals would activate the occasionally temperamental repositioning mechanisms. In any event, pictures could only be taken during the next two passes—if everything went well. It would get cloudy and dark by the third pass.

General Fregouze had already decided on one thing, however. His boys would go after the hijacker at the proper time and threaten to destroy him if he refused to land quietly at Vandenberg. He would then interrogate the pilot personally.

Until such time as he could let his fighters loose, he would have to check with Tom Bragan. Fregouze could not understand why a civilian had been granted such sweeping authority, but General Raymond Prominowe at the Pentagon had been adamant about it. Nothing could be done without Bragan's consent. Meanwhile, his fighters were burning fuel, going no place.

A colonel approached General Fregouze. He suggested, in whispers, that supersonic fighters flying at sea level could perhaps evade the hijacker's detection. It would take them fifteen minutes or so to reach the point where the 747 and the fighter were holding. At that moment, they could zoom straight up to thirty-six thousand feet and let the hijacker have it before he could react.

Fregouze turned purple. He adjusted his glasses one more time and, wide-eyed, looked at all the officers present in the control tower.

In a high-pitched voice he screamed:

"Let's get this perfectly clear, all of you. No one is going to stick his neck out. Nobody goes from anywhere until we get the green light from the Pentagon to shoot the sonofabitch down. I don't want to hear about any more harebrained schemes. That's final!"

In the cockpit of the 747, things by now had more or less settled down to a routine holding pattern.

Hadley, Bessoe, Faust, and Senator Wadsworth were craning their necks, trying to get a look at the fighter through the side windows, but their angle of vision was extremely poor.

"He's probably directly behind us and very close to our tail," Hadley said. "He knows it's impossible to catch a glimpse of him that way. Not that it matters at this point, but I'm curious to know just what kind of aircraft it is."

"I'll keep looking," Bessoe volunteered. "Maybe he'll get careless and drift a little in a turn. All we need is a little wider angle."

"I doubt he'll give it to you," Hadley sighed. He turned to Faust. "Herb, call Laura. Ask her how things are going in the cabin."

Laura had quietly called the eight other girls into the galley, four at a time. While she briefed one group on the situation, the others continued to circulate among the passengers. Lastly, she had summoned the two extra stewardesses deadheading to Honolulu, and had asked them to lend a hand.

Her charming good looks and good-natured disposition notwithstanding, Laura kept a tight rein on the junior cabin attendants under her supervision. Some of the girls stiffened with fear when they heard the news. Laura gave them a moment to recover. She then gently reminded them they should be the last to show any signs of apprehension.

"There's no sense in getting excited," she said with authority. "We have to set an example for the passengers. Captain Hadley is deciding what course to follow and I don't want any rumors running wild in the cabin. All we need is one high-strung individual to lose control and communicate panic to all the others. You let me know if anyone gives you any trouble. I'll handle it. Keep the passengers busy. Give them all they want to drink. Don't collect any money. We'll take care of the inventory and the paper work later."

Laura took aside Bea Adgie, a stunning onetime Miss America contestant next in the line of seniority on this flight.

"I have to report to the cockpit periodically for further instructions from the Captain. Will you keep a close watch on things when I'm not around?"

"You can count on me, Laura. We'll keep things smooth. Don't worry."

Bea walked down the tourist-class cabin with all the aplomb of a beauty queen, flashing warm smiles left and right, as if she were parading in Atlantic City.

There was very little talk and no laughter. The passengers all sensed an undercurrent of tension. Some of them were already complaining about the constant circling, and asking for airsickness bags. A few smiled weakly at Bea, raising their eyebrows as if to ask her to tell them the truth.

As she slowly made her way to the back, Bea was stopped by two gregarious hardware salesmen in loud clothes bound for a convention in Honolulu. They were sitting in a row by themselves.

"Hi! I'm Bruce," said the heavier-set man as he grabbed her hand. "This is Dick," he said, winking, pointing at his skinny weasel-faced companion. "Don't we know you from someplace?"

"That's possible," Bea said politely, controlling an urge to grimace at the stereotyped approach. "I'm on this run all the time."

"No, no. That's not what I mean," Bruce came back, squeezing her hand a little harder. "Didn't we meet you at a party in L.A. a couple of months ago? You know, that wild thing at our boss's place where everybody took their clothes off and jumped into the pool? Boy, were they all bombed out of their minds that night!"

"I'm afraid you have me confused with someone else," Bea said, wincing, trying to pull her hand away.

"But Dick here said . . ."

"If your friend Dick was intoxicated too, he couldn't possibly remember things too well, could he? Now be a good boy, Bruce, and let me go say hello to the rest of my passengers."

"You'll be back, won't you?"

"In a little while."

"OK. We'll be waiting. My buddy Dick, here, he's a little shy but he told me he's nuts about you. Don't disappoint him," Bruce said with a belly laugh. "By the way, I'd love to fly you myself. What's your name?"

"I'm Bea and you'll get all the excitement you want on this flight. I guarantee it," she said, smiling, unable to resist throwing this parting line as she freed her hand.

Bruce turned toward Dick, who was wearing a sheepish grin at his friend's audacity.

"What are you smiling about?" Bruce asked, annoyed. "Who the hell does that broad think she is, anyway, giving us the Queen of Sheba bit? I don't make passes at everyone, you know. I'm pretty particular, as a matter of fact. She doesn't seem to appreciate that."

"Relax, Bruce. She knows you're on the make. She sees a million guys every day. She's pretty refined, you know. Try another angle."

"Oh, you mean I'm not refined, huh? What's wrong with asking a dame if I met her at a party? You know me. I get right to the point."

"You don't tell people you met them at an orgy, especially a low-life one. She wouldn't have anything to do with guys like us. She's got class."

"You think so, huh? Well you just watch old Bruce operate the next time around. Maybe you'll learn something."

One of the other stewardesses came by with a tray of mixed drinks.

"Gentlemen," she said, smiling, "we have bloody marys, vodka martinis, manhattans, whiskey sours . . ."

"Vodka martini for me," Bruce said. "What about you, Dick?"

"I'll have the same."

She handed them the drinks and napkins.

"What do we owe you?" Bruce asked, putting his hand in his pocket.

"Nothing, sir. Compliments of PGA. Our way of apologizing for this unexpected weather delay. It's the Captain's treat."

"Oh, in that case," Bruce said, "give us a couple more. Save you the hassle of running back and forth."

"Certainly. Here you are."

Bruce turned to Dick as soon as the girl had moved on. He jabbed him in the ribs with his elbow.

"You ask for refills when we finish these. Might as well gas up on the house. For once, these cheap bastards are giving something away. At the fares they're charging these days, they can afford it."

Laura tiptoed into the cockpit, then silently made her way to the front past Wadsworth and Faust. She gently tapped Hadley on the shoulder.

"Captain, everything's quiet in the cabin. We're serving drinks but some of the passengers are getting restless. We've been in the air for forty-five minutes and they can't understand why we're still circling."

Hadley looked pensively at Laura, the Senator, the flight engineer, and the co-pilot as he removed his head set.

"Yeah! It's been a long time. Have all the girls been briefed?"

Laura nodded. "Bea's looking after things right now."

"Might as well give the passengers the bad news, then," Hadley sighed.

He picked up the cabin mike and cleared his throat.

"Good afternoon ladies and gentlemen. This is Captain Burton Hadley. Welcome aboard," he said cheerfully. "We're presently about 160 miles southwest of Los Angeles, at an altitude of thirty-six thousand feet, and, as you've noticed, we're circling." He paused.

There was absolute silence in the cabin. The stewardesses stood still wherever they were. Everyone strained to hear. Bea Adgie, standing by the control panel, turned up the volume.

"I'm afraid I have some disquieting news, ladies and gentlemen. We're being diverted from our normal routing by a military aircraft that is escorting us at the moment. We have been instructed to hold right here until further notice. He's asking for a ransom to let us proceed on our way." He paused again.

The passengers had their ears cocked to the loudspeakers. Most of them had a dumfounded look of astonishment. The reaction was one of stupor.

Bruce, the salesman, gulped down his first vodka martini and started working on his second. His friend Dick stared stonily ahead.

"Since our hijacker is not on board and we have no way of negotiating with him face to face, we're talking to him on the radio . . ."

Just at that second, one of the three babies on board let out a piercing wail of hunger, chilling everyone's blood.

"Shut that baby up, goddamn it," shouted a man sitting in the front.

The infant kept howling with annoying, shrill insistence. The passengers close to the baby's mother stared at her as if it were all her fault.

The woman, who looked frightened to death, patted the child mechanically, trying to quiet him, so that the rest of the passengers could hear what Hadley was saying. The Captain's words were lost.

"Give him a bottle or something," a woman screamed from the back.

One of the stewardesses ran to help. She picked up the baby and rocked him in her arms. The mother frantically looked through her tote bag for a pacifier. She found one and put it into the child's mouth.

In the meantime, Bea had called the cockpit, asking Hadley to repeat the last part of his announcement.

"As I was saying, ladies and gentlemen," Hadley resumed in his most reassuring tone, "we are communicating with our hijacker on VHF radio. His demands are being met. The authorities are doing their best to satisfy him in the shortest possible time. This much I know, and there's nothing to worry about on that score."

Some of the passengers began to unwind, but their relief was short lived.

"But I might as well be frank, instead of giving it to you in small doses. We're all in the same boat, so to speak," Hadley went on. "We have a little problem. The man, who is behind us in a fighter, has asked to be paid twenty million dollars in gold. Since this amount is not available locally, it is presently being flown to Los Angeles from Fort Knox, Kentucky. So . . . folks . . . you might as well relax. It's going to take a little time until we get back on the ground."

All the passengers instinctively leaned in their seats, in an attempt to look through the portholes at the airplane shadowing the 747. They met with no more success than the crew.

"I know some of you will eventually find this holding pattern uncomfortable but, unfortunately, there's nothing we can do. Our cabin attendants will remain at your disposal for antimotion sickness pills and the like. Please don't hesitate to ask for anything you need. We're at your service. Barring any unforeseen developments, we should be returning to Los Angeles within three or four hours. I'll keep you advised regularly on our progress. Thank you."

Laura heard loud, angry voices as she was walking down the spiral staircase on her way back from the cockpit. A heated argument was taking place in the first-class section occupied by the four executives. The chief stewardess stood discreetly next to the entrance to see what was going on, wondering if she should interfere.

Horace J. Transcombe, vice president of "Mutual Fidelity Financing and Investing," had blown his cool. He was taking things out on Brent Gilmore, the younger-looking analyst who had been shuffling papers on takeoff. The other two men were prudently keeping out of it.

The long, cadaverous Transcombe was standing in the middle of the aisle shaking a bony finger at a cowering Gilmore.

"What the hell did that pilot mean by 'barring any unforeseen developments' and by 'we SHOULD be back in L.A. in three or four hours'? There's obviously a doubt in his mind—something he's hiding from us. That fighter isn't just following us for no reason. He intends to shoot us down if anyone makes a false move."

"Please calm yourself, H.J. Everyone can hear you. I'm sure it's not as bad as all that. Think of your blood pressure."

"Blood pressure my foot. I told you we should have taken the evening flight but you insisted on booking this one, you idiot. Now look what you've done."

"But Mr. Transcombe, how could I possibly have known we were going to get ourselves hijacked? As a matter of fact, you even told me you were delighted to leave earlier so you could get in a little putting practice on the hotel golf course before dinner."

"I don't remember anything about any golf. I must have said that absent-mindedly to make you happy, so you wouldn't feel incompetent."

Gilmore was very upset. He began to stammer.

"Oh no, Mr. Transcombe. The four-o'clock plane was full. We had a choice of this flight and the one that left at 11:00 P.M. You picked this one."

"I didn't pick anything," Transcombe screeched. "Everything you touch turns to crap. Do you know how much money you've already cost the company?"

"Let's not talk about that. I warned you against speculating on soybean and pork belly futures. The market wasn't right for it. You wouldn't listen. You're the one who made the company lose its shirt. That was a typical asinine remark, H.J."

"You're fired. I always knew you were a jinx—you and your

imbecilic statistics. You couldn't wait to bug me with them, even before we took off. You just wait till we get back on the ground."

Gilmore looked imploringly at the other two men for help. They avoided his gaze. He suddenly noticed Laura, and felt a deep sense of humiliation at being scolded in public like a child.

He picked up his briefcase from under his seat and stared with loathing at Transcombe and the other two men.

"Doesn't look to me like we're ever going to get back on the ground, H.J." He let out a forced little laugh. "You're a man of perspicacity, aren't you? You don't really believe all this nonsense about the authorities handling the situation, do you?—especially if they're headed by bombastic morons like yourself."

Transcombe seemed on the verge of apoplexy. Gilmore, the worm, had turned. He couldn't think of a thing to say.

Gilmore sensed he had the advantage. Suddenly, Transcombe looked much older than sixty-two and quite pitiful.

"Transcombe," Gilmore said, almost compassionately, "you can't take the stress. I would suggest you start drinking earlier than usual and settle promptly into your normal six-o'clock coma. I'm going to the other section. I can't stand the sight of you. In fact, you all make me sick."

Transcombe stood there, transfixed for a moment, watching Gilmore being escorted to the rear by Laura. He gradually regained his composure and turned toward the other two men, who were sitting together now, seemingly in deep conversation. He glared at them.

"Well? Don't pretend you didn't hear what went on. Where's the Senator?"

The two men looked up at Transcombe and shook their heads.

"Last time I saw him, he was going upstairs," one of them said.

"He should be here with the rest of us. He's probably getting preferential treatment. Why should he? One of you go find him. I want to talk to him. There must be something we can do to get out of this mess."

One of the men rose and walked toward the staircase.

"And send one of the girls up here," Transcombe shouted after him. "Tell her I want an old-fashioned."

Captain Hadley's voice came over the loudspeakers.

"Since we have to wait a while until our hijacker releases us, I suggest you make yourselves as comfortable as possible. You may walk around the cabin if you wish but please be prepared to return to your seats and to fasten your belts if necessary. Our cabin attendants will soon be serving lunch, which was scheduled for about this time. We'll put on a movie for you after that. Naturally, the normal surcharge for viewing will not be collected on this occasion. The earphones which will be supplied to you can also be used to listen to a variety of recorded programs. The selection switches will be found on the armrests. Thank you."

Bruce, the swinging salesman, stood up and removed his plaid jacket, which he dropped on a seat.

"The last meal of the condemned before the execution, hey? Free entertainment too. How 'bout that? Captain Hadley, you're a real sport. A big spender after my own heart!" He tried to laugh but no one was amused. He looked at Dick then gestured at the stewardesses. "To hell with the lunch and the movies. Keep bringing the booze, girls. I don't wanna know 'whaaat's' happening."

Two rows behind, an extravagant-looking character with shoulder length hair, mustache, and dark glasses stood up. He was wearing faded dungarees, a T-shirt with a wedge of apple pie printed in color on the front, and a brown wide-brimmed hat.

"Hey, man!"

Bruce turned around.

"Yeah, you man. Right on! You got the right transcendental attitude, man. I love you. I'm with you, man. Peace, brother!"

Bruce did a double take.

The man was expertly rolling a joint. He licked the paper with relish, and silently offered to make one for Bruce, who refused by shaking his head.

Wearing a broad smile, he lit up, then took a deep drag. He blew the smoke right into the face of a squat, hard-hat type with a constipated look, who was sitting across the aisle.

"Man, if this is my last trip, am I gonna fly. Yeah! Wanna join me in orbit, brother?"

"Punk," mumbled the man, obviously disgusted. "Nothing but punks running around loose these days. Why don't you go take a bath or something and smell human?" He got up, brushed past Bruce, and found another seat.

"Don't argue with me, Major. I'm not asking you. I'm telling you," General Raymond Prominowe growled into the telephone. "Just get those ten supersonics ready at Godman Air Force Base at Fort Knox or else at Standiford Airport at Louisville within the next thirty minutes, all fueled up and in takeoff position. That's all. I know this is not regular procedure. . . . Well. . . . Where's the base commander right now? . . . I don't care if he's on a training mission. Contact him in the air. Tell him to come back down. In the meantime you make sure those fighters are ready to go, understand? . . . Tell the Colonel I said so and that he can check with me right here. Now get going, for Christsakes!"

It was beginning to get dark in Washington and the Secretary of the Treasury was in deep concentration.

He was about to stroke an easy two-foot putt on the eighteenth hole of the Burning Tree Golf Course. That birdie would win the match and one hundred dollars. His opponent was tight lipped, sweating the shot. Just as the putter was touching the ball, he heard the panting voice of a caddy who had run all the way from the clubhouse telling him he was urgently wanted on the telephone.

The Secretary missed. The opponent grinned. A tie was no bet. The Secretary did a slow burn. Then he threw down the putter in utter frustration. He gritted his teeth at the caddy.

"What is it now?"

"Sorry, Mr. Secretary," the caddy apologized. "It's long distance from Los Angeles. They said to tell you it was a matter of life or death."

"Since when has inflation become something that can't wait until a man finishes his putt?" the Secretary grunted as he jumped into his golf cart.

In the clubhouse, his eyes grew wider and wider as he listened and frequently interrupted the caller.

"Twenty million? . . . You know damn well I can't authorize a thing like that! . . . Fort Knox? . . . What's wrong with you? . . . You must be kidding. . . . Who did you say was on board? . . . Senator Wadsworth! . . . I'll have to clear it with the White House. . . . No, I cannot make this decision alone. . . . Why? Because this thing's way over my head, that's why. . . . Yes, I've got it. Bragan or Ayno at Los Angeles Tower. I'll get back to you as soon as I can. Of course I realize it's urgent."

Captain Fred Scarlata was shown into General Prominowe's office. He stood at attention, a thick folder bulging with computer printouts under his arm.

"We can dispense with formality right now, Captain. Put the file on my desk and sit down. What did you find out?"

"Sir, a first check indicates none of our aircraft are unaccounted for, except for those presently conducting missions over North Vietnam."

"I'm not satisfied, Scarlata. He must have stolen this fighter somewhere."

Scarlata looked through his file.

"General, verification narrowed down to the last thirty days, that is until last night, shows no aircraft or pilots missing, except in action. As far as the TX-75E type is concerned, the computer says we've lost sixty-seven of them in the last three years, since the escalation of hostilities in Southeast Asia. Some of these planes, however, were destroyed during training flights in the United States, Germany, Japan, and South Korea."

"How many pilots are qualified to fly these things?"

"The records show 5,236 men received instruction on this type aircraft. Some have been killed, of course. A few are presumed to be POWs. Others have since left the Air Force. Many have moved on to other duties. It is my understanding, however, General, that any qualified pilot who has operated similar swing-wing supersonics could have possibly stolen the aircraft. He could have taken the risk of flying it without prior check-out by an expert."

"That widens the field considerably, doesn't it?"

"I'm afraid so, sir. But we're rechecking everything. I should be back with more data within thirty minutes."

"OK. What about the voice prints?"

"Nothing on that as yet, sir. It's a big job, even for our computers. We should know more when I return with the next set of figures."

"Thank you, Scarlata. You're doing a fine job."

It was just past 5:00 P.M. in Washington and, at the White House, the lights were burning brightly in the Oval Office.

The President looked very upset. He was at his desk, sitting on the edge of his chair, talking on the telephone with the Secretary of the Treasury. One of his closest advisers was standing next to him, listening to the conversation on an extension line.

"I can't talk to you too long. I'm in the middle of a very important foreign policy meeting right now, but you did well to call me, Andrew. No. We don't have time to check anything about the constitutional legality of giving gold. We'll work out the technicalities later. I'll take the full responsibility, Andrew. I'll back you up all the way. You go ahead and authorize Fort Knox to ship the gold. I'll have my staff handle the rest from here on. Thank you, Andrew."

The President turned to his adviser.

"You heard everything. What would you do if you were in my shoes, Hoffman?"

The assistant was in deep concentration. He was thinking aloud.

"Mr. President, I have quickly tried to analyze the situation and to consider all the options at hand. I think it would be an indication of weakness to give in to such extravagant demands."

The Chief Executive raised his eyebrows.

"The gold is only the hijacker's first request, Mr. President. There will certainly be more, since he must pick up the ransom somehow. On the other hand, if the blackmailer's ultimatums are not met, he might, indeed, shoot down the airliner. I have also considered that possibility. I might add that such a disastrous outcome would be as good a way to get rid of the Senator as any."

The President appeared to be shocked.

Hoffman continued.

"However, Mr. President, this IS an election year and you cannot afford to have the airliner destroyed without having ostensibly tried everything first."

The President nodded.

"In any event, Mr. President, no one must ever know to what extent you were directly or indirectly involved in the decision-making process, no matter what the outcome will be. I also wish to say I find it hard to believe that with all the military might of this country, one single man could paralyze the whole apparatus with this kind of blackmail."

"For once, Hoffman, I'm afraid I disagree with you," the President said somberly.

The adviser looked surprised.

"I believe," the President continued, "that I should demonstrate proper concern in the face of such cold-blooded threats to an unarmed American civilian airliner. I will listen to suggestions from all quarters on how to best handle the problem and then make up

164

my mind. The people have a right to expect me to act in a situation of such magnitude."

Hoffman was not overly impressed with the President's reasoning. He remained impassive.

"Coming back to the Senator, Hoffman, my ruthless political enemies will accuse me of having deliberately killed him if this airliner does not return safely. And, as you well know, we have enough scandals right now. If, however, the airliner lands unharmed, I will have confirmed my qualities of forward-looking leadership which transcended all political considerations EVEN in an election year."

The adviser understood that the President's mind was made up. It would be futile to press any further arguments on him at the moment. He nodded.

"Cancel all my appointments until further notice."

"Including the Soviet Ambassador?"

"Yes."

"He's already here. He won't like it."

"That's too bad."

"I'll tell him myself."

"Good. Come back as soon as you can. I'd like you to find out who's been put in charge of the over-all operation at the Pentagon. Tell him to report to me. Have our technicians install a radio in this office immediately. Tell them to set up a relay to Los Angeles International. I want to listen directly to what's going on between the fighter and the airport."

"I'll get on it at once."

"Also, I wish to speak to the man in charge at Los Angeles Tower. Have someone put him on the line. Thank you, Hoffman."

CHAPTER 18

Grant was watching his radar scope.

There were no targets on the screen except for the airliner dead ahead, and he was satisfied his instructions had been obeyed. He rummaged through the knapsack between his legs and poured a cup of coffee from the thermos. It was still hot. He enjoyed it thoroughly, then drank a can of orange juice and munched on a few dry crackers. He'd have a more substantial meal later.

It was a little after 2:00 P.M. The news of the hijacking must have broken by now. Grant tuned one of the low frequency radios to KFWB in Los Angeles to hear how the authorities were reacting and what measures they intended to take against him.

An announcer on the all news station was giving the first sketchy details. For the moment, no action was being contemplated for fear of jeopardizing the lives of the people aboard Flight 81. He added that, in a short while, on an updated newscast, a famous psychiatrist, specialized in the "convoluted mentality" of hijackers, would be interviewed regarding this despicable new form of blackmail.

Grant smiled.

"And now a word from the friendly makers of 'Happy Puppy' dog food," the announcer went on cheerfully.

Bragan's office had been invaded by several controllers waiting for instructions. The FBI man was there with the PGA representative and the FAA director. An Air Force colonel who had been dispatched to the scene and a uniformed police captain were also present. Bragan asked a controller to bring in some more chairs.

Mike Ayno ran in from his office and pushed his way through the small crowd.

"Tom, the President's on the line."

Bragan blinked.

Everyone in the room stood perfectly still, waiting to hear the chief controller's side of the conversation.

Bragan crushed out a cigarette as he picked up the phone.

"Yes, Mr. President. . . . I'm the man in charge. . . . Bragan sir, Tom Bragan. . . . Right now there's nothing much we can attempt . . . he definitely knows what he's doing, sir. He's fully familiar with our procedures . . . he's always one step ahead of us. . . . Yes, Mr. President, I'll hold . . ."

In the Oval Office, the President put his hand over the mouthpiece and conferred briefly with Hoffman.

The people surrounding Bragan were hanging on his lips. They looked intently at him the moment he resumed the conversation.

"No, sir. We have no idea how he intends to pick up the gold. He has said nothing so far in this regard. He's delivering his instructions a bit at a time without giving us a chance to react and set up a counterplan. . . . No, sir. Nothing about Senator Wadsworth. There doesn't appear to be a connection. . . . In fact, the Senator was supposed to be on another airline. His reservation was changed just a few hours before he left. The hijacker probably had no way of knowing. . . . Yes, I'll hold . . ."

Again, the President consulted his adviser.

"Yes, Mr. President, I'm still here. I agree with you, sir. We should definitely not antagonize him. . . . Yes, sir. I have handled or been involved in other hijackings but the man was always on board—the crew could size up the situation. Here, we're dealing with a ghost. . . . Yes, sir, I'll stay on the line but please hurry. He doesn't want to talk to anyone else but me and he may call back any second . . ."

Bragan motioned for a cigarette while he waited. Someone gave him a filter. He shook his head. Ayno offered an already lit king size, which he accepted.

"I'm here, Mr. President. . . . Well, they can only last about eight hours—at least that's how much fuel there is aboard the PGA . . ."

Bragan took a deep drag. He was visibly shaken by what the President had just said. He clenched his fist but nevertheless maintained a respectful tone.

"It's true most of the others were bluffing, Mr. President, but I don't think this one is. . . . Mr. President, there are 201 people on board. There ARE unfortunate precedents, sir. An EL AL

Israel Airlines flight was shot down by MIGs over Bulgaria in 1956 . . . the Olympic Games massacre at the military airport in Munich . . . A Libyan 727 recently shot down by Israeli jets over the Sinai Desert . . . this man must know that we're aware of this. Yes, sir, I'll hold but I may have to leave if he calls . . ."

Bragan was getting frustrated with this conversation. He was doing all he could to contain himself.

"Yes, this is still Bragan, Mr. President. . . . We don't know if the Palestinian guerrillas are behind this. . . . Those phone calls you're mentioning must be the work of cranks, sir, but I'll have the FBI chief check into them. He's standing next to me, sir. . . . Very good, Mr. President. We'll leave the military end to your staff and the Pentagon, sir. What's that name again, sir? General Prominowe, OK. . . . No, I don't need the spelling, we can check that out. Sir, I must insist that nothing be done by the Armed Forces before clearing it with me. We just cannot work at cross-purposes. . . . Fine, Mr. President. Please make sure they're all notified, especially at Vandenberg. . . . Thank you. . . . Yes, sir, my assistant will keep you informed constantly. . . . Mike Ayno, sir. . . . It's spelled ALFA . . . YANKEE . . . NOVEMBER . . . OSCAR. . . . Yes, I'll hold . . ."

Bragan sighed and shook his head with impatience.

"Hello. Yes, I'm here. . . . No, sir. I don't think he's using an old surplus fighter modified for the purpose. He wouldn't have the necessary endurance to match that of the 747. Besides, the aircraft seems to have been positively identified by a United pilot as a TX-75E. I don't know how long it can stay in the air—that's classified, from what I understand—but you could check it with the Pentagon, sir, and let us know too. That way, we'd have an idea what we're up against. . . . No, sir. I say once again I really don't know why you think he's faking it. . . . All right, sir, I'll try to find out since you're ordering me to do it. . . . Yes, of course, we'll let you know at once. Thank you, Mr. President . . . we're all doing our best."

Bragan was annoyed at the President's insistence to test or, rather, as he had put it, to "carefully feel out" the pilot of "Shadow 81."

He lit another cigarette and thought for a moment while all those around him watched silently. He decided the best course of action would be to try a little diplomatic psychology.

The chief controller stepped out of his office, closely followed by all the others, and sat at an empty console.

He flicked a few switches, pressed the mike button, and called the fighter.

"Shadow 81—LA Tower."

"Hi, Bragan—Shadow 81. What can I do for you?"

In the cockpit of the 747, Hadley and the three other men stopped talking at once.

"Shadow 81," Bragan said firmly, "your instructions have been carried out to the letter so far. All airplanes are now beyond four hundred miles from LA International and the supersonics will be on their way shortly."

"Good, Bragan, you're doing all right. But I'm sure you didn't call to tell me just that. What else is on your mind?"

"Well, Shadow 81, as one pro to another, I realize you're an intelligent man. So, if you'll excuse me for asking—how do we know you're not bluffing?"

Grant chose not to reply at once but to let everyone squirm. He bided his time.

Hadley wondered with anxiety why Bragan had picked this particular moment to irritate his pursuer. Why should he even ask such a question? He looked at Bessoe, Faust, and the Senator. They were all holding their breath.

Bragan felt his pulse quickening. The waiting was getting on his nerves. He called.

"Shadow 81, did you read me?"

"I heard you loud and clear. It was a fair question, Bragan."

Grant gave a short, harsh laugh.

"I guess you're entitled to know for sure. You guys kill me, but I'm going to satisfy your curiosity. Tell you what, Bragan, I'll do even better. I'll have Hadley confirm to you that I'm not kidding. Is that good enough for you?"

Bragan found himself breaking out in a cold sweat. He knew he shouldn't have challenged the hijacker. He had now deliberately provoked him and would have to bear the consequences if anything went wrong. He decided to back-pedal immediately. He tried to sound composed, friendly, and cheerful.

"Didn't mean to insult you, Shadow 81. No offense meant, really. Sorry if I upset you. Forget it. Please . . . don't do anything foolish. We'd all regret it."

"Bragan, don't talk to me in soothing tones as if I were some kind of nut. You're dealing with a pro, remember? You said so yourself. So cool it, Bragan. Just sit back for a few minutes and leave the driving to us. Hadley, did you read what just went on?"

"We were listening—PGA 81," Hadley answered, making an effort to sound self-assured.

"Good. Hold off that lunch for your passengers. As for you, Bragan, I don't want you to interrupt for the next few minutes. Did you both copy?"

"PGA 81—we copy."

Bragan looked at the people surrounding him and shook his head with resignation as he clicked on his mike.

"We copy—LA Tower."

"OOOKAY, here we go."

Grant sounded almost delighted, as if about to pull a wonderful prank.

"You, Hadley. Pull back the power and let down immediately to five hundred feet." Grant then began to speak in a voice mimicking Bragan's pacifying tone during the last exchange. "No need to dive . . . nice and easy . . . I'm right behind you. We don't want to scare your passengers . . . do we now?"

"Roger, descending—PGA 81."

"Hadley. Verify and adjust your altimeter to the standard setting of 29.92 inches. This way, we'll both read them alike. When you reach five hundred feet and I mean five hundred, no more and no less—if you know what's good for you—fly straight and level on a heading of 010 magnetic. Do you read?"

"We read. Twenty-nine point nine-two inches, five hundred feet, zero one zero magnetic."

"Good. Let down at 3,600 feet per minute. Keep circling. We should be at five hundred in ten minutes. I'll call you back when the time comes."

"OK. 3,600 feet per minute is the rate of descent."

Hadley picked up the cabin mike.

"Ladies and gentlemen, this is your captain. Would you please return to your seats at once and fasten your seat belts. Our hijacker has just asked us to perform some maneuvers at low altitude. We assume he has his reasons and we won't argue with him. There is no cause for alarm. Please remain calm. Lunch will be delayed for a few minutes. Please refrain from calling on our cabin attendants for the moment unless you find it absolutely necessary. I would also like them to sit down and fasten their seat belts. Thank you."

Hadley realized that this was not the most comforting announcement, but the fighter pilot had given him no opportunity to rehearse a carefully worded speech.

The passengers were unashamedly terrified. Some scurried to their seats, fastened their belts, and instinctively gripped the armrests.

Hadley called Laura on the intercom.

"I know the atmosphere must be oppressive in the cabin, Laura. I'm counting on you and Bea not to let things get out of hand. I have no idea what he has in mind. I can't tell you more than what you've heard. I'll get back to you as soon as I can."

"Don't worry about us, Captain. We can take care of it. You've certainly got a lot more on your mind than we do."

In the tower, Bragan looked strained. Ayno and the others around him felt the tension mounting. No one said a word.

The chief controller remained seated at his console, in deep thought. He looked at the digital clock on the panel. It was 1412. The hijacking had now been in progress for exactly fifty minutes and a million things were happening at once.

Bragan turned to Ayno.

"Mike, we won't know anything until about twenty after the hour. Call the Coast Guard. Tell them to have cutters ready to proceed to the scene—just in case."

A controller manning a set of telephones a few feet away waved at Bragan.

"Tom, it's the President again."

Bragan grimaced and immediately sensed everyone's eyes upon him. Angry and resentful because of this further disturbance, he picked up an extension line by his console.

"Yes, Mr. President," he said in a neutral tone.

"Bragan, I now have a radio here on my desk and can monitor what you people are saying. What the hell is he doing?"

"I honestly don't know, sir. You asked me to test him. The man has a diabolical mind and this is the result."

"You don't think he's liable to do anything rash, do you?"

"I wish I could reassure you, Mr. President, but there's nothing

I can say. We have to wait and see and sweat it out. I tried to tell you there was a certain rapport established between the hijacker, Hadley, and myself—a professional understanding, if you will. I only hope we haven't destroyed that thin thread of mutual confidence and respect among the three of us. I'm especially concerned about Captain Hadley, sir. I don't want his faith in my competence to be shaken."

"OK, Bragan. You've made your point. I won't interfere. I'll leave things up to you from now on. I'll listen on the radio but I still want to be kept abreast of things."

"Yes, Mr. President. Let's just pray it isn't too late."

Barney Alcott was becoming a celebrity. He was getting telephone calls from every part of the country. Newspapers, radio, and TV stations, all wanted "exclusive" stories.

The "Aviation Editor" of the Los Angeles *Times* was being quoted from coast to coast as a "leading expert" with "high level contacts in airline industry circles" and fully familiar with the pertinent facts.

All the lines in the pressroom at LA International were busy. Barney had locked the door to prevent competitors from barging in on him and was talking on two telephones at a time.

Before he began dictating his articles, he made a little announcement.

He warned the editors calling him that it would be the nominal "standard" rate of fifty dollars per taped minute or fraction thereof for his services, personal comments, and appraisal of the situation. Only upon acceptance did he begin to spew out his yarns.

Barney kept track of the callers on his notebook.

But Barney Alcott was also an efficient journalist and his time was worth every penny. While he spoke into a headset, he banged out his stories for the news wires and handed the sheets to Dubbs. His apprentice could barely keep up the pace punching the copy on the telex. He had never learned "writing under pressure" at U.S.C.

At 2:22 P.M., Grant's voice broke the silence in the cockpit of the jumbo jet.

"Hadley. We're coming up on five hundred feet. Turn right to zero one zero. Maintain your altitude at five hundred and give me an airspeed of one six zero knots, no more. Got it?"

"Roger—PGA 81," Hadley answered with a frog in his throat. He noticed his hands were trembling slightly on the yoke and looked at Bessoe, who was equally uptight. Wadsworth was still standing behind them. Faust was sitting at his panel, watching his gauges.

"Stand by, Hal," Hadley said, "in case we're both needed at the controls."

"PGA 81," Grant called, "you're looking good now from where I'm sitting. Hold your airspeed."

"What are you going to do?"

"Keep quiet, Hadley, and listen. You just look down at the ocean—dead ahead—about three miles out. Tell me when you're ready."

"OK. I'm ready now—what should I be looking for?"

There was another long silence, which Bragan and the other men in the tower began to find almost unbearable.

Grant positioned himself exactly 1,000 feet above and two miles behind the tail of the 747.

He followed the airliner for approximately thirty seconds, making sure he wasn't gaining or losing ground on it.

Grant took careful aim, slowly squeezed the trigger, and fired one of his rockets located under the right wing.

Hadley and the three other men saw the blazing trail of the missile streaking by the nose of the jumbo jet toward the ocean.

Their eyes were momentarily blinded by a huge flash. It was immediately followed by a towering, mushrooming geyser shooting out of the Pacific at the sky.

The awesome column of water rose to over a thousand feet. It appeared to remain suspended in mid-air for several seconds.

The Boeing continued on the course ordered by the fighter pilot and passed through the mountain of water. Hadley and the three other men ducked their heads instinctively as tons of water falling back toward the surface crashed against the windshield.

Screams of hysteria pierced the quiet in the cabin as the passengers heard the cascade battering the fuselage and wings.

"Goddamn that sonofabitch," Hadley shouted in frustration as he fought with the yoke, the rudders, and the trim tabs of the erratic airplane, for what seemed an eternity.

Grant broke in.

"Tell Bragan what happened, Hadley," he ordered tersely.

"LA Tower—PGA 81." Hadley was furious. "Our pursuer has just fired a missile or a rocket, I don't know which, into the ocean, dead ahead of our airplane. It was so close the spray hit us. He IS armed. We're convinced of that. Our passengers can't take much more of this and . . ."

"OK, Hadley, that's enough," Grant interrupted. "Bragan, are you there?"

The chief controller's eyes were closed. He was picturing the scene and seething with rage at being so helpless.

"I'm here," he answered through clenched teeth.

Grant took no pains to conceal his sarcasm.

"Are you quite happy now, Bragan?"

The chief controller was in no position to fight back.

"Roger. There was no need to frighten the daylights out of them."

"OK. Now that the fun and games are over, it's your turn," Grant said caustically. "Tell me how we're doing with that gold?"

"It's being loaded and will be on its way any minute. ETA in about two hours and twenty minutes at LA International."

"It's your neck if you're lying, not mine," Grant warned. "Hadley," he continued, "get back up to thirty-six thousand feet. Keep circling as you climb. Resume holding as before once we reach altitude. Same checkpoint. Same radius. You can go ahead and feed your passengers. I don't think our friend Bragan is going to bother us for a while."

"Roger, climbing back to three six zero—PGA 81." Hadley sounded relieved.

Grant smiled.

Laura came into the cockpit.

"Captain, I see we're climbing. What do you want us to do now?"

Hadley gave Laura a little grin.

"I'm glad you're here. I was about to call you. He was just trying to scare us. He succeeded very well, I might add. Get ready to serve lunch. You can tell the passengers everything is under control. I'll make an announcement in a couple of minutes."

"I'll tell the girls immediately. When do you want me to check in with you again, Captain?"

"No rush now. You'll be pretty busy for a while. I'll call you if anything comes up."

"I'm on my way."

The stewardesses started rolling out the serving carts, but no one really felt like eating.

Grant called the tower.

"Bragan—Shadow 81. Get ready to copy while we're climbing back. It is now . . . 1428 local, or T minus two hours thirty-two minutes and counting."

"Ready to copy—Bragan."

"First: I want a large police paddy wagon with ten armed cops. It is to be positioned at 1440—that is in twelve minutes—in downtown L.A., in front of the Los Angeles Times Building. Have the L.A. Police Chief, in uniform, inside the wagon. Do you read?"

"We read. Stand by one, Shadow 81."

Bragan looked inquisitively at the police captain standing next to him. The man nodded in assent and reached for a telephone.

"Go ahead, Shadow 81—Bragan."

"Second: I want you to have a twin Widgeon amphibian all gassed up at LA International Airport before the supersonics arrive with the gold. Place it at the end of the active runway in takeoff position. Got that?"

"Shadow 81—Bragan. OK regarding the police paddy wagon and the Chief. We're getting on it. But where do you expect me to find a twin Widgeon amphibian? This is a thirty-year-old relic. I don't even know if there are any in California, let alone within range of this airport. Will anything else do?"

"No. I want a Widgeon. Do I have to tell you everything, Bragan? All you have to do is call every private airport around your area. You can also check the seaplane bases. I'm sure you'll have no trouble finding one."

"OK. We'll do our best—Bragan."

"That's not good enough. I want a Widgeon," Grant insisted impatiently. "I'll give you a clue, Bragan. Save us all a lot of time. Why don't you try Van Nuys Airport. It's only about thirty or forty minutes from you. Send someone up there to take a look around. Check, man, check."

Bragan couldn't help gritting his teeth.

"OK. We'll look," he snarled. "Stand by. We'll call you back."

"Now, that's much better, Bragan," Grant said in a mocking tone.

At NORAD headquarters, in Colorado Springs, General Herman Sandline was in his office, nervously waiting for the phone to ring.

As chief of the North American Air Defense Command, he had placed a call to the White House ten minutes earlier, saying he had the solution to the hijacking and that he should be put through to the President. He was wondering what was taking so long. After all, he was the man in charge of the fantastic tracking complex carved out of rocks beneath Cheyenne Mountain.

NORAD kept tabs on all satellites and chunks of space debris sent aloft by the U.S., the Russians, the Chinese, and miscellaneous European countries. Its spider web network covered every foot of the North American Continent and could, theoretically, pinpoint any airplane or flying object operating over the United States. NORAD was a critical part of the shield against enemy Inter Continental Ballistic Missiles.

A Cuban MIG had recently managed to evade NORAD's detection. The pilot, a defector, had simply flown to an air base in Florida and landed there unchallenged.

It had been an embarrassing moment. What if the MIG had been carrying atomic weapons? clamored the press.

The whole incident, quickly swept under the rug, had been lamely explained—a defective radar station and the pilot's good fortune. It was said he had flown dangerously low to escape tracking and could have killed himself.

General Sandline's phone finally rang. He grabbed it.

It was Hoffman, the President's assistant.

Sandline was disconcerted but, nevertheless, he presented his ideas to the adviser, who told him to hold on.

"The President wants to think about it. He'll call you back when he makes a decision," Hoffman said.

"We don't have much time. Please let me talk to him," Sandline begged. "It won't take thirty seconds."

The President was listening on an extension line. He cut in.

"General Sandline, I'm not interested in your plan right now. Mr. Hoffman has already told you I haven't made up my mind."

"Mr. President, please listen. The missile I'm talking about is the most sophisticated weapon in the arsenal. It can hit a mosquito at two hundred thousand feet and three hundred miles range. I'm sure we can get the fighter without touching the airliner."

"General, I can understand your enthusiasm. But to what extent can you guarantee the accuracy of your missile? . . . No, General Sandline, that won't do. I want closer figures than that. . . . I see your point, General. . . . But what would happen if the hijacker suddenly decided to change the present circling pattern, altitude, speed, or whatever?"

"Well . . . er . . . Mr. President . . . there's always a risk . . . of course. But, maybe now is the time to find out if our weapons can do what they're supposed to do. I can assure you every precaution . . ."

"General," the President interrupted, "I remember being guaranteed that only military targets would be hit in and around Hanoi. I was assured that your 'smart bombs' could tell the difference between a bicycle and a bag of rice. The next thing I knew, the French Legation was demolished, its chief was killed, and the Bac Mai hospital blown apart. Now you tell me you have missiles that can hit mosquitoes. Get this straight, General. As Commander in Chief, I definitely forbid any launching of weapons in the direction of the airliner or the fighter. Thank you, General. Good-by!"

Sandline remained crestfallen and speechless for a long time. The President turned to his adviser.

"You see, Hoffman, the type of idiots I have running our defenses? A general who wants to shoot mosquitoes!"

"Don't get upset, Mr. President."

"Upset! I'm already called a bloodthirsty monster by every liberal in the country. Now he wants me to risk shooting down one of our own airliners—just before the elections. Good thinking! That's really all I need right now!"

"Now, Mr. President, no one could possibly blame you for trying to do your best during this unfortunate turn of events."

"Hoffman, we must be very careful and, also, very subtle with all this stuff about gold. With the way things are going in Vietnam, the catastrophic state of the economy, rampant inflation, corruption and scandals in the government, this could be a plot concocted by the opposition to embarrass me."

"Mr. President, please guard against saying such things in public. This could be interpreted as another overreaction on your part."

"Don't be ridiculous, Hoffman. They're out to get me. I know it. Well, they won't!"

Hoffman saw the blood rushing to the President's face and decided it would be best to change the subject.

"Mr. President, the afternoon White House press briefing had to be delayed because of the hijacking. Reporters also have questions about the Strategic Arms Limitation Talks with the Russians and your forthcoming trip to Europe. What should the spokesman say?"

"Let him tell them there are no comments on the hijacking. He should say that the President is busy with pressing problems and that all of today's scheduled activities are inoperative."

"Inoperative? What's that, Mr. President?"

"I'll be damned if I know. Let them figure it out."

It was now 2:35 P.M. in Los Angeles and a police paddy wagon with screaming sirens was racing wildly through the downtown section.

The vehicle was escorted by half a dozen howling patrol cars trying to make way for it through red lights but snarling up the traffic instead.

At 2:40, as ordered by the hijacker, the paddy wagon screeched to a halt in front of the Los Angeles Times Building. Reporters from the paper came down from the upper floors to see what the commotion was about. They began taking notes.

Policemen jumped out of the rear of the paddy wagon and, helped by the officers in the patrol cars, began diverting all traffic from the area.

The Ringling Brothers Barnum & Bailey Circus was in town and added somewhat to the problems encountered by the police. A parade, with marching bands, elephants, bears, stagecoaches, trapeze artists, and dancing clowns, was proceeding to the Sports Arena. Crowds of children and adults were gathering in front of the L.A. Times Building.

Police Chief Walter J. Cowlan, in full uniform, was calmly sitting on a bench inside the wagon, next to the partition behind the driver. He was smoking a pipe and observing the scene while listening to a portable VHF set resting on his lap. A walkie-talkie was crackling beside him on the bench.

Cowlan summoned one of the patrolmen standing guard outside the wagon.

"Tell the circus people to make a right before they reach the end of this block and to conduct the parade on the street parallel to this one. Order the crowd to move over too. Don't let anyone give you any arguments. Get all the help you need. Move it!"

At Fort Knox, the Captain of the Guard stood outside the rear entrance of the "United States Bullion Depository" surrounded by MPs with guns at the ready. He was supervising a detail of puzzled privates in army fatigues loading dollies with the gold destined for the hijacker.

The Captain glanced at his watch. It was forty-one past the hour. He only had nine minutes left to send the gold on its way to the airport and for his responsibility to end.

Gaining access to the gold and sorting it out had been no easy task for the Captain. A mind-boggling total of 147 million ounces, worth over 6 billion dollars, was stored in the depository. The vault was protected by a door weighing more than twenty tons and no one person was entrusted with the combination.

Several members of the depository staff were required to dial, separately and unobserved, numerous combinations known only to them. Rounding up the various people involved under such short notice had taken some doing.

The Captain looked at his tally sheet. Thank goodness, there were only one hundred more ingots to go to complete the shipment of 1,000 five-kilogram bars. Luckily for everyone, the 5,000 one-kilogram ingots demanded by the hijacker had been easier to handle.

The privates were grumbling under the frantic pace imposed by the Captain.

"We usually take this stuff in, and do it slowly," one of them said. "I know I never took any of it out," he grunted as he placed six of the heavier ingots on top of a heap.

Another man stopped to wipe his brow.

"Jesus," he groaned. "There must be zillions on those dollies. What's the hurry anyway? Why do we have to rush like this?"

His curiosity got the better of him.

"Where's all this gold going, sir?" he asked the man in charge. "Mind your own business, Private," the Captain of the Guard answered gruffly. "The less you know, the better. Get on with it."

Four armored trucks loaded with MPs pulled up. They were surrounded by jeeps with machine guns mounted on the front and rear.

"All right, men, let's load the dollies in the trucks. Hurry it up," ordered the Captain.

The precious cargo was placed aboard the vehicles in a matter of minutes.

The Captain looked at the time. It was only forty-eight past the hour. He'd made it—with two minutes to spare.

Preceded by two jeeps, the four trucks moved slowly in a convoy down Gold Vault Road toward the steel fence surrounding the depository. Two other jeeps brought up the rear.

Once through the gate and out of the depository, the vehicles turned right onto Bullion Boulevard to exit from Fort Knox. They then made another right, got on Route 31 W, and started racing toward Godman Air Force Base.

All TV and radio networks were now putting on special newscasts.

The anchor men had every element for a good suspense story. Countdowns, airplanes, ransoms, gold, emergencies, and instant high level decisions. Senator Wadsworth was on board, which added spice. Last but not least, there was "human interest" drama at high altitude and the agonizing wait of relatives on the ground.

Science editors were summoned to the studios. They were asked to give "educated guesses" as to the chances of the hijacker getting his demands satisfied on time and before tragedy occurred.

Old documentaries on Fort Knox were dug up from the files. Featurettes on the Boeing 747 were aired. They gave the characteristics of the airplane, such as size, range, endurance, and, of course, the cost of the aircraft amounting to over twenty-five million dollars.

There were no details as yet on the hijacker's plane. The Pentagon was unco-operative and declined to be specific. A spokesman simply confirmed that it was a "fighter aircraft of undetermined origin and type."

The regular news was aired earlier than usual and intermingled with the coverage of the hijacking during "dead spots" when there was nothing new to report.

Film clips of the war in Vietnam were shown. They were followed, as a counterpoint, by videotaped reports transmitted by satellite, of the peace negotiations being conducted in Paris.

A correspondent's voice from the French capital said that the atmosphere was presently very "optimistic" and that peace agreements could now be finalized any day. Diplomats were seen exiting from a conference room, smiling and shaking hands. The prisoners of war, the correspondent concluded, could be coming home very soon.

An anchor man announced that his network had succeeded in tuning in to the frequency utilized for communications between the hijacker, PGA Flight 81, and Los Angeles Tower. Viewers and radio audiences of network affiliates would now be able to listen "live" to the "unprecedented saga" unfolding over the Pacific Ocean, 160 miles southwest of Los Angeles. Shortly after, the two other networks succeeded in patching in this transmission as well.

For a brief moment, Grant was heard asking the tower if a Widgeon had been located. Bragan replied there seemed to be one at Van Nuys Airport, as the hijacker had suggested.

For the benefit of the viewers who didn't know what a Widgeon was, an anchor man explained that the fighter pilot and the chief controller were referring to a vintage twin propeller aircraft. It was an amphibian capable of operating on land and water. He then drew the obvious conclusion that the Widgeon would apparently be needed by the hijacker to make his escape at a later time.

At Los Angeles International, Barney Alcott was now getting fewer and fewer phone calls. He had had his moment of glory and, for almost two hours, had reigned supreme. Now that every network was tuning in directly to the story, he was no longer needed except for background material.

Barney smiled philosophically. Modern technology was making him once again obsolete.

CHAPTER 19

Grant opened a can of ham, sliced a thin wedge, put it between two pieces of melba toast and bit ravenously into this "dainty hors d'oeuvre."

"Hey, Hadley?—Shadow 81."

"PGA 81—go ahead."

"How are things going aboard? The passengers nice and quiet?"

"We've got everything under control, thank you," Hadley answered curtly.

"Now come on, Captain, don't be mad at me. I'm just trying to be friendly. I didn't want to pull that stunt. You know it."

"What do you want now, Shadow 81?"

"Nothing much. Getting pretty lonesome up here. Just wanted to know how you were doing . . . feed the passengers lunch yet?"

"They're being served right now."

"What's on the menu?—Just curious, that's all."

Hadley was slightly perplexed by the hijacker's conciliatory attitude. He was really in no mood for small talk but, nevertheless, entered the spirit of the exchange.

"Oh . . . we have our usual 'Hawaiian Luau Feast'—with a choice of roast suckling pig . . . broiled lobster, I think . . . steak to order too, I believe."

Grant smacked his lips then looked down at his dry melba toast makeshift sandwich with disgust.

"You make my mouth water, Captain. Wish I could join you."

"Why don't you buy yourself a ticket and make a reservation on the next flight?" Hadley smiled.

"You're a good company man and a great salesman, Hadley. I think I'll take you up on that. Will you invite me for the grand tour of the cockpit?"

"Sure, why not?"

"I'll be your passenger one of these days. I promise. But you won't know who I am, of course. That's too bad. I'd really like to meet you."

"I'm not so sure I'd like to meet you."

"That's not nice, Hadley. You know this is nothing personal. To me, your airplane and passengers are a totally abstract thing—a means to an end. But I must say I'm happy you happen to be in command. I'd hate to have to deal with a panicky amateur."

"Thanks for the compliment, but flattery will get you nowhere," Hadley chuckled. "Now, if you'll excuse me, Shadow 81, I don't have time to chat. I've got to talk to my passengers."

"Certainly, Captain. Tell them it's no longer up to you or me, but to the guys on the ground, and that we two are co-operating. That should make them feel better. The faster they get moving down there, the sooner they'll be going home. So long now. Have a good lunch, Hadley."

"I don't have time. You're keeping me pretty busy."

"Sorry about that!"

Grant took another bite of ham and washed it down with a can of warm grape juice.

Senator Wadsworth was still standing between Hadley and Bessoe.

"Are the mikes off?" he whispered in the Captain's ear.

Hadley nodded.

"He seems to be in a good mood just now. Captain Hadley, would you let me talk to this man? Maybe I could have some influence on him. I believe my intervention might be beneficial."

"Senator, I think you'd be wasting your time. He's playing for enormous stakes and he's in too deep now. I'm convinced we're not dealing with an irrational man. He's much too meticulous and too good a pilot. He has all the bases covered. To him, it's a game of three-dimensional aerial chess and we're checkmated as long as he's behind us."

"He's human," Wadsworth insisted. "He can make a mistake."

"He hasn't made any so far. Think for a minute, Senator. Do you have any idea why he picked this particular flight?"

"I really don't know."

"Elementary for a pilot, Senator. He didn't want an airplane going over an inland route. Too many Air Force bases, missiles and what have you. He needed a flight proceeding over the ocean where he wouldn't be hindered. That's us. It had to be a long-range aircraft to give him time to get his gold from Fort Knox. We're it. He had to have as many passengers as possible as hostages. There's nothing bigger than a 747. And, finally, Senator, the right time. He needed daylight to find us and darkness to escape—just about eight hours. We left a little after 1:00 P.M. —an ideal moment for him. He's been planning this operation for a long time. He was waiting for us. He just said we're nothing but unimportant pawns to him. We might as well face it. He's not going to let go of us before nightfall. The only pieces that don't fit the puzzle are that Widgeon and paddy wagon. I don't have a clue what he wants to do with them, but I bet we'll soon find out."

"Let me talk to him anyway. What have we got to lose?" Wadsworth persisted.

"I doubt anyone could talk him out of it, Senator. Anyway, if I were in his place, I'd be mighty jumpy right now. He knows everyone's waiting for him to make a false move. I believe it would be foolish to upset him."

"I'd still like to try to talk to him, Captain. What do you say?"

Hadley looked at his co-pilot and flight engineer. They said nothing but, from their expressions, they seemed to be on the Senator's side. He looked at Wadsworth for a moment then shrugged his shoulders.

"If you insist, Senator. But please be careful."

Wadsworth nodded his thanks and picked up the co-pilot's mike. His voice came over rather timidly.

"Shadow 81? . . . This is Senator Wadsworth aboard PGA 81. Would you mind if I had a word with you?"

Grant was surprised at the call but not intimidated.

"Ah! Senator C. Felton Wadsworth himself and in person! This is quite an honor," Grant said pleasantly. "I didn't know you were on your way to Honolulu. Very nice this time of year, don't you think? Sorry I'm delaying you. Go right ahead."

At Los Angeles Tower, Bragan lost his temper.

"Goddammit," he shouted. "Why the hell does he feel he has to butt in?"

In the Oval Office, the President perked up and leaned closer to the monitoring set installed on his desk. He looked astonished, as did his adviser, Hoffman.

"This is worth a special tape," the President said breathlessly as he listened. "Put a fresh cassette in the machine, Hoffman—quickly . . . hurry. I want to keep a record of what Wadsworth has to say."

In the 747 cockpit, the Senator beamed. He winked at the crew, apparently satisfied with the effect his name had produced on the hijacker.

In the cockpit of the fighter plane, Grant settled back and grinned. He was going to enjoy this conversation.

"Shadow 81," Wadsworth went on, "I realize you're under pressure right now, but I still would like to discuss the possibility of our coming to an understanding."

"Keep going, Wadsworth. Say what you have to say without trying to humor me," Grant replied acidly.

Wadsworth was taken aback by the hijacker's unexpected change of tone and evident lack of respect. He looked at Hadley, who motioned him to tread very softly.

"Shadow 81, you're certainly aware that the people on this airplane are very frightened. You probably also know that your chances of getting away with this are very small."

"Go on. And, please, don't talk down to me or I'll cut this discussion short."

There was a moment of embarrassed silence. Wadsworth groped for words.

"Sir," he said for lack of a better form of address, "you must be a member or former member of our Armed Forces. I'm sure that, deep down, you know in your heart that your sense of duty and loyalty will inevitably prevail."

"I've already told you, Wadsworth. Stop patronizing me."

The Senator cleared his throat.

"I'll make you the following proposition, Shadow 81. I'll see to it that you're not prosecuted and that you're granted full immunity and pardon if you'll just let this airplane go. You don't have to give me an immediate answer. Think about it."

"Who appointed you spokesman to make me offers, Wadsworth? By what authority can you bestow any kind of immunity or pardon?"

"I'm sure I could arrange it so we could downgrade the charges to attempted blackmail of PGA. You'd be let off lightly as a first offender."

"Yeah, just like you fixed everything else, Senator? Hasn't it penetrated into your brain that I'm not blackmailing an airline? I'm holding up the U.S. Government."

"Please listen . . ."

"I hear you fine. Wadsworth, weren't you the one clamoring for a bill in the Senate advocating the mandatory death penalty for air piracy?"

The Senator hesitated for a second.

"Er . . . yes. But this is different."

"Why? Because you're on board, Senator? Because you're presidential material?" Grant laughed irreverently. "Right?"

"Wrong. As an elected official, I have a responsibility to these passengers and the crew. I'm not thinking about myself."

"Not much. You're a phony, Wadsworth. And holier than thou besides. My . . . My . . ."

"Now wait a minute . . ." the Senator protested.

"Wadsworth," Grant interrupted, "right now, I'm earning my money the hard way. I seem to recall a few episodes in your life that aren't the most exemplary. I don't think they'd do you much good if they were brought to light. What gives you the right to preach to me?"

The Senator's face flushed.

"I'm not discussing my life and I'm not trying to give any sermons. Can't we talk this over?"

In the White House, the President was listening intently, absorbing every word.

From coast to coast, millions of people tuned to the radio networks were eavesdropping on the exchange.

"Wadsworth," Grant sneered, "you're nothing but a hypocrite trying to cash in on this situation. You sound like you're about to make a speech—one of your revolting addresses beginning with 'My fellow Americans.' You know everyone's listening to you on the ground right now and you want to make the most of it."

The Senator felt like he was about to burst. He saw Hadley staring at him and contained himself.

"I don't know what makes you so hostile, Shadow 81. Maybe it's the war. Now if it's a matter of getting you an honorable discharge, son . . ."

"Who the hell do you think you're calling son? And you, of all people, YOU have the nerve to wave the flag at me. Where were you when they needed you in the Senate to put an end to the war? We're selling out right now and you're the Number One salesman. Who do you think you're kidding? I wouldn't trust your word on anything."

"You sound awfully bitter but my offer still stands," Wadsworth said quietly, making a last try.

"Can't you understand I have absolutely nothing to talk over with you? If you want some advice from me for a change, I think you'd better keep out of this before your stock goes way down. You've said enough. You'd better quit while you're ahead."

"What do you mean?"

"I mean that I didn't kill anyone in cold blood—not yet, anyway."

"What are you insinuating?" Wadsworth whispered hoarsely.

"I'm not insinuating. I'm just saying plainly what everyone suspects. You got rid of your friend because you were having an affair with his wife. He was going to blow the whistle on you; put an end to your political career."

"You don't know what you're saying," the Senator gasped.

"Get off this mike, Wadsworth, you pretentious bastard."

In the Oval Office, there was the shadow of a grin on the President's face as he turned to his assistant.

"I like this boy, Hoffman. He can see right through Wadsworth. He's got guts and fights back. Too bad he decided on this reckless course of action. Here I am, agreeing with a hijacker . . . paradoxical, isn't it? Yet he's sharper than all those fellows trying to corner him. We could use people with brains like that around this place."

"I admit he's a rather intriguing character, Mr. President. I know I previously suggested you do not get involved in this but do you feel you might want to talk to him now, since everyone is listening?"

"No, Hoffman. I don't think it would be appropriate at this time. He seems to have it in for everyone. Who knows how he'd react to me? I don't think it would play well in Peoria. Besides, I must preserve the dignity of this office."

It was very quiet in the cockpit of PGA 81. Hadley, Bessoe, and Faust were uncomfortable. Wadsworth's lower lip was trembling. He was looking down at the floor, shattered and in a daze.

Grant's voice over the loudspeaker broke the silence.

"Hadley?—You there?"

"I'm here, Shadow 81."

"Don't put any more clowns on the mike. That's final."

"Roger. Sorry. The Senator was very persistent."

"Hadley, you and I are in the same business. We speak the same language and understand each other. Both of us still have a lot of flying to do. The less we're disturbed, the better."

"I agree. Roger. PGA 81."

Hadley turned to Wadsworth.

"Senator, I warned you. Perhaps your place is now in the cabin. In fact, I'd appreciate it if you would help reassure the passengers as you, yourself, originally suggested."

Wadsworth was now very humble and almost unable to react.

"All right, Captain, as you wish. You know . . . it isn't true . . . what he said about me . . ."

"It's not important right now, Senator," Hadley said with great kindness as Wadsworth left.

Grant looked at his clock and squeezed his mike button.

"LA Tower—Shadow 81. Get ready to copy."

"Shadow 81—Bragan. Go ahead."

"It is now 1443 local or T minus two hours and seventeen minutes and counting. Mark."

"Mark—LA Tower."

"OK. Within the next two minutes, a man will come up to the police paddy wagon. He is armed. Furthermore, his body is booby trapped with dynamite from the neck to his ankles. He is a walking bomb. The Police Chief is to follow his orders to the letter. The cops are not to touch him. They must not try to capture him or interfere in any way. Got that?"

"Understood—Bragan. We're relaying at once to all concerned."

Inside the police paddy wagon, Chief Walter J. Cowlan was listening on his VHF set to Grant's instructions.

"Be advised that I am in radio contact with this man at pre-arranged times on another frequency unknown to you," Grant continued. "If I do not hear from him exactly on schedule, I shoot. I wouldn't try anything stupid. Bragan, relay this to the Chief and acknowledge."

Cowlan reacted at once. He picked up his walkie-talkie tuned in to headquarters.

"This is the Chief. No need to repeat. Tell Mr. Bragan we've got the message and to confirm compliance."

At Godman Air Force Base, the last of the gold ingots were

loaded in the bomb racks of the ten supersonic fighters requisitioned by Grant.

The hatches were closed. The canopies slid into locked position and the engines started.

The jets lined up, held short of the runway threshold and, upon clearance from the tower, took off in quick succession.

They assembled into formation as they climbed and headed west, toward Los Angeles.

At the Pentagon, Captain Fred Scarlata walked into General Raymond Prominowe's office with an impressive stack of statistics.

"Anything turn up, Scarlata?"

"Sir, we still haven't pinpointed any suspicious disappearance of fighters or pilots."

"Tell me about the voice prints."

"We ran copies of the tapes of the conversations between the hijacker, PGA 81, and Los Angeles Tower. Negative. The computer cannot identify the voice."

"Did you cross-check against samples of Hadley's voice and Bragan's running simultaneously on another computer?"

"We certainly did, General. There's nothing wrong with our equipment. We ran an original tape and a copy. Hadley, Bragan, and the fighter pilot's voices matched perfectly every time. However, there is nothing in the memory banks corresponding to the hijacker's voice."

"How do you explain that, Scarlata? We're supposed to have voice prints of every pilot with access to classified equipment."

"Well, sir, the hijacker's voice has a metallic-sounding characteristic. There's sort of an echo chamber quality to it. It's obviously electronically altered. He must have a frequency modulator of some kind to prevent us from matching his voice prints."

"Go on."

"My guess is that he has an electronic device. It must be connected to his mike and it somehow disguises his voice by distorting the pitch, the modulation, or by warping the frequency. Sir, I think we're dealing with a man who knows exactly how we would react and who has taken every precaution to throw us off. I hate to say this, but he's beating us at our own game."

"I'm surprised at you, Scarlata. Don't give up yet. This fighter can't possibly have more than eight to ten hours' range. If he planned this as carefully as you say, he must have taken off from somewhere in Nevada, Arizona, Utah, Oregon, Washington, Mexico or, even, possibly, Canada. Check reports on any unidentified aircraft which may have proceeded from any of these points to Los Angeles within the last three hours. This guy isn't going to make us look like a bunch of beginners."

"You're probably right, sir, but he must have flown low enough to evade radar detection. There's one thing that crossed my mind, General. The airplane could have been stolen in Vietnam and could have been part of unaccounted casualties."

General Prominowe smiled.

"You have a great deal of imagination, Scarlata. But how the hell would the guy fly it across the Pacific without being noticed? Even with a full ten hours of fuel, it would never have the necessary range. Assuming he would have made it over the ocean without refueling, where the devil would he have stopped to pick up a second load of kerosene to keep him in the air for the hijacking without getting caught? That idea I can't buy, Scarlata."

"Yes, sir," the Captain said respectfully. "It was just a thought. Perhaps it was shipped across."

Prominowe smiled again.

"You should be writing mystery stories, Scarlata. A boat? Out of the question. Do you realize the number of people who would have been involved in handling the airplane, sailing the ship, etc. Someone would have talked along the way. We would have known about it. I feel it's probably one of the airplanes that disappeared without a trace over the Nevada desert during training in this country. The guy probably managed to hide it for a year or two while waiting for the right moment to strike."

"Yes, sir. I'll go back to my computers and keep looking. I'll check with NORAD regarding unidentified aircraft movements up to two hours prior to the hijacking."

"One more thing, Scarlata. The Air Force doesn't want it to be known the fighter is a TX-75E. The Joint Chiefs of Staff concur. The endurance figures are top secret. They don't want the enemy to learn the airplane can stay in the air for as long as ten hours. The Russians, through intelligence, think it can remain aloft for only five or six hours. The policy of the Pentagon, therefore, is to minimize this hijacking and play it down rather than let the cat out of the bag."

"I understand, sir. I'll be back as soon as possible."

At Naval Headquarters in San Diego, Admiral Alfred P. Casters had finally managed to get through to the White House. He had succeeded in getting past Hoffman and could hardly wait to tell the President the news.

"Mr. President, by pure coincidence we happen to have a nuclear Polaris submarine practically below the two aircraft. It's the U.S.S. *Barracuda*, on its way back from Pearl Harbor to San Francisco."

In the Oval Office, the President looked at Hoffman, raised his eyes toward the ceiling and shook his head skeptically.

"Here we go again!"

Admiral Casters was astonished at the President's remark before he had even spoken his piece.

"Mr. President . . . were you talking to me?"

"Never mind, Admiral. It would take too long to explain. What about the *Barracuda*?"

"Well, you see, sir, the submarine does not have to surface to aim or fire a missile at the hijacker. That's taken care of by inertial equipment. . . . What's that, Mr. President? You've already heard the same thing from NORAD? . . . I understand your objections, Mr. President, but, with the submarine, we're at extremely close range and we can have visual contact. The *Barracuda* has a sophisticated high-resolution telescope within the periscope. It can scan vertically and zoom in on the fighter plane. It's virtually sitting on the hijacker's lap, sir . . ."

"I don't want to hear about it, Admiral. For some reason or other, these tinker-toys never seem to work well in critical situations."

"But, Mr. President, at least give us a chance to tell you if it's feasible. . . . No, sir, nothing will be done without your prior approval, you have my word. . . . I'll let you know what the submarine commander thinks after surveying the theater of operations. . . . No, sir, I assure you there is absolutely no risk that the submarine can be detected by the fighter. . . . Thank you for giving us this opportunity, Mr. President."

Senator Wadsworth sat alone for a while in the upper lounge, trying to regain his composure. He still looked dejected as he walked down the spiral staircase leading to the first-class section.

Horace J. Transcombe was waiting at the foot of the stairs. He pounced on Wadsworth, jolting him out of his meditation.

"Senator," Transcombe said in a booming voice as he grabbed Wadsworth by the sleeve, "as a taxpayer and law-abiding citizen, I demand to know what's really happening!"

Wadsworth gave him a cold, blank stare and pushed away his hand.

"I have no idea who you are," the Senator said, "but you'd better get hold of yourself. The Captain's already told you everything there is to know. And there is no need for hysterics."

The Senator saw the other two men slouching glumly in one of the back rows and decided he'd rather not return to his own seat. He brushed past Transcombe and went to look for Laura in the economy section.

The Los Angeles Times Building had been cordoned off. The entire block was surrounded by police officers and detectives, suspiciously eying all passers-by.

Swarms of motorcycle cops and foot patrolmen were rerouting the circus parade. They were outdoing each other blowing shrill whistles as they pushed the crowd into adjacent streets.

Someone had spread the rumor that a bomb was about to go off. People started screaming. Cops were trying to calm them by shouting instructions into bullhorns but only added to the mounting panic. Mothers clutched their children as they tried to run. Kids were yelling and refused to leave. Some sat on the sidewalk and went into crying tantrums—they wanted to stay and see the clowns.

"Hey, Ma!" a little boy shouted. "Wait. I want to see Santa Claus."

"What Santa Claus? Don't be silly," the mother said impatiently as she pushed through the crowd. "It's not Christmas yet. Come on. Let's go or I'll leave you right here, I mean it! We'll watch the parade on the next block," she pleaded as she tugged the child away.

"No, Ma . . . look . . . please . . . in front of the elephants . . . there's Santa Claus . . ."

"OK, OK—we'll wait for him around the corner. I promise. Now, come on."

There was, indeed, a Santa Claus. Weighing in at about three hundred pounds, he was happily frolicking in front of the elephants, jingling a large brass bell.

Still pirouetting and waving at the children, he danced his way through the crowd of onlookers. Busy herding people, the cops hardly paid heed to him until he was almost ready to climb into the paddy wagon through the rear door.

It suddenly dawned on them that Santa Claus was getting too close. Three officers surrounded him to ask why he wasn't moving along with the other circus people.

Chief Cowlan dropped his pipe, jumped to his feet inside the vehicle, and yelled:

"For God's sake don't touch him!"

Santa Claus had wires protruding from his big black belt.

Ignoring the cops, he stepped into the wagon and sat next to one of the doors. He deposited his bell on the floor, calmly put on a pair of dark glasses, and, with his index finger, beckoned the Police Chief to come closer.

"Any tape recorders planted in here?" he whispered in Cowlan's ear.

"No."

"You're sure now? Any of your cops wearing bugging equipment?"

"No. You have my word," Cowlan said quietly.

"OK. Get your boys in this wagon and let's go," Santa Claus ordered.

Cowlan waved at his men. The ten cops who had arrived with him hopped aboard and silently sat in the rear.

Santa Claus pointed at the doors. The Chief slammed them shut.

The paddy wagon started moving slowly down the street under the jolly fat man's direction.

At Van Nuys Airport, northwest of Los Angeles, a black limousine carrying six FBI agents dashed down a taxiway. It came to an abrupt stop in a cloud of dust in front of a Widgeon amphibian parked on the grass.

Four men, wearing sloppy clothes and obviously in excellent spirits, were loading fishing equipment aboard the aircraft, which looked about ready to leave. They were unaware that all air operations had been suspended.

The head of the FBI group approached the party and flashed a badge.

"I'd like to talk to the owner of this airplane," he said as his five companions surrounded the aircraft.

One of the four outdoor characters stepped forward. He was fortyish—a short, round, balding little man who affected an RAF handlebar mustache. Dressed in a greasy T shirt, frayed dungarees, and sandals, he was wearing a fishing hat with tackle pinned all around it.

"Who are you?" the owner asked.

"Special Agent Carmen Charles Marsi—FBI. Could we step aside for a minute, please? What's your name, sir?" Marsi inquired as he took the man's elbow, and gently led him out of earshot.

"Nayten—Russ Nayten," the owner of the Widgeon mumbled, looking more and more confused. He turned toward his friends. "I'll be right back," he shouted. "What have I done?" he asked Marsi. "If it's about the annual inspection of the airplane, I know I'm a little late but I assure you I can explain everything . . . I didn't know the FBI got involved in airworthiness certificate renewals and . . ."

"No, no. Nothing like that, sir," Marsi reassured Nayten. "Let's just go somewhere quiet. This will only take a moment."

Nayten's friends, watching him confer with the FBI man, suddenly saw him go into a sort of Indian war dance. Gesticulating wildly, he stamped his feet, while flailing his arms and wagging his head adamantly.

The Widgeon's owner appeared disturbed, but his cronies couldn't tell why. The five other FBI agents guarding them and the airplane maintained a stony silence.

Nayten's friends heard him howling in anguish but couldn't make out what he was saying. They saw Special Agent Marsi patting him on the shoulder, trying to quiet him down.

"Why pick on me?" Nayten was ranting to Marsi. "I don't have anything to do with this. It's none of my business. Do you know how long I've been planning this vacation? Two years! Do you hear? Two years to get us four guys together."

"Please, Mr. Nayten, try to understand the situation . . ."

"Understand? Have you any idea what it took to talk my wife into letting me go alone on this one-week fishing trip to Canada? I left her by herself to run my plumbing supplies store. You wouldn't believe the things I had to promise. No, sir! This is my airplane and nobody's taking it away from me. That's final!"

"I know how you feel, Mr. Nayten, but this is a national emergency. The hijacker specifically requested your type of aircraft. You're the only one in the area with this kind of plane in flying condition. How could you have the heart to go fishing in some Canadian lake when 201 people on board the airliner are depending on you for their very lives? Besides, all departures have been canceled until further notice."

Russ Nayten looked far from being convinced. He shook his head at the FBI man.

"From what you've told me, restrictions will be lifted in a few hours, that is as soon as both airplanes eventually run out of fuel. I can leave then. Look, I'm a patriot and all that jazz and I don't want to sound callous, but this is not my responsibility. The Air Force and the Navy have a million airplanes which would do just as well. Let them work it out. I'd like to help you, believe me, but I can't do this to my pals here. We've been planning this for too long."

"We're in no position to argue with this fighter pilot, Mr. Nayten. He wants your airplane because he is apparently familiar with it. Now, I hate to say this, but if you refuse to co-operate, the Government will have no choice but to requisition it. We're wasting precious time . . ."

"Just a minute, whoever you are. The Government has no right to impound anything in time of peace and this thing—conflict or action or whatever you want to call it—in Vietnam is not supposed to be a war. Don't try to bluff me or pressure me. Besides, assuming, just assuming, I let you have my airplane, when would I get it back and in what shape would you guys return it?"

Marsi looked perplexed.

"That, I admit, I don't know. Look, I'm not a pilot. We have no idea what he intends to do with your airplane and if it will ever be brought back."

Russ Nayten was outraged. He started jumping around again in a great state of agitation.

"In fact, you're purely and simply asking me to donate my airplane to some nut who's going to crack it up for me. You must take me for an idiot. Nothing doing!"

The FBI man was now getting desperate.

"Look, Mr. Nayten. If it makes you any happier, the Government will guarantee restitution, pay for any damage or buy it outright. How about that? We don't have much time. I'm pleading with you now."

Nayten scratched his chin and nervously twirled his mustache.

"How do I know I can trust you guys—FBI and all? . . . By the way, what did you say your name was?"

"Marsi, Carmen Charles Marsi."

"Carmen? That's a woman's name, isn't it?"

"It's both masculine and feminine. What's that got to do with it?" Marsi said, getting very annoyed.

"And Marsi? What kind of a name is that? What are you? Spanish? Mexican? Puerto Rican? Italian? I thought you FBI people all had to be Anglo-Saxons to get in."

"I'm of Italian extraction, if you must know. And for your information, we're not all in the Mafia," Marsi said with great irritation.

"Well, I'm half Irish and half Polish and I'm not ashamed of anything. I just want to know who I'm dealing with, that's all."

"You're dealing with the FBI—the Federal Government of the United States of America. Is that good enough for you? Now stick to the point."

"My airplane's not for sale. Let me think about it for a minute. I'm not alone in this. I want to talk it over with my friends."

"OK. But hurry."

The owner of the Widgeon walked over to the airplane and went into a huddle with his three companions under the watchful eye of the five other FBI agents.

Marsi restlessly paced up and down.

At 2:55 P.M., the police paddy wagon stopped in front of one of the main branches of the Bank of America, at the corner of First Street and Main.

With Santa Claus at his elbow whispering instructions, Chief Cowlan marched his uniformed squad into the bank.

The guards were at a loss to understand what was going on and were unable to react. They grinned sheepishly as they were disarmed by the policemen under Santa Claus's supervision.

Clients lined up before tellers' windows or filling out slips at various counters didn't know what to make of the situation. For a moment some of them thought it might be some sort of promotion to encourage the opening of Christmas Club accounts. This couldn't be a holdup. These men were law-enforcement officers.

The Chief summoned the manager. As both men stood in the center of the ground floor, Cowlan explained the circumstances in hushed tones, pointing from time to time in the direction of Santa Claus.

The manager turned ashen as the Chief's explanations began to sink in. He cupped his hands around his mouth, shouted for the doors to be closed and for everyone—guards, tellers, and customers —to freeze right where they were. Next he ordered three male employees to bring canvas pouches to the counters.

Covered by two police officers, the trio ran down to the basement and immediately returned with the bags.

Assisted by the policemen, Chief Cowlan and the manager promptly proceeded to clean out the tellers' and cashiers' drawers.

Leaving four officers to stand guard over the petrified crowd, Cowlan and a detail of cops then descended to the vault, which the manager was forced to open. Bills of every denomination were thrown in heaps into the canvas bags while Santa Claus looked on.

One of the officers operating by himself in a corner of the vault felt tempted to pick up a little easy cash in the confusion. He sneaked a look behind him, saw he was unobserved, grabbed a few hundred-dollar bills, and prepared to put them in his shirt pocket.

Just then, Chief Cowlan made a brief announcement.

"Let me warn you men that everyone will be searched after this is over."

The officer registered surprise at the Chief's lack of faith in his own cops. He thought better of his idea and reluctantly tossed the handful of bills into a bag.

Santa Claus looked at his wrist watch. It was almost 3:10 P.M.

"OK, boys, that'll do. It's a fine job, real professional," he said, dead pan. "Let's go load all this into the van."

Carrying the heavy pouches on their backs, the cops filed out and proceeded to the paddy wagon.

Chief Cowlan was casting dirty looks at Santa while a crowd of openmouthed passers-by watched the scene in wonderment.

Cowlan's cops, feeling very self-conscious and stupid at being the official escort of a holdup man, formed a chain to stack the bags into the vehicle.

From one of the deep pockets of his fur-trimmed red costume, Santa Claus produced a long-range walkie-talkie.

He extended an antenna, put the mike to his lips, pushed the transmitter button, and whistled the first few bars of "Santa Claus Is Coming to Town."

A few seconds later, someone whistling the beginning of "Pennies from Heaven," was heard on the loudspeaker of the set.

Santa Claus smiled at Cowlan as he put the walkie-talkie back into his pocket.

The Chief sized up the situation: This was one of the pre-arranged codes between the fighter pilot and Santa Claus. No one had any way of knowing the tunes or the sequence in which they would be transmitted. Also, it was obvious that Santa Claus was ready to blow himself up and everyone else around him if an attempt were made to overpower him. Cowlan realized that Santa Claus knew he was safe as long as he remained under police protection.

Santa Claus ordered everyone back aboard the paddy wagon.

"I'll let you know what the next stop will be after we get going," he told Cowlan.

The bank manager was now on the telephone, talking to the Deputy Chief at Police Headquarters.

"It was so sudden . . . we never had a chance to mark the bills . . . you've already told me the hijacker had stipulated he didn't want any cash, only gold," the manager said impatiently. "He conned everyone, that's all . . . caught us all with our pants down."

"How much did he take you for?" asked the deputy.

"I don't know exactly," the manager moaned. "I would estimate at least four or five million dollars in bills ranging from thousands to hundreds to ones. . . . What's that? . . . Of course we had no time to take down the serial numbers. . . . I'll tell you what I think . . . you'd better advise every bank in and around L.A. to start marking their bills pronto before he gets to them. . . . Yes, I'll let you know the total amount he got as soon as we can. Police Chiefs holding up banks! Who'd ever dream of such a thing. GOOD-BY!—AND THANKS!"

At Los Angeles Tower, Bragan was on the telephone with the FBI.

"Yes . . . someone just told me about the holdup. . . . All I can tell you is that it's impossible for a little Widgeon to carry that much gold and cash. It just doesn't have the load capability. He's probably got something in mind . . . I don't know what . . . I really can't figure it out . . . We'll just have to wait and see. . . . Your boys found a Widgeon at Van Nuys? That's great! Please get that airplane at any cost. Keep me advised."

Russ Nayten, his hands in his pockets, strolled over to Carmen Marsi. He was taking his time, a smug expression on his face. Nayten's attitude had radically changed. In fact, he now seemed eager to please. In the background, by the plane, his friends were grinning from ear to ear.

"Marsi, you say this is a national emergency? I have a little proposition for you," Nayten said, fondly stroking his mustache.

The head FBI man smiled and began to relax.

"I'm listening, Mr. Nayten. You'll find us most reasonable and co-operative, I assure you."

"Good. You know, I've always dreamed of having my own little twin Gates Learjet. It's the cutest little airplane in the world. Look, Marsi, just like this one."

Nayten pulled an aviation magazine from his back pocket, opened it to the center fold, and showed it to the FBI special agent.

"Isn't it gorgeous?" Nayten asked.

Marsi nodded.

"Yes, I suppose it is, but I don't understand . . ."

"Tell you what, Marsi. I'll swap my Widgeon for a Model 25D, just like the one in this picture."

Marsi's face fell. It was his turn to get excited.

"Why, this is pure blackmail, Nayten. You're no better than that goddamned hijacker. You think you can hold up the U.S. Government like that?"

"Well, our friend up there is doing it and getting away with it. I'm not threatening to kill anybody, or anything. . . . This is strictly a business proposition. Take it or leave it."

"You have some hell of a nerve asking for a million-dollar jet in exchange for this clumsy-looking piece of shit that you couldn't give away . . . this . . . this . . . this fucking Pidgeon, or whatever you call it . . ."

Nayten looked reprovingly at Marsi and shook his head as tears almost welled in his eyes.

"It's not a Pidgeon, it's a Widgeon. You're hurting my feelings. This is an antique . . . a part of Americana . . . an heirloom . . . one of a kind. You don't seem to realize the sacrifice I'm making. Do we have a deal or don't we?"

"OK, you little prick. Taking advantage of a situation like this . . ."

"Now, now, Marsi, let's not get excited. We don't have much time, remember? If you don't mind, I'd like to have this in writing. I don't mean to be disrespectful but I want it okayed by someone in authority in Washington—notary public—the whole bit. Not that I don't trust you, you understand, but I want my little jet by next week on a priority delivery basis. You know how the Government likes to drag things out. I'd get on the phone if I were you."

Marsi's eyes were almost popping out of his head.

"Oh, by the way," Nayten added, "while you're at it, I want all the options. Full solid state radio and radar equipment—all the avionics, the whole works. Also you guys are to pay for my training on this type of aircraft until I get checked out. Put all that on paper and you've got yourself a Widgeon!"

"Oh! You no good bastard!" Marsi screamed as he ran for a phone.

The police paddy wagon pulled up in front of Tiffany's in Beverly Hills.

Under the direction of Santa Claus, the cops picked up everything in sight. They then proceeded to the safes and emptied the contents into bags kindly furnished by the management.

With the exception of Chief Cowlan, the officers seemed to be enjoying themselves now. They had become absolutely legal burglars and could act out their craziest fantasies. With big smiles on their faces at the looks of the astonished people they were robbing, they gleefully went about their business, having the time of their lives.

Once everyone was back aboard the wagon, Santa Claus summoned Cowlan to his side.

"Chief," he whispered, "at our next stop, you'd better have a couple of men watch this van while we go about our business. I don't want it to get held up. We're beginning to attract attention and I think I noticed some suspicious-looking characters following us in a car."

Cowlan's eyes bulged. He would have loved to choke Santa Claus.

At Police Headquarters, the Deputy Chief was on the telephone trying to co-ordinate things with the FBI. His temper was rising as the agent kept asking more questions.

"He picked up about five million dollars in gems . . . that's all I know," the Deputy Chief said irritably. ". . . No. There is no pattern to this operation . . . these guys are like chess players . . . you can't anticipate their next move. . . . No, I don't have enough men to watch every bank and jewelry store in town. What good would it do anyway? It's obvious this Santa Claus has no intention of holding up similar places twice in a row. His disguise is perfect. You can't even tell how much he weighs. He's got the world by the balls right now."

"What about trying to grab *him* by the balls, and force him to whistle his little tunes?" asked the FBI man.

"Forget it. He's liable to blow up the Chief and ten other guys. Besides, even if we captured him, what would happen if he whistled the wrong thing? The hijacker would blast the 747 out of the sky. We can't take the responsibility. The President doesn't want to hear about it. We aren't supposed to take any chances. We'll just do as the President says. Look, you, don't tell me I'm being negative. I resent your attitude . . . I'm not telling you how to run your business, so don't tell me how to run mine!"

Senator Wadsworth was standing in front of the partition separating the economy- and first-class sections of the Boeing 747, holding the cabin intercom mike. H. J. Transcombe and his two sidekicks had crept up behind him from the first-class cabin and were trying to look over his shoulder.

"Ladies and gentlemen, I'm Felton Wadsworth and I suppose most of you know who I am," the Senator said. "I was just up in the cockpit discussing the situation with the Captain. I've also spoken with our hijacker. I can assure you that everything is under control. The ransom is being delivered at this moment. He seems to be a reasonable man who has no intention of harming us. I am confident that it will turn out all right." Wadsworth paused to survey his audience and to assess how he was going over. The passengers were receptive and he was in command. He continued his little speech.

"As you know, however, we have the dubious distinction of being participants in the first hijacking of this type. It's something new to the authorities and, naturally, it will take a little time for everything to get organized. We will not be back on the ground for another three or four hours, and when we get back, I'll conduct a full-scale investigation of this incident. I hope you'll all co-operate with me."

"You're a good guy, Senator," Bruce the salesman shouted as he rose to his feet in the back. "I'm going to vote for you when you run for President. Have a drink, Wadsworth, and join the fun!"

A few timid cheers of approval went up in the cabin.

"I don't mind if I do," Wadsworth said, smiling.

"Hey, girls," Bruce yelled, "give the Senator a drink."

The Commander of the U.S.S. *Barracuda* was looking through his periscope. He could clearly see the Boeing 747 and the fighter plane above him. The submerged nuclear submarine was lying dead in the water right in the middle of the circle the two aircraft were describing. He called for his executive officer.

"Put on the scrambler, get Admiral Casters, and give me a mike."

"Aye aye, sir. The Admiral is on. Scrambler set."

"Admiral," the Commander said, "I'm in perfect position for a clean shot. I must tell you, however, that the fighter is following the airliner very closely—no more than about half a mile. I could get him without hitting the 747 but I'm afraid the combined blast of my missile and the fighter's weapons, when they blow up, could certainly damage PGA 81. In my opinion, there's only a fifty-fifty chance this might work. Personally, I would not dare to take this responsibility."

"Thank you, Commander. Stay where you are and don't do anything until I let you know."

"Aye aye, Admiral."

Grant's voice came over the loudspeakers of Los Angeles Tower.

"Bragan, it is now 1530 local or T minus one hour and thirty minutes. How are we doing?"

"Your friend is holding up places and the supersonics should be here in about one hour and fifteen minutes."

"What about the Widgeon?"

"We found one at Van Nuys but the owner gave us a little trouble. He demanded a new Gates Learjet 25D in trade, which sort of slowed things down until we got an OK from Washington. In any event, it will be departing shortly and should be landing here within the hour."

Grant could not help laughing good-naturedly.

"Some people really have no scruples . . . Look, Bragan, I want the owner of the Widgeon to bring the airplane to LA International by himself. When my colleague arrives, I would like the owner to check him out since these things are old and have their peculiarities. I don't want any 'unfortunate accident' on takeoff. So be sure the guy is there to brief him on how every gadget works."

"OK. We'll see to it—LA Tower."

"Bragan, I also want a plentiful supply of heavy duty plastic bags placed next to the Widgeon. One more thing. Don't put any electronic beepers, homing devices, time bombs or other gimmicks aboard the airplane. I know what to look for. Let me caution you that if I don't see my friend flying this thing next to me at the proper time, it will be just too bad."

"Roger—Bragan."

Admiral Alfred P. Casters was back on the telephone with the White House.

"If he only stayed a little further behind the airliner, Mr. President, the submarine commander feels we'd have a good chance. . . . Yes, sir, I'm a little disappointed, but I'll let him know at once that you have vetoed it. . . . You're right, Mr. President. It could be catastrophic if something went wrong. . . . Yes, sir. I'll tell him to dive deep and to proceed to San Francisco as scheduled . . ."

At Los Angeles Tower, Mike Ayno tapped Bragan on the shoulder.

"Tom, the French Minister of Foreign Affairs is on the phone."

"What does he want?"

"He was here for an international conference. There's a special

Air France jet that was supposed to leave at two-thirty and take him back to France via the polar route. He says it's imperative he should be in Paris in the morning and wants to know why he can't take off."

"Tell him he'll have to stand by, like everyone else."

Ayno picked up the phone and got back to Bragan a few seconds later.

"Tom, he says France cannot wait."

"France will wait. Tell him that."

A small group of pilots and mechanics, curious to know what the FBI was doing at Van Nuys Airport, had gathered around the Widgeon.

They saw Carmen Marsi running from the terminal. His tie was hanging loose around his neck. He was out of breath and perspiring profusely. He shot a murderous look at Russ Nayten.

"Here are the papers, duly notarized, you sonofabitch."

Nayten smiled at Marsi and the onlookers, enjoying the limelight, playing it very cool for the benefit of the gallery.

"Why, thank you! Delighted to be of service."

"OK," Marsi said, still panting, "now you've got to fly this thing to Los Angeles International Airport. They're waiting for you there. You'll have to check out the man who's going to fly this bucket of bolts."

The FBI special agent stared with contempt at the ancient, battered high-wing aircraft which really looked in miserable shape. The left strut was low, making the wing dip toward the ground, giving the plane a lopsided air. The paint was peeling. The Widgeon was full of unsightly seams and patches. Pieces of tape placed over cracks in the Plexiglas windows had become unstuck. Hanging loosely, they looked like bandages fluttering in the wind.

"Hold it, Marsi!" Nayten gasped. "This was not part of our arrangement. Now you want me to be a ferry pilot and instructor besides. I'm not going anywhere near that hijacker. No way!"

"You're the only one who can fly this junk heap. You've got to do it," Marsi screamed.

"I just ain't going. Period!"

"OK. The deal is off. We'll find another Widgeon. I understand there's one at Compton Airport. You've just lost yourself a Gates Learjet."

"Just a second, Marsi. I've changed my mind. As a ferry pilot and instructor and, considering the circumstances, I think I'm entitled to danger pay. Besides, I have to get back here later. I'll accept my standard rate of two hundred dollars an hour from the moment I leave until I return to this airport. OK?"

"You miserable, no good . . ."

"Do you want me to go or don't you?" Nayten kept pressing, his eyes shining with greed.

"OK. But you just wait until I get my hands on you after this is over."

"It's perfectly legal, Marsi. Just one thing. Put it down on paper while I check out the airplane and do a preflight inspection."

Continuing on its rounds, the police paddy wagon stopped in front of a ground-floor establishment specializing in the exchange of foreign currencies.

The cops got out, invaded the place and picked up all the paper money. Japanese yens, German marks, French francs, British pounds, and Swiss francs were stuffed into pouches with great gusto while Santa Claus observed the scene through his dark glasses.

"OK, gentlemen, that's enough," Santa Claus said once he was satisfied the place had been cleaned out. "Let's go."

The face of the Police Chief was the picture of wretched frustration. Cowlan felt ridiculous. He looked on the verge of apoplexy, about to burst a blood vessel.

As the wagon pulled away, a curious crowd began to rubberneck in front of the ransacked foreign currency exchange office, wondering what had happened. No one knew for sure, not even the employees. It had all been so fast.

The Deputy Chief, sitting in his office at Police Headquarters, was again on the telephone, arguing with the FBI.

"He just pulled another job at Perera's. . . . They figure a little over two and a half million dollars in foreign bills. . . . No identification marks, no serial numbers. . . . How the hell should I know where he's liable to go next? . . . We don't operate on hunches in this department. We work on the basis of solid information. . . . Don't keep asking me stupid questions, I'm just keeping score."

CHAPTER 20

Grant kept the tail of the airliner in sight as he sipped the last of his coffee and listened to one of his radios tuned to KFWB news.

The announcer was telling him all he wanted to know about the progress of Santa Claus. He was also keeping him up to date on the activities of the civilian and military authorities in various parts of the country.

Grant wondered why the Government had never taken positive steps to enact legislation imposing a news blackout in cases of this nature.

It had been determined on several occasions that information supplied by newscasters gave hijackers an added advantage. It obviously helped them to plan their strategy, but no one seemed to care or want to do anything about it. Freedom of the press was all right, but there were limits, Grant thought. This was illogical. The hunters operated in a fish bowl while the hunted continued to move in perfect secrecy.

"The hijacking has now been in progress for almost three hours," the newscaster said. "As previously announced, we have assembled a distinguished panel of experts for a round-table discussion. They will give us their views on what could possibly motivate someone to attempt such an undertaking and what is likely to happen before and after it's all over. We have Dr. Samuel Blackstone, the noted psychiatrist, who has made a study of over fifty case histories and interviewed some thirty captured would-be air pirates. He is the author of the recent best-selling book *Hijacking—The Answer*, available at all bookstores for seven ninety-five in hard cover and at one dollar and seventy-five cents in paperback. We also have the Reverend Leonard Vegner, a prison chaplain of considerable experience, Congresswoman Donna Tsupnick, Liberal of the Fifty-first District, and anchor man Norman Sternfeld for analysis and commentary. But, first, this brief message from your independent life insurance agent . . ."

Grant turned up the volume. He didn't want to miss this for anything.

"We'll start with you, Dr. Blackstone," anchor man Sternfeld said. "Is there a predictable pattern to such behavior—to such irresponsible acts of . . . lunacy . . . for lack of a better word?"

"In reply to your question, I have found that most hijackers— or terrorists of every description for that matter—are homosexuals or, quite often, latent homosexuals. They sublimate their desires and fantasies by initiating some spectacular action during which they will become the focus of attention for a certain length of time. Money is usually not the primary object of the operation but exhibitionism—recognition of what they think is their superior intellect. With few exceptions, they were probably frustrated as children by their mothers. 'The repressed suckling instinct' is my personal terminology for it. This is explained at length in my book, by the way. I believe you mentioned that it is presently sold in bookstores, although I understand copies are fast running out."

"Yes, I did speak about your book, Dr. Blackstone, but to get back to the hijacker . . ."

"Yes—er, I lost my train of thought. Well, you see, I have concluded that these people want to commit suicide. They are bent on self-destruction but they don't dare kill themselves. Therefore, they seek to be obliterated by some anonymous force over which they have no control—such as the police, for example."

"Dr. Blackstone," Sternfeld asked, "doesn't it seem that in this particular case, the hijacker is *not* an exhibitionist? In fact, he has gone to great length to conceal his identity. He is apparently not looking for recognition. He is nothing but a voice."

"Aha!" Blackstone replied triumphantly. "That is exactly the point. It is the exception that proves the rule."

"I'm not quite sure I understand, but we'll get back to you in a moment, Dr. Blackstone, after giving our other panel members the opportunity of stating their opinions. What do you think, Reverend Vegner? I hear you've made extensive inroads into the psychology of prison inmates."

"That is true. I'm afraid I do not entirely agree with the renowned Dr. Blackstone. I am only a prison chaplain, but it has been my experience in the penitentiaries that such individuals actually crave, even relish sympathy and admiration. Some of them hate their surroundings, others really love incarceration, feeling it is the womb, the discipline they lacked at home. A few think they are against the war and take refuge in prison to escape the draft, but they are confused. Under the guise of pacifism, they seek revenge against society or the so-called establishment. Basically, I would say, it is not a sexual matter, as Dr. Blackstone chooses to believe. They are all poor, misguided men, who have never really found their place in the world. We must be kind and show compassion and understanding . . ."

"I've never heard such drivel in my life!" Dr. Blackstone interrupted. "I'm totally against this philosophy of coddling which the Reverend here is trying to propagate. Let him stick to religion and let competent people in the field of psychoanalysis tackle the problem . . ."

"More harm has been done by you shrinks planting ideas of sexual aberration my prisoners have never even heard of and, believe me, there's very little they don't know," Reverend Vegner retorted. "What makes you such an expert on homosexuality and exhibitionism, Blackstone? I would say it takes one to know one . . ."

"Now look here, you prayer peddler . . ." Dr. Blackstone cut in, "you just go sing your hymns and don't stick your nose into things of which you are totally ignorant . . ."

Grant was almost hysterical with laughter.

"Now, now, gentlemen," anchor man Sternfeld intervened, "I must ask you to keep this discussion on a higher plane. I understand and appreciate the intensity of your feelings regarding the approach to the problem, but our discussion will not be helped by trading insults. Gentlemen . . . please! . . . We will return after station identification . . ."

"This is KFWB news, Los Angeles. You give us twenty-two minutes and we give you the world," an announcer said. "And now, a word from . . ."

LA Tower broke in on Grant's loudspeaker.

"Shadow 81—Bragan."

Grant regretfully turned down the volume on the radio station.

"LA Tower—Shadow 81. Go ahead."

"In a short while, the Widgeon will be taking off from Van Nuys. You will, therefore, see him on your radar scope. Same thing for the ten supersonics. I am advising you of these movements so that you will be aware that they are not hostile."

"Roger—Shadow 81."

Grant couldn't wait to turn KFWB back on. Congresswoman Donna Tsupnick was now talking. He recognized the loud, grating, raucous voice which was her trademark. She was into one of her long-winded, endless tirades.

". . . the poisonous atmosphere created by the Vietnam war is influencing everything in this country. The Vietnam amorality is corrupting every sense of decency. My views on the matter are very simple. It is an obvious lack of leadership on the part of the administration and the brass at the head of our Armed Forces. What do you expect when we have a bunch of middle-aged juvenile delinquents running the nation—and I mean from the top on down . . ."

"Er . . . yes, Mrs. Tsupnick," anchor man Sternfeld interrupted, "but we're discussing a hijacking and we seem to be digressing . . ."

"Would you please let me finish what I have to say, Mr. Sternfeld," Donna Tsupnick rasped. "I know we're talking about a hijacking and there's nothing much we can do at this point regardless of whether the man has sexual or religious problems. All I want to say is that he is a product of the examples of corruption furnished by our leaders. Former governors going to jail for embezzling, district attorneys on trial for fixing cases, state supreme court justices impeached and disbarred for lining their pockets, police department detectives in penitentiaries for murder and dealing in narcotics, high government officials indicted for perjury, and I could go on and on. But I can tell you that I will definitely call for a congressional investigation after this incident is terminated. I want to find out how and why such a thing could happen when we're spending billions upon billions on defense at the expense of welfare, schools, housing, mass transit, etc. I will introduce a bill . . ."

"I'm sorry, Mrs. Congresswoman, but we're running out of time. I have just thirty seconds left for summing up and a comment. Thank you, Mrs. Tsupnick," Sternfeld said. "I certainly don't want to be accused of 'instant analysis' without being in possession of all the facts," the anchor man continued, "but I think there's definitely something wrong in all this. We have a right to be protected against aggression and our leaders have failed us—just as they have failed us in Vietnam. Let this be a lesson for those

209

who will shortly be running for office. This is Norman Sternfeld. Thank you for listening and stay tuned to this station for further developments."

The police paddy wagon halted in front of the brokerage firm of "Duncan, Osborne, Finch and Peters" in downtown Los Angeles.

By now accustomed to their little routine, the cops knew exactly what to do. They proceeded to the back room where the safes were opened. Under the guidance of Santa Claus, they collected bundles upon bundles of negotiable securities.

"All right, gentlemen, that will be sufficient for today," Santa Claus said, nodding approvingly.

Under the flabbergasted gaze of the branch manager surrounded by his account executives, Santa Claus, the Chief, and his men climbed back aboard the wagon. There was little room to move inside the vehicle loaded down with bags and pouches of dollar bills, foreign currency, and jewelry.

Chief Cowlan shut the doors.

"OK," Santa Claus said, "let's get to the airport."

On the way, the paddy wagon overtook a Brinks armored truck stopped in front of a red light. Santa Claus spotted it through one of the rear windows.

"Hold everything, Chief. Tell the driver to stop. I want that Brinks truck to come with us to the airport—just for good measure—in case we missed something in town."

"Don't you think you have enough already?" Cowlan grimaced.

"I don't want any arguments," Santa Claus hissed as his hand reached for the wires sticking out of his belt. "You get me that truck. Throw out the crew that's aboard. Have a couple of your men take it over and follow us. Hurry!"

Cowlan heaved a sigh of despair and gave instructions to the driver of the paddy wagon.

The Brinks guards never knew what hit them. The element of surprise was complete.

The paddy wagon allowed the Brinks truck to pass it on the left. It then turned on its sirens, overtook the armored vehicle, ran it off the middle of the road, and cornered it against the curb.

The guards inside the truck reacted instinctively. They reached for their shotguns and stuck the barrels out through the gunports in the front, sides, and rear of the vehicle.

Protected by four of his men, Chief Cowlan, his hands above his head, ran to the Brinks driver and identified himself. It took him about five minutes to convince the guards this was not a fake holdup—but for real.

The driver insisted on checking with his dispatcher to find out what all this nonsense was about. The Brinks headquarters got in touch with the Police Department. To the guards' astonishment, the Deputy Chief said it was OK and to do just as Cowlan said.

The four Brinks men were abandoned on the sidewalk, clutching their shotguns, feeling foolish and embarrassed, grinning self-consciously at astonished passers-by.

Two of Cowlan's cops jumped into the armored vehicle and followed the paddy wagon.

Santa Claus sat in the rear of the police van, occasionally glancing through a window to make sure the truck was staying close behind.

Russ Nayten was in the cockpit of the Widgeon. He was frantically pushing switches, pumping the primers, the fuel mixture control levers, throttles, and cursing like mad at having a generally hard time getting the engines to catch.

After several tries, the left engine whined, wheezed, coughed, spurted, and, just as the battery seemed about to die, it started.

Nayten closed his eyes, as if in grateful prayer, then brought back the throttle to idle at 800 RPM. He began to work feverishly on the second power plant, but, as if frozen, the right propeller refused to spin.

With the left engine idling, Nayten jumped out of the plane carrying a small aluminum stepladder and ran over to the balky propeller for a visual inspection.

He couldn't spot anything wrong. Nayten scratched his head, stamped his foot, cursed again, and kicked the tire of the right wheel in frustration. He hurt his toe, let out a yell, climbed on the ladder, then grabbed the tip of one of the propeller blades which he shook furiously from left to right in the hope of loosening it up.

Nayten ran back inside the airplane, hopping on his one good foot, sweating, while the FBI agents and his friends looked on skeptically from a distance, fearful the Widgeon would blow up.

He went once more through the whole procedure of starting the right engine, repriming and pumping the throttle wildly. The propeller spun reluctantly a couple of times, stopped, then finally started turning.

Nayten looked out of the cockpit window with a joyous expression, then smiled triumphantly at Carmen Marsi.

Advancing the overhead throttles, he released the brakes.

The Widgeon waddled off the grass like a crippled duck, turned onto the taxiway, and rolled slowly toward the active runway.

"I hope he breaks his neck in that contraption," Marsi grunted.

Nayten reached the runway threshold and ran up the power to 1,800 RPM for a mag check and verification of carburetor heat. The engines backfired several times and seemed about to shake loose from the wings.

The airplane had the airport all to itself, as the tower cleared Nayten for takeoff anytime he was ready.

He debated for a moment whether he should use Runway 34 left, which was eight thousand feet long, or the parallel runway, 34 right, measuring four thousand feet. He was at the edge of the shorter runway he always used under normal circumstances. It was amply sufficient and, now that everything seemed to be working—more or less—he didn't want to waste any time.

The Widgeon carefully nuzzled onto 34 right and lined itself up, pointing its long nose northward.

The airplane began to roll as Nayten added power but seemed hesitant to pick up speed. Halfway down the strip, the engines sounded as if they were intermittently cutting out and the Widgeon looked as if it would never get off the ground. At last, the tail lifted as the plane pulled up timidly with one wing low but mushed right back down onto the concrete. It roared and squealed as it skidded into a slight cross-wind, bounced back off the ground, then hit the runway again. It pulled up sharply in a nose high attitude, finally airborne. It was hanging on the props, on the verge of stalling, but just made it before running out of runway.

Nayten picked up a little altitude as he retracted the landing gear, crabbed into the wind, and trimmed the airplane.

Half a mile north of the airport, about five hundred feet off the ground, he made a 180-degree turn and flew back over the runway.

Swooping down, he made a low pass over the heads of Marsi, the other FBI agents, his friends, and spectators as he looked out of the cockpit window wearing an ecstatic expression. He was bouncing up and down on his seat for joy.

Marsi shook his fist at the tail of the Widgeon as it laboriously gained altitude, banked, and climbed on course to LA International.

In downtown Los Angeles, TV crews were taping the scene in front of the Bank of America. Mikes in hand, network correspondents were doing "man in the street" interviews.

A group gathered around a reporter who was questioning a spinsterly-looking woman of about fifty.

"Madam, may I ask who you are, what you do for a living, and how you feel about what's happening at the moment?"

"I'm Edna Zakovitch, I'm a schoolteacher—fourth grade—and I think it's shameful. This terrible, violent person, this . . . this . . . monster, is becoming a hero to the children. They were listening to him on transistor radios during classes. My goodness, they're comparing him to Superman and some of the characters in those foolish cartoons on television. Something should be done about him. Why, do you know, a little boy in my class just told me before recess . . ."

". . . Er . . . thank you, Miss Zakovitch . . . we understand how shocked you are," the reporter said as he turned toward another prospect. "What about you, sir?" he asked a revolutionary type, real cool, in an outrageous white suit. The tall, skinny man wore a wide-brimmed hat and sported a Vandyke. Chains and medallions were dangling around his neck. He was alternately leaning or slouching on a silver cane he gripped in his right hand, while puffing on a little cigar which he held between his teeth.

"I'm Leroy Hastings. I'm an independent businessman . . . sort of a free-lance entrepreneur . . . know what I mean? . . . I do a little bit of this and a little bit of that," he said, waving his cigar under the reporter's nose. "Promotional ventures, you might call 'em . . . Don't put all my eggs in one basket, man . . . know what I mean? . . ."

The reporter was sorry he'd chosen him.

"Yes, I think I get the picture, mister . . ."

"Hastings . . . LEEROY Hastings, Leroy means 'the king' in French." He smiled condescendingly, straight into the camera, flashing a gold front tooth. "Well, since you're askin' me, man, I think the dude's OK . . . know what I mean? . . . He's showin' the establishment he ain't gonna let nobody push him around . . . y'dig, man?"

Hastings grabbed the mike out of the reporter's hand.

"Right on, man," he shouted. "If you're listenin', I'm for you, baby . . . know what I mean? . . ."

"I'm sure we know what you mean," the reporter said, tugging to regain possession of his mike, ". . . er . . . please let go . . . er . . . thank you . . . Mr. . . . let go . . . er . . . Mr. . . . Hastings."

Across the street, a correspondent from another network got hold of a fat, middle-aged, sweaty-looking man.

"What about you, sir? What do you think?"

"I'm Milton Felzer, I'm an accountant and also an attorney. I'm originally from New York. Are we on 'live' or is this a tape you intend to edit?"

"Oh no, sir! We're 'live,' " the reporter said proudly.

"Good. I don't want to be misquoted."

"You won't be Mr. Felzer."

"What I'd like to know," Felzer snarled, "is who's paying for all this? Airplanes flying around . . . gold—twenty million, no less . . . robberies in broad daylight by the Police Department . . . who's paying? . . . PGA? . . . The Government? . . . The insurance companies? . . . Or is it the taxpayer?"

"Well . . . hum . . . I'm sure I don't know, Mr. Felzer . . . and . . ."

"Of course you don't know. You don't have to tell me that. Do you realize how many cops are being put on overtime right now? The Armed Forces are presently on alert all over the West Coast, if not from one end of the country to the other. Do you have any idea what this is going to cost? And do you know who's going to foot the bill?" Felzer screamed.

". . . er . . . no . . . not really . . . Mr. . . ."

"The taxpayer! that's who's going to be paying for these shenanigans. As an experienced accountant and tax attorney, I recommend the following until the matter is clarified. I would advise the taxpayers to refuse to file their statements or to deduct a pro-rata amount from their returns for what was stolen from the treasury. Otherwise, you'll see, it's the little guy who's going to be paying for this, just as he always does. I think . . ."

". . . Well . . . yeah . . . OK . . ." The reporter stopped Felzer, who was beginning to like the sound of his own voice. "Thank you for giving us a chance to air your views, sir . . ."

"Why don't you ask me what I think?" a man in a tattered shirt and torn pants shouted from one of the back rows in the crowd.

The reporter looked with surprise, as the man, a derelict of about sixty, made his way to the camera holding a brown paper bag "by the neck."

The man took a swig, wiped his mouth with the back of his hand, and, swaying a little, looked the reporter in the eye, then winked.

"You wanna know what I think?" he belched. "I think this is a Commie plot engineered by the CIA . . . that's what I think," he slurred, as he turned around and smiled victoriously at the bystanders.

The Widgeon made a sloppy landing on Runway 25 right at Los Angeles International.

Bragan got on the mike and told Nayten not to bother using the taxiways. He instructed him to make a U turn on the runway proper and to proceed back to the threshold. Once there, Bragan added, Nayten would have to make another 180-degree turn into the wind to line up the airplane in takeoff position on the twelve-thousand-foot runway.

As soon as the props stopped spinning, the Widgeon was immediately surrounded by police officers and airport security guards. All the men were under strict orders to keep intruders away. They were not to touch the airplane or interfere with Santa Claus in any manner after he arrived.

A gas truck pulled up to fuel the Widgeon to capacity as Nayten got out of the airplane to be greeted by the unusual welcoming committee.

In the economy-class section of PGA 81, Senator C. Felton Wadsworth was holding his sixth scotch. He was flying high. So were most of the other passengers, including Horace J. Transcombe and his two remaining loyal flunkies.

The Senator was standing in the middle of an aisle, conducting a community sing. Inebriated voices were bellowing "In the Good Old Summer Time."

Bruce the salesman and his friend Dick had recruited two other gay blades and formed a barbershop quartet to provide the background harmony for Wadsworth.

Passengers were standing in the aisles, their arms around each other's shoulders, glasses in hand, waving for more drinks.

Laura, Bea, and the other stewardesses were racing up and down with trays of liquor.

No one seemed to give a damn any more, except for the three women passengers with children. The infants were sleeping, in spite of the din. The mothers had huddled together for moral support.

Bragan called Grant.

"Shadow 81—LA Tower."

"Go ahead, Bragan," Grant replied, his voice breaking slightly.

"The Widgeon's here. No sign of Santa Claus."

"He'll be there soon. Stand by for further instructions after his arrival," Grant said, his voice breaking again, as if he were in pain.

"Roger—Bragan."

The chief controller turned to Mike Ayno.

"Did you notice anything strange, or is it my imagination?"

"He sounded tired to me, Tom. Maybe the circling is getting to him too, or something."

"No. I don't think so. He seems to have a problem, Mike. I'm beginning to wonder if he's all right?"

"He can drop dead, as far as I'm concerned. I hope he has a heart attack."

"That's not the point, Mike. Captain Hadley's listening too. I'm afraid he might feel the same way we do and try to make a break for it. I just hope he doesn't. If anything is really happening to the hijacker, it might incite him to take PGA 81 along with him. This may sound preposterous to you but I'm praying he's OK."

Grant was feeling an irresistible urge to go to the bathroom.

In his planning, he had figured he would be able to last for the duration of the hijacking operation. He had conducted several tests while crossing the Pacific on the *Solitude* and had found that he could contain himself without difficulty for up to eight hours.

But, he suddenly realized, he had not been under pressure and the experiments had taken place at sea level. He had now been sitting in the airplane for more than four hours since his departure from Baja California.

The necessity of having to go to the toilet was beginning to interfere seriously with his concentration. He was feeling dizzy, then drowsy. His breath was getting short and his vision was becoming blurry.

"I can't foul up this thing just because I have to go to the can," he muttered angrily to himself.

There was only one thing to do. He relieved himself into the thermos bottle now empty of coffee and screwed the cap back on. At least he would be all right for a few more hours.

But the drowsiness persisted. In fact, Grant was beginning to experience a feeling of euphoria.

For a moment, he thought he might have blood poisoning. He found it more and more difficult to breathe and to think lucidly.

Grant checked his oxygen mask. There was nothing wrong with it. He began to sweat and felt about to pass out. He wondered what the hell was wrong with him.

And then his eye caught the oxygen regulator gauge. The needle was fluttering next to the zero mark.

Grant felt a twinge in his bowels. There was a leak somewhere. He knew he had an eight-hour reserve when he had taken off.

His head was pounding. He had to make an immediate decision. But, above all, his voice must not betray his predicament.

"Hadley—Shadow 81," Grant said, as firmly as he could manage.

"PGA 81—go ahead."

"Descend . . ." Grant slurred, "descend . . ." he said slowly, "descend at once to ten thousand."

Hadley was now certain something was wrong.

"Shadow 81, are you feeling all right?"

Grant gritted his teeth and forced himself to breathe every last whiff of oxygen his nostrils could inhale. His eyes were almost popping but he could think clearly for the moment, although he knew it wouldn't last.

"Dive immediately, or else," he managed to shout. "I've got my finger on the trigger, Hadley. This time I mean it!"

It took Hadley a fraction of a second to decide he couldn't take a chance. He pulled back the power and went into a steep descent.

Grant followed him, fighting for a breath of oxygen, like a fish struggling to stay alive out of his element. He wasn't capable of concentrating on his gauges. He just kept the tail of the airliner in sight as a reference point.

In the cabin the singing stopped and was replaced by shrieks of panic as the passengers tried to grab on to something before they went sprawling along the aisles. Glasses shattered as trays went flying. Ears popped as people turned livid.

The co-pilot got on the cabin intercom to try to explain what was happening. His voice was drowned out in the chaos.

Within three minutes the 747 had let down from thirty-six thousand feet to twenty thousand. The color was gradually returning to Grant's cheeks but he was still pale and nauseous.

At fifteen thousand feet, Grant removed his oxygen mask and tried to breathe normally. He could focus on his gauges now but he was still panting.

Grant began to feel normal once again as the airplanes passed through twelve thousand feet. He rubbed his forehead, swallowed hard to clear his ears, and wet his lips.

"Hadley, level off at ten thousand and resume circling as before."

"Roger," Hadley said, as evenly as he could. "Shadow 81," he added, "you know we're going to be using a lot more fuel at this altitude. We won't be able to last too long. Neither will you, for that matter."

"You worry about your own problems. Don't be so concerned about mine. How much time do you have left at 160 knots?"

Hadley looked at Faust, who raised three fingers, then a fourth, then shook his hand to express doubt.

"Shadow 81, we have three hours—four at the most."

"That'll do, Hadley, that is if they don't try to stall us on the ground. Bragan? you there?"

"I'm here—Bragan."

"Did you read us?"

"We've got the message. We'll activate."

"Good!"

Grant took a deep breath.

The paddy wagon, followed by the Brinks armored truck, stopped by the side of the Widgeon sitting on the runway.

Santa Claus ordered the police to transfer all pouches and bags from the wagon into the large heavy-duty plastic bags Grant had ordered Bragan to provide. He then asked for all the pouches in the armored truck to be dumped on the runway for inspection.

With the help of the officers, Santa Claus sorted out the Brinks pouches. Those containing coins were discarded. The selection consisted of about fifteen pouches of bills of large denomination, which were also placed into plastic bags.

Together with the items brought in the paddy wagon, the bundles of Brinks loot were placed alongside the fuselage of the Widgeon, ready to be loaded after the arrival of the gold from Fort Knox.

Nayten was observing the scene, dazzled and openmouthed, as he tried to make a mental calculation of the fabulous amounts of money lying at his feet.

He was shaken out of his reverie by Santa Claus ordering the owner of the aircraft to step out of the crowd of cops and guards surrounding the Widgeon.

Nayten approached timidly, nervously twisting his fishing hat in his hands.

"Did you fly this thing in here? What's your name?" Santa Claus asked gruffly.

"Nayten, sir—Russ Nayten. The airplane belongs to me. I just brought it in from Van Nuys." Nayten cringed, swallowing hard.

Santa Claus turned to Chief Cowlan, who was standing next to him.

"Tell this guy what the score is."

"He's wired with dynamite. Don't touch him. Just do as he says."

Nayten's hat dropped out of his hands.

"Dy . . . dy . . . dy? . . ." he stuttered, shaking from head to foot, his eyes bulging, his Adam's apple bobbing up and down.

"Relax, Nayten," Santa Claus tried to reassure him. "Just co-operate and you'll be OK. Did they hide any electronic beepers or explosives on board the airplane at Van Nuys?"

"No, sir. I swear. No one came near the aircraft. I'm the only one who touched it."

"What about right here? Anyone go aboard with any packages?"

"Absolutely not. Believe me. Just a gasoline truck to top off the tanks. I got in a few minutes before you arrived. I didn't move from here, never let the airplane out of my sight."

"You'd better be telling the truth."

"I am, sir. I am," Nayten bleated. "As one fellow pilot to another, I would never mislead you and . . ."

"Oh, shut up and get into the cockpit. I want you to check me out on the panel."

"Can't you go in by yourself?" Nayten pleaded as he looked, fascinated with fear, at the wires protruding from Santa Claus's belt. "I'm sure I can explain everything you want to know from the outside, through the window . . ."

"Get into the cockpit," Santa Claus bellowed.

Santa Claus went aboard first and sat in the left seat. Nayten squirmed into the right seat.

"OK, show me what's wrong with this piece of garbage."

"Oh, it's in fine shape . . . sir. I only use it to go fishing on Sundays, when the weather's good," Nayten said diffidently, sounding like a used-car salesman. "Just a few minor items here and there . . . but, I assure you, it goes like a bomb once it's in the air . . ."

Santa Claus gave Nayten a dirty look.

". . . I mean like lightning . . . Ha! . . . Just a figure of speech . . . stupid of me to be talking about bombs at a time like this . . . Ha! . . . Ha! . . ."

"Cut out the crap. I've flown this type of airplane before. Now, I'm asking you again. What is there that I should know about?"

"Well, you see, the left magneto on the right engine needs a little work. The landing gear leaves something to be desired . . . so . . . you've got to give it a lot of left rudder on takeoff. But, on the water, it's fine, really . . . fine . . ."

"What makes you think I'm going on the water?" Santa Claus scowled.

"Nothing, sir. Nothing." Nayten cringed. "Since you asked for a Widgeon, I just assumed . . ."

"Stop assuming and get on with it."

"Right away, sir. Well . . . you see . . . the radios are getting a little old. If the VHF cuts out, you've got to hit it on the top right-hand side, like this, a couple of times, gently, of course, but only once in a while . . ."

"What about the VOR and the ADF?"

"They're pretty good. Maybe a couple of degrees off. If the needles stick or fluctuate, tap the dials gently with one finger. That'll loosen them up."

"Give me the power settings."

"She cruises at about 120 MPH at 2,450 RPM. This particular airplane has a tendency to sink fast when you reduce power on landing, so I would bring the throttles back very gradually. The left float is a little bent. But, otherwise, it's fine . . . really. Watch your air speed on takeoff . . . with the kind of load you'll be carrying . . . none of my business, of course . . . you'd better wait until it hits 90 miles per hour or so before you lift off . . . but . . . you'll be fine . . ."

"Anything else?"

"No, sir. That's about it."

"You're sure now? I've got a good mind to take you along with me, just in case something should go wrong."

"Oh no, sir. You don't want to do that. I'd only be in the way . . . dead weight . . . Ha! . . . Ha! . . ." Nayten laughed hysterically, in a high-pitched falsetto. "You'll be fine, sir . . . honest! . . . I guarantee it . . ."

"You stick around outside in case I need you if I have any trouble getting this thing started. Now get off."

Nayten felt so relieved he almost managed to smile.

"Yes, sir! . . . Thank you, sir . . . Have a good trip now . . ."

"Get off and shut up, goddammit! You talk too much."

Santa Claus waited until Nayten had left. He then proceeded to inspect the cockpit and the cabin before stepping out to check the exterior. He had to satisfy himself the owner of the airplane had not lied to him and that no electronic tracking equipment had been hidden aboard or taped to an outside surface.

The ten supersonic fighters from Fort Knox landed in rapid succession on Runway 25 left. They were instructed to taxi at once to the threshold of Runway 25 right and to park next to the Widgeon. They opened their hatches, exposing their cargo of glittering bars of gold.

Santa Claus watched the unloading as he stood next to Chief Cowlan.

"Have your men count out one thousand, one-kilo ingots. I want them to be placed inside plastic bags then spread out along the entire length of the floor of the airplane. Next, place the pouches inside the other plastic bags on top of the gold. Tell them to make sure the weight is distributed evenly. I don't want to be tail-heavy."

"What do you want us to do with the rest of the gold?" Cowlan wanted to find out.

"That's all I can carry right now. Have your boys prepare the rest in more plastic bags. I'll be back for another load later. Hurry it up!"

Grant's voice came over the loudspeakers of Los Angeles Tower. "Bragan—Shadow 81. It is now 1650 local or T minus ten minutes. Give me a status report."

"Santa Claus is here. So are the supersonics. The Widgeon is being loaded. It'll take a while before they're through."

"OK. Maintain radio silence from now on and until I get back to you."

"Roger—Bragan."

Grant tuned one of his radios, put the mike close to his lips, and began to whistle "Goldfinger."

Santa Claus heard him, took out his walkie-talkie, and answered by whistling "Happy Days Are Here Again."

Business was getting slow for Barney Alcott in the pressroom. There was little talk now between the hijacker and Bragan. He decided to go to the tower to see if he could pick up anything new. He proceeded directly to the chief controller's office.

Bragan wasn't expecting him and greeted him coldly.

"Got anything I can chew on, Tom?" Alcott asked.

"Sorry, Barney, I've nothing more to add to what you've heard on the radio."

"How about some human interest? Your personal feelings under this kind of pressure with everyone breathing down your neck, that sort of stuff? Got to keep my customers happy, you know," Alcott said, trying to sound friendly.

"You've already said enough, Barney. I don't have the time for personal interviews right now. As agreed, we'll keep you advised when necessary. Now, I don't mean to be rude but I'd prefer if you went back to the pressroom and kept listening to the radio. We have too many people in this place as it is."

Alcott was cut to the quick. He was no longer *persona grata* in Bragan's domain. He tried to think of something to say but the words wouldn't come. He turned to leave, when Mike Ayno, his eyes glued to a piece of paper he was holding, walked in without bothering to check if anyone else but Bragan was present.

"Tom, the Pentagon just gave me the figures on the TX-75E. It seems . . ."

"Mike!" Bragan stopped him.

Ayno looked up and saw Alcott. His face reddened.

"So long, Tom. By, Mike," Alcott said, acting as if he hadn't heard.

Within a few minutes, Alcott was back at his desk. He began to thumb rapidly through a pile of *Aviation Week and Space Technology* magazines.

In the cockpit of PGA 81, Hal Bessoe was in deep concentration. He was frowning and biting his lip as he scanned the fuel gauges.

Hadley noticed his co-pilot's intense mood. He glanced at Faust, who was sitting at the engineer's panel, smoking a cigarette, looking equally concerned.

"What's on your mind, fellows? Is there anything I don't know?"

"We're going to be running low on fuel in a couple of hours, Captain, and we'll still have to cover about 160 miles to make it back to L.A.," Bessoe said. "He doesn't even have to shoot us. All he has to do is let us run dry and go into the drink. There must be something we can try to get away from this guy."

"What, for instance, Hal?"

"Well, Captain, he's forcing us to stay at ten thousand feet and he's certainly not doing too well on fuel either. He sounded awful at thirty-six thousand and now he seems to be OK. Obviously, he ran out of oxygen. Too bad he didn't pass out when we were still up there."

"I figured as much when he ordered us to descend in a hurry, but I couldn't take a chance. I never heard of any kind of fighter that could stay in the air as long as this one, but I doubt he can outlast us. So, what do you suggest?"

"Do you think we'd have a chance if we took him by surprise and made a break for it on a straight climb to high altitude?"

Hadley looked at Bessoe, then at Faust, and shook his head.

"As he said at the beginning, forget it. I don't know if he'd really have the guts to shoot. But he sure as hell could nail us before we even reached twelve thousand. He could even follow us up to twenty thousand without oxygen for a few minutes. No. The only thing we can wish on him is some kind of mechanical failure which would force him to abandon his plan. The way he's been going, that possibility doesn't look too likely to me. I'm not so sure he wouldn't try to harm us, just out of spite, if anything should go wrong."

"I have one more suggestion, Captain," Faust said. "How about trying to ditch the airplane when it starts getting dark. I don't believe he'd shoot us in cold blood in the rafts."

"As a last resort, Herb," Hadley said calmly.

The loading of the Widgeon was completed.

Santa Claus looked at his watch. It was just past 6:00 P.M. He took Chief Cowlan by the elbow and steered him aside, out of earshot of those surrounding the airplane.

"Send one of your men to the tower. He's to tell them I won't call on the radio and that they should not try to contact me. You stay here and keep an eye on things. I'll be back for more gold in about an hour. All traffic must remain suspended. I'll be using this same runway when I return. Got it?"

Cowlan nodded.

Santa Claus went aboard the Widgeon and closed the door. He made his way to the cockpit with difficulty, climbing over and around the bags cramming the small cabin.

It took him about ten minutes and a good deal of cursing to get the engines started. Russ Nayten prayed as he stood in front of the nose of the airplane, gesturing to Santa Claus to keep pumping the throttles.

At 6:15 P.M., Santa Claus pulled out his walkie-talkie, stuck the antenna out of the left window, and whistled "Anchors Aweigh."

Grant answered by whistling "I'm Sitting on Top of the World."

Santa Claus ran up the engines to 1,800 RPM for a mag check.

Grant called Bragan.

"Do not attempt to have the Widgeon followed, even at low altitude. I can see everything on radar from where I'm sitting."

"Roger. No one will interfere—Bragan."

"Good."

The Widgeon was so overloaded it used more than ten thousand feet of the twelve-thousand-foot runway to get airborne. It gained altitude slowly over the ocean. When it reached about a thousand feet, it banked gently to the left and headed southwest in the direction of the fighter and the airliner. It soon disappeared from view in the smog.

Bragan turned to Ayno.

"Mike, track him on primary radar. See where this Widgeon is really going."

"We're doing just that, Tom," a controller who had overheard him called out. "He's about five miles out right now. We're getting a faint signal. He must have let down already. He's flying pretty low."

Grant called again.

"Bragan—Shadow 81. In case you haven't been told yet, my friend will be coming back soon. I want you to leave everything as is. I'll let you know what time to expect him. Hadley, you keep circling."

"OK—LA Tower."

"Roger—PGA 81."

"Mike," Bragan said, "I think he's conning us this time. They keep harping on this 'coming back' bit. I don't believe the fighter has enough fuel to last much longer. Besides, that Widgeon couldn't take a second trip like that, considering the condition it's in. Unless they've got a boat close to shore to pick up the load from the Widgeon—which would surprise me—they're going to make their getaway soon. In fact, I'm sure of it."

"What about all the gold they've left behind? Santa Claus only took a couple of thousand pounds," Ayno said skeptically.

"Don't you realize what they've done? The sonsofbitches tricked us. They never really wanted the gold in the first place. Santa Claus took some just for the hell of it. At about three thousand dollars a pound, that's more than six million bucks. He already had a fortune in cash and jewels."

"I still don't get it, Tom."

"My guess is that the hijacker demanded the gold in order to throw everyone off. He used it as a decoy—to create a diversion—in the best military tradition. He panicked everyone, starting with the President. He never gave the banks a chance to mark or note the serial numbers that were stolen."

"Tom, you make a lot of sense. What do we do now?"

"Make sure the supersonics are completely unloaded and have them refueled. Call General Fregouze at Vandenberg. I want these fighters to participate in the search when the time comes. Request him to clear it through proper channels and to give me an OK as soon as possible. Ask him if his satellite has picked up anything on the fighter, the 747, or the Widgeon, especially the Widgeon."

"OK."

"Wait, Mike. Have all the controllers and everyone else stand by. It'll be dark soon and the weather in their area is getting cloudy. They'll have to make their move soon. Santa Claus won't talk on the VHF. He's too smart for that. He knows we'll get him on tape and maybe identify him through voice prints. That's why he whispered his orders to the Police Chief or whistled into the walkie-talkie."

"Yeah. And from what the police told me, he wore thick gloves and dark glasses all the time."

"These guys are no beginners, Mike. The fighter knows we can track him on voice transmission alone. When he maintains radio silence after co-ordinating with Santa Claus, that'll be the time for their escape. Keep a sharp ear, Mike. This is it."

Captain Hadley looked at Bessoe and Faust and sighed in frustration.

"We'll be in darkness shortly. How much fuel have we got left, Herb?"

Faust glanced at the dials on his panel.

"About an hour and fifteen minutes, an hour and a half at the most."

"Shit," Hadley grunted. "And look at those goddamned thunderheads building up over there. Something had better happen fast or I'll have to seriously consider your ditching plan, Herb. You boys start going through the emergency checklist. Call Laura and brief her, just in case."

In the Widgeon, Santa Claus was listening to the news on the automatic direction finder tuned to KNX News—an affiliate of CBS.

"This time, Santa Claus came to town to take, not to give. He availed himself of many expensive gifts," the announcer said as a lead-in. "As best as can be determined at the moment, here are the latest facts on the hijacking which is still in progress: The man disguised as Santa Claus has robbed a total of about fifty-two million dollars in gold, U.S. and foreign currency, gems, and negotiable securities. He left most of the gold at Los Angeles International Airport. This is apparently because gold ingots can be traced by their mint marks and are difficult to sell, even to professionals who are equipped to melt them down. The man said he would be returning for more, however. In any event, he is presently allegedly carrying somewhere in the vicinity of twenty-four million dollars' worth of stolen items in his amphibian airplane. And now this late word just in. Aviation expert Barney Alcott says that after extensive research, he has determined that only one type of fighter could possibly be capable of this hijacking. It is a TX-75E. This doesn't mean much for the layman, but Alcott adds that this is a top-secret aircraft and that the Pentagon is in an uproar. It seems the Air Force officially claimed that the airplane had a range of only five hours. Foreign powers unfriendly to the United States are now fully aware the aircraft can stay in the air for almost double that time. We will continue with minute-by-minute coverage of this breaking story after this message . . ."

Grant's voice broke the silence in the cockpit of PGA 81.

"Hadley, let down to fifty, repeat five zero feet. Keep circling at the same time. Do not put on your landing lights."

"That's a little low over the water, isn't it?"

"Don't give me an argument, Hadley. Let down to fifty feet."

"Roger—fifty feet," Hadley confirmed, his voice trembling slightly.

At Los Angeles Tower, Bragan called Ayno.

"That's it, Mike. He's getting ready to let them go. Where's the Widgeon?"

"We've lost him. He must have landed or else he's just above the water. General Fregouze said it's OK about the supersonics. He also says General Prominowe at the Pentagon just gave him hell about the leak on the TX-75E."

"We'll explain the circumstances later about that no-good bastard Alcott. What about the satellite?"

"General Fregouze said his satellite isn't picking up anything. Must be a malfunction."

"Call him back. Tell him to have his fighters at Vandenberg ready. Get the supersonics here to fire up their engines."

"Will do."

Followed by Grant, the Boeing 747 was letting down very gently. It was now dark. Hadley, Bessoe, and Faust were straining to see, trying to spot whitecaps as a reference point for depth perception, not daring to depend entirely on the altimeters.

Hadley picked up the cabin mike.

"Ladies and gentlemen, this is Captain Hadley. We are apparently close to the end of our problems. The hijacker's demands have been satisfied. He wants us now to descend to an altitude which will be just above the water but please do not be frightened. He seems to want to get as low as possible to avoid being detected by radar when he leaves us. We will have to skim the ocean for a little while and then we'll climb back to altitude and return to Los Angeles. Please go back to your seats, fasten your seat belts, and refrain from smoking for the moment. Thank you."

Most of the passengers who had continued to drink heavily were sobered by the announcement. There was absolute quiet in the cabin.

Senator Wadsworth felt compelled to say something. He picked up Laura's mike.

"You can believe what Captain Hadley's telling us. He's a fine pilot. He knows what he's doing. I assure you we'll be all right. Just be a little more patient."

Grant called Hadley.

"PGA 81, we're reaching one hundred feet. Begin to level off. Stop circling. Proceed due west on a heading of two seven zero."

"Roger—two seven zero—Hadley."

Grant looked all around to make sure no airplanes were in sight, his own radar being unreliable at this altitude. As the airliner continued to fly west at reduced speed, Grant made a steep 180-degree turn to the east and added power, heading toward the California coast at just under 700 MPH.

"Stay right on this heading, Hadley, you're doing fine. I'm right behind you," Grant lied, as he kept getting farther away.

About five minutes after this last message, Bragan became concerned. He began to wonder if anything could possibly have happened to either aircraft flying so dangerously close to the ocean.

"Shadow 81—Los Angeles Tower," Bragan called.

There was no answer.

"Shadow 81—Bragan here."

Still no answer.

"PGA 81—LA Tower."

"Go ahead—PGA 81."

"Are you OK, Hadley?"

"Affirmative, but a little too close to the water for comfort."

"Stand by, Hadley. Be back with you in a second."

Bragan turned to Ayno.

"This is it, Mike. Tell Vandenberg to turn their fighters loose. Send the supersonics on their way."

Ayno was ready. He had an open line to Vandenberg. The fighters scrambled out in the direction of the hijacker's last known position. The supersonics began to take off in pursuit.

Bragan's voice came over the loudspeaker in the cockpit of the jumbo jet.

"PGA 81—Bragan. I think you've lost your shadow. You may proceed back to L.A."

Hadley's face broke into a joyous smile of relief.

"Roger. Understood. No shadow. Request clearance to climb to 17,500 feet and return direct to the airport. We'd like to make a straight-in approach if the wind is right."

"Clearance approved. See you in a little while—Bragan."

"You bet your sweet ass, my friend—Hadley."

The passengers felt the airplane climbing.

Bruce, the salesman, let out a joyous cry. He slapped his friend Dick on the back and ran up toward Senator Wadsworth to shake his hand.

"Girls," Bruce sang at the top of his lungs, "bring out the booze. Let it flow. We're going home!"

PART THREE

CHAPTER 21

The Widgeon was sitting in the water, its propellers idling, a few miles from land. It was almost pitch dark.

The fighter-bomber approached at slow speed, barely skimming the waves. It hovered for an instant before the nose of the Widgeon, then flew past it.

Approximately two hundred yards from the amphibian airplane, Grant hovered again and opened the canopy. He gently set the fighter-bomber on the water with the landing gear up and shut down the engines.

There was a loud hiss, accompanied by a cloud of steam, when the burning exhausts touched the surface of the ocean.

As the belly of the airplane began to fill with water, Grant stood up. He picked up the dinghy, held it against the exterior left side of the fuselage, and triggered the CO_2 cartridge. The rubber craft inflated instantly. It remained attached to the aircraft with the rope Grant had previously secured with a slipknot to the grip handle of the canopy.

He ripped out the little black box he had taped under the panel, its connecting patchcord and the airplane's microphone, then threw them into the ocean.

Grant stepped out onto the left wing.

Holding onto the frame of the windshield with his left hand, he fished into the cockpit with his right hand. In turn, he quickly took out the little outboard motor, the waterproof knapsack, and the paddles, which he lowered into the dinghy.

The wings, almost empty of fuel, gave the aircraft buoyancy. It wasn't sinking fast enough.

Groping nervously into the knapsack, Grant pulled out his ax, then furiously punctured the left wing and fuselage. The water rushed in. The aircraft began to go down like a stone.

Grant unfastened the slipknot and slid into the dinghy. He as-

sembled one of the snap-on paddles in an instant and started pulling with all his might toward the Widgeon.

The wide door in the side of the aircraft was open. Holding the
dinghy's rope between his teeth, Grant climbed aboard, pulled in
the rubber boat, and closed the door. His helmet, life preserver,
boots, and dripping flight suit were promptly removed, then placed
into the dinghy.

Clad only in his Jockey briefs, Grant crouched and struggled to
make his way to the right seat of the airplane over the piles of
plastic bags containing the booty. A discarded Santa suit was lying
at the top of one of the heaps.

The man in the left seat had his back to Grant. His raised right
hand was on the overhead throttles. The airplane was advancing
slowly in the water.

Grant contorted to get into the co-pilot's seat feet first.

General "Zach" R. Enko turned toward him.

"Well, boy, how'd it go?"

Grant flashed a victorious smile.

"Pretty smooth, General, considering . . . How about you?"

"No complaints, except for the half-wit who owned this crummy
airplane. He almost fouled up everything with his demands for a
Learjet. No sense of citizenship these days," Enko laughed. "Take
a look behind you at what we've got."

The General pushed the throttles slightly forward and increased
the taxiing speed toward their destination. He was also in
Jockey briefs, with a revolver resting on his bare lap.

"This reminds me of the good old days in World War II when I
learned to fly these goddamn Widgeons in Alaska," Enko commented.

Grant turned toward the back, extended his hand, squeezed one
of the bulky plastic bags and let out a long, low whistle.

"Can't see a thing. Too dark. Can't tell by the feel. How much do
you figure we have back there?"

"The radio said over twenty-four million in miscellaneous un-
traceable items. That should keep us going for a while."

"Yes, sir! We certainly did it."

"By the way, Grant, I hope you brought my clothes. As women
are always fond of saying, I don't have a thing to wear."

"Your stuff is in the knapsack, General, together with mine."

"Good boy."

"Twenty-four million . . ." Grant said dreamily, "twenty-four million . . . that's beautiful . . . really beautiful . . . and not a drop of blood spilled for it . . . beautiful . . ."

"Yeah, Grant—just about the price of a fighter-bomber or a Boeing 747. They want to kill my airplane, they'll have to pay for it. A drop in the bucket of the defense budget. They'll never feel it. Even then, I wonder if they will ever have paid enough for what I've gone through."

The General's mouth was hard. He was very intense and trembling a little. Grant's joyous mood began to fade. Enko made him suddenly uneasy. He changed the subject.

"How did things go, back at Da Nang, General?"

"Oh, fine. They're still hunting for you. We sent out about a dozen search and rescue crews for your airplane. They never found anything, of course, to my dismay. I put McSnair in charge during my absence. He's still looking."

"McSnair? That jerk?"

"He's a pompous buffoon and a lousy pilot. Why I ever got stuck with him I'll never know. He was wished on me, I guess. But it's just as well. He's the kind of moron we need for a perfect alibi. He'll swear up and down I almost became distraught when we lost you. He turned into my lap dog the minute I gave him a little responsibility. Thank goodness Bill Keegan is there to assist him. He's a bright boy. Without him, McSnair couldn't even count blankets in the storeroom—that drunk!"

"How long do you think it will be before we're in sight of shore?"

"We're still about ten miles out and we'd better taxi this thing slowly. I'd love to fly it there but we can't take a chance on being picked up by radar. At this speed, I'd say we'll be there in about thirty minutes. We have plenty of time. Relax, Grant."

"What happened at the Pentagon?"

"Harmon and the Secretary gave me a hard time. I put on a big act—worried sick about my boys and all that stuff—a real tear-jerker. What a sob story! I think they bought it. But I know one thing now. As far as they're concerned, my career is over. I'm through."

"That's too bad, General. Are you sure?"

"I'm very sure," Enko sighed. "They need a scapegoat for the screw-ups on our fighter-bomber. I'm it. They're setting me up."

"Isn't there anything you can do about it?"

"I could fight back, but who cares, anyway," Enko said with a trace of bitterness. "I'm no longer interested. I've got to be back at the Pentagon day after tomorrow—with plans for renewed bombings. They'll have them. They'll be the best plans they ever dreamed of—Enko's swan song."

"What about your wife? Where did you say you were going?"

"That part was a little more difficult to handle. I had to pick a fight with her to find a pretext to get out of the house. She never knew what hit her. Poor thing. You know, Grant, I still really love her—after twenty-two years. She doesn't believe it. She thinks I'm a moody guy, and that I went out on a binge somewhere. I'll make it up to her. She'll get over it."

Grant remained silent for a moment, wondering about Enko's feelings on everything.

"There's another thing I meant to ask you, General. What was Wadsworth doing on that flight?"

"Just a coincidence. He was on his way to Honolulu for a political rally or something. You really gave it to him, though—but good. I heard a replay on the radio while I was waiting for you. I'm proud of you."

"Well, General, you can bet he's not going to let it go at that. There's going to be a monumental investigation and hell to pay because he was on board. We're going to have a hard time."

"I know, I've been thinking about it. There are other factors as well. I'm afraid I've got a little bad news for you, Grant—nothing too terrible that you couldn't handle."

Grant closed his eyes. He was very tired. He took a deep breath.

"OK, General, let's have it."

"Our original plan has to be modified somewhat. You're going to have to get captured by the North Vietnamese."

Grant jumped in his seat as if he had been jolted by an electric shock.

"You can't be serious. The deal was that I should make my way through the Cambodian jungle back to Saigon."

"I know, kid," Enko said calmly. "But you were at sea for over three weeks and many things of which you're not aware happened during that time. The negotiations are running hot and cold. At this moment, things are more or less at a standstill. They won't be for long, however. The war could be over any minute now. The presidential elections are coming up and this is a race against the clock. Yesterday, I found out at the Pentagon that our buddy—the negotiator in Paris—is about to sign a peace agreement any day. That's why we'll now have to put the pressure on with renewed bombings."

"What the hell does all that have to do with me?"

"It simply means that you'd have no alibi fucking around in the jungle if the accords are concluded while you're still on your little Cambodian excursion. On the other hand, it'll be a little while before the prisoners of war are released, even after the agreement is signed. We'd be in the clear then, don't you see? You'd be a hero, boy!—just like all the rest of them. All it means is a few weeks in the Hanoi Hilton, that's all. From what I understand, you might even be home by Christmas."

"That's easy for you to say. Suppose I get killed in the process of being captured?"

"Unfortunately, that's a calculated risk we now have to take."

"A risk WE have to take? Calculated? And who's doing the calculating?—you, General? You must be kidding. I'm not doing it. I'm going according to plan."

Enko pulled back on the throttles. The airplane stopped well near dead in the water. Except for the hum of the idling engines, the cockpit became almost deathly silent.

The General was shaking with rage. He turned his face toward Grant's and glared at him. For once, Enko didn't look dignified wearing nothing but his Jockey briefs. He tried to contain himself but his tone, nevertheless, betrayed his anger.

"Grant, I'm sorry to have to remind you of a few things but whose idea was this in the first place?"

"It was your idea," Grant said quietly, now on the defensive.

"OK. Who figured everything out? Who made all the plans?"

"You did, General," Grant replied softly, feeling his own temper rising.

"OK. Who put up the money for the operation? Who went into hock up to his eyeballs to get the $180,000 to finance the purchase of the ships plus the other $5,000 for the rest of the equipment in Hong Kong? Who?" Enko roared at the top of his lungs.

"You did, goddammit, you did," Grant yelled back. "But who the hell put his ass on the line to pull it off for you at Hoa Binh and just now with the 747? I did it," Grant screamed, getting almost hoarse. "You remember that, General, I did it. Not you."

The two men's faces were no more than six inches apart. They both looked ludicrous, as they perspired freely, arguing in their underwear in the tiny cockpit.

Enko pulled his face back and looked Grant up and down. His eyes were narrow slits. He regained possession of his normal timbre of voice.

"OK, so you played a part," Enko said through clenched teeth. "But you don't seem to realize that you're nothing but a hired hand."

Grant flinched.

"That's right, Grant. Better get off your high horse. You just carried out instructions and don't you forget it. What about me taking the risk of getting blown up with all that dynamite under my Santa Claus costume? I did my share too. You're no hotshot, boy. You were taking a cruise on the Pacific while I was setting up alibis. You were buzzing around in the air following a helpless 747. You still had a chance of getting away if things got tough. I was on the ground, surrounded by a bunch of Keystone Kops. Had one of them panicked, we wouldn't be here right now. I kept control over the situation, never let things get out of hand. That's why I'm a general. Now you obey orders, period."

Grant was livid. He was biting his lip and staring straight ahead, out of the cockpit window, into the night. The Widgeon, its propellers still idling, was drifting aimlessly. He was surprised at the low, monotonous tone of his own voice when he spoke out.

"General, you set up the alibi but you never told me exactly what you had in mind. I'm not as cynical as you are—yet. I would never have had the guts to send out so many guys on wild goose chases to search for me . . . taking the chance of getting them killed looking for an airplane that wasn't there. It's only thanks to the monsoon the rescue crews didn't get wiped out. Otherwise, you would have sent them to their deaths without turning a hair."

Enko gave Grant a crooked smile.

"You've got a lot to learn, boy. People are like dogs. You train them. You condition them. They obey orders. It's no more complicated than that."

"For you it's vengeance, General, but I didn't know it. A vendetta against Harmon, the Pentagon, all those who passed you by, who left you by the wayside to play with your airplanes. For me, General, it was a way to get out of the clutches of the virtues of mediocrity. I was tired of being used."

"Don't give me that philosophical horseshit," Enko said, sneering. "Don't you start feeling sorry for yourself. I don't want to listen to that kind of crap."

"General," Grant continued, still staring out through the cockpit windshield, "I wanted to get out of the war business because I felt I was being programmed, propagandized, manipulated. You promised me freedom. Now I find that *you're* manipulating me. What was the point? Nothing's changed. Instead of working for them, at the Pentagon, I'm now working for you. For a moment there, I was dumb enough to believe I was my own man."

"That's ridiculous. You're going to have a lot of money, kid. You're going to be a rich man. You'll have all the women you want. Not another worry in the world for the rest of your life. It was worth it, wasn't it?"

"I don't know any more, General," Grant replied evenly. "I still think I've been had."

"Of course you know. You just don't want to admit it. Who the hell convinced you there was no such thing as conscience and that you never have to feel guilty about a thing?"

"You did. But I cannot be hypocritical to the point of trading on the POW issue. They're being used as bargaining pawns by the Administration and by the North Vietnamese. Now you want to use me in the same way, General. You want to take advantage of their misery."

Enko was exasperated. He resumed the verbal fistfight full force.

"You sucker! I get no lump in the throat. I don't feel any compassion for those crybaby prisoners of war who were clumsy enough to get caught. They're professionals. They knew what they were letting themselves in for. In the Hanoi Hilton, I want you to be a long-suffering, shining example of American fortitude under adversity. Now you follow the plan."

"I'm not getting captured, General. I've already done my share."

Enko made one last try:

"Grant," he said soothingly, "we're not going to get anyplace arguing about who did what. Why are we fighting, anyway? We've just pulled off one of the biggest coups in history and here we are at each other's throat. Think for a minute . . . think! There are several very good reasons for you to have to go to North Vietnam."

"I'm not going, no matter what."

"Shut up and listen. They've found out the airplane was a TX-75E. Don't ask me how they know. I just heard it on the radio. Maybe someone spotted you. I'll pump some people at the Pentagon. We should have wrapped up this operation in six hours and it took us eight. I guess they figured only a TX-75E could have done it."

"What else?"

"There's the imminent signature of the peace treaty. And let's not forget that goddamn Wadsworth. If I know him, he'll be leading the Senate investigation—just to grab headlines. He'll be damn thorough about it too. Believe me, Grant, I'd go to North Vietnam myself, if it were possible. But we have no choice. We can't leave ourselves wide open now."

"You'd better figure out something else, General. I've already told you. I'm not going."

"I'll offer you an alternative then. You can remain dead. You'd have to change your identity and you would probably never be able to return to the United States. There's no other solution."

"Nothing doing, General. I'm going according to plan."

Enko grabbed the gun that was resting on his lap and pointed it at Grant. There was a wild gleam in his eye.

"Look, son. I've been in this business longer than you have. They're not complete simpletons at the Pentagon. Remember, you're missing in action. I'm not. As far as they're concerned, you could be missing right here instead of over there. So, why don't you be a good boy and listen to Daddy. Maybe you can fly an airplane but, in the brains department, I'm a general and you're still nothing but a lousy captain."

Grant stared Enko straight in the eye.

"Put that gun away, General," he said softly. "I've got a sealed letter in a bank vault to be opened one year after I'm officially dead. I may be only a captain but I'm not THAT dumb."

Enko placed the gun back on his lap.

"*Touché*, Grant," he conceded. "So you wrote out your last will and testament, hey? I never thought you wouldn't trust me."

"Sorry, General. You're a great teacher. I just don't trust anyone any more."

Enko burst into good-natured laughter.

"You have a point there, Grant. But I still say my strategy is foolproof. Why don't you just listen for a minute?"

"OK. Let me hear it," Grant said dejectedly.

PGA 81 made its final approach into LA International just before 9:00 P.M. It had been a long flight to nowhere.

Hadley had the airport all to himself. Bragan had maintained the embargo on all operations until he was sure the 747 was safely back on the ground.

Bragan opened one of the tower windows. The airport was perfectly quiet. He listened for the whine of the jumbo jet's engines. A few seconds later he saw the landing lights of the aircraft lining up with the runway and getting closer. He watched the 747 flare out, and broke into a big smile when he heard the screech of the main landing gear tires on the concrete. He called Hadley.

"PGA 81, you're cleared to taxi to your company terminal as soon as you're able to turn off the runway. Welcome home."

"Roger," Hadley acknowledged, as though it were a routine landing.

Bragan turned to Ayno.

"You can resume normal operations. Advise all concerned. Thanks, Mike. I'm glad you were around."

"We all earned our pay, Tom. Buy you dinner later?"

"You bring the food. I'll bring the champagne."

"Fair deal," Ayno said, giving the thumbs-up sign to the controllers standing by at their consoles.

The normal chatter between the tower and pilots who had been sitting in their cockpits ready to start their engines picked up at once. LA International resumed its normal routine.

The arrival gate of PGA 81 was swarming with relatives and friends. TV cameramen assigned to correspondents from all the major networks and local stations jockeyed for position. Radio newsmen tested and readied their tape recorders. Reporters and press photographers from several prominent newspapers and magazines competed for the best spots. Everyone pushed and shoved, trying to get past a cordon of airport security police. Curiosity seekers swelled the crowd and added to the general confusion.

Sighs of relief and tears of joy welcomed the exit of the hostages as they slowly emerged into the terminal to fall into waiting arms.

The cameras were grinding away. Reporters stuck mikes under dazed people's noses. They asked bright questions—such as if the passengers were glad to have escaped with their lives. They also wanted to know how it felt to be back on the ground and if anyone was going to ask for a refund or sue the airline.

The newsmen promptly abandoned their helpless preys when they spotted Senator Wadsworth. They flocked about him. He would be good copy.

"Senator," asked a reporter, "could you enlighten us on your radio conversation with the hijacker? What exactly did he mean when he implied . . ."

"No comment." Wadsworth glared as he brushed the man aside and looked desperately for Vito Di Stefano in the crowd. He needed assistance and Vito wasn't there. The message was clear. He was being dropped like a burning coal after the fighter pilot's accusations, heard from coast to coast.

With newsmen and photographers dogging his footsteps, Wadsworth hurried toward the terminal exit and dashed into a taxi, totally unconcerned about leaving his suitcase behind. He would have it picked up later.

He waited until the cab was out of the airport and he was sure no reporters were following him before he gave the driver the address.

"Take me to the Beverly Hilton," Wadsworth said, and then broke into uncontrollable sobs.

Captain Hadley removed his headset, took a deep breath, and remained seated in the cockpit. He was in a pensive mood. He told Bessoe and Faust to go to the operations office, where he would join them in a moment. He calmly proceeded to fill out his logbook.

In the space reserved for "remarks" Hadley wrote: "Flight not completed to destination due to threat by unidentified military aircraft—full details on tape with LA Center." He signed the book and was last to leave the plane.

A dozen or so reporters pushed by the guards and jumped Hadley as he walked into the terminal. Cameras and floodlights were aimed at him from every direction. He was annoyed with all the commotion but tried not to show it.

Using his three-suiter and flight case to help him plow through the group, he quickly excused himself saying he would have no comment until he made his report to the proper authorities.

At about 9:30 P.M. Hadley stepped out of an elevator into the glass enclosure of the tower. He asked one of the controllers where he could find Tom Bragan. The man pointed toward the center of the room.

His feet propped up on his desk, Bragan was sipping a container of coffee when Hadley walked in. He rose and walked toward him.

"Bragan?" Hadley asked.

The chief controller nodded. "Hadley?"

The two men shook hands silently.

"Glad to meet you, Captain. You're no longer just a voice."

"Same here. You did a fine job, Bragan. We're much obliged. My thanks to you and the rest of your crew."

"We all had to sweat it out. Still, we were better off down here than you up there. How about joining me and my assistant Mike Ayno for some dinner?"

"Nothing I'd enjoy more. But first I must go to company operations, then make a couple of phone calls. I also want to change into civilian clothes so I can get away from these newshounds. See you in the restaurant in about an hour. The drinks are on me."

"Sorry, Hadley," Bragan said, shaking his head from side to side with a sad look on his face.

Hadley shot a look of surprise at the chief controller.

"I've already beaten you to it," Bragan broke out in laughter. "I'm buying the champagne. Next time it'll be on you."

"Let's just hope there will never be a next time. I don't wish it on anyone, not for all the champagne in the world," Hadley said, smiling wearily.

The mood was grim at Vandenberg Air Force Base Tower, which was now co-ordinating the aerial hunt for the hijacker and his accomplice.

A total of sixty-two Air Force, Navy, and Marine Corps aircraft were in the air. They included supersonic fighters, slow twin-prop transports, and helicopters. The planes had been dispatched from eight bases along the California coast with orders to relay their findings at once. So far, the reports coming in over the loudspeakers were discouraging.

The plan called for an inch-by-inch sweep of a vast area in record time, starting the moment Tom Bragan gave the green light from LA International. It allowed the hijacker in the fighter-bomber no more than a ten-minute head start to proceed in any direction toward the coast.

The search boundary was in the shape of a rectangle. It protruded 200 miles out over the ocean—30 miles beyond the farthest point where the TX-75E had last been spotted on radar in the company of PGA 81. On the shoreline, the perimeter extended approximately 400 miles north and south of LA International. It ran from San Francisco, down to Rosario, on the coast of Baja California, 250 miles southeast of San Diego.

Each aircraft had been assigned a designated altitude within a specific sector to be methodically combed in overlapping square and circular patterns.

The paths of the airplanes were to crisscross at different flight levels, thereby forming a theoretically inescapable web of radar detection for anything that was airborne.

The airplanes participating in the search kept calling in with negative reports.

The comments were almost identical from all sectors. No moonlight—pitch dark. Weather clouding up, no pickup on radar. No trace of the fighter-bomber or the Widgeon.

General Paul Fregouze, who was in charge of the sweep, called the Federal Aviation Administration. He gave his consent to the resumption of commercial flights with the exception of operations over the Pacific until further notice. He also asked the FAA to advise every airport in the United States, Canada, and Mexico, including private strips and seaplane facilities, to be on the lookout for the fighter-bomber and the Widgeon.

By 10:00 P.M., the fighters, operating far out at sea on full power and at low altitude, began to report they were running low on fuel.

The jets were instructed to return to their home bases, refuel, and stand by for another sortie.

General Fregouze got on the phone to the Pentagon and was put through to General Raymond Prominowe.

"I'm afraid we've drawn a blank so far. It's like looking for a freckle on a porcupine," Fregouze said with disgust.

"What do you think happened? What's your status at the moment?" Prominowe asked.

"The interception of PGA 81 took place about nine hours ago. No fighter in the world could stay in the air for that period of time operating as long as he did at low altitude. My feeling is the hijacker must have ditched his plane in the ocean. He must be floating around on a raft or dinghy unless he was picked up by a third accomplice. I don't think the Widgeon and the fighter would have tried to rendezvous at sea."

"I agree, these guys would not be crazy enough to try a stunt like that in the darkness. Any other ideas?"

"There is, of course, the possibility he might have made it to some point on the coast without being tracked. I doubt it, though. I just don't see how he could have slipped through our radar net.

"What about that goddamn Widgeon?"

"He left LA International at about 1830 and disappeared from the scopes a few minutes later. The bastard had a good ninety-minute head start on us by the time we got the go-ahead for the search."

"What did he have—three, four hours' range?"

"That's about it. But at 120 miles per hour cruising speed, flying low, he could have gone anywhere within 180 miles of LA International before we went after him. My guess is that he proceeded one way while the fighter flew in a different direction just to throw us off. That Widgeon has probably reached its destination if it backtracked to the coast by taxiing on the water after he was sure radar had lost him. For all we know, he may have cracked up in that overloaded piece of junk. There's another theory. Both airplanes may have stretched things just a little too far and met with separate accidents."

"This is very frustrating, Fregouze. How the hell are we going to explain that not only one but two airplanes managed to give us the slip in an area as heavily defended as the West Coast?"

"We had no option. The orders from the White House were to lay off until the fighter had let go of the 747."

"We can't go on blaming things on the White House forever, Fregouze. Try to come up with something better—like technical reasons why we couldn't take a chance and jeopardize the lives of innocent civilians on board the airliner. We should be the good guys who preached moderation."

"I'll see what I can come up with. What do you want us to do right now?"

"Continuing the search in the dark seems like a waste of time, money, and effort, doesn't it? Suspend operations for the night. Send the planes back in the air at daybreak. Maybe they will spot some wreckage. Keep me advised."

"Yes, sir."

General Fregouze relayed the orders.

CHAPTER 22

Just as Vandenberg was calling it a day, the Widgeon was proceeding at a snail's pace on the water on a northeasterly heading.

At about 10:15 P.M., Grant spotted a glimmer in the distance, directly to the east. He looked at Enko.

"We're getting close to Santa Catalina, General. See those lights at about two o'clock?"

"I got 'em," Enko said. "We're still three or four miles out from where we want to go. Better start taking bearings on the VOR and ADF. I'll take care of the taxiing."

"OK," Grant acknowledged.

The General groped under his seat. He found a small paper bag which had previously been hidden under his Santa Claus costume. It contained a marine chart, a miniature flashlight, a pencil, and a small ruler, which he handed to Grant.

"Here's what you need. Let me know when we're two miles off the northwest tip of the island. I want a fix at the intersection of the following lines of position from the mainland—exactly thirty-five miles southwest of Los Angeles International and fifty miles due west of Laguna Beach."

Grant unfolded the map and cupped his hand over the flashlight. He tuned the VHF radio omnirange to LA International, then to Santa Catalina, and the low frequency ADF to a local radio station in Laguna Beach.

"Keep her steady on this course, General. We're lined up perfectly with both the airport and Santa Catalina on the VOR. Let me draw the lines on the chart now . . . OK . . . that does it . . . now for Laguna on the ADF . . . OK . . . I've got it . . . it's not coming in very strong . . . this airplane's a real wreck . . . nothing works right . . . the needle is fluctuating a bit . . . let me mark the spot . . . it's not one hundred per cent but I guess it'll have to do . . ."

"What's our position now?" Enko interrupted.

"We're not quite there yet. Stay on a heading of 020. We should reach your spot in about five minutes. I'll recheck it then."

"OK. My walkie-talkie's in the back. Throw it out. I already got rid of the dynamite. Hand me the ax and get everything else ready in the meantime."

Grant extricated himself from his seat and crawled between the plastic bags to the back of the cabin.

He found the ax in the dinghy. Before giving it to Enko, he used it to split his flight helmet into slivers. He then grabbed it by the blade and pushed the handle toward the General over the pile of bags.

With a sharp knife taken from his knapsack, Grant cut up the Santa Claus costume, his flight suit, and his boots.

He opened the cabin door and little by little threw out the walkie-talkie, the pieces of clothing, and the helmet. They were carried away by the prop wash as the airplane kept advancing in the water. He tied one end of the dinghy's rope with a slipknot to the door handle and installed the tiny outboard motor on the stern bracket.

"You finished?" Enko called.

"Be right up."

Grant crept back into his seat and took a new set of bearings.

"Correct ten degrees to the right, General. Steer 030. There seems to be a strong current around here."

"OK. How much farther? We'd better hurry now. I don't want to take any chances. One of those low-flying search planes might still be around, although no one's talking on the VHF. I'd hate to have one of them spot the phosphorescent trail of our wake, as narrow as it is at this speed."

"I'm taking a last bearing, General. We should be there in a minute. Laguna is coming in fine now on the ADF. OK . . . We're exactly two miles off the northwest tip of Santa Catalina . . . I've got it marked."

"OK. Get the boat ready. I'll be right with you."

Grant went to the back of the cabin once again.

Enko pulled back on the throttles and put the mixture levers into idle cutoff position. The engines sputtered and died. The Widgeon shuddered for a few seconds, then started drifting.

The General took the ax and began swinging at the Plexiglas windshield, then at the side windows of the cockpit. They cracked, splintered, shattered, and crumbled under the blows. He then struck the fuselage with all his might, gouging big holes into the metal skin above the water line. Finally, Enko hacked at the floor of the cockpit until the blade pierced through the hull and the water began to shoot up through the punctures.

"Here it is. Take it," Enko shouted as he pushed the ax toward Grant, while he crawled between the bags toward the rear as fast as he could.

Grant donned his life preserver, lowered the dinghy into the ocean through the cabin door and grabbed the ax. In turn, he started chopping into the floor at the back of the cabin. When the water started squirting, he hit the sides of the tail section. The Widgeon was sinking slowly.

"Wait here. I'll be right back," Grant yelled as he jumped feet first into the water holding the ax in his right hand. He swam a few feet toward the float under the left wing and climbed on it.

Holding onto the strut with his left hand, he hit the lower part of the wing with the ax, rupturing the fuel tank and getting doused with gasoline in the process. He then bent down and hit the float under the water line.

Grant let himself back into the water and quickly made his way around the nose of the aircraft to the other side. He climbed onto the right float, punched a gaping hole into the wing above it, then swung at the float and pierced it.

Still holding onto the strut, Grant hurled the ax as far away as he could. As it went to the bottom, he swam around the tail of the sinking aircraft back to the boat and propped himself aboard.

"OK, hop in," Grant shouted at Enko, who was crouching by the door of the Widgeon, now half submerged.

The General lunged forward, his arms extended, in an attempt to grab hold of the bow of the rubber craft. He missed. Grant caught a glimpse of Enko going under. He waited a few seconds, certain that his head would reappear on the surface, and prepared to give him a hand to get aboard. Nothing happened.

Grant felt panic gnawing in his throat. He couldn't understand what was going on.

"General . . . General . . . where are you?" he called. "I can't really see too well . . . hurry . . . the plane's going down fast."

There was no reply from Enko.

"Where the hell are you?" Grant screamed in alarm. He leaned over the side to grope in the water all around the boat, still tied to the sinking Widgeon.

No answer.

The wildest suppositions went through Grant's head. Could Enko have suffered a seizure trying to swim a couple of strokes when the boat was no further than ten feet from the plane? What could possibly have gone wrong?

The high-swept tail of the Widgeon was now half submerged.

There was no time to lose. Grant had to untie the rope linking the bow of the boat to the cabin door or get dragged under with the sinking airplane.

He grabbed the line, slid off the boat, and started pulling his way toward the aircraft to unfasten the slipknot.

Halfway to the Widgeon, Grant felt something under his feet. Still holding onto the rope, he groped below the surface. His right hand clutched at a tuft of hair.

Grant fumbled a little lower and caught hold of an arm. He pulled with all his strength and got the General's torso out of the water.

Although he had been under less than a minute, Enko was limp and barely conscious.

"My foot," Enko groaned as he spat and coughed. "My foot . . ." he gasped, trying to catch his breath, "it's caught in the rope . . . tangled . . . I can't swim too well . . ."

Grant felt the rope getting taut as the sinking Widgeon picked up the slack. The General was being pulled down, this time for good.

Acting on reflex, Grant untied his life preserver and fastened it around Enko's chest.

The top of the tail was already under the water. The General and the boat would soon follow.

Grant thought feverishly fast. It would take him some time to loosen the tight and complicated knot in the boat's bow if he groped in the dark. Also, it would now take too long to get back aboard the rubber boat, find his knife in the knapsack and cut the rope. Since he was already in the water, it might be simpler to free Enko and the boat by just tugging at the slipknot. To do this, he had to reach the cabin door—and fast.

He took a deep breath, submerged, and followed the rope to the sinking Widgeon.

The short underwater swim was a suffocating nightmare until Grant reached the door, which had been purposely left open to let the water in faster.

The airplane was almost six feet under when Grant's searching fingers found the short end of the slipknot. He tugged at it and the rope went limp.

Holding the line between his teeth for fear of losing his way back to the rubber craft, Grant kicked with all his might toward the surface.

Enko was half dead but had instinctively managed to drag himself to the boat. He was holding onto it with one arm draped over the side as he spat out the huge quantities of salt water he had swallowed.

In a virtual state of exhaustion, Grant needed all his remaining will-power to force himself to climb back aboard the tiny boat. He paused for a couple of deep breaths, then hauled Enko aboard.

The two men sat there, panting for a good half hour, too tired to move a muscle while the dinghy drifted slowly.

Grant opened the knapsack and pulled out a small bottle of gin. He handed it to Enko.

"Here, General, maybe you can use some of this."

Enko took a deep swallow. It made him shiver from head to toe. He gave the bottle back to Grant.

"You certainly think of everything. That came in handy, I must say."

Grant took a long drink.

"I had it packed to celebrate. But I guess we need it more for survival now. Why didn't you put on a life preserver?"

"I looked for one while I was waiting for you at our rendezvous point. The jerk who owned the airplane didn't have any on board. Can you believe that? An amphibian without life preservers? It never entered my mind to ask him when he delivered it at LA International. Besides, why should he have known I might have intended to use one. I wasn't worried about swimming a few feet but I must confess I didn't anticipate getting my foot caught in a stupid rope."

"We'll have to report him to the Coast Guard," Grant chuckled. "That guy is a public menace. His pilot's license should be revoked."

"Tell me something, Grant," Enko asked in a perplexed tone. "All you had to do was to cut the bowline and free the boat. Why did you come looking for me? You could have easily let me drown, boy. You could have had it all to yourself."

"What? and leave your body floating around Santa Catalina as evidence when you're supposed to be in Washington? Now you're the one who's not thinking right, General—if I may say so," Grant laughed.

"I'm sure you don't really mean that," Enko said very seriously. "The sharks would have probably taken care of me. Thanks anyway."

"Don't mention it, General. Besides, I didn't want to leave that slipknot tied to the handle of the Widgeon door. Suppose someone finds the airplane? Why should they know we had a rope that was probably attached to a dinghy? First security rule, remember? Don't leave any clues."

"They'll never find the Widgeon. Why do you think I picked this spot without even telling you about it. It's buried under exactly eighty feet of water. It will absolutely not cross their minds we sank it right under their noses, thirty-five miles out of LA International from where it took off. They probably think I flew this thing to Canada or Mexico."

"I hate to admit it, General, but you're a genius."

"I know. I also know how the military mind works."

"How about something to eat? Might as well get rid of some of the cans I brought along."

"Great idea. I'm starved now that I'm back from the grave."

"What would you like? We have meat loaf . . . ham . . . chicken . . ."

"I'm just in the mood for chicken with . . . er . . . a little more of that gin."

"Dinner will be served in a minute," Grant said, grinning as he picked up a can opener from the knapsack.

It was now midnight, and time to proceed to Santa Catalina.

Grant pulled the starter cord of the tiny outboard motor and pointed the boat toward the lights in the distance.

On the way to the island, Grant got rid of every unnecessary item still in the knapsack. He threw overboard the remaining cans of food and drink, the can opener, the empty bottle of gin, the binoculars, the marine chart torn into little pieces, as well as the ruler, pencil, and his circular slide rule. He just kept the knife.

Grant groped one last time into the knapsack and found his gun. He sent it to the bottom.

"By the way, General, this reminds me, where's your gun? We'd better get rid of it. You won't be needing it any more."

Enko pulled his revolver from the crotch of his Jockey briefs and tossed it into the sea.

"All we have left now is our clothes, General. Since we only have one life preserver, I'll drop you off first with the knapsack then go back out and sink the boat."

"OK."

About five hundred yards from their destination, Grant cut off the motor, unfastened it from the stern bracket, and let it sink. Both men paddled the rest of the way to the southwest shore of Santa Catalina.

Enko jumped onto the sand and pebble beach and pulled the boat ashore. They had landed close to Sentinel Rocks, less than half a mile from Escondido Road, which would lead them into Old Stage Road, the main mountain trail to Avalon.

Both men crouched and remained perfectly silent for about ten minutes, listening for any sounds.

Enko looked at the luminous dial on his watch. It was just past 2:00 A.M. He took off his life preserver and handed it to Grant.

"We're about ten miles from town and everyone around here in the sticks is fast asleep," he whispered. "Maybe you'd better go now. I'll put on some clothes in the meantime."

Grant donned the life preserver. He laboriously unfastened

the wet rope from the bow and threw it into the boat, which he pushed out to sea.

After paddling for a good ten minutes, Grant figured he was about half a mile from shore. He unsnapped the paddles and threw them over the side, together with the rope.

With his knife, he slashed at the dinghy and trampled it under his feet as it sank, before swimming back to shore.

Enko was dressed and sitting by the knapsack when he arrived. Grant put on a sports shirt and dungarees.

The two men brushed the sand with their hands to erase any telltale tracks possibly made by the boat. They put on their socks and, holding their shoes in their hands, made their way to the winding road to Avalon, located on the southeast coast of the island.

They began their long trek to civilization at 3:00 A.M.

Enko stayed on the right side of the road. Grant remained a few steps behind, walking on the left, covering the General in the unlikely event anyone would seek to challenge them.

Were it not for their extreme fatigue, the two men might have enjoyed the hike. The night was cloudy but warm and still. Although there was no moonlight, they had no difficulty following the road.

Grant still had one more chore to perform. As he went along, he used his knife to cut the life preserver and the knapsack to ribbons. He threw the remnants by the wayside and over cliffs where they would never be found. Lastly, he got rid of the knife.

The General and Grant reached the outskirts of Avalon as dawn was breaking.

Enko untied a chain around his neck. Two keys were dangling from it. He gave one of them to Grant and put the other one in his pocket.

The two men conferred in whispers for a moment by the roadside, then separated.

Enko went to the ferry terminal and left on the first crossing to Long Beach, on the mainland.

Grant made his way to the seaplane air taxi service and bought a ticket to Long Beach as well.

After arrival on the coast, each man took a taxi to Los Angeles International Airport.

Grant arrived first. With the key provided by Enko, he opened a locker where he found a suitcase with clothing, money, a passport, and a ticket. He went to the men's room, shaved, then entered a toilet where he could change and wait unobserved.

At 11:00 A.M., Grant heard someone whistling one of the Beatles' hits, "It's Been a Hard Day's Night." He opened the toilet door.

Enko was whistling in the washroom, alone, also with a suitcase. He was wearing a hat and dark glasses.

"Glad to see you," Enko said. "Did you hear the news?"

"Yes, in a diner where I had breakfast. I also read the papers."

"They're all screwed up," Enko whispered with a smile. "They don't have a clue to what the hell is going on. I've got to catch my plane. I'm going nonstop to New York at 11:30—sleep on the plane. I'll take a connecting flight at Kennedy Airport. I think it's wiser not to go back directly to Washington—just in case. This way I'll have a chance to find out what's going on by listening to the radio in New York."

"What airline are you using?"

"PGA, of course. A very reliable and competent outfit," Enko laughed.

"I've got another hour to go before my own Pan Am flight leaves for Bangkok. I think I'll go check in my bag and sit in the waiting room. See you in a few days. So long, Santa Claus."

Enko stuck out his hand.

"You look very handsome and dignified with that beret, gray beard, and mustache. So long . . . Mr. Dentner!"

CHAPTER 23

Traveling under the name of Wilford Sprague, General Enko arrived in New York on Wednesday a little after 8:00 P.M. Eastern Standard Time.

While waiting for the departure of his connecting flight to Washington, he bought the New York *Times*, the *Post*, and the next morning's early edition of the *Daily News*.

Almost twenty-four hours after the event, the hijacking was still taking up a considerable amount of space.

"PASSENGERS AND CREW SAFE AND SOUND," was the headline of the *Post*. "SANTA CLAUS—JET PILOT—MASTER-MIND BIGGEST HEIST OF ALL TIME," screamed the *News*. The *Times* devoted one column to the story on the front page. It was followed up by an editorial in the back of the first section lamenting the "sad episode."

The *Times* pontificated, praising the authorities "for their moderation in handling the situation on the one hand." But it criticized them, "on the other hand," for their "lack of vigilance and preparation in meeting threats of this type."

Enko didn't really understand what the paper was trying to say. Muddled thinking and foggy, as usual, he thought.

In any case, the details in all the papers about the progress of the investigation were sketchy and quite stale by now.

Enko listened to WINS and WCBS on a small transistor radio. Everyone was completely baffled.

He boarded his flight, arrived at Washington National Airport just before 10:00 P.M., and took a cab to the Sheraton.

On Wednesday night, at 11:00 P.M., fifty-three hours after he had left his house in a huff, General Enko was taking a shower in his hotel room.

He made himself a drink and lit a cigar. He got into bed and made sure the sheets and the pillows were rumpled then flicked ashes on the carpet and on the tiles of the bathroom floor.

Enko put on his uniform and called his wife.

"Susan?"

"Zach? Where are you?"

"I'm at the Sheraton. I've finished my report and I'm sober. I've been thinking a lot about you, Susan."

"So have I, Zachie baby . . ."

"I love you, Susan. About that house . . . I think we can talk some more if you really have your heart set on it . . ."

"I don't care about the house. I'm worried about you. Zach . . . I love you too."

"I believe I'm in a position to arrange it after all. I'll see about a loan in the morning. How much of a deposit do they want?"

"Fifteen thousand dollars should be sufficient. But if that's what's bothering you, Zach, it can wait."

"I'll take care of it. You'll have the necessary papers before I leave the day after tomorrow."

"Zachie . . ."

"Yes . . ."

"Why don't you come home? . . ." Susan murmured softly.

"Maybe I'd better not . . ."

"Please, Zach . . . I want you . . . so badly . . ."

"You're sure? . . ."

"Yes, please come . . ."

"I'll be there in thirty minutes."

Enko checked out and took a cab to his house.

By midnight, he was making love to his wife, as if it were a second honeymoon.

On Thursday morning, at 11:30, Enko reported to General Lawrence F. Harmon's conference.

The meeting was brief. Harmon collected the reports from the fourteen participants and asked if there were any questions.

There were none.

"I'll study your reports today," Harmon said. "We will meet again tomorrow at 0900. We should be through by 1100. Please make arrangements for transportation back to Vietnam immediately following the conference. Thank you, gentlemen."

The generals and admirals rose and began to file out. Harmon put his hand on Enko's arm and asked him to step aside for a moment.

"I tried to call you at home yesterday, Zach, but you weren't there."

"A little argument with Susan. I stayed at the Sheraton. I needed a little peace and quiet to prepare your plans."

"Sorry I asked."

"That's all right. I guess you have your domestic problems too."

"Who doesn't? I suppose you saw the news. One of your airplanes seems to have gotten into trouble again."

"Oh, you mean that hijacking thing? How did they find out it was a TX-75E?"

"A United pilot saw it. No markings, no numbers. A snoopy newspaperman overheard it at Los Angeles Tower. There were no leaks from here. The Russians and the Chinese know all about the range of the aircraft now."

"Not really, Larry. It could have stayed in the air a couple of hours more, if necessary. The whole thing was over in about eight hours. They're probably still guessing. Two hours is a long time. Let them try to build one. They'll never match it."

"I suppose not."

"At least the airplane proved it wasn't defective and that it could do something, if nothing more than a hijacking," Enko said sarcastically. "Do they know who the pilot was? Any idea where the aircraft came from?"

"A complete blank so far. General Raymond Prominowe is in charge of the investigation. Do you know him?"

"No."

"He may need you when the time comes. Since you're the expert, he'll probably ask you for technical details—that sort of thing."

"Of course, I'll be glad to help."

"How about dinner tonight, Zach? Carrie says she'd love to get together with Susan and you. Did you patch things up?"

"Yes."

"How about you picking us up at seven?"

"OK."

"See you later, Zach."

Enko went to his bank, arranged for a $15,000 loan, and gave the necessary papers to Susan. They went to visit the house in Silver Spring that afternoon. He said he liked it, although he really didn't give a damn.

The dinner party with the Harmons at a fashionable French restaurant was most enjoyable. Enko drank very little but remained in an excellent mood. Everything was going great.

Enko kissed Susan good-by on Friday morning and arrived at the Pentagon a few minutes before nine.

Harmon said he was satisfied with the plans submitted by the participants and thanked everyone for their suggestions. He added that they would now be studied in depth in light of the peace talks, which should be concluded very shortly. Further orders would be transmitted in the near future. In the meantime, full scale bombing operations would be resumed as soon as the conferees returned to Vietnam.

"One last thing, gentlemen," General Harmon said. "Please make yourselves available when the prisoners of war return home. The President's instructions are that all C.O.'s must personally greet and decorate their men when they arrive from Clark Air Force Base, in the Philippines. Ceremonies will be organized at Air Force or Navy bases closest to the prisoners' home towns."

An admiral raised his hand.

"Yes?" Harmon asked.

"That will mean a lot of fast traveling from base to base, General Harmon."

"Things will be scheduled accordingly. Special planes will be at your disposal to give you time to proceed from point to point in the event there are several arrivals on the same day. There will be ample TV and radio coverage. Just remember this: Every prisoner of war is a hero. This is what the President has decided after consultations with the Joint Chiefs of Staff. This will be the final stage of the 'Peace with Honor' program, gentlemen."

A Marine Corps general motioned he had something to say.

"Yes?" Harmon recognized him.

"What about those who fraternized or co-operated with the enemy while in captivity?"

"They're heroes too. Let me make this very clear. EVERY PRISONER OF WAR IS A HERO. I repeat. This is a Presidential order. It is now official government policy and he doesn't want any bickering to mar the homecoming. This is going to be a patriotic event. You make it look good, gentlemen—very good!"

Enko fought hard to suppress a smile.

At 1500, at Andrews Air Force Base, General Enko boarded a C-141 jet transport to go back to Vietnam.

Counting almost forty-eight hours of travel and taking into consideration time zone differences, which had canceled each other out on the round trip, Enko arrived in Da Nang exactly eight days after leaving.

He was greeted by Colonel Bernie McSnair and Captain William Keegan.

McSnair felt cheated. Enko had promised he'd be in charge for two weeks. Keegan was glad to see him if for no other reason but to get McSnair off his back. He eagerly grabbed the General's bags.

Enko proceeded to his office immediately and closeted himself with McSnair.

"How did things go while I was away, Colonel?"

"Fine, sir. No casualties. A few problems with the weather but that's all."

"We have new directives from the Pentagon. Summon a staff conference for tomorrow morning at 0800. I want all the flight leaders to be present."

"Will do, sir."

Enko briefed McSnair on the resumption of bombing operations.

"After the meeting, I'll be going to Thailand. Set up transportation for me. I must co-ordinate fighter protection with the B-52 boys at Udorn. Bear in mind I have to be at that base by 1600 at the latest."

"Yes, sir."

"Anything new on Fielding?"

"I'm afraid not, General. We've had a total of fifteen sweeps over the area since he was lost. It looks pretty hopeless. He's either dead or a POW."

General Enko shook his head sadly.

"That bugs me, McSnair. He was a good man. Did they extend the search to a fifty-mile radius, as I had ordered?"

"I even took the liberty of widening the boundary around Hoa Binh to one hundred miles during your absence, sir. No luck."

"I'm still not satisfied, Colonel. The only way I'll be able to get this thing out of my system is to go looking for that airplane personally—if it's still there. If you want something done right, you do it yourself."

"Begging your pardon, General, don't you think a man of your importance shouldn't be taking such risks flying over enemy territory?"

"You're right, McSnair, of course. But hell, man! I've got the nagging feeling they didn't look in the right place. I just want to be sure that airplane was destroyed. Besides, I liked that boy."

"That's very noble of you, sir, but . . ."

"I want to see with my own eyes. This way, I won't have anyone to blame but myself."

"As you say, General."

"McSnair, on second thought, I've changed my mind about

that transportation. Have an OV-10—fully armed—ready for me to take off tomorrow at 1000, after the staff meeting. I'll fly it myself to Udorn. Call Nakhon Phanom. I'll stop there on the way and have them show me the territory covered by the Sandys and the Jolly Greens. I'll take a look myself after that. It won't be much of a detour and I'll make it to Udorn in plenty of time."

"You want an OV-10, General? Are you certain you wouldn't prefer a single-seater jet?—maybe a TX-75E?"

"No, Colonel. The OV-10 is perfectly suited to my needs. It'll be ideal for the kind of search mission I intend to conduct."

"Who do you want for co-pilot in the back seat, sir?"

"No one. I'll fly it alone. This is my problem. I don't see why I should risk anyone else's neck searching for Fielding at this point. Just have that airplane ready. I'll sleep at Udorn and return the next day—maybe take another look on the way back. That's all, Colonel. Thank you."

"Yes, sir."

Enko conducted the briefing at a brisk pace the next morning. He relayed General Harmon's orders and specified the selected targets. Disregarding Harmon's instructions, he overstepped the boundaries of his authority and informed the flight leaders that these punitive expeditions would be missions of harassment. He stressed that nothing in his eyes would justify the taking of unnecessary risks with men or equipment.

At 0945, the General went to his quarters and donned his flight suit and helmet. He then picked up a large blue B4 canvas bag and his briefcase.

McSnair was waiting outside and offered to help when he saw the General was ready to leave.

Enko insisted on carrying the heavy bulging bag himself to a waiting jeep but allowed the Colonel to take his briefcase.

At 1000, the General dropped his belongings into the rear seat of the OV-10 and sat in the front of the tandem airplane.

With graceful lines similar to those of the famous World War II P-38 "Lightning," the OV-10 was also known as the "Bronco" or the "Workhorse." The sleek-looking, high-wing, twin-prop, twin-tailed aircraft was equipped with dual controls, separate canopies and separate doors for its two occupants. Each seat had its own ejection mechanism. The tandem aircraft was superbly designed for short takeoffs and landings. Its range of speeds from slow flight at 65 knots to high performance at over 240 knots rendered it extremely versatile for a variety of missions over all types of rugged terrain.

Enko was airborne by 1015. He arrived at Nakhon Phanom, Thailand, one hour later and went to the briefing room while the airplane was being refueled.

The General was shown the Fielding file with pilot reports and detailed maps of the search areas scrutinized by the rescue teams. He said very little, looked concerned, and nodded gravely.

McSnair had made arrangements for an escort. Enko canceled them. He would proceed alone.

At 1230, the General took off again. He headed northeast, beyond the Mekong River, over Laos and toward North Vietnam.

Ten miles out, he descended to treetop level as he made a steep left bank. He crossed the river once again and turned northwest, back into Thailand.

Hugging the terrain, invisible to radar, Enko headed toward the town of Nong Khai, located on the Thai side of the Mekong, south of the Laotian capital of Vientiane.

At 1255, precisely, the General gunned the engines twice as the OV-10 made a low pass over a brick-red dirt road winding through abandoned rice paddies gouged by bombs during counter-insurgency and "mopping up" missions.

Anti-Thai government rebel terrorist activity had recently ceased in this sector. Enko discounted the possibility of ground fire but, nevertheless, remained alert as he surveyed the barren fields and deserted villages.

The muddy trail continued west, toward Nong Khai, five miles distant, as it first bordered then disappeared into a teak forest charred by napalm.

He made a 180-degree turn and flew back slowly over the narrow strip of earth.

Still disguised as Harold Dentner, Grant emerged crouching from the forest. For a brief moment, he stood full height in the middle of the path, waved, then took cover in a ditch.

Enko spotted him, about a mile ahead of the nose of the airplane. He reduced speed further and touched down lightly at less than 70 MPH. As the airplane rolled closer to Grant over the potholes, he cut the right engine.

Grant swung open the back door, hopped aboard, and sat behind Enko.

The General started the right engine, added power, made a short soft field takeoff, and was off the ground in less than a minute.

"Your parachute's in my B4 bag," Enko said.

"What about the rest?" Grant asked.

"Everything's in the bag. I had a hell of a time carrying it, pretending it wasn't heavy," Enko laughed.

Flying low, at full power, the General pointed the airplane toward Sam Neua, in northern Laos, close to the North Vietnamese border.

The cockpit was small and the bag took up a considerable amount of room. Grant had a hard time wriggling out of his clothing. He cracked open the door and threw the items out of the airplane one at a time. Next, he took off his beard, mustache, and beret, got rid of them as well, then closed the door.

"Any problems getting to the rendezvous? How do you feel?" Enko inquired.

"It took me three days via Bangkok and Vientiane. I hardly got any sleep at all since I left Los Angeles, in fact since I took off from Baja California. Just caught a wink here and there, cat naps mainly, on airplanes."

"Good. You look tired and beat—exactly what we need."

"Thanks."

"Were you spotted? Anyone suspicious follow you?"

"Didn't give them a chance. I landed in Vientiane posing as a respectable historian gathering material for a book about Southeast Asia. Everyone and his brother is writing books on the subject . . . No one was surprised when I said I thought I had the solution to the Asian problem. They just smiled."

"Go on."

"I took a sightseeing tour on a bus immediately after I got to town. I left the group of tourists listening to the guide in front of some temple or other and slipped out of the city without ever checking into a hotel. In the evening, I tipped the ferry guy ten bucks to cross the river incognito to Nong Khai. I snuck out as soon as I got there and walked the rest of the way to where you picked me up."

"Good boy!"

"What about you, General? Anything new in Washington or Da Nang?"

"They'll never figure out how we pulled it off. They've got a million theories but they're groping in the dark. Believe it or not, the General in charge of the Pentagon investigation—Prominowe is his name—wants to consult with me about the TX-75E, hoping I can give him a lead. How do you like that?"

Grant laughed as he unzipped Enko's bag.

He found underwear, a flight suit, boots, a helmet, rations, a jungle survival kit, a pistol, and the parachute. It took him a good fifteen minutes, plenty of cursing and contortions to get dressed again.

"Are you all set now?" Enko asked.

"I just have to buckle up the parachute, General, but I think I'll do that later. No need to be uncomfortable. How long before we get there?"

"No rush. We've got another forty-five minutes or so to go yet. It's a little over 250 miles. We'll be there by 1400. You get yourself captured quickly and you should be at the Hanoi Hilton in time for dinner à la carte. A real vacation compared to all the running around we've been doing during the last month. You'll get all the sleep you want."

"I'm still not too crazy about the whole idea, General. I sure hope I don't regret this. Suppose the war goes on?"

"It won't. We've already sold out. General Harmon assured me the POWs will be home by Christmas or New Year's at the latest. Anyway, it's too late now. You no longer have any choice and neither have I."

"You'd better be right, General. By the way, are you sure this parachute will work?"

"You still don't trust me, hey, Grant? In spite of that letter in your vault. We've been through all that. We need each other. Fishing out the stuff from the Widgeon will be a two-man operation. I couldn't do it alone and I certainly don't need another partner."

The OV-10 was coming up on Sam Neua. It was 1346. Enko turned to the right on a course that would put the airplane ten miles to the east of the town.

"OK, Grant. Better get ready. We're about to cross the border. We'll be southwest of Hoa Binh in about fifteen minutes."

263

Grant bent down into the cockpit to adjust his parachute straps, taking his eyes off the horizon.

"Duck!" Enko shouted. "We've got company, goddammit! Get as low as you can. Put on an oxygen mask. I don't want anyone to see you."

"What is it?" Grant yelled back as he crouched behind the General, his nose almost touching the floor of the cockpit.

"Don't know. Looks like a Phantom . . . an old single seater F 4C. It's at ten o'clock—about three miles—heading straight for us," Enko answered, putting on his own oxygen mask to hide his features.

"What the hell does he want?" Grant moaned as the blood rushed to his brain. He was doubled over, trying to keep his head between his knees in an attempt to roll himself into a ball.

"No idea. He seems to be in trouble . . . he's rocking his wings. You just sit tight . . . listen in on your earphones. Here he comes . . . don't move!"

The F4 Phantom approached, reduced speed to match the 270 MPH of the OV-10, and lined up in formation off Enko's left wing.

Skip Spence, a lanky, slow-speaking captain from Racine, Wisconsin, had problems indeed.

The Phantom was in sad shape. It had been badly shot up, apparently by ground fire. A direct hit had pulverized the black radar nose cone and substantially damaged the instrument panel. A chunk of the left wing tip was missing. Tracer bullet holes ran in rows down the fuselage from the back of the cockpit to the tail. Hydraulic fluid was leaking from the wings and the undercarriage, leaving red trails along the outer metal skin of the aircraft.

Skip looked at the General and cupped his right hand over his earphone repeatedly, indicating with his hand signals that he wanted to talk on the radio. His face was covered by his oxygen mask but Enko could see his eyes. They were half closed and tearing. The man was obviously in agony.

Enko cupped his left hand over his earphone and nodded he understood. He then waved his hands in front of the side window of the cockpit to tell the pilot of the Phantom he did not know which frequency to use.

Skip nodded and answered by raising one finger, then two, then four.

Enko turned his VHF dials to 124.0.

"Phantom, go ahead. Bronco is on one two four point zero."

There was no reply.

Skip looked at Enko, shook his head to say he was not receiving, and motioned for him to try 122.5.

The General called again on the second frequency.

This time, Skip nodded and grabbed his mike.

"Boy! Am I glad to see you. I was just about to give up. Couldn't make up my mind whether to bail out or belly land."

"What's your problem?" Enko asked, trying to conceal his annoyance.

"I'm lost, man. Radar and radios are gone. Lucky I got you on this frequency. I think it's the only one left that's working. Don't even have a compass any more. Haven't got any idea where the hell I am, except I know I was heading west. I got hit in the right leg. Can't tell if it's a bullet or shrapnel. Hurts like hell, and I'm bleeding like a pig. I need medical attention."

"What do you want me to do?" Enko inquired, forcing himself not to sound bored.

"Which way to Thailand?"

"Where are you going?"

"Udorn."

"You'll never make it, Phantom. You've got fuel pissing out from under your right wing. Better go to Nakhon Phanom. It's closer. You'll have a better chance."

"OK. Take me there."

"Can't now. Urgent rescue to perform south of Hanoi. I'll point you in the right direction."

"I don't give a shit about your other stuff. I'm more urgent. I need a transfusion. Now you take me to Thailand. That's your job!"

Enko bit his lip and swallowed hard in frustration. He couldn't tell the Phantom pilot who he was and order him to proceed to Nakhon Phanom. His main concern at the moment was to drop Grant. Time was short. He had to think.

"Phantom," he said, "we're going the wrong way. I'm entering a 110-degree turn to the right. You get behind my tail and follow me."

"Why can't I stay right where I am. I like it fine off your left wing."

"Because I don't want you next to me in case you blow up with all those fuel leaks. No need for both of us to go at the same time. I'll feel more comfortable if you stay in the back."

"Thanks for the encouragement," Skip said as he threw Enko a hateful look. He understood the Bronco pilot's logic, however, and slowly began to drop back behind the OV-10.

Enko made sure his transmitter was off.

"Grant?" he shouted. "Did you hear? This guy's a pain in the ass. That's all we need. Tales of woe and sob stories."

"Well, we've got to help him somehow."

"Why?"

"Because he's hurt and he's lost, that's why. I don't understand you."

"That stupid bastard! Can't even find his way without his radar and radios. What the hell is he doing flying a Phantom if he can't even read a map."

"He says he's in pain. Maybe he can't concentrate. Maybe he can't reach his maps."

"Bullshit. One little scratch and these jerks panic. He comes barging in just before I'm about to drop you off. Of all the rotten luck . . ."

"General, listen to me. Take him to Nakhon Phanom then bring me back. It'll delay things a couple of hours. That's no tragedy."

"Can't do that, Grant. Don't have enough fuel to make it there and back then go to Udorn. Total endurance is less than four hours. I can't land at Nakhon Phanom to top off the tanks with you inside. Besides I'm expected at Udorn at 1600. I'm late already. They'll be wondering what the hell I'm doing. Also, I'm not so sure this jerk didn't spot you. That, Grant, is a chance we cannot take. I'm supposed to be alone in this airplane."

"What do you suggest we do?"

"Don't know—yet. I'm thinking."

Enko remained silent for a few minutes then switched on his transmitter.

"Phantom? You still there?"

"Right behind you."

"OK. We've got about an hour to go."

"Roger," Skip acknowledged.

Enko made sure his mike was off.

"This situation remind you of anything, Grant?" he shouted.

266

"Yeah. PGA 81. Only now *we're* being shadowed."

"Grant, I've made up my mind."

"What are we going to do?"

"I've just flipped the toggle switches to arm the rockets. I'll talk to him as I add power and make a sudden 360 to the left. Shoot him down broadside when you get a good angle while I concentrate on the flying."

"General, have you gone mad?"

"We can't have any witnesses. Shoot him. That's an order."

"But that's killing a defenseless man in cold blood—one of our own."

"Fuck him. He's got no business getting lost. Shoot him, you idiot. Don't argue. Now get ready."

Enko squeezed his mike button.

"Phantom, are you OK?"

"Getting a little woozy. Still losing blood but I guess I can hold out. How far to go yet?"

"About fifty minutes. You relax now. Everything's going to be all right," Enko said soothingly as he abruptly pushed the throttles and banked steeply to the left to circle around the jet fighter.

Grant raised his head just above the back of the General's seat, his finger on the firing button for the rocket under the left wing.

The Phantom suddenly came into his line of sight.

For a fraction of a second, Grant was in perfect position for a deadly shot. His hand trembled. He took his finger off the button as if it had been burned and ducked back toward the floor of the cockpit.

"What the hell are you doing, buzzing around me?" Skip asked Enko.

The General thought quickly while he kept showering Grant with profanities.

"Thought I saw a MIG for a second above us at two o'clock. I figured it would be best to protect your tail. Sorry I couldn't warn you."

"You scared the hell out of me, man. And here you were telling me to relax."

"I think I'd better sit on your ass from now on," Enko said. "I'll give you the necessary course corrections if you drift off. This way I've got you in sight and I can see what's coming. We're over the Ho Chi Minh Trail now. You keep your eyes open too."

"OK. I'll try but I'm very busy up here. Nothing's working on this airplane. Just let's get there for God's sake."

The General lined up the Bronco behind and a little to the left of the Phantom. The fighter kept pitching and rolling as Skip tried to keep it under control.

Grant raised his head again and took a peek over Enko's shoulder. The airplanes were at eleven thousand feet, heading southeast over mountains. There was a thick bank of clouds about ten miles ahead.

Enko called Skip.

"Correct about ten degrees to the left, Phantom. You're drifting."

"OK."

Skip banked, exposing the side of his fuselage, but Enko kept going straight.

"You're doing fine, Phantom. Just turn a little more," Enko said, setting himself up for an ideal broadside shot as Skip unwittingly obeyed his instructions.

The General's finger was on the button for the rocket under the right wing. He couldn't miss.

Grant watched, horrified. In a second, the Phantom would be blown to bits. He closed his eyes, feeling he was about to get sick.

"Just a little more," Enko said gently. "That's it, Phantom, you're looking good . . . just right . . ."

Grant grabbed the back seat control stick, pulled it violently toward him, and turned it to the right as Enko pushed the button.

The OV-10 pointed its nose toward the sky, then began to fall off on the right wing as the rocket streaked past the top of the Phantom's canopy, just missing the tip of the right wing.

Skip disappeared into the clouds ahead.

"What the fuck's wrong with you, Bronco? What are you shooting at? Where are you?"

Enko was trembling. Again, he thought fast.

"I saw that MIG again. I took a crack at him with a heat-seeker."

"Well, you almost got me, you stupid bastard. I didn't see him. Where are you now?"

"I lost you in those clouds while I had my eye on that MIG."

"What do I do now, Bronco?"

"You just let down to nine thousand . . . Oh, I forgot . . . your altimeter isn't working either. Tell you what. Get below the cloud cover. You'll have plenty of clearance above the terrain," Enko lied. "I'll try to find you. Otherwise, you just follow the river. It'll take you to Nakhon Phanom. If you can add a little power, you should be there in about twenty minutes."

"OK. But you come back and look for me, hear?"

"I'll do my best to locate you. Don't you worry about that," Enko said.

The mountaintops were at about ten thousand feet and Skip almost hit a peak as he let down according to Enko's directives. He managed to avoid a ridge in the nick of time and found himself in a valley. The Mekong River was below him. He followed it to Nakhon Phanom.

Enko looked frantically for the Phantom but couldn't find it. He was furious.

"I suppose you're happy now, Grant. You've done your good deed for the day."

"General, I couldn't let you shoot down one of our own men. It's bigger than I am."

"You're proud of yourself, hey? You idiot. One more casualty, one less, when we've already lost more than fifty thousand men. What the hell's the difference? No one would ever miss that guy. Do you realize what your stupidity is now liable to cost? Twenty-four million bucks, not to mention going to jail?"

"It isn't worth the money to me. I didn't let you drown when I could have kept everything. Why should I shoot him or let you kill him? He doesn't have much of a chance anyway, now that you sent him into those mountains. But, at least, the odds are better of his making it by himself than with your 'helping him along.' "

"Listen to that shit!" Enko fumed as he kept chasing after the Phantom. "Grant, you'll never learn. He must be over the river by now. I'll find him. I'm going after that sonofabitch and, this time, I'm going to get him."

"General," Grant said between his teeth, "you're not going after anyone. Now you take me to the drop point or the deal is off. I mean it!"

Enko hesitated for a moment, then banked the aircraft to the left, made a 180-degree turn, and headed back for North Vietnam.

"OK. You win . . . but you're stupid! I only hope I can straighten out this mess if this jerk wants to make something of it. Otherwise, we're in big trouble."

"You'll figure something out, if I know you, General."

At 1430—thirty minutes behind the schedule he had set for himself—Enko was hugging the ground southwest of Hoa Binh. There was good cloud cover.

"OK, Grant, this is it. Get ready."

"I'll be through buckling up this parachute in a minute," Grant said as he bent down and groped for the straps.

"See you soon. It's going to be a real vacation. Have a good rest."

"Stop trying to sell me the idea it's going to be a picnic."

"I told you. It's a matter of days before the peace accords are signed, a few weeks maybe—a couple of months at the most."

"I'm ready now," Grant said.

"I'll take you up into those clouds. They're at about fifteen hundred. That'll give you plenty of time for a nice easy ride down."

Enko put the OV-10 into a steep climb. He leveled off at 1,850 feet, well inside the clouds, slowed the aircraft down to under 80 MPH, and cut off the right engine.

Grant opened the door, slipped out onto the tiny handrails welded to the side of the fuselage and climbed on the wing behind the still propeller. He crawled toward the back of the fuselage, and let himself fall into the gaping hole between the twin tail booms of the aircraft.

Enko started the engine, secured the rear door, and descended immediately to hug the ground once again. He saw Grant's parachute floating down.

The General reached Udorn half an hour late but without further incident.

He attended his meeting, went to the Officers' Club for drinks and dinner, then immediately got into bed.

The next morning, he took off for Da Nang, where he arrived at 1100. He called McSnair into his office.

"Colonel, I took a look around. You were right. It does look pretty hopeless. Let's just pray he destroyed the aircraft. Cancel all further searches for Grant Fielding."

Captain Skip Spence had been lucky enough to find his way to Nakhon Phanom. He made a successful belly landing after his damaged undercarriage refused to function and was rushed to the infirmary.

The next day, while Enko was returning from Udorn to Da Nang, Skip asked for a debriefing officer to be brought to his bedside. Captain Gilbert Grelley came at once.

"You probably won't believe this," Skip said, "but the damnedest thing happened to me yesterday with an OV-10."

Captain Grelley was a squat, no-nonsense career man, of little patience.

"What was the problem?"

"I had the weirdest feeling this guy wanted to use me for target practice. So help me, I thought he wanted to finish me off. He was imagining MIGs all over the place. I never saw one. I tell you, this guy wanted to kill me!"

Captain Grelley gave Skip Spence a peculiar look.

"Where did this happen?"

"I'll be damned if I know. All I can remember is that it was someplace south or southwest of Hanoi. My instrument panel was shot to hell. I couldn't tell where I was. That's why I asked him to help."

"Did you get the number of the OV-10 you're talking about?"

"Who the hell was thinking of taking down numbers? I was almost out cold with pain and loss of blood."

Skip saw the incredulous look on Grelley's face and became very agitated.

"What's the matter with you?" Skip shouted. "Don't you believe me? I'm telling you that guy shot a rocket at me. He was trying to get my ass."

"Calm yourself," Grelley said. "You've been through a lot since yesterday. You lost a considerable amount of blood. You wouldn't have made it without the transfusions. You've suffered some kind of shock."

"That's right. Tell me I'm crazy!"

"Now, now, Spence, relax. The doctor said you shouldn't get excited."

"Excited? Balls, Grelley! Do you know it's a good thing I didn't listen to him or I would have ended up on the side of a mountain.

271

He steered me right into a ridge, the sonofabitch. I just don't understand it!"

Grelley decided he'd better play along.

"Did you see the man's face? Can you describe him?"

"No. He was wearing an oxygen mask. So was I, for that matter."

"And you have no idea where all this took place?"

"I've already told you. It was about twenty minutes south or southwest of Hanoi. I was in a Phantom. You figure out the distance. It was over very rough terrain. Ten-thousand-foot peaks. I found the Mekong a short time later. It must have been somewhere along the North Vietnamese-Laotian border."

"What time was it?"

"About 1400."

"Were there one or two crewmen aboard the OV-10?"

"I just saw one guy in the front. He seemed to have some bundles in the back seat. I think he was carrying parachutes or something in the rear."

"OK. We'll check it out. There are a lot of OV-10s around, Captain Spence. We'll have to track down the ones that operated in that sector at that hour. It's going to be hard to pinpoint."

"I'm telling you the guy who was in that Bronco is a homicidal maniac . . . a psycho . . . a nut. Find that sonofabitch. I want to give him a piece of my mind—and have him put away—before he kills somebody!"

Grelley left and went back to his office. His first conclusion was that Spence had become paranoid with battle fatigue. He was obviously suffering from hallucinations caused by his wounds. He imagined the rescue planes of the U.S. Air Force were trying to shoot him down. Ridiculous! He decided to refer the matter to the base psychiatrist.

Grant had landed about a mile from the spot where he had originally disappeared during the raid over Hoa Binh a month before.

He immediately gathered his parachute, buried it, and hid in the brush.

All he had to do was wait to be escorted to the Hanoi Hilton.

As luck would have it, no one had seen Grant's parachute. He didn't have dinner at the Hilton that night as suggested by Enko.

In fact, he lived off his rations for the next five days in the damp North Vietnamese jungle.

He became nauseous from the pungent odor of chlorophyll and the rancid smell of decay permeating the jungle. He grew weaker by the day and developed an overwhelming fear of snakes.

Grant was begging to be captured, but no one was looking for him. He began to worry about North Vietnamese patrols and the likelihood of getting shot accidentally by an overzealous member of the people's militia.

He decided to come out into the open on the sixth day.

Looking haggard, unshaven, and emaciated from hunger, Grant timidly made his way toward Hoa Binh.

Around sunset, he heard sounds coming from a rice paddy. He hid in a ditch and took a look. Peasants!

Grant ran toward the villagers with his hands up and collapsed, exhausted, at their feet.

It took Grant another week to get to Hanoi, traveling by night, in a broken down truck, over gutted dirt roads, crossing rivers over pontoon bridges or by makeshift ferries. He finally arrived at the old municipal prison in the center of Hanoi known as the Hilton.

He was led under an archway and taken into a yard surrounded by low buildings. A heavy iron gate was opened and he was ushered into a second yard bordered on two sides by two buildings at right angles to each other. They were the POW compounds. The dorms were shared by sixty or eighty men. They were at ground level. In the middle of the second yard there was a fountain where some of the American prisoners were washing their laundry. Grant waved at them as he was taken to the interrogating officer.

Clean-shaven and pale, dressed in a striped prison uniform pajama, Grant stood before Colonel Nguyen Van Duc, who spoke good English and who was otherwise known as "Duckie," "Donald Duck," or "Daffy Duck" to the habitués of the Hilton.

"From what we have gathered," the Colonel said, "it has been over a month since you say you were shot down. Where were you all this time?"

"I was unconscious and ill the first few days. I waited in the jungle, hoping someone would find me and get me to a hospital."

"And then?"

"I began to feel better, and I started to think of how I was going to get back to South Vietnam. I decided to head west, toward Laos then possibly into Thailand."

Colonel Nguyen Van Duc was an old hand at interrogating American prisoners. Grant's story left him quite skeptical.

"Where did your airplane go down?"

"Somewhere south of Hoa Binh. I activated the self-destruct before I jumped."

"What type of airplane was it?"

"I'm not at liberty to say. The Geneva Convention . . ."

"Don't start with that nonsense about the Geneva Convention. There was not too much activity around Hoa Binh during the last few weeks, Captain Fielding. We did not find many remains of airplanes. Those that we located had their pilots near them. We found nothing so far to match your version of the events. I could have you shot as a spy."

"I am not a spy. I was shot down over Hoa Binh."

The Colonel was making notes.

"Captain Fielding, we will pursue the matter of the exact circumstances of your arrival in North Vietnam at another time. As a matter of personal interest, I would like to know what you think of your disgusting imperialistic war now that you are here, in my custody?"

"I have no political opinions, Colonel. I was just doing my duty and serving my country," Grant answered with patriotic fervor.

He received a slap across the mouth by one of the guards for his trouble.

The interrogation was adjourned to the next day.

Grant was assigned to a dormitory where he gave the former arrivals the latest news. He became a model prisoner, a real morale booster for the others. He also became the local chess champion.

CHAPTER 24

Grant expected to remain a prisoner for about six weeks and to be home by Christmas, as promised by Enko.

As it turned out, he was the guest of the Hanoi Hilton for over five months. He cursed the General every day of his captivity.

Grant maintained a dignified pose throughout the harrowing interrogations. He refused to meet with visiting peace apostles from the States. Politely but with contempt, he declined to send messages home on the radio or to express any political opinions.

As the weeks went by and the bombings continued, Grant became apprehensive, thinking the conflict might be prolonged indefinitely. He was especially concerned about the letter in the vault he was using as protection against Enko. It would be opened in a few months if the North Vietnamese did not list him soon as a POW. No matter how hard he tried, there was no way he could find out if his name had been released.

Grant was beginning to despair when, finally, a C-141 "medical evacuation transport" landed in Hanoi. Without a word of explanation, Grant was led out of the Hanoi Hilton, put into a bus, and taken to Gia Lam airport.

Together with another 64 men, he was flown to Clark Air Force Base, in the Philippines.

A red carpet was placed before the aircraft while a military band played marches.

An admiral in full regalia stood at the bottom of the steps. He enthusiastically returned the prisoners' salutes as they came down and shook his hand.

The families of servicemen stationed at the base formed the welcoming committee. They cheered while cameras recorded the event, which was relayed "live" to the United States via satellite.

Wives, children, sweethearts, parents, relatives, friends, and neighbors huddled around television sets from coast to coast to watch the historic return.

Mothers fainted. Fathers beamed with pride and joy when their sons appeared on screen. Their emotions were dutifully taped by TV crews who had set up their cameras in the returnees' homes.

Grant was one of the last men to leave the airplane. And back in Stamford, his mother screamed with delight. Mr. Fielding cleared his throat.

Grant was led with the others to a podium where he waited his turn to say a few words into the mike.

Many of the men spoke with a lump in their throat. Some, who had spent a few years in Hanoi, cried openly without shame upon tasting freedom once again. They were loudly applauded.

Grant was asked to speak. He decided to be brief.

"I only tried to do my duty," he said with feeling. "I can hardly wait to get back home. So many wonderful things are in store."

Now reassigned to the Pentagon, General Enko was staring at his TV screen with more than passing interest. He started making plans.

The prisoners were scheduled to remain at Clark for a few days. Medical attention was to be lavished upon them. Psychiatric programs for "readjustment, rehabilitation, and readaptation" were designed to enable them to meet the challenges of the free world back home.

Grant asked to return to the United States at once.

The psychiatrist assigned to his case was baffled. He could not get over the fact that Grant kept maintaining he was feeling fine, that he was not bitter, and that he had no complaints.

This was extraordinary as far as the psychiatrist was concerned. He insisted on putting Grant through a complete battery of tests.

Grant was very patient and understanding with him. He explained at length that he had been a prisoner for only five months. He had no wife or children to worry about. His emotional problems had, therefore, been minimal, he assured the therapist.

Within a few hours, Grant had passed the tests with flying colors. He left the psychiatrist shaking his head at the astonishing degree of will, stamina, and determination shown by his patient.

The second day after his arrival at Clark, Grant was asked to report to debriefing. He was also told that a seat would be available to him aboard a jet transport leaving for California in the evening, if he so desired.

Grant was driven in a jeep to the operations building. He was shown into a drab, depressing office.

"I'm Colonel Guy Klavell, from Military Intelligence. Welcome, Captain Fielding," said the bald-headed man in charge, as he shook his hand.

"Delighted to be here, sir."

"Would it be all right if I had a few words with you, Captain? That is, if you're not too tired to answer a few questions? They tell me you're feeling OK. But I can wait if you don't think you're up to it right now and wish to remain here a few more days."

Grant's heart sank.

"I'm fine, sir. Go right ahead."

"It's about your airplane, Captain. I have a request from the Pentagon to find out whatever happened to your TX-75E in North Vietnam after you were shot down over Hoa Binh."

"The aircraft was destroyed, sir."

"How?"

"I managed to arm the self-destruct mechanism at the last second before I succeeded in bailing out."

"Why didn't you confirm that to your flight leader, who was calling you at the time?"

"I did, sir. I had a fire in the cockpit. The wires were burning. My radio must have gone out at that moment."

"That explains it. You're sure the airplane was destroyed, though?"

"Colonel Klavell, I personally guarantee no trace of this aircraft will ever be found."

"Excellent. That's good enough for me. You're probably wondering, Captain, why I'm asking all these questions?"

"Frankly, yes."

"In the first place we wanted to make sure the enemy didn't get their hands on it. Secondly, since you've been out of touch with things for almost six months, you're probably not aware that a TX-75E was used to conduct the hijacking of a PGA airliner proceeding from Los Angeles to Honolulu."

"I can't believe it. When did this happen?"

"Oh, about a month after you were shot down.

"Please tell me more, Colonel."

Klavell related the story to Grant, who looked surprised at first, then genuinely shocked by what he heard.

"So, you see, Captain Fielding, Intelligence thought for a moment it might have been your airplane used by the North Vietnamese for a propaganda stunt. They could have shipped the plane by freighter and launched it from the deck somewhere off the California coast. There was a theory that a turncoat in captivity could have become a North Vietnamese sympathizer and pulled it off, to give Hanoi the money."

"Really? That's incredible!"

"Of course, he would have needed your airplane in good condition. Now that we know it was destroyed, that takes care of that."

"Where did he get the airplane, then?"

"That's what we don't know. We're checking out every man who's ever flown a TX-75E. One of them might be able to give us a clue, some fresh ideas, a lead."

"Well, I wish you luck, Colonel Klavell. Oh, by the way, was the money ever found?"

"The TX-75E, the Widgeon, and the money disappeared without a trace. The owner of the Widgeon got a brand new Gates Learjet—the greedy bastard. For a while, we thought he might have been an accomplice but upon questioning him, we discovered he was much too stupid and panicky. Apparently the hijackers had previously checked out Van Nuys and knew there was a Widgeon there. They had thought of everything. It doesn't look as if anyone will be able to figure this one out for quite a while. But I'm keeping you, and you certainly have other things on your mind. Thank you, Captain Fielding. You've been most helpful."

"I thank you, Colonel Klavell. You made me feel much better. Good-by, sir."

"Have a good trip home, Captain."

In a brand new uniform, under a marvelous California sun, Grant stepped out of a giant C5A parked in front of the terminal at Travis Air Force Base.

Grant had traveled from the Philippines with eleven other POWs. The welcome of the local residents matched the enthusiastic arrival at Clark a few days before. Again, Grant was asked to say a few words.

"I'm certain I speak for all of us in saying we're thrilled to be back home. Although I come from Connecticut, I have a very soft spot for California—it's a place of rich memories for me. As soon as I'm able to do so, I assure you I will return. This is where I intend to recover. Thank you all for your welcome. We feel very proud."

At Travis, Grant learned that his back pay and bonuses for the time he had spent in captivity didn't amount to much—just a few thousand dollars. Nevertheless, he thought, this little nest egg would come in handy. It would permit him to circulate until such time as he straightened things out with Enko.

Some of the men who had remained in prison for several years received over $150,000. Grant reflected that, if he had had a choice, he would have never exchanged his freedom for any amount of money.

There was no Air Force base close to Grant's home in Stamford, Connecticut. Forty-eight hours after his arrival in California, Grant was informed that the official welcoming ceremony honoring his return would take place at Bridgeport Municipal Airport. He would be flown there the next day, together with two other POW pilots from the same general area. They would be dropped off on the way at McGuire AFB, New Jersey, and at Stewart in Newburgh, New York.

An elaborate reception had been planned for Grant at Bridgeport in the late afternoon.

The elegant little passenger terminal was decorated with bunting. Little flags had been passed around to the crowd of about five hundred by the American Legion and the Veterans of Foreign Wars. Children waved them with ardor. A military band and a school band played marches.

Antiwar members of the Yale Political Union staged a small protest. They tried to boycott and disrupt the festivities by lining up a few pickets carrying signs with slogans such as "WHAT PEACE? WHAT HONOR?" There were a few scuffles. The students were promptly hustled out of the airport by the police assisted by diehards belonging to the veterans' organizations.

Grant's parents were crying with emotion. His girl friend Jennifer had arrived from Hartford and was standing a little to the side of his family.

Grant exited from the rear door of the Air Force transport, smiled, and waved from the top of the steps as the military band played "God Bless America." He came down quickly and fell into the arms of his family. For the benefit of the television cameras, he gave Jennifer a long, passionate kiss.

General Enko came out of the terminal when the tumult had died down. He shook Grant's hand and patted him on the back as photographers from the local papers clicked away and kept asking for "one more."

Enko led Grant to a podium.

The General delivered a five-minute speech extolling the virtues of the returning hero. The address was constantly interrupted by thunderous applause.

"The country will never be able to repay Grant Fielding for his sacrifice," Enko said, as he pinned a medal on Grant's chest and smartly saluted him.

Grant returned the salute as the crowd went wild.

"It is my pleasure to inform you," Enko said, beaming, "that upon my personal recommendation, the Department of Defense has promoted you to the rank of major. You deserve recognition for your brilliant performance. I am delighted for you. Now it's your turn to say a few words, MAJOR Fielding."

Looking overwhelmed, humble, and modest, Grant stepped up to the mike.

"I only want to say that I cherish the time I spent in the service of my country under the wonderful and stimulating leadership of men like General Zachary Enko. I consider it a privilege to think of him as having been my friend and partner in the fortunes of war. I found the experience most rewarding, I assure you."

The veterans led the cheering and the applause.

Grant raised his hands above his head to quiet down his admirers.

"However, my friends, I regret to tell you that I have decided to leave the Armed Forces, although I thank all those responsible for this promotion. I will remember all of you, and the General in particular, with great affection."

Murmurs of disappointment rippled through the crowd. Enko looked surprised and saddened by Grant's announcement.

"Would you like to tell us what you intend to do now, Major?"

"I did a lot of thinking while I was a prisoner. I believe I should now undertake what I've always wanted to do. I want to study law and criminology, together with sociology and psychology. I intend to go to Harvard or Yale on the GI Bill, that is if they'll have me, General."

"I'm sure their doors will be wide open for a man of your talents, Major."

"Thank you for your continued confidence in me, sir."

"We'll be sorry to lose you, Major. But this, I hope, will not affect our personal friendship in any way. Keep in touch with us. The country needs men like you!"

"I'll keep in touch. You can bet on that, General."

Enko waved at the leader of the military band, who struck up another march as the crowd applauded, then disbanded. After shaking hands with Grant's parents, the General took him by the arm and they walked out of earshot, toward the airplane that was shortly to take Enko back to Washington.

"I've got to decorate a couple of more guys in the next few days—in Savannah and someplace in Florida, I think. Don't try to call or see me for the moment. I read the report on your debriefing at Clark. I'm waiting for the one from Travis. You're doing great but be very careful if they should ask you any more questions. Nothing new on the Pentagon side. They're still fooling around with their computers, but the CIA has also been asked to investigate."

"When are we going to get together?"

"I'll meet you in a few weeks at the White House gala reception. After that, I can take a couple of weeks vacation and go with you to the 'dive-in' bank."

The General's crew was approaching to ready his plane for departure.

"Good-by for now, Major Fielding, and good luck," Enko said aloud.

Grant shook the General's hand, saluted, and walked toward his father's car.

During his recuperation period in Stamford, Grant made sure the letter was still in his bank vault. He settled his pending affairs, brought his papers up to date, and applied to several universities for admission in the fall.

Grant had a few stormy meetings with Jennifer during which he broke things off.

It was a messy, painful, and tearful separation.

Although he tried to make her understand he had changed, during and because of the war and his captivity, she still wanted to cling to him.

She finally went back to Hartford, convinced that his new sense of values and his desire to pursue an academic career were totally opposed to her romantic conception of life.

There were no loose ends. Grant was now free of all ties and ready for Enko.

At the Pentagon, Captain Fred Scarlata was shown into the office of General Raymond Prominowe.

"Yes, Scarlata? What's on your mind?"

"Two things, sir. Senator Porter Bancroft is very unhappy. One of his constituents, Captain Skip Spence from Racine, claims he's being maligned. He was a Phantom pilot in Vietnam and he's sending letters to newspapers charging that the Pentagon is party to a cover-up. Apparently he's been grounded for psychiatric reasons—a nervous breakdown after being wounded in North Vietnam at the tail end of the hostilities. Spence insists he was attacked by one of our own rescue planes—an OV-10—after being hit by ground fire."

"What's this got to do with us? Why doesn't the Air Force look into it?"

"They have, sir. But Spence has told Senator Bancroft they're trying to brush him off as a mental case because no one wants to rock the boat. The Senator wants us to conduct a full investigation before the matter reaches undue proportions. As you know, Senator Bancroft sits on the Armed Forces Committee . . ."

"I know, I know," General Prominowe said impatiently. He sighed and shook his head. "OK. Put the file on my desk, Scarlata. I'll take a look at it and discuss it with you later. Now, what else?"

"It's about the 'Shadow 81' hijacking file, sir."

"Oh, anything new?"

"I'm afraid not, sir. Interviews of TX-75E pilots are still being conducted but, so far, we've had nothing to go on."

"So?"

"Well, General, it's been almost seven months since the hijacking took place. I still have two men working full time on the dossier. I'm also handling incoming reports on those Russian arms shipments to the Middle East. I'm flooded with them. Their new SAM is giving us a lot of trouble. I just can't gather enough intelligence on it."

"And you don't have the adequate manpower to handle the hijacking and the arms shipments at the same time. Is that it?"

"Briefly put, yes, sir. I have to do one or the other, depending on your priority assignments."

"The Middle East is more important right now. That comes first. Tell you what to do." The General sighed wearily. "Take the Shadow 81 file out and leave it on my desk. I'll follow it up personally."

It was one of the most lavish affairs ever to take place at the White House. Tents had been set up on the lawn. The food was superb and the champagne magnificent. There was dancing under the stars to the accompaniment of the best musicians in the country.

The President was in his glory. Dressed in a tuxedo and fully aware of the TV cameras, he stepped up to the mike. He made a resonant and vigorous speech exalting and idolizing the former POWs, their wives, their children, and the rest of their families for their heroism under adversity. He lauded their devotion to duty, courage, gallantry, strength of character, doggedness, patience, and perseverance.

In "passing," the President pointedly reminded everyone listening that his policy of negotiating from "a position of strength" had paid off, although it had required sacrifices. His determination to "stick it out" had proven correct, he insisted. The decision had not been easy, he said, adding, with a controlled sob in his voice, that he had spent many sleepless nights thinking of the plight of the POWs.

The applause was well orchestrated.

Generals, admirals, and senior POW officers spoke. They commended the tenacity shown by their men while in captivity. They all sang the praises of the President and his wonderful leadership. He had been one of the few men with enough vision to see "the light at the end of the tunnel."

During the speeches, Enko picked up two glasses of champagne and led Grant aside, under a tree, then looked around to make sure they couldn't be overheard.

"I've got a boat set up in Long Beach," he whispered. "We'll buy the scuba diving outfits in Los Angeles."

"I just read the price of gold is soaring," Grant said, clinking glasses with Enko. "When do we go?"

"Next week. I'm sending my wife to Germany to see our son. Got to get her out of the way. I'll meet you at LA International, in the same men's room we used last time—on Monday at 1000 hours."

"Now that we've done it, General, what are we going to do with all this junk. How did you plan to get rid of it?"

"After we park the stuff, we'll have to buy an airplane. We'll sneak out of the country and go to Switzerland a few times to launder the money gradually."

Grant took a sip of champagne as he thought for a moment.

"How about a Chinese laundry?"

"What are you talking about, Grant?"

"Well, there's one in Hong Kong owned by my old friend Jimmy Fong."

"Hey, that's not a bad idea. We could get a boat or a plane and . . ."

"Hold it, General. The speeches are over. They're coming our way. We'll settle the details later."

With his adviser Hoffman at his elbow, the President now circulated among the various small gatherings that had formed on the lawn. He threaded his way from group to group, smiling and shaking hands with former POWs and their wives.

The President finally got to Grant, who was still standing next to Enko, drinking champagne.

Enko made the presentations.

"Mr. President, General Zachary Enko," he said, standing at attention with a glass of champagne in his hand. "This is Major Grant Fielding, one of my best men."

"Glad to meet you, Major," the President said, extending his hand. "How long were you in North Vietnam?"

"Just under six months, at the Hanoi Hilton, sir."

"I'm sorry you had to suffer that long, Major."

"It was worth it, Mr. President."

"Fine spirit, Major. Fine morale. Did you get a promotion?"

"I was a captain when I was shot down and captured, Mr. President."

"I'm happy they made you a major."

"Thank you, sir."

The President turned to the man next to him.

"General Enko, Major Fielding, this is Mr. Hoffman, my adviser."

"How do you do, sir?" Enko said, shaking hands.

"Delighted to meet you, Mr. Hoffman. Thank you for all you did for us during the negotiations," Grant said, smiling as he also shook hands.

"Major Fielding is leaving the service, Mr. President," Enko said with regret in his voice.

"That's too bad, Major," the President said. "The country can use men of your breed—not enough people with the right aggressive spirit these days. I hope you change your mind. In any event, what you need now is a little rest and relaxation. I want you to take good care of yourself."

"Oh, I will, sir."

"What did you have in mind for a vacation?"

"It's kind of you to ask, Mr. President. I think I'll go soak up some sunshine, maybe in Florida or California, do some surfing, perhaps a little skin diving."

"Sounds like great therapy, Major."

"I agree," Enko said, smiling. "I need a change myself. Wish I could join you, Fielding."

"Be my guest, General, love to have you along."

"Maybe I will."

The President beamed benevolently and patted Enko and Grant simultaneously on the back as he turned to leave.

"Wonderful idea. Have fun, gentlemen. The war is over!"

ACKNOWLEDGMENTS

I wish to express my gratitude to the staff of Doubleday & Company, Inc., and to all those who contributed information, advice, encouragement, and patience:

Verl H. Doolin   Chief Pilot SAFAIR Flying Service, Teterboro Airport, N.J. What he doesn't know about airplanes isn't worth knowing.

Ann Loring   A great warmhearted lady—efficient and direct, harshly critical but always right. Best teacher of screenwriters around.

Gus Nathan   The most enthusiastic businessman on the East Coast of the United States. He thinks big and never gives up.

Myer Rosen   They don't make newspapermen like him anymore.

Captain Clifford W. Sandberg   A living encyclopedia of maritime knowledge. A rugged and charming old salt with a great sense of humor.

Walter L. Speth   Unquestionably the best sounding board and analytical mind.

Friends and colleagues who humored me when I was unbearable:

H. Genkens, N. & O. Goldman, F. Greenfield, T. Joseph, M. & E. Levy, H. Roy, M. Struhl.

BA, RB, MC, RC, GC, LD, GD, CD, HF, PF, PL, GG, LH, MH, WK, JLISS, BM, CCM, RPM, IR, PRN, FS, VS, AT.

My wife, Velma, who put up with living with a hermit.

My son Gerard, who unselfishly typed, chauffeured, researched, criticized, suggested, pleaded, quit, was fired, rehired, and is still waiting to get paid.

And to all those I may have forgotten. This was not intentional. They restored my faith in human nature—for a while, anyway.

LN

Printed in Canada